An Inconceivable Deception

DEFIANT HEARTS BOOK 4

Sydney Jane Baily

cat whisker press
Massachusetts

Published by cat whisker press

Cover: Philip Ré
Book Design: cat whisker studio
Editor: Chloe Bearuski

ISBN-13: 978-1957421025

DEDICATION

To Philip
Who is more like me than not

*The beginning of our story, quite auspiciously,
interrupted the middle of this one.*

OTHER WORKS

The RAKES ON THE RUN Series

Last Dance in London
Pursued in Paris
Banished to Brighton
Gretna Green by Sunset

The RARE CONFECTIONERY Series

The Duchess of Chocolate
The Toffee Heiress
My Lady Marzipan

The DEFIANT HEARTS Series

An Improper Situation
An Irresistible Temptation
An Inescapable Attraction
An Inconceivable Deception
An Intriguing Proposition
An Impassioned Redemption

The BEASTLY LORDS Series

Lord Despair
Lord Anguish
Lord Vile
Lord Darkness
Lord Misery
Lord Wrath
Eleanor

PRESENTING LADY GUS

A Georgian-Era Novella

ACKNOWLEDGMENTS

Absolute gratitude from the dead center of my heart to the readers who continued to ask me when Rose's story was going to be released. Honestly, your emails spurred me on when I nearly gave up on *An Inconceivable Deception* myself. It was an obscenely long amount of time to wait, and I apologize. I truly hope I've done justice to the last Malloy sibling.

Thanks to my beta readers who pointed out a few anachronisms (gasp) and plot points that weren't quite right. This story is better for your input: Toni Young, Renee Sevelitte, and Lisa Mackin. Lastly, to fellow writer E. Ayers, who did so much more than read this story. Your copious notes spurred me to recheck, rethink, and rewrite. Thank you for the gift of your time away from your own writing. I know how precious that is.

CHAPTER ONE

Ever so quietly, Rose eased the high wooden gate closed behind her. Not sparing a glance for the row houses directly opposite, with their shutters closed against the night air, she hurried along the brick alley behind her family's house on Mount Vernon Street.

Passing their coachman's front door, she pulled the hood of her traveling cloak more tightly around her dark hair. Having tiptoed down the rear staircase before slipping out the back door of her family's gray-shuttered home to the lane behind, she was determined not to alert her mother, or the servants, to her latest escapade.

As she turned left on Willow Street, Rose let out the breath she'd been holding, and then she started to run. She continued to do so until she reached the long oval patch of grass surrounded by the Greek Revival homes of many of her friends on Louisburg Square.

With the expansive grassy Common behind her, all but deserted at such a late hour, Rose traversed Beacon Hill. She knew it was foolish to be out so late and unaccompanied anywhere in Boston.

More than foolish, it was downright dangerous. Her heart pounded with exhilaration and excitement.

Her brother would wring her neck if he ever found out. Her mother would faint on the spot. Her sisters would shake their lovely heads in dismay.

Rose continued moving quickly until she reached her best friend's house on Myrtle Street and saw the promised carriage discreetly awaiting her a few yards past.

Giving a whispered thanks and a penny to the lad who'd agreed to wait with the runabout in the moonlight until she arrived, Rose climbed aboard the lightweight vehicle. A wave of relief accompanied the gentle swaying as the mare started forward.

Bless Claire for helping! She was always there when Rose was in a prickly situation. And this one was pricklier than most and ever so important. Rose simply had to see Finn before he left once more. He would be out at sea for nearly a month.

One wretchedly long month. She couldn't stand it. Unfortunately, she would have to, unless she stowed away on his vessel. And even she was never so bold. Her family would disagree, no doubt, especially if they knew the extent of her involvement with Phineas Bennet. She smiled, feeling a shiver of anticipation as she approached the rooming house on Bowdoin Square.

Knowing Claire's docile horse would stand for hours without fussing, Rose left the carriage pulled up close to the sidewalk, the reins tied tightly around a hitch. As she approached the three-story brick building, she couldn't help looking up at the second floor, the first window on the left. Was he watching for her?

Darting up the short flight of stone steps to the main door, she let herself into the foyer.

A lamp was lit, and a shiny black candlestick telephone sat on the hall table alongside a pile of mail for all the building's residents. She hurried up the stairs and rapped softly on Finn's door. Instantly, it was wrenched open, and Rose nearly found herself sprawled across the threshold. Instead, she fell into Finn's arms.

"My Rose," he murmured against the top of her head, his lips on her hair. She loved the way her name sounded with his Maine accent.

With her face against his chest, she breathed in the brisk ocean scent of him that somehow clung deliciously to his skin and his clothes.

"I don't like you coming out so late, love," he said. "You should have let me come to your house."

What a dear man he was for worrying over her.

Unbuttoning her cloak, she removed it, laying it over the chairback while choosing her next words carefully.

"You know you cannot do that," Rose told him, looking up into his beloved face.

Finn took a deep breath and released her abruptly, walking to the window and keeping his broad back to her.

"How long do you plan to keep 'us' a secret?" he asked, looking out into the dusky evening, lit by the flickering gas lamps that dotted the neighborhood.

Rose sighed, watching Finn fold his strong arms over his chest and look like an immovable mountain, stubborn and silent, but she didn't want to have that conversation with him. Not again, and especially not on the eve of his departure.

"Please, let's not discuss this now."

She ventured closer, eventually wrapping her arms around his trim waist, pressing herself against his solid back, and leaning her cheek between his shoulders.

Rose could feel the tension in all the lean muscles of his body, although the longer she nestled against him, the more relaxed he became. His breathing steadied. At last, he turned in her embrace.

"We'll have to settle this sometime. We can't hide forever. Your family will have to accept me."

Would they? Rose knew there would be a confrontation, which she hated. She imagined the repercussions and stern discussions.

Lastly, there would be disapproval. She couldn't stand to think of the look on her mother's and brother's faces as they learned of her decision, one they would consider rash and ruinous.

Moreover, they would be crushed by her deception.

"I'm your husband," Finn said, running his hands down her back and pulling her even closer. "There's not a bloody thing they can do about it."

Rose shivered at his seductive touch while a frisson of fear danced through her. Her brother, Reed, was renowned for his legal mind. Oh, she had no doubt there was something he could do about their hasty marriage. Especially as they hadn't yet consummated it.

As if reading her mind, Finn lowered his head and kissed her, sweeping his tongue into her mouth without warning, stealing her breath and her senses as he always had. His hand left her back and slipped inside the opening of her silk dolman, his fingers brushing across her blouse to tease her breast beneath.

As usual, she wanted him desperately. And as usual, she denied them both.

Leaning back, Rose shook her head. "I'm sorry."

Finn gave a groan of frustration and sat down on the bed with her still in his arms.

Resting upon his muscular thighs, she nestled against his chest and tried to calm her rapidly beating heart.

"When, Rose?"

"When everyone knows about us," she promised. "Besides, it's too late to do anything about it tonight. If you go away tomorrow, and I'm with child, there won't be a shred of me left to come home to after my family finds out."

"Don't be silly," he said, nuzzling her neck and causing fingers of pleasure to run up and down her spine. "I've listened to your stories about them. They love you beyond words. As I do. When they find out you've fallen in love, they'll be happy for you."

Rose wanted to believe that. Except her mother was never going to like the fact that Finn's father was a joiner working in yards on the rugged coast of Maine or that Finn made his living as a shipbuilder and would sometimes go out to sea on test sails. That was the part Rose dreaded most, the times when he would have to leave her.

Moreover, this was the first such sailing since they'd met five months earlier.

She still found it hard to fathom it had been such a short time. From the first, her heart had cried out for him. Her body had followed suit, tightening and pulsing in all the right places whenever he was near. She'd been walking where she shouldn't have been, on the East Boston docks with her best friend, Claire, after eating lunch at the Maverick House.

There, across the harbor in Eastie, they had decided to view up close the spectacular cruising vessels at the Cunard dock, dreaming of a time when they, too, might take a long sea voyage. Finn worked on merchant vessels on a nearby dock.

As Rose and Claire strolled, some unknown movement momentarily blocked the sun. That was when she'd spied him climbing the rigging of a tall ship, looking like a modern-day pirate. Shielding her eyes from the sun, she'd stood and simply stared at the fine specimen of a man until Claire stopped walking, realizing Rose was no longer beside her.

Somehow, Finn had caught sight of her as well, staring right back. Later, he told her he felt she'd bewitched him with her dark-haired beauty. He had climbed down while she'd grabbed Claire by the hand to continue walking. Within a few moments, however, he'd chased her down, asked her name, and made sure he could find her later.

Under Claire's watchful eye, Rose had flirted, as she was wont to do, all the while thinking she'd never again see the brash sandy-haired man, full of dash-fire and spirit.

Rose had not only been wrong about never seeing him again, she'd married him. Why exactly, she couldn't say, except that nothing in the world could have stopped her. From the first moments they spent alone together, when he'd ambushed her the following Sunday afternoon as she came out of her house to visit friends, she'd felt as if Finn were hers, and she, his.

When he was anywhere close, both her body and her brain were always aware of him. Indeed, she swore when he entered a room or even glanced at her, she knew with a prickling sensation.

Their courting involved picnics out of town and far away from anyone who knew her. They took carriage rides in her father's old enclosed brougham hidden from prying eyes, walked the East Boston docks as Finn pointed out vessels he admired, or shared a bottle of wine in his room.

Between them was a current of understanding, of like-mindedness, and of the deepest desire to enjoy each other and to make the other one happy.

True, Rose was a tad impetuous. Some would say more than a tad. Yet standing before a judge, just the two of them, with only Claire knowing about the marriage beforehand, Rose had felt it to be precisely the right thing to do.

Telling her family, however, had seemed impossible, and Finn had not pushed it, until that moment.

He rolled backward onto the bed, taking her with him. Splayed across his chest, Rose let out a peal of delighted laughter.

"I suppose you're right," Finn said, surprising her. "I wouldn't do that to you, leave you in such a precarious position. If only you had let me go to your family...," he trailed off when she climbed to a sitting position, straddling his thighs and looked down at his handsome face, gazing into his eyes which seemed to her to be the color of a stormy sea.

"I can't think straight, love," he admitted, "with you looking at me like that. All I can think about when I have you in my arms is kissing you. And a few other things."

Rose smiled demurely, and he grinned back. However, she simply couldn't give herself to him, even though he was her husband of nearly a month, not without her mother's approval of their marriage first. She'd had no idea she would want that approval so desperately, yet she did. Like Reed with his beloved Charlotte and like her two older sisters, one with a banker for a husband and one with a doctor, Rose wanted her family not only to accept her husband but also to welcome and love him.

She could not simply spring on them her shipbuilding man, with his tar and resin and solid-oak scents that she'd come to love as part of him. All things she feared they would despise.

"Maybe when you return," Rose began, but he shook his head.

"Don't think about it now. In a month, we'll deal with it. I know what you worry about, sweets. I know I'm not exactly a Boston Brahmin. Still, I'll make a good living for us and our family. You'll see."

She knew he would. She would start to prepare her family for the shock of her being the wife of a shipbuilder while he was away. After all, at the young age of twenty-four, he was already a quarterman, not an unskilled laborer, not a small cog like a riveter in an iron shipyard. Whereas some men his age were still assigned cordage duty, he was helping to design and build.

When Finn returned, she would take him by the hand, march up to her mother, and confess how her heart had been taken by this incredibly kind and intelligent man. That he looked like Michelangelo's *David* didn't hurt either.

A month, not that long to wait really. Yet as she looked down at his relaxed face, with his quirky smile and single dimple, she felt foreboding wash over her. A whole month, it was an eternity!

"Sweets, what's the frown for?" he asked.

Pulling her down on top of him, he gently took her face in his hands and held her in place while he kissed her.

"It's too long a time to bear," she said when he, at last, let her breathe.

"I know." And he held her close. "When I'm out at sea with a bunch of rude sailors, I'll think on this moment and try to recall how it feels to have you in my arms." He kissed the top of her head, his warm breath on her hair. "I know my memories won't come close to this. You are my heaven, Rose, and I'll leave my heart with you."

She didn't want to cry, didn't want to leave him with that image of her, red nosed and teary eyed. So she lifted her head and gave him her brightest smile.

"I'll keep your heart safe for you," she vowed. "I promise."

He kissed her again, and she felt him move under her, felt the familiar sensations of her mouth going dry as her body went soft and hot for him.

Suddenly, she couldn't wait another moment to join with her husband. Sending her own tongue darting into his mouth, she slid her hands down the length of his torso, stopping at his waist. She slipped her fingers into the band of his trousers and tried to touch his skin.

He froze while she struggled with the layers of his shirt and unmentionables, eventually able to stroke the skin across his hips.

"Rose," he warned, and she felt his own hands take a journey down to her backside, which he then cradled in his palms.

"Finn," she teased back, but then she pushed against him and sat up. Looking down at this comely man, it didn't matter a whit that their love was a secret. Before the eyes of God and the Massachusetts legal system, he was hers and she, his.

In short order, she slipped off her jacket and began on the buttons of her blouse. *Forget her shoes. Leave her stockings.* Although maybe she should have started with—

His hands closed over hers, stopping her movements.

"What are you doing, love?"

She stared into his gray-blue eyes. "Undressing. For you."

He swallowed, blinked, then gave her a wry smile.

"Like a sacrificial lamb?"

"No." Her voice had turned husky. "Because I want you."

That wiped the smile off his face. In about half a second, she found herself rolled under him with Finn looking down at her. The expression on his face warred between uncertainty and desire.

"Rose, why now? I'm so used to your resisting me with all the stubbornness of a Johnny Reb." His gaze dropped to her lips, then back to her eyes. "You've thrown me off-kilter, like a sailor on his maiden voyage."

He lowered his head and put his mouth to hers until she parted her lips. The weight of him upon her yielding body was delightful, and he seemed to fit into the cradle of her hips and sink into the sensitive place between her legs. Finn was careful not to crush her breasts as he plundered her mouth. Her body pressed up against him of its own accord, until finally, he lifted his head and gazed into her eyes.

"I want to be really and truly your wife. Right this very moment," she added, lifting her hips as much as she could under him, which was barely at all.

"Sweet girl. You *are* my real wife, and you'll always be mine regardless. And we'll keep you as a virgin bride until I return."

He looked to where the neckline of her gown gaped slightly and lowered his head to place a kiss on the upper swell of her breast.

She gasped, wishing he would do more, perhaps draw down the bodice of her dress. Instead, he trailed his kisses upward to her collarbone and her throat, up her slender neck, along her chin line and back to her mouth. She enjoyed every single kiss, every rasp of the faint stubble on his face, as it ran over her sensitive skin.

Then, to her surprise, he slipped his hand into the top of her gown and ran the back of his knuckles across one of her breasts, brushing her peaked nipple.

She moaned and heard him echo the sound.

"If we continue to lie here like this," Finn added, "I fear you won't be a virgin much longer." He sat up, pulling her gently to a seated position. "Come on, love, I'll walk you home."

She shook her head. "I have a carriage. I want five more minutes in your arms. That's not too much to ask, is it?"

She stretched out in the warm place he had just vacated, offering him her most pleading pout and come-hither gaze. He looked down at her and sighed.

"Rose, you're not playing fair."

"Whatever do you mean?" she asked, fluttering her lashes at him.

"You know exactly what I mean. You're too tempting for a man."

"You're not simply any man," she teased.

"No, I'm the one who loves you more than anyone or anything on earth."

Rose sobered. This was no game, and he was not an idle flirtation.

"I know. And I, you. Please hold me a few moments longer," she said, wishing the fear of separation weren't clouding the joy of being near him.

"Shall I ask Liam to keep an eye on you while I'm away?"

Finn's closest friend at the yard was a quick-witted Irishman who helped whittle the scaled wooden models of the ships before they were built. She'd heard of him but never met him.

"I thought he would be going with you," she said.

"As did I." Finn twisted a lock of her hair around his finger and studied it. "He told me this afternoon he'd been pulled from the roster. I thought it only a fluke, but then he asked if I wanted to be pulled, too. When I asked him how he could arrange that, he said he was only joking and putting on airs."

She felt him shrug.

"Anyway, I have to be on that ship," he continued. "Someone's got to make sure she stays afloat." Then by the captured skein of her dark hair, he tugged her face closer, and she forgot about the small surge of fear she'd felt at his casual words of staying afloat.

"I don't need Liam to check up on me," she told him as his talented lips nibbled along the column of her neck. She had enough watchful eyes among her mother and older siblings.

"Besides, it's only for a month. You haven't told him about me, have you?"

Finn's mouth stopped its pleasurable journey.

"No," he said, sounding irked. "You asked me not to, and I didn't."

She relaxed, immediately sorry she'd touched on the sore point between them once again.

"Please," she begged. "Continue. Except on my lips this time.

Then she let his mouth claim hers, and five more minutes slipped into an hour.

One month became two and then three. And then a year. A year became two, and now, it had been over three years since Finn had kissed her lips. Rose had long since stopped haunting the Eastie waterfront for any news of the sunken vessel, weary of taking the ferry back and forth, of crossing over the very waters that blanketed her husband's body.

Perhaps some of her friends had thought her a little strange with her fascination over the loss of the *Garrard*, one of the prototypes of the new steel-clad cargo ships. Her family appreciated the more grown-up, less-wild Rose, but then, in the face of her uncharacteristic solemnity, they began to worry.

Finn had said the ship's center of gravity was too high, with its five masts towering over the deck that rode low in the water, aided by a steam engine deep in the bowels of the vessel. He had railed against his superiors who'd built a ship that had a freeboard set too low. Waves would wash over the weather deck, he'd predicted.

Nevertheless, he'd done his job and headed out with others from the shipyard to test her for its wealthy owner.

The day the Boston *Post* announced the capsizing on the front page, Rose had been out riding with Claire. She'd come in to see her mother drinking tea and scrutinizing the paper.

"Such a shame," Evelyn Malloy said. "Have a cup of tea, dear, you must be parched, what with all that running around you and your friend do."

"What's a shame, Mama?" Rose asked, taking a cup and pouring tea from the pot steeping on the sideboard. She chose two lavender wafers, as well. They were among her favorites from their cook's specialties.

"A ship went down off the coast." Her mother had rattled the newspaper loudly as she straightened it and checked the details. "Somewhere slightly west and south of Yarmouth."

Wordlessly, Rose had set her cup down and sat beside her mother. She had known even before she read it. Still, she slid the paper closer and looked at the headline. Then she scanned the first paragraph and saw the ship's name.

She didn't gasp, nor did she cry out. She let out the breath she was holding and managed to drag in another. She took a sip of tea with a trembling hand and tried to see past the tears that filled her eyes.

"Rose?" her mother said. "Are you crying?"

She couldn't hide it. She nodded and dropped her teacup onto its saucer with a clatter, spilling its contents everywhere. Evelyn ignored the mess and put her hand over her daughter's trembling one.

"Why ever for, dear?"

Rose could only shake her head as the tears streamed down her cheeks.

"Oh, my dear girl, you have such a soft heart."

"All those poor men," Rose said at last, needing to relate something of what she was feeling, needing to feel comforted by her mother.

Sure enough, Evelyn put her arms around her youngest daughter.

"I hope it was quick for them," her mother said. "They are buried at sea under God's watchful eye. And their families will remember them, every one of them. There will be a memorial service, it says in the paper. Next Sunday. We can go if you wish."

Rose nodded. Yes, she would remember Phineas Bennet every day that she lived.

Had he died resenting her for not telling her family about him?

Had he died wishing they'd consummated their marriage?

Had he died loving her?

CHAPTER TWO

1891, Boston, Massachusetts

Charlotte knew her husband was worried about his youngest sister because he sat, staring out of the window at the sea, his brow furrowed. He didn't seem to notice as she entered their main room, which served as the parlor and drawing room, as well as the place where they took their morning coffee and enjoyed a late-night glass of brandy.

She'd seen that look before, when one of his family members came to him with a problem. This time, he'd been closeted with his mother, Evelyn Malloy, for over an hour. When Charlotte had knocked on the door with tea, Evelyn had obviously been crying, and Reed was grim-faced with his lips set in a tight, white line.

"Are you going to brood all night?" Charlotte asked after standing beside him for a moment in silence. She'd put to bed their two younger children as well as her two young cousins whom she and Reed were happily raising as their own.

At that moment, she simply wanted to soothe her husband's furrowed brow.

He turned his head slowly after her words sunk into his distracted brain.

"I don't brood," Reed said, grasping her hand and pulling her onto his lap.

As he cradled her face in his hands, she gazed into his deep-blue eyes and felt the familiar warmth of love along with the rapid rush of desire.

"I contemplate," he added.

He lowered his head and kissed her. Her hands slipped around his neck and held him fast against her, pulling back only for a necessary breath.

"Well, Mr. Malloy, are you going to stare at that vast ocean and *contemplate* all night?"

Reed's handsome face lit with a smile, and Charlotte's toes tingled at the obvious message in his roguish expression.

"No, I believe I'll take my lovely wife to bed. I have neglected her since dinner and owe her some special attention."

"Do you want to talk about Rose first?"

His face darkened momentarily. "Tomorrow morning at breakfast, we can talk more about our melancholy Rose."

Then he stood up, and Charlotte couldn't stifle a gasp as he lifted her into his arms.

Carrying her from the room, her husband turned toward the stairs leading to their bedroom, which she loved for all its memories and for the promise of more to come. She rested her head against his broad chest, smelling his sandalwood scent that immediately made her feel both serene and excited at the same time.

Reed represented home to her, and their love was currently her only source of excitement as she'd halted a successful journalism career until their four children were older. Nowadays, adventure was confined to their bedroom—or occasionally, to the soft rug in front of the fire in his study.

"Tonight," he added, "no more words." Pushing their bedroom door open with his shoulder, he carried her inside and kicked the door closed behind him.

Rose sat on a tufted red velvet sofa next to Claire Appleton and surveyed the room full of people, some old and sedately talking, some young and breathless. The noise level was only moderate as the band was taking a well-deserved break. She wished she hadn't come, but her brother and mother were starting to worry overmuch, and Rose had to begin making an effort at normalcy.

She knew nearly everyone at the dance. At twenty-two years, she'd already been to more of these gatherings than she could count. All her peers and her friends, married and not, were there, and even some relatives. She spied her brother, Reed, and his wife, Charlotte, and her oldest sister, Elise, with her spouse, Michael.

When Rose did attend an event, she tried to avoid her siblings since they always seemed to scrutinize her behavior. By their expressions, they found her lacking. Earlier, her mother had worn a preoccupied mien, as she did so often of late, and had told Rose to go to the dance without her. This gave Rose a measure of freedom she didn't usually get to enjoy.

However, her jubilance was tempered by Reed having come by their mother's home and spoken with her earlier. Without mincing words, he'd let her know her family was extremely worried about her withdrawn behavior and if it didn't cease, she'd better be prepared to explain herself.

To where had the mischief-maker disappeared, he'd wanted to know, for he sorely missed her. Where was the firebrand, the plague of his existence?

Rose had very nearly told him where that mischievous, lighthearted girl had gone—with her husband to the bottom of the Atlantic over three years earlier, but she'd held her tongue.

Instead, she'd discussed with her brother what was bothering her of late.

"I want to *do* something with my life. Something important. Like Charlotte or Sophie," she said, thinking of her journalist sister-in-law and her middle sister who was a world-class pianist out West. "But what can I do? Everywhere you turn, you trip over a suffragette, even Mama and Elise. They will fail or succeed without me, as I have no interest in that regard beyond hoping they're successful. There are women doctors and scientists, and I have no aptitude for that type of thing. Why, Mrs. Cochrane has already created an automated dishwasher, for goodness sake. How can I top that? What more could anyone want?"

She'd sighed. "I am too old to be a painting prodigy or any type of prodigy, for that matter. What can I do?"

Into her brother's stunned silence, Rose had added, "Perhaps I should become an actress."

After all, she'd spent the past few years acting the part of a normal person, one who hadn't secretly married the man of her dreams and then had her heart torn asunder when she'd lost him.

"Don't you dare," Reed had said, and she could see by the look on her brother's face he was absolutely serious.

It didn't bother her. She had no wish to go on the stage anyway. To be thrust into the limelight might have worked for the old Rose. This Rose wanted none of that.

"I'm only jesting, dear brother. There is all that memorizing to do," she added, trying to sound blithe. "And I daresay the heavy makeup is terrible for one's skin."

"Look. There's Franklin," Claire whispered behind her hand, bringing Rose's thoughts back to the present.

Rose's best friend had become even closer since the loss of Finn. As the only one who had known about their brief marriage, Claire was the sole person in whom Rose could confide and on whose shoulder she could sob out her broken heart. And Claire had performed admirably, shoring Rose up as needed, trying to lift her spirits, and as time went on, dragging her back into the social scene.

Moreover, after Rose's marriage to Finn, Claire no longer tried to push her into the arms of the other Appleton sibling, Claire's twin brother, Robert, with whom Rose felt only familial affection. For Rose's taste in the opposite sex obviously ran to a more adventurous sort, a rugged man.

Certainly not a hobbadehoy like Robert Appleton. Finally, Claire had informed Rose she'd relinquished her dream of having her for a sister by law as well as by heart, as she understood her twin would never suit.

Yes, Claire was an absolute peach. Rose squeezed her friend's hand ever so slightly. It was definitely her turn to help her. Claire had been sweet on Franklin Brewster for the past three weeks and had yet to speak to him or to dance with him.

Rose couldn't help shaking her head. If she'd been interested in Franklin, she would have marched right up to him already, batted her eyelashes, and shaken her follow-me-boys curls, demanding he notice her. She would have made her intentions plain or simply asked him to write his name on her dance card. Not that Rose had felt like doing anything of the sort since Finn had come into her life and then all-too-soon left it.

Watching the young couples, she regretted she'd never been to a proper dance with him. Yet they'd found plenty of ways to have fun together. She'd drawn him out, refusing to dwell on his serious musings, and she'd enjoyed coaxing out his soft smile and his puckish laughter. She still missed both of those traits and found her own had disappeared along with his.

Even if she didn't feel like laughing, she always felt like helping her dear friend. Although hardly the retiring type, Claire was far too hesitant when it came to the male of their species. Rose made a decision.

"Wait here," she said to Claire, who immediately tried to grab for Rose's arm and make her stop.

Looking into her friend's widening green eyes, Rose said, "Do not worry."

"Impetuous trouble," Claire murmured, reminding Rose of what old Mrs. Barnes had said when she'd seen the two girls entering the party.

Too late, Rose thought, already four steps toward Franklin Brewster, who stood with three other youthful Brahmin. His late father, whom he greatly resembled—both being tall and handsome—was a developer, not only in Boston but also in New York City. Mr. Brewster was a leader in the effort to fill in the Back Bay with over seven hundred acres filled and converted into buildable land.

Franklin was indeed an eligible bachelor worthy of her sweet Claire!

The well-to-do blue-bloods were talking and laughing, all the while scanning the room, surveying the female company.

Rose walked right into the middle of them, silencing their laughter. They stared at her and she looked back at each in turn, not the least bit uncomfortable. Finally, John Claymore, whom out of sheer boredom she'd allowed to briefly flirt with her the previous summer, found his voice.

"Well, Miss Malloy," and he offered her a saucy look as if she'd come over there to speak with him, "is there something *I* can help you with? Perhaps a slot on your card."

She glanced down at the dance card dangling from her wrist. Always empty and by her own choice.

"Not the likes of you," she retorted, watching two spots of color bloom on his cheeks.

Oh, he was handsome enough, but she'd found him soft in certain unappealing ways. His hands were delicate, his laugh was too quiet, and he kissed like her grandmother. In other words, he was absolutely nothing at all like Phineas Bennet. As expected, her husband had become the impossible touchstone against whom she measured every other man.

Also as expected, she found every single one of them to come up short.

As for John Claymore, she'd cursed herself for even bothering to try to recapture a little happiness. John's failure to come close to Finn's appeal only made her sadder and lonelier.

"I'm here to speak with Mr. Brewster," Rose said, turning her vivid-blue Malloy gaze to ward Claire's heart's desire. The others exclaimed aloud.

"Now you're for it," said Thomas Craigston, whom Rose had never fancied despite his good sense of humor.

They all chuckled at his friendly warning.

"Are you attached?" she asked Franklin, ignoring the others.

Franklin looked taken aback.

"I . . . That is . . . Are you . . . ? No . . . why?"

"Do you always stammer?" Rose asked. "Because while my friend might have an interest in dancing with you, I will not recommend you to her if you cannot also carry on an amusing conversation."

She saw him look over her shoulder to where Claire sat as it dawned on Franklin to whom she referred. No doubt the two of them locked since her best friend was most likely watching the exchange.

Rose noted with satisfaction how a small smile appeared on his appealing face, along with an interested spark in his cocoa-brown eyes and a becomingly humble blush upon his handsome cheeks.

Perfect. She had a feeling they would be well matched. Claire was an intelligent young lady with flaxen-blond hair, a lovely face, a sweet disposition, and blessed with a certain vivacity. Rose's impression of Franklin was that he, too, was clever and easy-going. What's more, Claire's father and her grandfather before him were extremely successful financiers.

Any man should be pleased to gain Claire's interest.

"Are you speaking of Miss Appleton?" Franklin asked, still looking past Rose.

"If I were, are you agreeable to such an association?" Rose asked, wanting to hear an affirmative before she said any more.

Franklin coughed. Rose knew her direct approach bothered some and scandalized others. So be it. She usually got results, and more quickly than beating about the bush.

"I would very much like to dance with Miss Appleton," Franklin admitted. "However, it seems she is otherwise occupied."

Rose turned to find her seat had been taken by a forward young man, who clearly was attempting to monopolize Claire. For her part, Claire's green-eyed gaze was still trained on Rose and Franklin's encounter while admirably trying to wrest her hand from her admirer's grasp.

Rose rolled her eyes. *Good God!* She couldn't leave her alone for one minute.

She turned back to Franklin. "My dear friend is not in the least interested in Mr. Sonders, I assure you. I suggest you and I rescue her since the next two dances on her card are free. I will engage the gentleman while you whisk away Miss Appleton to the dance floor. Agreed?"

Franklin merely nodded, seemingly quite impressed by Rose's forthright manner.

With a "good evening, gentlemen" to his companions, leaving them with her most dazzling smile, Rose swished her gray-silk skirts as she turned on her heel and headed back to Claire, secure in the knowledge Franklin was following on her heels like a good pup.

"Mr. Sonders!" Rose exclaimed as she approached the blond-haired fellow. "I was so hoping to run into you." She grabbed his wrist so suddenly he released Claire's hand and looked up.

"Miss Malloy," he greeted her and, as a gentleman, immediately stood.

Out of the corner of her eye, she knew Franklin had taken her advice and was indeed striking while the branding iron was burning hot. He grasped Claire's hand, brought it to his lips, and, in another instant, made off with her to where couples were dancing a slow Boston-style waltz.

"What can I do for you?" Sonders asked.

Rose stared at him, a man with unfortunately large teeth and an even larger fortune.

"Oh, *um*. I believe if I'm not mistaken my dear brother is looking for you."

With that vague intimation, Rose curtsied and hurried away. Circling the edge of the room, she sipped at a drink she'd grabbed from the refreshment table, something fruity, and wished she had an interest in any man there. She tapped her toe softly to the music, once more feeling the tug of regret she'd not had the opportunity to dance in public with Finn.

Taking another sip of her drink, she admonished herself against self-pity. After all, one glorious night, they had danced together, swaying to the sound of a young violinist practicing one floor above at his boarding house. The unskilled musician was terrible, but she'd enjoyed every second of being in Finn's arms.

Rose came out of her reverie to realize John Claymore was approaching her from one side, no doubt wanting to try and take up where they left off the previous summer. Her eldest sister, Elise, and her beloved Michael were approaching from the other. Moreover, she had a look of purpose on her lovely face.

Rose slipped through the doorway behind her.

Intending to go back into the Tremont's ballroom through the door at the other end of the hallway, she stopped stock-still upon seeing her brother already down there. Reed and his wife, Charlotte, her unmistakable auburn hair drawing Rose's gaze like a beacon, were chatting with the big-toothed James Sonders.

"Drats!" she muttered, feeling surrounded. She didn't need Reed interrogating her on her doings of the past week. She'd been caught by their mother trying to go out without a chaperone after dinner two nights ago. It had been harmless enough. Rose had wanted to listen to a band on the Common and desired only her own solitary company. Yet one would have thought she'd been secretly going to meet a man in a rooming house, by the way Evelyn Malloy had carried on with a long lecture about propriety.

How she wished that had been the case. Rose's heart gave its usual painful squeeze at the delicious memory of secretly meeting Finn.

Rose remained motionless until she realized her family hadn't seen her. Although she wanted to watch Claire and Franklin have their first dance, she walked in the opposite direction. Same people, same dances. Same, same, same. No wonder her other sister, Sophie, had gone clear across the country to live in California, as far from home as one could get and still live in the United States.

Rose sighed and began a slow meander along the spacious hallway. When she reached the end, she climbed the wide stairs with its pretty floral runner. As she reached the landing halfway, she thought she heard footsteps begin at the bottom, and she faltered a moment. Perhaps another partygoer was exploring the venue, or maybe it was a hotel guest with a room on one of the three upper floors.

She continued upward until she reached the next floor, where another long hallway stretched out before her. She strolled toward the other end, intending to descend the far staircase and make a complete circle.

Hearing the steps behind her again, she increased her pace a little, her heart racing slightly. When she could stand it no longer and with nowhere to hide, she whirled about to face her tracker, hands on her hips.

Still twenty feet down the hall yet with his eyes fixed determinedly on her was William Woodsom—a few years older than her, handsome in a classic way, always good fun at a gathering, although a tad cock-sure of himself in her opinion. No doubt that was due to his father being an expatriate from England and an earl or a duke of something or other. His family had arrived in Boston when young Woodsom was already in his teens, and he'd maintained a slight accent that seemed to make all the female hearts beat more quickly.

But not Rose's.

Luckily, she was immune. In fact, her pulse slowed when she realized who it was, despite not being entirely sure there was no threat to her person. After all, they were barely acquaintances, and certainly not friends.

"Mr. Woodsom," she said, greeting him with a nod of her head when he was ten feet away. She hadn't noticed him downstairs. How odd that he would be up there on the second floor.

"Miss Malloy," he returned, slowing his steps when he reached her. "How is it that you can make a greeting sound like a challenge?"

She tilted her head. *What did he mean?* Then she couldn't help but laugh at his expression. There was something about him that made her feel spirited.

"It's no matter," he added when she didn't answer. "Are you tired of the party already?" His eyes looked her up and down, not with insolence yet with definite interest.

Rose considered her answer. "In truth, I am a little weary of the party." *This and every other one,* she thought to herself. Then she tried to be more sociable and added, "Although I do love to dance."

"Odd. I don't believe I've seen you dance, not lately at any rate," he said, his well-formed lips ending with a half-smile. "However, the party loses its luster in your absence."

She smiled back at his light banter. William Woodsom was a known flirt, nearly as bad as she used to be when she was a precocious youth. Yet somehow, they'd never connected, nor had even the briefest of attachments. He had entered her circle rather late, having spent his formative years in Britain and the Continent. Rose had always been interested in someone else in their group. *Before* Finn. And after him, she'd felt nothing.

Yet "lost its luster" was a good line, she had to admit.

"Does it really?" she asked, tilting her head. "Has Maeve Norcross grown tired of you already?"

He raised an eyebrow but gave no indication she had hit a sore spot.

"Have you been keeping track of my attachments?"

Rose didn't blush. After all, she had no designs on him. She merely knew Claire had seen Maeve and William riding along the Common because her good friend had been keeping an eye on Franklin Brewster, who was Maeve's cousin and thus had been riding along behind.

"So, she *has* discarded you?"

"What an awful way to put it!" William protested, with mock indignation. "Discarded, indeed, like an old stocking."

However, he didn't deny it or look the least bit upset.

Rose gave an unladylike shrug. "I am returning to the ballroom now. The luster will be restored momentarily."

William laughed. "You ought not to walk around by yourself."

"I sought only to avoid too many of my family members." She turned away, realizing she'd spoken without thinking. She probably shouldn't have revealed something so personal.

Nevertheless, when he fell into step beside her and they started once more toward the far staircase, she decided he meant her no harm. Thus, she compounded her familiarity with another such disclosure.

"Everywhere I turn, it seems there is a Malloy."

After a brief pause, he nodded. "Being the *only* offspring does have its privileges," he offered, sounding sincere.

Hm. He'd always struck her as someone who enjoyed his privileges. That was certain. Perhaps a tad spoiled, perhaps he considered himself entitled. Perhaps he would end up inheriting a castle or country manor back in his parents' home country. She didn't know. She knew only that his father was an ambassador with an office at the State House and that William worked with him in some capacity.

Actually, Rose knew one other thing —too many of her acquaintances had fallen for his good looks only to have their expectations dashed.

For her part, Rose appreciated his wit and charm when she'd been briefly exposed to it, and his lively disposition, even his pleasing face and figure. However, she was not the type to fall at a man's feet, especially knowing as she did his reputation for a wandering eye. She'd never given up the smallest part of her heart, neither before nor since Phineas Bennet, and she didn't intend to start with the likes of William Woodsom.

They were nearly at the bottom tread when, unexpectedly, he rushed a step ahead, abruptly cut in front of her, and turned at once to face her. Unlike her oldest sister, Rose was not overly tall. However, with William a step below, they were nearly nose to nose.

"What *are* you doing?" she asked, grinding to a stop, their faces inches apart.

"I'm going to kiss the prettiest girl at the Tremont."

CHAPTER THREE

"**I** beg your pardon," Rose said, while a tremor of anticipation shot through her at his bold words. "That is completely beyond the pale."

"As is your strolling by yourself through these corridors. Good thing I came along and rescued you. For that at least, I deserve a kiss."

"You deserve nothing of the kind," she began when, to her astonishment, he laid hands on her, one at her waist, one cupping her head under her glossy black curls.

Good thing her hair was up, she briefly thought, or he would have mussed it terribly. And that thought was chased by the next one: *Good God, he's touching me. He's really going to—*

William didn't brush her lips with his as a few of her suitors before Finn had done, nor did he offer her a peck at the corner of her mouth. No, his lips closed over hers, then he tilted his head, and their mouths fit together like two sides of a coin.

Rose stilled a moment, a flash of fear at what was happening, followed closely by a blaze of sensation so exhilarating, she felt breathless. For the briefest of moments, she could pretend it was

Finn, for this felt the closest to his kiss she could imagine while not being him.

William moved his mouth, and then the tip of his tongue touched the seam of her lips. Unthinkingly, she parted them, and he slipped his tongue inside. Briefly, she felt his tongue touch hers, and then he withdrew. In that instant, though, something changed in her. Low, between her hips, she felt a flush of warmth. Just as with Finn.

Before she could react, to push him away or pull him closer, he broke it off. They stared at each other for what felt like forever.

Was that surprise on his face, as well? She knew she ought to slap him for what he'd done, but she didn't want to. She wanted him to kiss her again.

Perhaps something in her face expressed this, for he took in a quick breath and started to lower his head once more.

"No," she whispered.

He froze at the single word she'd uttered, and then he drew back. She said nothing more, still trying to regain her senses and decide how she felt.

"I ought to apologize, I suppose," William offered, although she could tell he didn't intend to, nor would he mean it.

Besides, how could she demand an apology when she'd not only enjoyed the kiss but practically invited a second one?

"I think I'd best return to the dance," she said, wondering if he was going to want to form an attachment to her. She hated to dash his hopes, but she couldn't imagine becoming a couple so quickly on the heels of him and Maeve, or him and Sarah before her, or him and . . .

God, what an idiot she was! And why was she thinking of becoming a couple? This kiss meant nothing to William Woodsom, and it should mean nothing to her. She was a widow and had remained true to Finn, no matter how long he'd been dead. No doubt William fancied himself quite stellar, working as he did for their esteemed lieutenant governor, but his political position didn't impress her one bit.

He didn't impress her either, she reminded herself.

"You need to release me. At once," Rose added, realizing his hands were still on her.

He hesitated, then drew his hands back to his sides.

She pushed past him down the last step, hurried across the landing, and continued her descent. The hallway was empty, thankfully, for he was close at her back.

"Let me go first," she hissed, imagining her brother's expression if he saw them entering the ballroom together.

"Rose," William began, reaching out to detain her.

She would not be one of his conquests. She made sure to stay out of his reach and hurried away.

"Rose," he said again as they entered the ballroom. "May I have the next dance?"

She barely paused in her desire to put more distance between them.

"I think not," she said, and then looked back at him. *Was he surprised by her refusal?*

"I do not dance," Rose added to soften her words, holding up her wrist as if he could see that every dance on her detested card was unclaimed by any gentleman's name. Then she thought she'd better put him back in his place. "And I am *Miss Malloy* to you."

Or Mrs. Bennet, she amended silently, unable to tamp down the guilt at letting another man kiss her.

She hurried to find Claire.

Should she tell her friend what had occurred? Absolutely not! *Would she?* Most likely.

In a group made up of Rose, Claire, Franklin Brewster, Claire's brother, Robert, and Rose's young niece and nephew, Lily and Thomas, with Claire's housekeeper as chaperone—they made up a merry roller-skating party.

After a heated discussion as to whether to go to the Cyclorama or the large rink on St. James's Avenue and Clarendon Street, the group sat on the benches at Winslow's rink in the Back Bay and strapped on their skates. For nearly a decade, Rose had been a skating enthusiast since first trying it out in New York on vacation with her middle sister, Sophie, who had gone only because there was an orchestra playing every night at the Albany rink.

Despite being quite adept, Rose let Robert hold her arm as they went around.

"Faster," Rose urged.

Robert gripped her arm more tightly.

"I think not," he said as Claire and Franklin whirled past them.

Oh, for goodness sake! Rose rolled her eyes. She found him to be old beyond his years and stuffy, so unlike his amusing sister.

"Even Thomas is going by us, and he's only twelve," she complained to Robert before yanking him along willy-nilly. "Full speed ahead!"

Two seconds later, Claire's twin brother stumbled, let go of Rose, and crashed into the rink wall.

Thank goodness he'd released her, she thought, looking at his crumpled form. Claire and Franklin helped him up.

"I think I'll sit for a little while," Robert said, heading for the gate and the nearest bench.

"So sorry, Robert," Rose called after him, glad to be unfettered at last.

She and Finn had skated at this very rink at midnight, fleeing only when the night watchman eventually showed up. A little surprised by her daring nature, Finn had nevertheless matched her speed. Together, they'd raced around, laughing like children. She'd felt perfectly safe holding Finn's hand.

At that moment, she wanted to skate alone and remember.

"You can hold onto Franklin's other arm," Claire offered, interrupting her thoughts.

Rose nearly laughed, seeing as how Claire was a crack skater, too, and neither of them needed to hold onto a man for support.

Rose simply smiled and waved her thanks before skating off at breakneck pace around the oval. Soon, she was away from her entire party.

Gliding down one end, she looked back to see where Reed's children were—safely with Claire's housekeeper, and then she looked ahead again. A figure cut across her path. Rose gasped. Too late to stop or even turn, she slammed into the other skater who managed to catch hold of her as they went down.

Landing on top of him, she looked down to see the grinning face of William Woodsom.

"You!" she exclaimed. "You oaf! You could have injured us both."

"Could have? How do you know I'm not injured?" he asked, his head still resting on the polished wooden flooring.

"It would serve you right," Rose said, although she tried to soften her tone. "Are you?"

"As it happens, no. Except my pride. I'm usually known as an excellent skater."

By this time, Claire and Franklin reached them.

"Are you hurt?" Claire asked while Franklin offered his arm to Rose and pulled her to standing.

When they were both upright again, William reached for her hand.

"Since we have already fallen together, will you skate with me?"

She wanted to pull her hand from his, but that seemed petty. Besides Claire was watching with her large, curious eyes, and her good friend knew about the stolen kiss. Better to be casual and skate with William, and then leave him at the other end of the rink.

"I suppose," she demurred, and with a quick wink to Claire, Rose let William lead her away. They skated easily, well-matched, and Rose let the comfortable silence stretch on.

After a moment, without looking at her, he said, "I wish you had let me dance with you at the Tremont."

She stiffened.

"Why did you run away?" he persisted.

"You were behaving outrageously."

"You didn't seem to mind. I've heard you used to be a lively girl."

Rose gasped. Good God, did she have a reputation as someone whom a man could kiss at will? True, she had been lively but never immoral. Never that! Was she considered loose? Her mother would kill her if such an opinion was floating around Boston. That was, if her mother ever came out of the fog she'd been in for so long.

What that woman was pondering for hours on end, Rose had no idea.

As they approached the opposite end of the rink, she yanked her arm from William's

"You are as insulting now as you were boorish the other night."

"Please, Rose, I didn't mean to insult you."

"No matter your intention, you did. Moreover, you will call me by my family name until I give you leave to do otherwise." She exited by the closest gate before he could stop her. *What a jackass!* The kiss had been nice, true, but if he thought she was going to fall all over him or let him do it again, he was sadly mistaken.

William blasted Woodsom! He could go to the devil.

She ended up on the bench next to Robert Appleton.

"Everything satisfactory?" he asked.

"Yes, fine." Quickly she unbuckled her skates from her shoes and made quick work of shoving the metal contraptions under the bench. "I'm going to get a beverage, maybe lemonade. Would you like anything?"

He started to stand. "I'll come with you."

"No!" she blurted out. "I mean, you've still got your skates on. I'll be back soon enough." With that, she hurried away. She seemed to be much in demand at present, although she doubted Claire's brother had anything in mind like William.

She doubted he could kiss like him either.

Rose! she scolded herself. *What a thought!* Good thing her improper notions stayed locked in her head.

At the refreshment stand, she waited while the gentleman pressed some lemons. All at once, she realized it was Maeve Norcross at her elbow. *What timing!*

"Maeve, how are you? I didn't see you at the Tremont the other night. What a fabulous dress you're wearing!" Goodness gracious, she was babbling, but she couldn't stop herself. "The color, a lovely lavender-blue, perfect for your hair and eyes."

Maeve smiled as warmly as ice water. "Nice to see you, too, Rose." Her pretty violet eyes didn't look happy however. "Did I see you skating with Mr. Woodsom? Are you two forming an attachment?"

Goodness, there were at least three hundred people there. Maeve must have eyes like a hawk to have spotted her and William. How quickly rumors could begin.

"No, not at all," Rose assured her. "Mr. Woodsom crashed into me. I'm here with the Appleton twins and my own niece and nephew." She gestured to the rink where her friends were starting to come out of the gate. "Oh, and your cousin Franklin is with us, too."

"Well, in that case, I'll warn you off from Woodsom, dear. That is, if you don't mind my telling you something."

"Do tell," Rose urged her. She wished she could say she was above enjoying gossip, but it was at least half the fun of her otherwise tame life.

Maeve needed no further encouragement. "You may be fine in such a public place as this with *him*. However, I caution you, do not find yourself alone with him. In fact, I beseech you."

"I beg your pardon?" Rose asked, hoping she wasn't blushing at having already been alone with him. "Whatever can you mean?"

Maeve gestured with her head that they should walk away from the listening ears of the lemonade server. Rose picked up her glass, and they walked toward a large window that looked out onto St. James Street.

"I hate to speak out of turn, but since my great uncle was the mayor, I try to help my fellow citizens."

Rose nearly rolled her eyes and only managed to stop herself by widening them and not blinking. She was sure she looked like a barn owl. It was well-known that Maeve liked to work her connection to Boston's former mayor into practically every conversation.

When the danger of any such rudeness as eye-rolling had passed, Rose blinked and urged Maeve to speak.

"Mr. Woodsom attempted to take liberties with my person," Maeve said. "I had to firmly rebuff him. Of course, I told him then that any attachment between us was impossible. I, for one, will have a marriage license in hand before any man tastes my lips."

Rose couldn't help her mouth dropping open slightly. *Really?* Did Maeve truly intend to marry, or at least become engaged to marry, before even kissing? What if the man kissed like an eager puppy, all sloppy and wet, or like parchment paper, dry and light, and Maeve found out such crucial information too late?

William Woodsom kissed very well, although perhaps that was because he had practiced quite a bit on willing females, which was not a particularly good thing. Rose frowned. Especially if he wanted to practice on Maeve one day and on her the next.

"I shall keep that in mind. Thank you for confiding in me."

Maeve made a moue of her mouth and tilted her head to the side.

"We ladies must stick together when the likes of Mr. Woodsom are preying upon us." With a small wave, the brunette wandered back to order her own glass of lemonade.

Rose frowned. Maeve's story made her feel uncomfortable at best and taken advantage of at worst. What had occurred at the Tremont could have been far more serious if she hadn't escaped William Woodsom when she had.

Reed's children ran up to her. "Will you buy us lemonade, too?" Thomas asked.

"It's not polite to ask," Lily said. "You should let Aunt Rose offer first." Her niece stared pointedly at her.

Rose smiled. "Right you are, both of you. And I *am* offering. I shall buy you each one." She handed Thomas her glass. "Will you return that for me, please." Then reaching into her reticule dangling from her wrist, she gave them both a coin.

"Come right back. We'll be leaving soon."

The sooner, the better. She didn't want to be caught again by William Woodsom, who seemed to stop at nothing, neither following her and ambushing her in a hotel hallway, nor knocking her off her feet at a public rink.

Thus, it was with little surprise a few minutes later—though with equal parts exasperation and excitement—that Rose saw him approaching her once more, this time in his street shoes. Luckily, Claire, Franklin, and Robert reached her first.

"Are you ready to depart?" Rose asked, watching nervously as William got closer. She grabbed Robert's arm and held on.

"All recovered?" she asked him sweetly.

"Quite so," he replied, looking startled by her attention.

She tugged him toward the main exit. Luckily, Claire's housekeeper gathered the children and in two carriages, they left. Rose couldn't help but look back at the rink one more time. Woodsom stood outside the door by a large maple, arms crossed, staring after her.

She had a feeling he wasn't finished with her yet.

"You seem jittery," Claire observed as they sat in Rose's mother's front room, tying ribbons into bows for one of her mother's suffragette events the following Saturday.

"What makes you say that?"

The door opened abruptly. Startled, Rose dropped her spool and half her bows on the floor. Yet it was only her brother entering with his young son, Emory, in tow.

"That's precisely what makes me say that," Claire pointed out.

Rose made a sour face at her friend. Truly, she was anticipating her next encounter with William, although she couldn't decide if she felt dread or desire.

"Hello, ladies," Reed said, and young Emory ran up to Rose to throw his arms around her, standing on and squashing her scattered ribbons as he did so. She hugged him fiercely.

If Finn hadn't perished, perhaps she would have her own little one by now. She squeezed her nephew hard until he squirmed for release. Then she started to scoop up the blue satin, hoping her creations weren't too crushed to hand out at the event.

"Have you seen Mother?" Reed asked. "I have about ten minutes to discuss whatever it is she wants and then—"

"Ten minutes!" Evelyn Malloy exclaimed upon entering the room behind her son, and Rose dropped the stack again. Claire giggled.

"Is that really all the time you can spare your own flesh and blood?" Evelyn continued, pausing to bend low and receive a hug from her grandson.

Rose and Reed shared a glance of amusement, then he winked at her.

"Where's wee Wesley?" their mother asked, releasing Emory.

"*Wee* Wes," Reed said with a chuckle, since his youngest boy was nearly four and built to become a bruiser, "is at home with his mama. Charlotte took pity on me. I can get a few things done with this one," he nodded to Emory with a loving smile upon his face, "but not with both. Speaking of which, will you ladies keep Emory? Mother and I will go into Father's study."

They all still called it exactly that, *Father's study*, despite Oliver Malloy having been gone for nearly a decade.

"Come, sit by me, Emory," Rose said. "See that lovely box. You can help me put these carefully in it." After all, he couldn't possibly crumple her work anymore than she already had.

The six-year-old did as he was told, and they went back to work. Rose didn't mind the distraction of her nephew. She simply added his busy little fingers, his humming, and his giggling to the distractions already coursing through her busy brain ever since the encounter at the rink. She'd kept an eye out for William, thinking she would see him popping out from behind a tree or whenever she opened her front door to step outside.

She anticipated the notion, while fearing it at the same time.

However, a week had passed and, surely, he had moved on to some other female. Besides in another week, she would be at the Bijou watching *Iolanthe*, with all of Boston's young Brahmin in attendance, mingling before and after. William might be there and she would see for herself whether he had his eye already upon another.

In the meantime, there was another house party to attend, although Rose didn't know if he was a friend of the Lowells, who were the hosts, or if William would attend in any case.

Later, with Emory back safely in his father's care and Claire on her way home, Rose headed to Mr. Mullett's famously ornate post office with her mother's correspondence tucked into her cotton carry-all.

As she alighted from her carriage on Congress Street, there *he* was, William Woodsom, coming across the square from the direction of Milk Street.

Rose felt a rush of something—excitement at seeing him perhaps, causing her heart to beat a speedy *rat-a-tat* in her chest—yet also, she couldn't deny a tinge of sadness. If she felt anything for this man, did that mean she was finally over Finn?

Did that mean she had to let her husband go?

Her chest tightened with confusion. If Finn had taught her one thing, it was that she was worthy of a man's undivided love. He'd said she had captured his heart and soul with his first glance and her first words. She simply would not take an interest in a man who split his attention amongst more than one woman.

"Good day, Miss Malloy," William said, as he approached.

"And to you, Mr. Woodsom," she returned.

"I feared you had moved to the hinterland since I had not seen you in so many days."

She raised an eyebrow at his slick banter. "The *hinterland*? Is that German?"

"Yes, Miss Malloy, I believe so. A more genteel way of saying the backwoods, don't you agree? In all seriousness," he added, "where have you been hiding?"

"Hiding, indeed!" she scoffed. "I assure you I have not been hiding, but merely going about my daily business. That we meet at all in a city this size is a wonder in itself."

He smiled. "There's a party in two nights at the Lowells'. Will you be there?"

She was sure his abrupt question was meant to catch her off guard.

"I couldn't say." She feigned disinterest. "Why?"

He blurted out with laughter, and she felt her cheeks infuse with warmth at her own coyness.

"Because I want more than anything to finally dance with you."

Blushing further, she realized she would like to dance with him as well. But what about Maeve's words of caution?

"Is that so?" she asked evenly.

"It is. Perhaps we could even arrive in the same group," he said.

She shook her head. She couldn't possibly invite him into her circle when she knew she would be going with the twins, Claire and Robert. Naturally, Claire had invited Maeve along in order to make it utterly acceptable to invite Maeve's cousin Franklin, as well. And the last thing Rose wanted was to toss William and Maeve together, creating an awkward situation.

"Impossible," Rose told him. "However, perhaps I shall see you there," she added, offering him no other encouragement, despite wanting to do so. When a pang of guilt assaulted her, she quickly tamped it down. Finn was long dead, and she did not dishonor her memory of him by feeling a little happiness at the idea of dancing with another man.

CHAPTER FOUR

When the night of the party arrived, Rose dressed to dazzle. It was the first time she could recall worrying about her appearance in a very long time. She strode up and down her front hall impatiently, waiting for her party of friends, and Maeve, to pick her up, and she couldn't deny the anticipatory excitement fluttering inside her. *How unexpected!*

When she entered the Lowells' spacious foyer, she noted that Reed and Charlotte were already speaking with William Woodsom. *Coincidence or had he sought out her family?*

Approaching at her brother's beckoning, she let Charlotte enfold her warmly in an embrace.

"So glad to see you," her sister-in-law said.

"And you," she answered. "Having a break from all the little ones?" Rose teased.

Her brother and his wife had four at present, two of their own and two adopted, and who knew if more were on the way.

Charlotte beamed. "You know I adore them all, the way a hummingbird adores nectar, but it's nice to be out with only adults." She let Reed take her hand and pull her to his side. It was apparent the only adults. they were truly interested in were one another.

Rose watched with something akin to awe as her brother and his wife gazed into each other's eyes for a moment, Charlotte's hand still clasped in Reed's, as if no one else in the world existed. They were so in love Rose found it difficult not to bask in their affection when she was around them. In her heart, she knew she and Finn would have had a similar relationship.

Of course, it was only a guess, and a nostalgic, sentimental, futile one at that. Yet her immediate attraction to Finn and her subsequent lingering loving memories made her believe it was true.

"Do you know Mr. Woodsom?" Reed asked, bringing her out of her reverie.

Rose focused her gaze on William's handsome face.

He gave her a brief smile, his eyes questioning, even cautious.

"Yes, we're acquainted. However, I didn't know you knew each other." Her glance returned to her brother.

"Mr. Woodsom's father was a client of mine," Reed explained. "As long as you two are already acquainted, I'm not remiss in leaving you to talk. I'm going to dance with my lovely wife."

They strolled off toward the Lowells' well-lit ballroom where a waltz had given way to a lively two-step with Sousa's music emitting joyfully from a small group of musicians.

"Shall we dance, too?" William asked.

She took a step backward.

"I'm quite safe," he added. "I won't bite."

"I know that," she said snappily. "It's just that I only arrived a minute ago."

"And that precludes you from dancing? Or only precludes you from dancing with me?" He crossed his arms. "Are you looking around for someone better to your liking? Here, let me see your card, and I'll point you in the direction of the best dancers."

She knew he was speaking in jest as the Lowells had forsaken the use of dance cards at their parties, letting people organize themselves more haphazardly or keep the same partner all evening long if they wished. It made for slightly more chaos regarding dance partners but often turned into a more relaxing evening.

In any case, Rose was looking for Claire but spied her already dancing with Franklin.

She sighed. As long as she wasn't alone with William and giving him leave to make advances, what was the harm?

"Fine. Let us dance," she said quickly and not very graciously. "It seems that's been on your mind for weeks."

He chuckled as he took her proffered hand. "Why wouldn't I want to have a lovely lady in my arms?"

"I suppose any one will do," she said tartly.

He stopped laughing as they entered the ballroom. Standing still, he looked down into her eyes.

"That's not the case at all, Miss Malloy. I've been wanting to dance particularly with you, and you only, or I wouldn't keep putting myself in the potentially humiliating position of asking."

Feeling chagrined and happy at the same time, Rose gave him a slight nod of acceptance, and he led her onto the dance floor.

A half hour later, her pulse raced, her breathing seemed slightly taxed, and her ears buzzed from the band's lively playing. She hadn't felt such intensity since the morning of the awful news that Finn's ship had sunk. Moreover, the brittle enclosure in which she imagined she'd placed her heart—along with her dead husband's for safekeeping—had cracked open ever so slightly during the brief time of dancing with William.

He was humorous without being snide or cynical. He was witty without being boastful. He made her laugh, kept her amused, and was a splendid dancer. In short, charming.

Rose was suffused with a lightness that felt like happiness.

When she went with Claire to the powder room, they talked about their partners and nothing else. Hair tidied, lace straightened, noses powdered, they looked at each other in the mirror.

"I'm so glad for you," Claire said. "I know it's been hard. You haven't been yourself for the past few years." She never brought up Finn's name, knowing how desperate Rose was to keep her clandestine marriage a secret. "I'm so glad you've found some joy at last."

"It's early days yet," Rose cautioned. "We are only dancing."

"And smiling. And laughing. And your eyes are sparkling."

Rose shrugged but glanced at herself in the mirror, looking into her own sapphire-blue Malloy eyes.

"Are they?"

"Come on," Claire said. "Let's get back to the menfolk."

However, the first thing that met Rose's gaze when she approached the refreshment table was William Woodsom speaking with Maeve, who had high spots of color on her cheeks and a sweet smile on her face.

Rose couldn't contain a sigh of exasperation, nor could she help from frowning. Was she really going to put up with a possible philanderer? Did she have enough feeling for him even to care what he did? She searched her heart. In some small corner, she was coming to like William. Only the tiniest bit, of course.

Claire had already sought out Franklin, so Rose strode over to the couple.

"Mr. Woodsom," she said with a nod to him. "Miss Norcross, you look lovely as always."

Maeve blushed.

What game was Maeve playing? Rose wondered. Franklin's cousin had so pointedly warned her away from William as if he were the devil incarnate, and yet quite of her own volition, she was talking to him. Perhaps *he* had approached *her.*

"Are you finding Mr. Woodsom's advances more acceptable this evening?"

Maeve's mouth dropped open in shock.

Rose smiled beatifically and tilted her head. "I mean, are you going to rebuff the poor gentleman again?"

"What?" William exclaimed, as Maeve flushed deeper and looked wide-eyed from him to Rose. "Miss Norcross, what is Miss Malloy talking about?" he asked.

Maeve only offered a shallow curtsey and ran off.

"Hm," Rose said, crossing her arms and watching her go.

William put his hand on her arm and turned her to face him. "Would you mind telling me what that was all about?"

Rose eyed him squarely. "Are you interested in pursuing the lovely Miss Norcross?"

His expression was one of puzzlement.

"She is indeed lovely, and as you know, we previously formed an extremely brief attachment. However, I can assure you I have no interest in her beyond the fact that she came over to say hello. I was merely being polite, as my mother raised me to be."

He took Rose's hand. "I am standing with the singular lady in whom I have any interest in pursuing. I promise you that."

"Is that because *I* let you kiss me and Miss Norcross did not?"

She had spoken in a normal tone of voice. Unfortunately, as she spoke, a couple of older women were walking close enough they overheard her words. Mrs. Cabot faltered in her footsteps and glanced briefly at Rose and then at William.

Rose only rolled her eyes at the old biddy, who grabbed the other woman's hand and hurried on.

William couldn't help laughing. "It'll be all over Boston by midnight and the rest of New England by midday tomorrow."

Rose shrugged. She had not been the object of gossip in a number of years. "I care not a whit," she retorted.

"In that, you are unique. Yet I wouldn't dismiss Mrs. Cabot so readily. She is about the most powerful woman in our sphere."

Indifferent, she shrugged again. "Answer my question or I will walk away, and we will never speak or dance again. Ever."

He stopped smiling. "You have no reason to believe me, although I have never lied to you. I did not try to kiss Miss Norcross, nor do I wish to do so."

He sounded sincere.

"Why did she break it off with you?" Rose persisted.

William looked down at the floor for a second, seemingly considering his answer.

"Apparently you and Miss Norcross have had a discussion. However, for my part, I would rather not discuss the lady out of turn."

Rose raised an eyebrow. *How gallant!* However, since Maeve had spoken "out of turn," it was, in fact, William's turn to do so, and Rose would wait all night for an explanation.

She told him precisely that.

His nostrils flared slightly, plainly not liking being issued an ultimatum. They stared at each other for a long moment. Then apparently, he decided to concede.

"If you insist, then I will tell you."

Rose found herself holding her breath.

"Miss Norcross is rather too simple for my tastes."

"I beg your pardon," she said. That was the last thing she'd expected him to say.

William cleared his throat. "She is not engaging in her discussion. Her conversation is always silly and frivolous, and her interests lie only with the fashion of the day."

Rose nodded in agreement, while at the same time, she felt a little shocked at his harsh judgment of Maeve. Was she, Rose, any less interested in fashion? Was she not also silly and frivolous?

"And you don't find me to be *simple?*"

He looked surprised by her question. "Of course not. I find you exceedingly interesting. You are able to discuss the issues of the day. You have an opinion, and you offer it readily."

She laughed at that. "True enough. I have been known to share my views with anyone who'll listen. Yet how would *you* know that?"

He smiled. "Truthfully?"

She nodded.

"I've watched and listened from afar."

"Like a Pinkerton detective?" she exclaimed.

"You see," he said. "How many women know about that agency?" He smiled. "I like that about you. In truth, I like a lot about you. Immensely. I was going to ask you to spend some time with me weeks ago, but my direct path to you was intercepted by Miss Norcross one evening. It seemed rude not to return her interest, just in case."

"In case she was more engaging than you suspected."

He gave a wry smile. "Well, she *is* attractive. However, there is nothing else there. At least, not for me. I'm sure she'll be well-suited for some other man, a man who likes to be reminded that her great uncle someone or other was once the mayor of Boston for about a minute."

Rose couldn't help laughing at how swiftly he had been subjected to Maeve's name-dropping.

William glanced around. "Since we're beginning to attract attention by standing here having our tête-à-tête, shall we get back to dancing?"

She nodded and let him take her hand. She liked William Woodsom more and more, and he was not the churl she'd feared.

As he led her onto the dance floor, she realized he hadn't directly answered one question.

"I take it she did not break it off with you. Rather the opposite."

William merely smiled, and Rose thought all the more of him for his gentlemanly discretion.

When he asked her to go driving the next day, she did so. On the following Sunday, he sent her an invitation to meet him after he left the State House for an early supper on Thursday, and she readily agreed. While she shouldn't have been allowed to dine with a man in a public restaurant without a chaperone, her mother allowed it as long as she followed her instructions— Rose must come home at a reasonable hour in her own carriage and never be alone with William. Then Evelyn wandered off to stare out at her gorgeous back garden in her distracted way.

Alighting at the Parker House Hotel, Rose found him awaiting her on the steps. William took her arm and her insides felt warm. Yes, she could get used to this man. It was not the same as the immediate yearning that had bowled her over with Finn, but it was satisfactory nonetheless, more than satisfactory, and it was blossoming.

In truth, she had as much desire to learn more about William and to kiss him again, as she used to feel with Finn.

At least, she thought so. It was hard to recall now. Their time had been so brief.

"What are you thinking?" William asked her as they were escorted to a table in the elegant dining room where every white tablecloth was perfectly pressed and the crystal chandeliers shone like icicles in brilliant sunshine.

She felt guilty. Thinking of her dead husband was definitely not the right way to start off an evening that held such promise.

"I was thinking how pleased I am to be with you." Then she smiled at him.

He looked surprised and immensely happy. "Thank you. I am honored."

A little while later, while sharing the lobster salad, he confessed, "I've watched you over the past few years. You seemed to withdraw from our society more than a little. You haven't been as outgoing as you once were. I didn't know if you were bored by all of us or if it was something else."

She could not tell him the truth—not all of it, anyway—but she could tell him something.

"There was an . . . an incident, no, it was more than that. Anyway, it happened about three years ago," she admitted, "and it left me greatly saddened."

"I am sorry to hear it. If you ever wish to tell me more, know that my ears, as well as the rest of me, is at your disposal. And I'm glad you've chosen to finally start reaching for some happiness again and are doing so with me."

The night went well. They each chose the mutton cutlets with mushrooms and a glass of burgundy. She told him about her family, and in return, he engaged her with stories about his. Rose hadn't been so relaxed and entertained and enthusiastic, all at once, in a very long time.

When their meal was over and he returned her to her carriage, they stood close.

"I should very much like to kiss you again," he told her, his gaze locked on hers.

She could be honest. *Why not?*

"I would like that," she told him, watching as a slow smile spread over his handsome face.

"Not here, of course," he said, not bothering to glance at the stream of people walking on the sidewalk. The murmur of the passers-by was a gentle background hum.

"Of course." She smiled back, not letting her eyes leave his.

"Soon, though?" he asked, his voice dropping to a delightful whisper.

She nodded, feeling a thrill of anticipation.

He helped her onto her carriage, which she prided herself on driving well, and stood watching as she drove off at a frightfully early hour, as she'd promised her mother.

"My goodness," she said aloud once alone. William Woodsom was certainly awakening a few things that had laid dormant since she'd become an untimely widow. What's more, she could easily imagine bringing him to meet her family. Why, Reed and Charlotte already knew him. Everything would be smooth as silk against one's skin.

For the first time, she wondered if because of her previous marriage, there was some formality she had to go through if things were to progress with William. Obviously, as a widow, she was free to enter into a new engagement.

Although if it came out she'd been married before . . . and she hadn't told him. *Hm*, Rose could imagine that would not sit well.

She decided to discuss it with Claire. Reed, as a lawyer, would be a better choice. Yet after all this time, she couldn't easily mention to her brother how she had once upon a time been a wife.

CHAPTER FIVE

Five months to the day they'd dined at the Parker House, William held out a small, pale-blue porcelain jewelry box while he and Rose drifted around the Public Garden lagoon in a swan boat. Despite room for eight, there were only the two of them, piloted by a young man in a white shirt and dark hat, all but hidden behind the large copper swan.

William had scooted close to her on the seat that could easily hold two more, and then he'd presented her with the box.

"Rose Olivia Malloy, will you do me the honor of becoming my wife?"

Rose looked down at the smooth porcelain and felt all the blood leave her head. *Dear God, was she going to faint in the middle of the lagoon?*

At that point, he lifted the hinged lid, presenting its contents to her.

Rose's breath caught in her throat at the sight. Inside, nestled on a bed of cream satin, was a delicate milgrain-worked ring of silver and rose gold. In the very center sat a bezel-cut diamond. Around this, dark rose-colored rubies circled with an outer halo of twelve diamonds giving the ring a scalloped edge. It was unusual and exquisite.

"As soon as I saw it," William intoned, "I knew it was meant for you."

With her heart pounding wildly in her chest, she looked up from the ring to William's eager face. So familiar to her, so beloved. He was offering her a new start at a married life.

She felt the smile tug at her cheeks, and then she nodded. He slipped his arms around her, bent his head, and kissed her. She dropped the ring box onto her lap and kissed him back soundly.

When he pulled back, he laughed. "Please don't let that fall out of the boat, dearest. I'm not sure there's another one like it in all the world, as I'm certain there's no one else like you."

He picked the ring out of the box, took hold of her trembling hand, and slipped it onto her finger.

"A bit big," he said, tilting his head, "but we can get that fixed easily enough."

"I'm engaged."

Rose allowed Claire to shriek and then shriek again. Then she grabbed her in a hug to stop her.

"Are you really?" Claire asked. "That's wonderful! I do hope I'm next. That's twice for you and not once yet for me."

"Shh," Rose cautioned. She wished Claire wouldn't bring up her past so casually. She had still not breathed a word of her previous marriage to anyone. Instead, Rose had allowed her attachment to William to grow over the past months, and when he'd asked her to marry him, it was easy to say yes. Her heart was full and happy.

She smiled thinking of how the boat had rocked when he'd jumped up and yelled to anyone within hearing, "Rose Malloy has agreed to marry me!"

"Tell me everything," Claire insisted, grabbing Rose's hand and dragging her to a bench in the back garden of her home on Myrtle Street. "Don't leave anything out. What's it like to kiss him? Let me see the ring again. It's lovely. You never had a ring with," she lowered her voice a little, "with Phineas. Everything is so perfect. This is how it is all supposed to be."

Rose didn't have to speak. With her friend radiating excitement, she knew she would never get a word in anyway. *This was how it was supposed to be*, Claire had said. A handsome young man in love with her. She, in love with him. He dined with her family on occasion, got on well with her mother, her brother, and her sister. It was uncomplicated.

And that caused her a pang of guilt for Finn. *How would it have ever worked out?*

William had even gone to Reed to ask his permission and had been granted it readily.

"Maybe Franklin will get the hint," Claire chattered on. "You do think he likes me in that manner, don't you?"

"Of course," Rose assured her, although she couldn't help wishing the man wasn't so slow to act. She would love to have been second to be engaged in this case. However, as far as Rose could tell, Franklin's mother was partly, if not entirely, to blame. In the eyes of Mrs. Brewster, a woman with an inflated sense of self and far too much reliance on harsh henna by the look of her hair, no woman would be good enough for her son. What's more, Franklin's mother had let every female in Boston know it.

If anyone could win over the woman, however, it would be Claire, with her endless good nature and soft manners, quite superior to Rose's own less-reserved, less-patient nature. Luckily, she didn't have to worry about her own future mother-in-law, as William's English parents were nearly always abroad.

"When and where?" Claire asked.

"In September."

"A safe month," Claire said.

Rose nodded. September was usually not too hot while also too early for the first fall cold snap.

"We shall probably have the ceremony at King's Chapel where Reed was married. That was a lovely wedding."

"It was, but yours will be even lovelier," Claire insisted. "You deserve it. After everything."

Rose shrugged. She didn't deserve it any more than the next woman. She counted herself very fortunate to have been loved by not one but by two wonderful men.

"What does your mother say? Is she sad or relieved to be losing her last child?"

"I hadn't thought of it that way. She hasn't expressed anything except happiness for me." Rose considered her mother's situation. They had talked about it briefly the day before when she'd returned from the Public Garden. "Why? Do you think she'll be sad?"

Claire looked thoughtful. "Well, that house has become increasingly empty. What will she do in a house that used to hold six and now will hold only one?"

Rose frowned. Had she been selfish in the face of her own impending happiness? Would Eleanor indeed be lonely? Goodness gracious, her mother had never been alone before!

They had closed up two of the bedrooms already, and she and her mother kept one each and one for guests. Rarely, Sophie and her husband, Riley, visited from the West Coast along with their children. At such times, they opened up another room and the house seemed lively as it had when she was a child.

Rose would have to discuss it with Elise and Reed. Maybe one of them wanted to move their family into the house. More likely, they would suggest selling it. William's parents had already given him their house for he and Rose to live in after they were married.

She sighed.

"Oh, Rose," Claire exclaimed. "I didn't mean to make you melancholy. Let's go into town and look at dresses."

"What? This moment?"

"Yes, immediately."

Rose nodded. "Yes, let's."

That night, she would make an effort to speak with her mother and find out her true feelings on the matter of the marriage of her youngest child.

However, over their evening meal, Evelyn seemed positively delighted when she heard the last of her three daughters bubbling about two different dress styles that had caught her eye. They sat at the table alone as they did most nights, each with a glass of wine and with their cook, Emily, providing a light supper.

"The Highlands isn't far, Mama," Rose added to the discussion she'd been attempting, imagining setting up her own household in William's home on Walnut Avenue. "We can go to the opera house on Dudley. Why, I'll still see you all the time."

Evelyn laughed. "You won't see me all the time. Nor should you. Why are you saying this now?" She took Rose's hand. "Why are you suddenly worrying over me?"

"Not suddenly, Mama. But I am the last to go. I can't stand the thought of you alone in this house." At least her mother was fully present and engaged at dinner, not daydreaming or looking out the window into the back garden.

Evelyn looked thoughtful. "I always thought I'd be enjoying these later years with your father, bless his soul. However, I have become used to life without him. I have good friends, and I'm never lonely. Except for Sophie, you're all still close by."

Rose nodded. She almost wanted to share how she, too, had lost the man she'd loved, but she knew her experience could be nothing like her mother's. For over thirty years, her mother had had Oliver before losing him so suddenly to illness, whereas Rose had barely enjoyed half a year with Finn, and only a few weeks married to him.

Besides, there was no point in shocking her mother at this juncture.

"I like Mr. Woodsom," her mother said unexpectedly.

Rose smiled. "As do I."

"He will treat you well. I can tell he dotes on you."

William had indeed shown his adoration and devotion a dozen times over. And Rose felt extremely lucky. The bothersome guilt of never having told him about Finn had faded, as with telling her mother and the rest of her family. *What point was there to doing so now?*

A day later, Rose sat fidgeting in Elise's study. Her oldest sister had decided she must have a fabulous engagement party, despite the fact that Elise hadn't had one herself, nor even a proper wedding ceremony. Or maybe *because* of those very facts!

"We'll have a small soirée at home," Rose protested for the umpteenth time.

"Nonsense," Elise said, brushing aside Rose's words with a sweep of her hand. "It will be fun for all of us. Or course, it will be at the Tremont where Mr. Woodsom first kissed you."

Rose blushed. She didn't know why she'd told her oldest sister about the scandalous encounter on the stairs. However, instead of being surprised, Elise had smiled at the story with a rather wicked grin. After all, she'd had a more-than-improper encounter with Michael, her husband, before they'd married, and she had confided in Rose about it.

"We won't get Sophie and Riley to cross the country with their little brood if not for a big occasion. They won't be able to attend the wedding, you know. Sophie already has a huge commitment with the orchestra in September."

"I can't even believe they're coming at all." It was always a treat when the Dalcourts came to Boston as it happened so infrequently since Sophie had moved away.

"And you'll help instead of hinder?" Elise asked.

"I suppose," Rose agreed. "Let's discuss the food."

Elise pulled a leather-bound notebook out of her writing desk.

"What on earth?" Rose asked.

"It's my organizer," Elise said.

"I swear, you get more eccentric all the time."

"I am not the least bit eccentric," Elise protested. "Anyone can have a stack of stationery, but this," she ran her hand over the blue-dyed leather, "this is for serious projects. You know, like the suffragette meetings I go to with Mama. Now, where were we? Ah, yes. Charlotte said her French chef will make everything to perfection. We have only to give him an idea of what you like."

"And William, too, of course," Rose added with a mischievous twinkle in her eye.

"And William, too, of course," Elise repeated before the two of them burst out laughing. As if he would have a say in any of it!

When they had gathered themselves and could talk again, Elise said, "Charlotte is writing a special toast for her and Reed to deliver. So sweet." Not to be outdone, she added, "Michael has a special surprise for you, too."

Elise was aglow with excitement. Rose shook her head, warmed by the fond feelings she felt for her sister.

"I think this party is as much for you as for me."

Elise opened her mouth in surprise. "No! Well, maybe a bit. I may be a long-married woman, but even so, I love the idea of romance and weddings and finally seeing you all settled."

It was Rose's turn to look surprised. "Finally seeing me settled? Why? I'm not exactly an aging spinster."

"I didn't mean that. Yet you were so light and gay a few years ago, and then you did not seem so happy until Mr. Woodsom came along."

Rose only nodded. At first, she'd had no idea her family had noticed her bereavement. By the time she came out of her own grief enough to realize the distress she was causing them, she hadn't the energy to do anything about it. In any case, she thought they would prefer the subdued Rose to the wild one who'd never listened to her elders if she could get away with it.

"Back to the food," she said, watching Elise lick the end of a stubby pencil that she'd pulled out from her pocket. "I want those little fairy cakes with orange bits. And the citrus rum punch that made you fall down."

"Goodness gracious!" Elise exclaimed with a shake of her head. "You remember that?"

"I may have been only fourteen, but I knew a tipsy sister when I saw one."

"Moving along," her sister muttered, a slight frown on her forehead. "What about actual food? Not merely cake and drink."

"Cubes of roast beef," Rose said, "tucked in individual puff pastries. Perhaps with some horseradish on the side. Do you think Pierre would do that?"

"I'm sure he would. I am a bit surprised, though, that you already have something so specific in mind."

Rose smiled. She was bursting to tell her sister about her latest desire, to attend the Boston Cooking School. Ever since her conversation with Reed about doing something with her life, even during the delightful romance with William, she had continued to think about what stirred her. One day, as she'd exited the Common on Tremont Street, she'd come face to face with the school.

Of course she'd heard of it. Moreover, she knew that not only did women attend who wanted to be employed as cooks, like their Emily, but also women who simply wanted to offer more nutritious and tempting meals to their families. What's more, some of Rose's peers went to the Saturday lectures to listen to the likes of Mrs. Richards discuss food chemistry. How thrilling to listen to the first woman admitted and graduated from such an institution as the Massachusetts Institute of Technology!

Immediately, Rose had gone inside, only to be met by some of the most delicious aromas she'd ever had the pleasure of encountering. Her mouth started watering while she was still in the foyer, and her brain began deciphering what ingredients she was smelling.

Eventually, she'd been introduced to the assistant principal, Miss Fannie Farmer, who'd tried to steer her to the Saturday lectures attended by other well-to-do young ladies until Rose expressed in no uncertain terms that she wanted to actually learn to cook.

"You understand," she'd told the heavy-set lady with her clean white lacey blouse and wavy brown and white hair, "I want to cook with my own two hands."

"Yes, indeed, Miss Malloy, now I do understand, and I believe our school can help you. You shall use your hands and all ten fingers and your arms and sometimes your back. And more importantly, you will use your brain. For cooking is *not* a slipshod and estimated endeavor. It is a science and thus responds to measurements and precision."

Rose thought of her brother's French chef. She'd always considered Pierre's cooking to be a calling and that the talented man was as driven to it as her sister Sophie was to playing the piano. Certainly, when she had dined with Reed and Charlotte, she'd discovered Pierre was not above tossing in an unexpected ingredient, turning an expected dish into something magical.

Perhaps this lady had no such beliefs.

"Do you not think there is an art to it as well?" Rose asked, feeling a little timid with this woman, despite the kind eyes that sparkled behind her spectacles. There was something determined and formidable about Fannie Farmer.

The assistant principal had smiled at her. "Of course. Yet you cannot have a Renoir or a Monet or a Harriet Peale, for that matter, until there has been the precision of da Vinci or van Eyck. Do you see what I mean?"

Yes, she certainly did.

"I do." Rose had enrolled on the spot. The next new course of lessons would begin in a week's time. She'd gone home immediately to ask their cook if she would mind Rose using some pots and pans and trying things out at home.

Emily had laughed. "If you want to putter in the kitchen, miss, be my guest."

"I have quite a few particular ideas about cooking," Rose told her sister, "and I intend to try them all out when I start taking cooking classes."

"Mm." Elise was writing on her small pad. "Then what do you think we should serve with it? Minted peas, perhaps?"

Oh dear. Rose sighed. Elise was not listening, too wrapped up in the party planning. If she'd needed a favor, it would have been a good time to ask her and receive an inattentive yes. Or perhaps it was a good time to ask about something that had worried her lately.

"Have you noticed anything odd about Mama?"

Elise looked up and sharply eyed her sister, fully present once more.

"Specifically?"

Rose shrugged. "Being a bit preoccupied for months, especially recently. I wondered if maybe she felt sad over her last child leaving the proverbial nest."

Elise shook her head. "She would never begrudge you your future or your happiness."

"I know. Still, have you and Reed discussed her being all alone?"

"As a matter of fact, we have."

"I knew it. I'm so relieved," Rose told her. "I'm not the only one concerned. What will we do with her?"

"*Do* with her?" Elise gave a wry smile. "It was not so much a discussion of such magnitude as it was setting up a casual schedule. If she dines with Reed and Charlotte once a week and with Michael and me once, and perhaps, after you get settled, with you and William, then if we also take turns going over to her house, why she'll hardly ever be alone for her evening meal."

"That's a good idea. Of course, she shall start coming over to dine with William and me immediately after I set up house."

Her sister nodded. "Back to the party planning." Then Elise took a quick breath. "Did you say something about cooking classes?"

Rose laughed and explained to Elise her new interest.

In the days that followed, she felt swept along by her sister and Claire and even by her mother and Charlotte. Everyone seemed to be extremely excited by a homegrown love match and the upcoming wedding. Sophie's nuptials had taken place in San Francisco, so they hadn't had a real Malloy wedding since Reed married Charlotte. Goodness! Was that already seven years past?

All of Boston society, every Brahmin, whether bourgeois or aristocratic, was abuzz with wrangling an invitation to either the engagement party, the wedding, the reception supper, or all three. Rose had not felt her heart so full of joy in years. The hum of excitement grew as the date got closer.

"I'm so very pleased you're here." Rose said to Sophie the night before the grand engagement party. Her middle sister had arrived the day before from the West Coast with her family. "However, I can't believe this is actually happening."

Sophie paused in brushing Rose's hair, something she'd always done when they were growing up. They locked eyes in the mirror over the vanity. "In a good way, you can't believe it?"

Rose laughed. "Of course. I'm very happy." And she was, even though, in a dark corner of her mind, she felt a sliver of fear that something would happen to William. In moments of quiet, she would suddenly imagine the devastation to her heart if anything befell him.

If something happened to him, how would she bear it?

"I'm relieved, dearest," Sophie said, resuming brushing. "He seems wonderful and smart. And clearly, he's madly in love with you."

Rose shrugged. She almost took for granted William's love, so used to basking in its warmth, and except for the fear of losing him, she knew no lapse in her happiness.

"If I'm as happy as you and Riley . . . ," she trailed off, while her sister grinned at her in the mirror hung over the dressing table.

"You will be," Sophie said. "We had a difficult start and a few obstacles to overcome in order to be together, but that made it all the sweeter." Sophie had the dreamy look she always wore when discussing her husband.

Sophie and Riley, Riley and Sophie. Rose could not imagine one without the other. The only reason they weren't together that moment was because Riley was putting their children to bed while Sophie enjoyed some private time with Rose.

"Is everything ready for tomorrow?" Sophie asked, laying down the brush and taking a seat on her sister's bed.

Rose turned from the vanity.

"Yes, it seems so."

The staff of the Tremont would spend all the next day putting the finishing touches to the main ballroom. Chef Pierre had left Reed and Charlotte's home and taken up residence in the Tremont's kitchens, cooking and baking all day and would continue the next day.

Lastly, Rose had found the perfect party dress in a blush color that would look fetching against her dark hair. She opened her wardrobe and there it was, hanging ready.

For the briefest second, the sight caused her a pang of sorrow. And, as always, the sorrow was linked to Finn, who'd never seen her in anything splendid like a party gown. Still, it comforted her to believe he would have liked it. She could easily recall the desire and wanting in his gaze whenever he looked at her.

"I can't wait to see your William's expression when he sees you in that gown," Sophie said, dragging Rose's thoughts back to the present.

Assailed by guilt over pondering a dead man on the eve of her engagement party, Rose thoroughly berated herself. Immediately, she conjured William's laughing, handsome face. Why, she had only to picture him, and her spirits lifted.

CHAPTER SIX

As it turned out, her fiancé's expression on the night of the party was positively awestruck causing Rose to blush, her cheeks matching her dress color. She had never felt so beautiful in her life.

William took her hand. "Can you wear this on our wedding day?"

She laughed. "Don't be ridiculous!"

"How can you top how magnificent you look at this moment?" he wondered. "It's impossible."

"We shall do it, nonetheless," remarked Elise, overhearing as she approached them.

"Everything is perfect." Rose grabbed her sister's hands. "Thank you for this. It is as special as you promised."

She surveyed the room where candles and mirrors made everything and everyone sparkle and dazzle with light. There were flowers on every available surface. Crystal punch bowls and heavily laden tables of the most heavenly smelling food beckoned the guests. And of course, there was music, which Sophie had planned.

Rose knew her musical-minded sister would be hovering over the small band all evening, directing them as to the choices. Sophie had already sat down at the piano once, pushing the alarmed pianist to the side of the bench, before sending out a happy tune over the ballroom.

At that moment, though, her sister, rustling in her skirts of deep purple taffeta, strolled over to where they stood. Of course, Riley strode along beside her, tall, ruggedly handsome—with something a little western and wild about him, despite being a physician.

Riley shook hands with William, who'd got on well with Rose's California branch of the family. "You had better follow me," Riley said. "Reed has something for you."

William raised his eyebrows and looked at Rose, who shrugged.

"Knowing my brother, it's a legal document spelling out the terms of our engagement."

Everyone laughed.

"You mean our *marriage*," William said.

"Oh, they'll be one for that, too."

They laughed again. "Go ahead," Rose told him. "Hurry back, though, and tell me what it is all about." She watched William walk away, striding next to Riley. Two such handsome men. And one of them was hers!

Sophie watched them go, too, then she turned to Elise. "Go rescue Mama."

They followed Sophie's gaze. By the dessert table, their mother was chatting with Ethan Nickerson.

"Not I," Elise said, her face flushing pink.

"Why ever not?" Rose asked, surprised at her oldest sister's reticence. She usually took charge of whatever needed doing.

Sophie laughed lightly. "I think she still feels discomfort about nearly getting engaged to the man."

"What?" Rose exclaimed so loudly her sisters had to shush her. She rounded on Elise. "Tell me," she demanded, for she couldn't picture Elise with anyone except Michael Bradley to whom she'd been ecstatically wed for the past ten years.

"You remember," Sophie said when Elise remained silent. "She was trying to make Michael jealous."

"With old man Nickerson?" Rose lifted her eyebrows.

"No, it wasn't like that," Elise protested. "It was more complicated."

"Couldn't you find someone closer to your own age?" Rose asked, wrinkling her nose and taking another look at Mr. Nickerson. True, he'd been ten years younger, but he was clearly the age of their parents. "He's well-preserved for a man Mama's age. Really though!"

"Enough," Elise said. "In any case, someone else can go draw Mama away."

"Maybe she doesn't want to be rescued," Rose surmised. "They seem to be having a pleasant discussion."

They all looked again as their mother, gorgeous in a peach-colored gown, laughed at something Nickerson said. She put a hand up to her hair, with its unfashionable gray streaks at either temple, the only sign she was aging, and very gracefully at that. Rose was quite glad her mother eschewed the popular dyes and let her beautiful hair alone.

"I'll do it," Sophie said, and she marched over to Evelyn Malloy.

"When did she become so bossy?" Elise asked, and then suddenly her own husband appeared at her side, sliding his arm around her waist. Before she could say anything, he bent down and murmured in her ear. Rose watched her oldest sister's cheeks deepen from pink to scarlet. Then Michael looked Rose in the eyes.

"My wife has done a wonderful job," he said. "And at present, she deserves to have some fun. Excuse us." He dragged her quite willingly onto the dance floor with the countless other couples, all in their finery.

How lucky her sisters were to have found their love matches. Now it was her turn. Just then, she saw a movement out of the corner of her eye and turned. For an instant, she had the impression a man might have been staring at her, but her view of him was blocked immediately by dancers. And then Claire, Robert, and Franklin appeared.

"Where did you three get to?" Rose asked. They each had a drink in hand.

"We were taking it all in," Claire said. "If I were to ever have an engagement party," she said, glancing sideways at Franklin, who suddenly seemed to find his collar a size too tight, "then I think I would ask your sister to organize it for me."

"I'm sure she would do it, too," Rose said. "She thoroughly enjoyed the planning and implementation." She looked at Robert, who was smiling affably, still being dragged around by his twin sister. *Could she set him up with someone?* He seemed so reserved and docile. Why, she couldn't even imagine him kissing. And then it struck her.

If any part of what Maeve had said was true, that she didn't want to be kissed before she was engaged, then Robert was most likely the perfect man for her.

Rose considered how terribly rude she'd been to Maeve months earlier. Perhaps she could make amends by encouraging Robert to turn his attention to the lovely girl. After all, Maeve's cousin, Franklin, was already—almost—a part of the Appleton family.

"What is that rather mischievous smile for?" William asked, suddenly at her side.

"You survived my brother," she said. "Was he harsh with you?"

"No, not at all," William said. "You were correct as to the nature of the conversation. I'll tell you about it later."

"We're going to dance," Claire announced. "Can't let all this lovely music go to waste." Franklin bowed and they walked away, Robert in their wake.

Rose watched them go. "What do you think of Maeve Norcross and Robert Appleton as a couple?"

William froze then blinked at her. "I don't think of them at all to tell you the truth. Right now, however, I believe Robert is somehow going to try to dance *with* his sister and Franklin." He laughed a little at his own quip.

In reality, however, Robert merely stood on the edge of the dancing and watched.

"If we see Maeve, we'll direct Robert toward her or vice versa," Rose decided. "Meanwhile, shall we join the dancers?" Rose asked. Truthfully, she was eager to feel her dress swish and swirl as they pirouetted and twirled.

"In a few moments," William said. "Let's go to where it all began first." He grinned at her, and she smiled back, feeling a little wicked. Then she nodded.

Together, they slipped from the main ballroom and along the corridor to the far staircase. Rushing up it like children while holding hands, they then ran along the upper hallway before starting down the other stairs.

"You know, we could have simply come to the bottom of these stairs," he said, breathing hard, as he stopped in front of her precisely as he'd done months before.

"I know," she agreed, laughter bubbling from her lips until he caught hold of her waist and drew her to him.

His earnest eyes looked both loving and serious at the same time.

"I am so happy, Rose."

"As am I," she assured him.

"May I kiss you?" he asked.

"You didn't ask me the first time, as I recall. You said I owed you a kiss."

"I would have said anything," he confessed. "At present, though, I owe you my heart and my soul, as well as my happiness. I am in debt to how you've changed my life."

She sobered. He had brought happiness to her again, as well. Before she could tell him that, he leaned in to kiss her. As their lips touched, she felt the last icicle of sadness melt away.

Breathing in his familiar scent, she allowed him to press her mouth open, to deepen the connection. They kissed much longer than they had the first time. And they might have stayed there all evening if Charlotte hadn't come to find them.

"Very improper!" she scolded before shooting them a broad smile as they broke apart. "In truth, I would tell you to carry on except people are starting to wonder where the couple of the evening has got to, including both of your mothers."

That was enough to break the spell. Rose knew her own mother wouldn't mind, but she didn't want to anger her soon to be mother-in-law.

"Hurry," she said, grabbing William's hand. "Let's get back."

With Charlotte following behind them, they raced to the ballroom. A murmur went up as they entered, arm-in-arm. The crowd parted, seemingly funneling them toward the dance floor, even though the musicians were taking a break. No doubt it was the respite from dancing that had caused people to wonder where the betrothed couple was.

Still, it seemed as if they were wanted in the center of the room. Thus, Rose let William lead her there. She saw so many familiar faces—her mother beaming, William's parents standing close with benign smiles, Claire, Robert, and Franklin. Riley and Sophie. Elise and Michael. And all of Rose's many friends.

Then Charlotte approached and handed them each a fluted crystal glass. Rose realized most people had a drink in hand already.

Ah! It was time for a toast.

Charlotte's green eyes sparkled as she took her drink from Reed. Then she faced the couple and pulled a piece of paper out of her sleeve. She flipped it open with her free hand, but then she frowned and crumpled it up before beginning to speak.

"Rose, I have been blessed to have your friendship since I entered this family. You and your sisters have been the sisters I never had. However, you are special, with your spark of liveliness, which some might call impetuousness."

A few people in the crowd laughed good naturedly.

"Add to that spark, your humor, your sweet disposition, and your quick mind, and Rose, in total, you are a delight. I've also known you to be very thoughtful over the past few years, even melancholy. Before Mr. Woodsom enlivened your life, exactly as your dear brother did mine." She glanced at Reed, who nodded. Then Charlotte looked at William.

"As Rose welcomed me in, I am welcoming you, William. You're a valued addition to this family."

She stepped closer and kissed Rose's cheek and then William's, who nodded gratefully.

It was Reed's turn, Rose realized, as he looked fondly at her.

"To my youngest sister," he began, then turned his eyes heavenward for a moment. "You have caused us all a great deal of worry." Everyone within earshot laughed. "More than the rest of the Malloys put together. Am I correct, Mother?"

Evelyn nodded, although she also blew Rose a kiss, and mouthed the words, "I love you."

Rose blew a kiss back, sipped her drink, and let her brother get on with his ribbing.

"Before I had children of my own, I think you started to give me my first gray hairs. However, every single one was worth it, especially to see you so happy tonight."

Reed turned to William.

"You may not know this. Our father said to our mother on the day Rose was born, this baby is a wild one, like the beach roses. And Mother said, then we'll name her such."

Everyone clapped, and Rose wiped the tears from her eyes, wishing her father were there.

"We're happy to deliver our Rose into William Woodsom's care. We wish him much luck with her, and patience," he added.

The guests laughed and raised their glasses toasting the couple, and then everyone drank. William shook Reed's hand before clasping Rose tightly to his side.

"My wild Rose," he murmured into her hair.

Rose felt her heart expand and could barely breathe. Her pulse was racing. She took another sip of the drink Charlotte had handed her and began a slow turn to survey the room as the music started again. So much love. So many friendly faces, some belonged to people she'd known all her life, some—

Finn.

In an instant, everything changed. The breath left her lungs in a whoosh that left her lightheaded, and she gasped out loud. Or did she scream? She wasn't sure.

Her blood was pounding in her ears, drowning out other sounds. She blinked to end the illusion. Yet impossibly, Finn still stood there. One moment, he was staring at her with his dark, anguished eyes, and the next, he was pushing his way between two guests and disappearing from her view.

The glass slipped from her hand, though the sound of it shattering on the floor was barely audible in the crowded room.

"Rose?" she heard William's voice.

Her head was spinning. Lights, brighter than the mirror-reflected candles or even than the electric lamps far overhead, filled her vision from all sides. Her stomach contracted and a wave of nausea rolled up from inside her.

Good God, she thought. She was going to be sick. But she would not. *Blast it.* She tamped it down, even as she felt a clammy coolness break out over her entire body. She closed her eyes as her legs gave way, confident William would catch her.

CHAPTER SEVEN

Rose heard her name. It was a man's voice. It seemed to be coming from a long way away. She didn't want to open her eyes. There was something terribly wrong. Something disturbing that she knew she didn't want to face, yet she couldn't remember what it was. She had a feeling if she raised her lids, she would either see or remember an awful occurrence.

"Rose." This time the gentle voice of her mother was accompanied by a slight tap on her cheek. Then a moment later, the acrid smell of ammonia assaulted her nostrils. She coughed and slowly opened her eyes, as Riley removed the vial of smelling salts.

All around her, Rose saw women, her mother on her left, Elise on her right, and next to them, Sophie and Charlotte respectively. Right beside her, though, was Dr. Riley Dalcourt, looking concerned.

"Here she comes," he said.

"How are you feeling?" her mother asked, running a hand over her youngest daughter's forehead.

"Too much excitement, do you think?" asked Sophie.

"It wasn't too much to drink," Elise said. "She was sipping her first glass of champagne."

Rose let her eyelids drift closed again. *What had happened? What was wrong?* She had an inkling she absolutely should remember something but dreaded thinking of it at the same time.

"Rose." It was Charlotte this time. "Come back to us, sweetheart."

Rose opened her eyes again.

"What happened?" she asked to no one in particular.

None of them answered her directly. Instead, Riley said, "Let's sit her up slowly. She'll feel better."

Rose felt them raise her up and prop pillows behind her.

"Breathe deeply," Sophie said, and Rose opened her mouth, sucking in a few deep breaths. The buzzing in her ears that she hadn't noticed until it began to subside ceased all together.

"What happened?" she repeated.

"You fainted," Elise said. "Dropped to the floor like a rock into the harbor."

The harbor. Then it came back with the speed of a summer storm—Finn. *Finn!*

Rose groaned.

"Darling, what is it?" her mother asked. "Do you hurt?"

Did she hurt? Yes, her heart felt as heavy as lead, and her stomach started to churn again. *Was she possibly going mad?*

"Would you all take a step back and let her breathe," Riley said firmly. He bent low and murmured in her ear. "You seem to have had a shock. Do you remember what it was?"

She could not tell him. She simply shook her head.

"Are you in any pain?"

She shook her head again. Then she asked, "Where is William?"

"He's downstairs," Charlotte answered. "They let us bring you up here to a vacant room."

"We're still at the Tremont?" Finally, she looked around at the unfamiliar wallpaper. "Is it the same night?"

She saw Sophie and Elise exchange a glance.

"Yes," said Elise. "William carried you up here, just a few moments ago."

How strange. She felt as if she'd been sleeping for ages.

"I'll be ready to go back downstairs in a minute," she assured them.

Riley handed her a glass of water, which she sipped and felt better.

Evelyn touched her daughter's hand. "Take your time, dear. The evening is young. Everyone is still in good spirits." Then she chuckled. "That's two of my daughters who have fainted on the floor of the Tremont."

The women all laughed.

"Technically," Sophie said, "Elise didn't actually faint so much as she passed out."

"Sophie!" Elise protested, clearly embarrassed by the mention of when she'd drunk too much punch and fallen into her now-husband's arms, nearly sliding down the front of him onto the dance floor. At the time, Michael was barely an acquaintance although she'd already been carrying a spark for him for years.

Riley shot his wife a fond look and offered her a wry grin.

"I remember when *you* fainted away at my feet. You frightened me half to death."

Sophie blushed. "You caught me as I recall, exactly like William caught Rose."

"I feel much better," Rose said. "I want to see William. Let's go downstairs."

Slowly, they went downstairs and walked into the ballroom, like a cluster of lovely flowers, with Riley taking up the rear. The rest of their menfolk were beside them in an instant.

"You gave me quite a scare," William said to Rose. "Are you well?"

She nodded, glad to set eyes on him and to hold his hand. He was real. He loved her.

"What happened?" he asked as she leaned into his side.

What *had* happened? She'd seen a ghost, a realistic-looking ghost. So tangible, in fact, that he'd been flesh-colored and breathing. However, she knew he had been a mere figment of her imagination.

"I honestly don't know, but I feel quite recovered. I'm even ready to dance."

William's face broke out in a smile. "If you're up to it." He took her hand. "I've been dying to show you off all night."

"Take it easy," Riley called after them.

Rose finally got to experience dancing in the arms of the man she loved, feeling like a queen, dressed in the loveliest garment she'd ever worn. She enjoyed hours with her family and friends, eating, drinking, and definitely making merry.

During it all, however, she felt strangely detached, as if she was watching the party through another person's eyes. What's more, Rose spent the first hour after awakening looking for Finn's ghost at every turn on the dance floor.

When she realized how foolish that was, she tried to stop herself and nearly succeeded. Yet even as she focused on William's handsome face or her sisters' loving smiles, Rose was aware of a shadowy discontent. Her own ridiculous hallucination had cast a pall over her engagement party, and she was determined to hide it from all those who had worked so hard to make this a special night.

She hated feeling slightly relieved when the party was over. Yet she couldn't deny she was glad to climb into her bed that night under her mother's roof. In the dark and quiet, Rose pondered what she'd seen.

The apparition had been so real—looking slightly older, Finn's wheat-colored hair a wee bit longer, yet his clothing had been in fashion. She wrinkled her nose, trying to understand what it meant. Wouldn't a ghost have looked exactly as Finn had looked when he'd died over three years earlier, nearly four? What's more, if he were merely a figment of her imagination, wouldn't he have been as she remembered him from their last night together?

She sighed in frustration. She was *not* going insane. She was merely tired. After all, it was two in the morning. Obviously, at the beginning of the evening, she'd been overexcited by the event. Her agitated brain had conjured up another exciting time from her past and summoned Finn.

Besides, the party had been a great success, and William was the perfect fiancé. She could ask for nothing more.

So why did she wish it was a few hours later when she could go to Finn's old rooming house? Merely out of curiosity, of course. A compulsion to go preoccupied her as she drifted off to sleep.

Ludicrous notion, she scolded herself, but she drove her carriage across Beacon Hill anyway and eventually stood before the front door of the residence on Bowdoin Square.

"Utterly absurd," she muttered, going into the foyer and then to the door of his room. Before she could decide whether to knock and be judged a fool, the door opened and an older gentleman came out. He was looking at his feet until he nearly collided with her.

"Oh! You startled me, young lady. May I help you?"

"No, sir," she said, bending down to retrieve a pint milk bottle that sat with its delivery note by his door. "My mistake."

Wordlessly, she handed the bottle to him before turning and fleeing. Not back home, however. No, she directed her horse toward the waterfront, not admitting she was heading toward East Boston. *What was the point in going there?* Yet there had been no point in going to his old rooming house, either. Had she truly imagined she would find his ghost had taken up residence at his old bedsit?

She shook her head at her own foolishness yet couldn't help taking the Charlestown Bridge all the way up to the Chelsea Bridge. Finally, she crossed the small Free Bridge on Meridian Street into Eastie, as close to the waterfront as possible. It was a path she had taken many times after the sinking, except for the times when she'd taken the penny ferry across the harbor.

Kelly's, or Finn's shipyard as she thought of it, was at the end of Saratoga Street. Today, Sunday, it was deserted since Mr.

Kelly was Irish Catholic as were most of his workers. Finn, had been an anomaly amongst them, a French Canadian, whom they'd apparently accepted. He'd spoken fondly of his fellow builders and their after-hour *shenanigans* at the many pubs in the neighborhood.

Rose shivered. Jovial times for Finn and his shipmates were far in the past. She tied up her horse at the main entrance to the shipyard's docks. It was achingly familiar. For months after he'd died, she'd haunted these docks, senselessly looking for him. On this side of Boston's harbor, they'd all known she was Finn's woman. Thus, those left behind at the yard had allowed her to stay as close as was safe, although she'd spoken to none of them.

It had been years since she'd gone anywhere near Finn's old workplace.

So, what was she doing there at that moment? she asked herself. Not merely an idle walk by the water to clear her head. She could have done that without traveling all the way to Eastie. But perhaps Finn was the one now haunting her.

She walked the same path she'd first taken with Claire and found herself pausing to look up at the closest ship, a large cargo clipper whose steel sides were being repaired. She glanced up at the three masts towering above her.

In her mind's eye, there he was, exactly as before. Strong, handsome, capable, catching her eye and holding it. She smiled at the memory, but the vision disappeared as quickly as it had come, along with her good humor.

Of course Finn wasn't up the rigging. He was at the bottom of the Atlantic.

Rose wandered farther along, breathing the ocean air and listening to the sounds of the gulls and of the seawater lapping against the wooden pilings.

Up ahead, at the very end of Kelly's dock, a lone figure sat on a bench and was looking out to sea, with a black knitted hat pulled down over his hair despite the sunshine and the barely discernible warm morning breeze. He wore well-worn dungarees and a blue shirt rolled up at the sleeves to reveal muscular arms.

Rose hesitated. These imaginings were becoming tedious. This man's body reminded her of Finn's with his broad shoulders and the way he held his head. Even the way he lifted his arm to shade his eyes with his palm as he looked at the shimmering, sun-dappled horizon, was exactly as Finn would have done.

She was inexorably drawn to the silent figure. No matter the impropriety. No matter the danger. Rose walked closer, then closer still. Eventually, she drew up level with the end of the bench.

Precisely when she would have either spoken to him or turned away, a white and gray gull cried loudly and swooped into the water in front of them, making her jump.

The man watched as the bird dove for a fish, and then, quite casually, he turned to her. His familiar eyes, a stormy gray blue, locked onto her startled gaze.

Everything fell silent, even the waves and the gulls—silent compared to the roaring in her ears.

The gasp that escaped her lips, though, that sounded overly loud.

He stood up, facing her, and she stopped breathing completely for an instant.

Taking a small step back, frowning at him, shaking her head in disbelief, she uttered only, "Finn?"

It came out as a whisper and a question.

Would he vanish? Was he a ghost? Or perhaps he was merely a man who looked like her dead husband, a man who would scorn her as a bedlamite ready for the asylum.

She realized she was reaching out a shaking hand toward him.

Then he spoke.

"Rose." Not a question, more like an affirmation that he knew who she was, spoken in a familiar voice.

With every part of her being, she knew it was indeed him.

Snatching her hand back, her knees started to tremble and her heart pounded in her chest. She fought against the buzzing in her head that warned of fainting. She would not give in to it, she was determined, sucking in great inhales of air until her head cleared. Then her feet carried her toward him at a lightning fast pace, and she struck her fists against his solid chest, while hot tears coursed down her cheeks.

She continued to beat her hands against him, unable to stop herself as rage and fear, sadness and confusion coursed through her.

How dare he? How dare he stand there, alive and calm, and as if they'd only parted company that morning?

She became aware of the feeling of his shirt fabric under her palms and, below that, the warmth of him. His pounding heart, his blood coursing, his lungs working. He was very much alive!

CHAPTER EIGHT

Afftter a few moments, Finn gently took hold of Rose's wrists and held them still.

Gasping in air, she could do nothing except stare up into his familiar face. So beloved to her, she had nearly wished her own death rather than live without seeing him again.

In his eyes, she saw terrible sadness, and what else?

"Rose," he said her name again, softly.

All the fight went out of her, leaving her with the intense desire to sleep. Wrenching her arms free, she plunked herself down upon the bench. A moment later, Finn sat beside her.

"Rose!" she sputtered, looking not at him but at the ocean, the beautiful and fearsome ocean that had supposedly swallowed him whole over three years past.

"Is that all you have to say? How can it be you? You're dead!"

"People don't die and then come back," she heard him say, causing her to whip her head around and gawk at him.

"That's exactly what you've done," Rose argued. "It *is* you? Isn't it?"

"Aye," Finn admitted, "but I didn't die." He shook his head, his mouth a grim line.

She took her eyes off of him again because it was almost too painful to look at him and, instead, stared out toward the horizon.

"The ship went down, all hands lost, no bodies recovered." She spoke the words that had echoed in her brain over and over in the first few days after the sinking.

Rose could see he was staring at her profile, yet she couldn't look at him again. She was overwhelmed—her brain buzzing with the impossibility of it, her heart squeezing with pain and then with intense gladness.

At last, Finn began to speak. "Storm clouds came up so fast, it was as if they were being pulled and pushed on purpose until they were directly over us. Thick and gray." His words were flat, unemotional. "The wind howled like a banshee. None of it was predicted for that April day. The ship was doomed from the start. Poor design," he added matter-of-factly.

"The center of gravity was too high," she said quietly, recalling his words when he'd told her his concerns.

"You remembered. Yes, it did precisely as I feared when a few waves washed over her bow. Tipped like a top-heavy tree in a hurricane. I saw the first men washed into the sea, and then we all went in."

Rose realized she was listening with her eyes closed, simply taking in the sound of his voice and making sure it was real and familiar. That this man was truly her dead husband.

"When it was over, I ended up clinging to a plank no bigger than a door. Another two sailors grabbed on. Eventually they died."

"Eventually?"

"I lost track of time," Finn explained, "but I think I floated for about four days, maybe five."

"With no food or water," she murmured, recalling how she, herself, had existed on a few cups of tea and little else for the first few days after he'd been reported dead. To think that he was on the sea on a board, without even the comfort of a sip of water.

"I started seeing things," Finn continued. "I saw you walking toward me one day, and I was so damn happy. When you got closer, you disappeared, of course. My heart felt as though it didn't beat evenly, and my leg muscles started to twitch. I went to sleep at some point, and when I awoke, I was being hauled onto the deck of a fishing vessel, like a bloody great tuna."

"Where have you been?" *Was that really her own voice?* It sounded frail and desperate.

"After I was rescued, I was taken up into the Icelandic waters. They were going out for four months, and no amount of bribery would turn them around. After all, I didn't exactly have anything to offer them except a promise of future payment. There was nothing I could do."

"Nothing you could do," Rose repeated. "Surely, you haven't been fishing for over three years."

"No, only about two and a half months," he said. "I had strange visions, and of course, I had lost a lot of weight. Apparently, I was out of my head when the fishermen found me. I woke every night for weeks in a cold sweat, screaming until the captain made me sleep on deck away from his men."

If she'd been with him, she would have put her arms around him and held him while he slept. She'd heard of men coming back from the war between the states having terrible nightmares even while awake and worse, becoming violent. She would not ever have felt afraid of Finn, no matter how he behaved.

"Eventually, the visions stopped, and I learned to fish, but I hated it." He sounded fierce about that, the first passion he'd displayed since she'd come upon him.

"It was a good thing they found me and kept going. If someone had brought me straight to land, I think I never would've gone to sea again. Eventually I got passage on another fishing vessel that came close to the first. It was heading for Great Britain. I was put off in Plymouth and made my way north to Newcastle."

Rose shook her head, unable to comprehend his going in the opposite direction to home. And to her.

Finn shrugged. "Shipbuilding at its finest. That's what was in England and Scotland. I needed to learn more, and I learned from the best."

She nearly asked, "What about me?" yet held her tongue. She was, after all, neither frail nor desperate, and so much time had passed, she could wait a little longer to hear if he had thought of her at all.

"After half a year, I went to Glasgow. They'd had a hard lesson after the capsizing of the *Daphne*. You may remember that. It was in all the papers."

She nodded. In all the papers, just like the *Garrard*.

"I needed to learn more, so I did. Their university has the best naval architecture program in the world." Finn crossed his arms and looked away from her.

Rose let that sink in—the priority he'd placed upon educating himself, which apparently far surpassed his feelings for her—and then she asked the question that popped into her bewildered brain. "When did you come back?"

"Last month, I landed in Portland."

A month! He'd been on the same soil as her for that long. Why did it feel like a personal failing that she hadn't known somehow?

"I went home for a bit," he added.

Home? Naturally to him that meant Maine. He hadn't been in Boston all that very long when she'd first met him.

"When I got there, my father said he almost didn't recognize me. I wasn't the same."

Finally, she let herself turn and study his profile. More lined perhaps, and a new scar on his brow by his right temple. He was wearing his hair a little longer, and when he realized she was examining him, he turned to her with a serious look in his eye that hadn't been there before.

"I would recognize you anywhere," she declared, wondering at the distant way in which they were speaking to each other. That she wasn't in his arms being soundly kissed seemed unthinkable. Yet he was like a stranger, and she couldn't imagine wrapping herself around him as she once did.

Finn gave her a wry smile, returning her scrutiny with a brief flicker of his gaze over her face.

"You might not have, not if you'd seen me as I was when I got to England. It took a long while to seem like myself again. I still have such strange dreams sometimes when I think I'm awake." He gave her that curious, new serious look. "You could be a dream right now for all I know. I've had this conversation with you a hundred times over the past few years."

She felt tears collecting. "I *am* real. I've been here all along. You could have found me any time you wanted." She couldn't help the bitterness in her voice. "I don't understand why you didn't send word after you reached Plymouth or Newcastle. Or even a month ago."

Inadvertently, she'd put her hand on his arm, and he covered it with his own. She looked down at their touching hands as did he. Then they locked gazes.

"I told you Rose, I wasn't the same. As soon as I reached England, I started trying to get back to you."

"I guess you didn't try hard enough." She knew she sounded bitter and simply couldn't help it.

He stared at her, long and hard, before he spoke again.

"I had no money and no proof of identity; no one to recommend me or to vouch for me. I had to find work so I could earn my passage home."

Finn withdrew his hand from her and crossed his arms.

"I did the only thing I could, I found a shipyard and got a job. Then I decided it would be better to make something more of myself before I came back.

Rose knew why, too. Because she hadn't introduced him to her family. She felt a hot rush of shame.

Into her silence, he continued, "What if I'd shown up unwell as I was, with strange dreams plaguing me, and you suddenly had to introduce me to your mother and the rest of your kin? Your strange, off-kilter husband!"

She had no one to blame but herself for his feeling that way. She dropped her glance from him. In the next instant, she raised it back to his face. It was too incredulous that he was even actually there, and she feared taking her gaze off of him in case he disappeared.

When he remained silent, she asked, "Why did you come back now?"

His gaze returned to the horizon. "Do you wish I hadn't?"

"Why would you ask that?" Even as the words were out of her mouth, she considered what his return meant. The end to all her plans. For the first time since she'd run toward Finn, she thought of William.

Her expression must have told him something.

"I've certainly complicated matters," he said. "After all, you are getting married." He didn't say it as a question, rather in a strange tone as if her doing so were extraordinary.

"I . . ." *What could she say?* She'd mourned deeply and then finally fallen in love again. The full ramifications of Finn's return dawned on her. "Obviously, I cannot marry. I *am* married."

"Aye," he said, and it came out on an exhalation, like a weary sigh. After a pause, he added, "What do you want to do, Rose?"

She hadn't expected that question. She didn't think she had a choice. They were married despite having never lived as man and wife.

"I don't know what you're asking. Oh, Finn!" She closed her eyes and groaned.

"You're not the only person to call me that, but when you say my name and make that noise, it reminds me of our last night together."

Her stomach fluttered, and she realized it was a familiar feeling, one she hadn't felt in years. Something similar but not the same, she experienced with William.

Dear William! He would be hurt beyond words.

"What if you'd come back too late?" she asked, imagining the horror of becoming Mrs. Woodsom only to find out later that she was not legally married after all, that she'd committed bigamy. "Why did you even let me get engaged?"

"I came as soon as I read it in the paper. The English follow Boston's society as we Americans do that of London and Paris," he said. "You were already officially engaged by the time I started my voyage, so it didn't matter if I went to Portland first."

"When exactly did you get here?" Rose asked. "In Boston, I mean."

"Three days ago."

Again, she wondered at the idea of Finn being so close, with her being completely unaware.

"Why didn't you come straight away to see me?"

A strange look came over his face. "I didn't want to startle you."

A laugh escaped her, sounding anything but happy, thinking of what happened at the Tremont.

"Then why did you show up in the middle of my engagement party?"

Finn shook his head. "I tried to get close to you the day before, but you were surrounded by females. I only knew Claire, and I couldn't let her see me before I'd spoken to you. Then I heard about the party." He looked sheepish.

"I had to see you," he added, "though I didn't think you would see me. Suddenly, you were standing there, looking right at me. I wasn't sure you would know me. Then you looked scared, and I panicked and left."

Finn looked away, back to the sea, then directly into her eyes. "You looked beautiful, by the way."

"Thank you." She'd never had a reason to wear anything like that gown when she'd been with him. They'd ridden horses and walked in the countryside away from everyone. They'd gone on adventures and strolled along the beach. They'd gone sightseeing to the quaint coastal town of Newburyport. But they'd never done anything remotely fancy.

One time, they'd climbed a tree when a family interrupted their picnic in Mount Auburn Cemetery, north of Boston. Rose had thought it great fun to hide out in the branches of an apple tree while a husband and wife and their children passed unawares below.

Always away from other people at her insistence.

"Your family obviously admires your fiancé. I heard the speeches."

What could she say? Rose nodded, thinking how strange her husband had been present while her family toasted her engagement.

"And this man loves you. That was clear, too."

Yes, William dearly loved her.

"Then again, who wouldn't?" he added, his voice a low murmur. "So, what do you want to do, Rose?"

For a second, she thought he meant at that very moment. *What did she want to do?* She couldn't have answered him. She knew the urge to hug him and wanted to feel his solid arms around her. Yet warring strongly with that feeling was the desire to lash out at him again, to cause him pain for letting her believe him dead for so long.

What did she want to do?

"Are you asking me if I intend still to marry William, now that I know you're alive? Are you offering me a . . . a divorce?"

She could barely say the word, had never in her entire life considered she would be the type of woman who would need one.

Finn seemed to bristle at the suggestion, straightening up on the bench. "I wasn't offering you anything of the kind."

"Then what are you asking?"

He took a deep breath. "Do you love him?"

Rose didn't have to consider, and she couldn't lie to him.

"Yes, of course. I wouldn't have become engaged to William if I didn't."

What did Finn think? That she would pine for him and then agree to marry just anyone who came along and asked her.

His unspoken question was, of course, did she still love *him?* Similarly, she wondered what were *his* feelings?

"Why did you come back at this time?" she asked him for the second time.

"My apologies," he said, his manner curt. "I didn't mean to spoil your plans."

How dare he inject a tone of bitterness! As if she'd been trying to marry someone secretly behind his back.

"That's hardly the point," she said. "Tell me why now."

"I told you. The news of Boston's high society reached me in Scotland," he said.

Finn hadn't bothered about her until she had decided to move on. Obviously, the announcement of her engagement and of the subsequent party at the Tremont had drawn him back to his long-neglected wife. *How terrible!*

"I couldn't stay away any longer. I had to know—"

Right then three sharp whistle blasts sounded from across the harbor, as the Boston and Maine train to Portland left its Haymarket depot. Neither of them moved although Rose realized it was probably the same rail line that had brought Finn back to Boston from up north. From his home.

"Had to know?" she prompted into the silence.

"How you had fared," he said at last, yet she didn't think it was what he originally intended to say.

"I grieved a long time for you," Rose told him, thinking of the countless hours of unnecessary sorrow. "Since meeting Mr. Woodsom, I have felt happy again." She almost added "finally" for it had seemed a long time of nothing apart from overwhelming sadness and of everything around her being dimmed and colorless.

To find out that Finn had been alive the whole time, studying in Glasgow!

"That's no small thing," she told him, wanting him to understand precisely how much William meant to her. "Before I met him, it was as though I were living under water. It's a poor analogy to make to you, after what you went through," she added, "but you will perfectly understand the sensation. My father often took us in the summers to escape the oppressive heat. We went northwest, about twenty miles."

Rose remembered being with her brother and sisters, canoeing and swimming in the Sudbury and Concord rivers.

"You know what it's like," she continued, recalling swimming down to the shallow riverbed, "not seeing clearly and being unable to hear sounds around you." The isolating feeling of being under water, unlike anything else, had stayed distinctly with her.

"After William began to court me, I . . . well, I breathed more easily again, colors were brighter, experiences were richer." And she'd laughed with him, with so much gaiety between them. However, in the face of the serious man beside her, she didn't mention that.

"I'll have to tell him about you," she added, thinking aloud.

Finn nodded. "What will you say to him?"

What indeed! Rose dreaded the scene, explaining how she had neglected to mention getting married before. She had been a widow who now wasn't one. And hiding being a widowed wife was bad enough. Now she had to disclose a dead husband who was not really dead at all.

Groaning, she put her face in her hands and exhaled. To her surprise, she felt Finn's arm go around her, and then he pulled her against him.

Stiffly at first, she held herself away, lowering her hands to her lap. His scent, familiar but until that moment forgotten, tickled her nostrils. She breathed deeply. Strange, yet also not strange.

Little by little, she relaxed, letting her shoulder remain tucked under his arm, and finally allowing her body to soften so her head made contact with the side of his chest.

He squeezed her shoulder gently, and a second later, she felt his chin touch the top of her head, resting there. This was not helping her determine what to tell William. This was muddling her brain and causing her pulse to race.

If anyone she knew saw her, alone, being embraced by this stranger and apparently being unfaithful to her fiancé! *Dear God!* The recriminations, the ostracism from her social group, and the disappointment of her family as she brought shame upon the Malloy name, it would destroy her.

Rose sighed. This was precisely the type of mess Reed was referring to at the party, the type that would give him more gray hair.

"I'm sorry," Finn said, his voice a gentle murmur. "I know I've put you in a bad situation."

To put it mildly. Yet she didn't bother to voice her thought.

"I had better go," she said straightening. She ought to sit alone in her room and examine her feelings. She ought to think about the best way to tell William. She ought to—

"Did you come by carriage?" he asked.

When she nodded, he said, "I'll walk you to it."

She hesitated. If they were seen . . . On the other hand, it was still early on Sunday, most people yet in church or at home.

"All right," she agreed and felt his arm slip from her shoulders as she stood. Rose shivered, still sensing where his touch had been.

Stepping away from the bench, she watched him rise to his feet, a head taller than most men she'd ever met. He turned toward her and took a slow step and then another.

"Finn?" she queried.

He shrugged. "I'm fine."

Yet he wasn't. He had a pronounced limp, like Miss Farmer at the cooking school, although he walked steadily enough. Rose fell into step beside him. She had discovered that the school's assistant principal had had a stroke at a young age. *What had caused Finn's injury?*

Unfortunately, so estranged from the man beside her and so shocked at his living, breathing presence, she could not find the words to ask him. It would feel like prying into a stranger's life.

"I can scarcely believe I'm walking along the dock with you," he said, stating the very thought that had flitted across her brain.

In silence, she went over their brief conversation. Finn hadn't made any declaration he still wanted her or that he'd come back to claim her, even though he had crossed the ocean only after discovering her engagement.

On the other hand, she knew precisely where she was with William.

"Where are you residing?" she asked as they neared her carriage. Perhaps after she drove off, he would disappear again, leaving her to think this was all an incredulous dream.

"I'm staying above The Restaurant Parisien on Winter Place. Do you know it?"

Of course she knew it! It was right across the Common from her home, and being aptly named, it served delicious French cuisine, which Rose had sampled in the second-floor dining room, which allowed women. She'd even told her cooking teacher, Miss Sweeney, she wanted to learn how to make *coq au vin* in a similar fashion to Chef Ober's.

"Then you know where to find me," he said, as if he imagined she would start dropping in at his room the way she had done as a foolish girl of eighteen.

Her horse stamped its foot and whinnied, and she patted its glossy neck. How would she and Finn part? *With a handshake?*

"You'll be fine getting home?" he asked.

"Perfectly fine." Yesterday, and for all the yesterdays she could remember, Finn had let her think him dead. Now, he was worrying whether she could make it safely from East Boston to Beacon Hill? "How will . . . that is, will I see you again?"

"I didn't come all this way to talk to you once on a bench." He took her hand and lifted it to his lips. He'd never been the type of man to kiss a woman's knuckles like a dandy. Instead, bowing his head, Finn turned her hand over and held her palm against his mouth, pressing her fingers to his cheek. Briefly, he closed his eyes.

Rose could feel his warm breath through her thin summer glove. That he breathed at all was a miracle to her still.

For a long moment, he remained that way while her heart beat a wild tattoo in her chest.

Then he lifted his gaze to hers. "Somehow, I knew you would come here today."

She nodded. It had been inevitable.

"You look even more lovely than I remembered. If that's possible."

"Thank you." The words stuck in her throat. She would have forsaken any compliments for the rest of her life if he'd only sent her a letter one, two, or even three years ago.

"I don't suppose you want me to stop by your home and meet your family, now that I'm back." Finn said it lightly, jesting with her, yet she had the distinct impression her refusal when they first met still irked him.

His appearance on Mount Vernon Street would not be any better received now than when she'd married him. No, it was a thousand times worse in the face of her engagement to William.

"I'll meet you wherever you want," she said, withdrawing her hand from his, "and then we'll talk." And figure out this impossible mess, she prayed silently.

A shadow crossed his face, shuttering his eyes. "Tomorrow then, at three o'clock, at Ober's restaurant."

Dine in public together? *Impossible.*

"I cannot—" she began.

"Trust me, Rose. I won't do anything to jeopardize your reputation. Or your engagement," he added before turning from her. "We'll dine privately upstairs."

She watched him walk away, frowning at his limp in an otherwise healthy-looking body. *What had happened to him?*

CHAPTER NINE

Unable to eat that night, Rose partook only of a large mug of cocoa before retiring to her room where she remained secluded for the evening. She'd wished she could go straight to Claire's house before dinner and pour her heart out. Inconveniently, her friend was in Newport for a debutante ball.

The Rhode Island branch of Appletons had done very well for themselves, and while Claire didn't know personally young Miss Wetmore who was being presented, she'd been invited, along with Robert, to Chateau-sur-Mer for the grand coming-out.

If Rose hadn't been so diverted by the sheer preposterousness of Finn returning from the dead—and consumed with guilt over the devastation that could ensue with William—she would have been extremely jealous of Claire's exciting opportunity. After all, there was nothing quite like the eager excitement of a seventeen-year-old's extraordinarily wealthy parents when it came to throwing the most divine ball possible.

Yes, Claire was going to benefit from that eagerness by experiencing an extravaganza. She would come home with tales of ice sculptures, champagne, quail dishes, and plate after plate of *strawberry Charlotte*, not to mention the music and the decorations, both floral and otherwise.

Meanwhile Rose paced. Then she sat and contemplated. She ought to unburden herself to her brother. He would give her wise counsel—after he gave her a dressing down, of course. She paced some more and finally took up the needlepoint she was always trying to finish. In five minutes, she tossed it down to the carpet.

Finn had missed years of her life, and she, his. He'd missed an entire governor coming and going. He hadn't had to struggle through The Great White Hurricane, as they called the 1888 blizzard that happened the winter after he died. Or rather didn't die! While she was wading through thirty incredible inches of snow, Finn was . . . where exactly?

Eventually, Rose wandered downstairs to her father's study and chose a book. Climbing into bed, she tried to read. It was almost more frustrating than the needlepoint. She tossed it at the wall, watching with satisfaction as it caused a small tear in the wallpaper. Bollocks! Before she was reduced to knitting or practicing the harpsichord, she put out her light, hoping the same question would not reverberate in her beleaguered brain all night.

How would she tell William?

Should she ask him to walk with her prior to their regular weekly dinner and explain about her youthful impetuousness? Usually he left his State House office where he clerked for Lieutenant Governor Haile and came directly to her on a Thursday evening. They ate with her mother, his parents if they were in town, or at a restaurant. On Fridays, William was free even earlier, and they usually went riding if the weather was fine and made plans for the weekend's activities over their evening meal.

Rose couldn't imagine what circumstance would be best for disclosing her past to him. It would have been an easy confession when Finn was still dead. *Why, oh, why hadn't she done it then?*

Now, the confession would end with the startling revelation she was not a widow but a wife. She was not free to be William's fiancée. Indeed, she could not be anything to him, to the man she loved.

Rose had been up since dawn, restless and anxious, and the day before her seemed interminably long until it would be time to go to Chef Ober's restaurant. Her mother cornered her in the dining room where it was apparent Rose was not eating, instead only sipping tea.

"Out with it, my girl."

Rose actually jumped. That was hardly her mother's normal way of speaking to her.

"Don't look shocked. Do you think I will get anywhere with you by beating around the bush? Something is wrong, and I fear it is to do with your engagement. Or worse."

Worse? Rose considered what could be worse than what actually had happened.

"Are you unhappy with William?"

"No, positively not." Rose sipped her tea and watched as her mother took toast from the sideboard and poured her own cup of tea, doctoring it perfectly with sugar and milk. "I have always been happy with him."

"*Hm,*" her mother mused, sitting diagonally to her at the head of the table. "Then what? Quite honestly, you've seemed distracted since the party. You didn't eat last night, and this morning, it seems you have no appetite."

Since when had her mother been so observant? She usually paid far more attention to her garden than the comings and goings of her adult children.

"I can think of one situation that could cause this behavior, and I want you to know, dear, that you can confide in me. This is not the eighteenth-century. If certain circumstances have occurred . . ." With a meaningful arch to her mother's eyebrow, Evelyn waited.

Rose frowned. It was the lack of sleep causing her to catch on slowly, but all at once, she realized her mother was wondering if she were with child. *Good God!* At least that hadn't occurred. If she'd given herself to William as she'd almost done more than once when they were in the clenches of passionate kissing, and she was at that very moment carrying his child while married to another man, she imagined she would have to flee New England all together. Perhaps she would have started a new life in California near her sister.

She shook her head, took a deep breath, and thanked the Lord for small favors.

"Mama, I assure you my lack of appetite and my being distracted are not caused by anything you are imagining."

And suddenly, thinking how much more dire her situation could be, she felt a little better. She was still married to only one man and she was not carrying another's child. What's more, she still had her virginity to give to whomever was left standing when this nightmare was over.

Deciding to walk rather than fight Boston's entangled traffic, Rose reached her destination early. Looking at Ober's Parisien, she thought it not very impressive from the outside with dark-stained wood and four plain windows. Nevertheless, her stomach fluttered as if she were entering Buckingham Palace to meet Queen Victoria herself. How could she be going to meet Phineas Bennet? It was surreal.

She could not hesitate long as the gentle stream of passers-by nearly carried her along and away from the entrance. Later, in another hour, it would be a strong tide of pedestrians when the streets flooded with bankers and lawyers and other businessman pouring out of their workplaces. Most likely, her brother would be one of them.

The notion of bumping into Reed caused her to quickly open the door and step inside.

The restaurant was deserted, save for an older gentleman sitting by himself at a table by the right-hand wall, eating a meal with apparent great gusto. Until he looked up and saw her. At which point his brow took on a thunderous look, and he began to scan the restaurant. No doubt he sought a waiter to toss her out or show her upstairs to the rooms in which a lady was permitted to dine.

Nodding to him, Rose kept moving, keeping her eyes averted from the infamous nude painting of Mademoiselle Yvonne. Obviously, the restaurant was between the luncheon crowd and the dinner set, and even more obviously, she was not welcome there.

Before she could decide what to do, however, the *maître d'hôtel* hurried out from a door in the back of the room. Suddenly a sliver of worry skated through her at the thought of being recognized so close to her home, and she tried to keep her head down while gracing him with a smile.

"Are you dining alone, mademoiselle?" he asked in a thick accent, looking shocked at the prospect. However, as soon as she told him whom she was meeting, he bowed low.

"Come this way." He led her through the ornate dining room with its mahogany furnishings, Italian sculpture adorning pedestals, and richly detailed European paintings on the walls. She remembered pressing her face against the glass as a young girl and looking in for the first time when walking with her father. She'd been unable to take her eyes off the sparkling crystal chandeliers, certain they were dripping with large diamonds.

Allowing her to pass through ahead of him, the *maître d'hôtel* held the door open to the kitchen from which a wave of warmth assaulted her along with the delectable aromas of roasting meat and sautéing onions. Finn leaned against a counter, arms crossed, talking with a tall, wiry man in a traditional chef's uniform with a kerchief knotted around his neck. The man was efficiently slicing mushrooms, his hands moving at lightning-quick speed.

"Rose," Finn greeted her, coming forward as soon as he saw her, his limp still obvious yet less startling.

Her heart lurched. She wondered if she would ever be accustomed to seeing him alive again, in the flesh instead of only in her memories. And then there was the unsettling surge of anger that followed. *Could she ever forgive him?*

"Louis, this is the lady I was telling you about. Monsieur Louis Ober," Finn added for her benefit. "This is Miss Malloy."

Rose felt a rush of alarm. What had he been telling this man who paused only briefly, sparing her a welcoming glance, before bobbing his head and turning his attention back to his task?

"Excuse my back, mademoiselle," the chef said. "I must keep working. We will have a full house tonight." Then he chuckled. "As every night we are open."

Indeed, not only was he working, but two other men, one kneading dough and the other cutting up a chicken, worked at different counters. Neither of them said anything or even seemed to notice her.

She relaxed a little and released the breath she'd been holding. If Finn had told this man more, then certainly he would have introduced her to Chef Ober as Mrs. Bennet. She'd hardly thought of herself that way, except the day they stepped out of the magistrate's office as husband and wife.

"You're mine now, Mrs. Phineas Bennet," Finn had said to her, but then she'd stopped him from kissing her on the public street.

"I already was yours," she'd told him to soften the rebuff until they were alone again when she could show him how much she loved him.

"It's nice to meet you, Monsieur Ober," Rose said.

"The pleasure's all mine, mademoiselle. You may call me Louis." At last with the mushrooms sliced, he laid his knife down, wiped his hands on the apron wrapped around his waist, and clapped Finn on the back. "It's so good to have you back in town. Take this lovely lady upstairs to your table, and I'll have Joseph bring your meal up. I must start my roux."

Finn put his large palm in the small of Rose's back and directed her to the back stairs. When they got to the smaller of the two second-floor dining rooms, it was deserted. He escorted her to a table for two, set with a crisp white tablecloth and fine china.

"What did he mean by 'your' table?"

Finn shrugged. "Louis is the first friend I made when I moved to Boston, before I met you. My mother was French-Canadian, you remember?"

She nodded.

"I walked by here one day and smelled what I would have sworn was her cooking. Louis said it was one of the greatest compliments he'd ever had."

"Why do you sit up here?" she asked as he pulled out a chair for her, then moved to the other side of the table and sat down.

He shrugged. "It's a little joke. I helped Louis design a vent to draw the oven fumes and smoke out of the kitchen and keep it cooler as well as making it easier for him and his cooks to breathe. In return, he dubbed this my table and said I could eat here whenever I wanted."

That was like Finn, Rose thought. Always thinking of some way to improve design, either a ship or a kitchen, it made no matter.

"Chef Ober was not shocked to see you when you returned?" Rose asked, watching Finn spread his napkin across his lap.

He looked up at her quickly, and she caught it—a flash of guilt.

"He already knew," Finn began slowly, "that I was alive."

"Oh." *What could she say?* He'd contacted his friend but not her. "You had written to him. When?"

"Last year."

His words struck her as if he'd actually laid hands upon her and delivered a blow.

Last year. Before she'd fallen in love with William. Before it had become too late. She nearly got up and left, except she had to hear more, no matter how painful.

Keeping her voice steady, she said, "You should have let me know, too, even if you didn't feel you could come see me."

His gaze remained on hers. At last he shook his head.

"I didn't think a letter was the right thing to do. I couldn't imagine you finding out without me here to—"

"To what? Watch my world fall apart?" Rose snapped, then pursed her lips. She hadn't meant to say that, and certainly not with the level of hostility her tone expressed, yet that was most certainly what was happening.

"No. That's not what I wanted."

They fell silent a moment, and it was into the silence that a man, presumably Joseph, brought in two plates of food. Rose thought it might as well have been a mound of dirt on her plate for the little appetite she had.

Like the chef, the man clapped Finn on the back before leaving. Rose couldn't imagine a man whacking William on the back with such familiarity. Of course, she couldn't imagine William withholding the simple truth from her that he was alive. William seemed so in love with her he would find his way back to her no matter what.

"I am not hungry to tell you the truth," she said. "I was hoping we could speak plainly."

"We always did," Finn said, and he used the side of his fork to cut off a piece of one of the twin crepes in front of him.

She couldn't help looking down at her own plate, with two delicate crepes slathered in a creamy sauce and sprinkled over with parsley. It smelled divine.

"There's chicken inside," Finn told her, chewing thoughtfully, "and celery."

Rose's stomach turned at the notion of even tasting it. In truth, it seemed indecent to enjoy food while thinking of her unintentional deception toward William.

"I will tell my fiancé when next I see him," she said.

"Tell him?" Finn prompted.

"That you exist."

"I see. Then what?"

"Then he'll ask what I intend to do." Rose felt more wretched when she thought about it.

Finn popped another forkful of crepe into his mouth.

"Which is?" he asked, his words making their way out of his mouth around the food.

Again, out of sheer frustration, she felt the urge to slap him. How could he calmly sit and eat? He had given her no indication of his intent.

"You are being insufferable."

Laying down his fork, he looked as if she'd delivered him a nose-ender with her fist.

"How can you say that? I'm giving you the freedom to do whatever you want, just as I always did. You never wanted to tell your family about us, and I didn't make you. If you don't want to tell William Woodsom I exist, then don't. If you do, then do so."

Rose's temples were starting to throb.

"This is a different situation entirely. If I don't tell William, then he will expect me to marry him. Clearly, I cannot do that."

"If you want to, you can," Finn said quietly. "I won't stop you. We can get a divorce, very discreetly, and no one has to know we were ever married."

"You said yesterday you weren't offering me a divorce." *Hadn't he?*

"I did. I'm not *offering* it, but if you want one, that's another matter."

Did she want one? She looked across the table at Finn, *her Finn*, the same man she had felt so strongly about she'd married him without her family's blessing, simply on the strength of her instinct that they were meant to be together.

However, this Finn was a stranger, who had left her alone and bereft, and except for a few inconsequential compliments, seemed to view her as no more than an old friend. Whereas William, he was her steadiness, her warmth, the reason she had smiled and laughed and loved again.

"All right," she said, watching Finn's face. "Let's proceed with a divorce. I'll speak with my brother."

She rose, unable to sit across from this unfamiliar Finn Bennet a moment longer. Her words had caused his expression to tighten. Regardless, all he did was offer a wry smile as he stood.

"So, someone in your family will finally learn of me."

Guilt twisted her stomach, but she could not change the past. Bidding him farewell, she did not even want to discuss meeting again. With her eyes burning from unshed tears and her heart pounding, she was in no fit state to go out the way she'd come in through the kitchen, or give her compliments to Chef Ober.

Instead, Rose strode through the first dining room and into the second on her way to the main staircase. As her eyes scanned the room, she locked her gaze onto her red-headed sister-in-law.

CHAPTER TEN

Rose stopped short, and Finn, who'd been close on her heels, slammed into her, causing her to gasp and lurch forward. Of course, all eyes turned to her, including Charlotte's and the man she was sitting with.

What could she do? Certainly not back up and disappear the way she had come. If only Finn were not, as she feared, standing directly behind her. She took a few steps, hoping he didn't follow, and then made her way slowly to Charlotte's table. It took all her willpower not to glance back.

"Hello," she said, bending down to kiss Charlotte's cheek as her dining companion stood up.

Charlotte's inquisitive eyes scanned Rose's face.

"This is my husband's youngest sister, Miss Rose Malloy," Charlotte introduced her. "This is Mr. Greene, publisher of *The Boston Post*." The distinguished man gave a slight bow.

"Are you having a late lunch?" Charlotte asked her, sounding as if she thought something else entirely. Or was that Rose's own guilt at being caught, projecting itself onto Reed's perceptive wife.

"No. Yes." She laughed as Charlotte lifted an eyebrow.

"I know the owner. Slightly. Chef Ober. And . . . well," Rose trailed off, gesturing around the dining room.

Suddenly, inspiration hit. "I was thinking about the wedding luncheon and how grand it would be to have his cuisine."

"An excellent choice," said the newspaper publisher, looking down at his plate of food growing cold.

"Please," Rose insisted, "return to your meal."

The man happily lowered himself into his seat and immediately took a bite of the food in front of him.

"You will excuse me," he added. "I was at my desk all day, and this is the first I've eaten."

"I will not hold you up a moment longer," Rose said, grateful for the gentle nudge to stop intruding on their meeting. Charlotte had a pad of paper out and a fountain pen in hand. She'd clearly been taking notes, probably for a potential story, while the man dined.

"Please give my love to my dear brother," Rose said, taking a few steps backward in preparation for fleeing down the stairs. "I'll see you soon."

"No doubt," her sister-in-law murmured. "Take care, Rose."

"Yes, of course." With that, she escaped, knowing Reed would hear all about the episode and would instantly start speculating whether there was any mischief involved.

Just as the glossy green door closed behind her, Rose glanced back into the restaurant's interior. Finn Bennet, very much alive, was in there. Her husband.

And he was granting her a divorce.

Claire's eyes had never looked so large, not even when Rose had whispered to her of her hasty civil marriage ceremony to Finn. This time, she made sure her friend was seated, a soothing cup of tea in hand. Still, Claire stared, gaped, and then set down her cup with a rattle.

"It's too much to take in," she said.

Rose knew exactly how her friend felt. She was reeling from the speed of the events that had occurred since her engagement party.

"Phineas Bennet, back from his watery grave," Claire mused.

Rose cringed at the poetic imagery.

"You say he gave no indication as to why he returned?" Claire asked. "Other than he saw your name in the society pages? Surely, he came back to claim you."

Rose shook her head. "He made no declaration, and he seemed distant at best. Even when I risked everything to meet with him. He sat in front of me and polished off a plate of crepes."

"Well," Claire said, offering a small shrug, "Monsieur Ober's are so very delectable. Practically irresistible."

"Good God, not you, too," Rose scolded. "In any case, the only thing I know for certain is that he will give me a divorce."

"Is that what you want?" her friend asked, eyes wide.

"When I think of William, I can't imagine not being with him."

"And when you think of Phineas?"

"Honestly, I don't know *this* Phineas Bennet. If I were meeting him for the first time today, I probably would have thought he couldn't hold a candle to my William. Indeed, he still cuts a strapping figure and is fetching, but I can't say that I would have given him a second glance."

Claire looked shocked, and Rose felt a pang of remorse. After all, her friend had sat through the countless hours of Rose gushing about Finn after meeting him that first fateful day on the waterfront. Claire had also supported her when she'd decided she simply had to marry him. Most of all, she'd consoled Rose for more hours than she could recall after Finn was lost to her at sea.

It seemed disloyal to Claire after all of that to admit she was giving up on the relationship.

"You admire William, too, don't you?" Rose asked, feeling suddenly unsure she had any ability to choose a man at all.

"Of course," Claire said. She cocked her head. "You've never asked my opinion on a man before. Do you know that? You've always known whom you liked and whom you wanted. Don't let this change you."

This? This was huge. This was marriage . . . and divorce.

"Do you think I shouldn't tell William? I mean, if Finn and I get a divorce, does anyone need to know we were ever married?"

Claire looked thoughtful. "I think in your heart of hearts, dear, you would feel badly not telling William, wouldn't you?"

Rose considered. It would be a strange secret to keep from one's husband.

"You haven't done anything wrong or anything to be ashamed of. I don't believe he'll think any less of you if he knows the whole story."

Claire was undoubtedly correct. There was nothing terrible about the secret, except keeping it would be a blight on their relationship.

"You're right, of course. I was an impetuous young woman, practically a child still. I'll tell William. Today, in fact." She sipped her tea, then looked at Claire's sweet face. "Or should I wait until I obtain the divorce?"

"Perhaps you should speak with your brother first," Claire advised. When Rose rolled her eyes, Claire added, "He loves you very much, you know. He will try only to help you."

Yes, Reed loved her but often with the results of a swaddling cloth. At least she could consult with him without delay—it was handy having a top legal mind in the family—and then speak with William with some idea of what was facing her.

When she told her mother she was going to visit Reed that very afternoon, Evelyn narrowed her eyes.

"Whatever for?"

Rose chastised herself. She used to be so quick to come up with ways to have whatever amusement she wanted. Now she felt positively slow-witted.

"Mama, I have a question regarding my upcoming marriage, of course."

Her mother hugged her. "I thought you might ask him to give you away. I'm very glad of it."

Give her away! Of course, the perfect reason for seeing her brother. Why hadn't she thought of that?

"I'll be back for dinner, naturally."

She forsook her carriage to walk to Scollay Square. It would be faster than dealing with the chockablock of horses, carriages, and trams that clogged the streets of Boston from morning until night. The only time she could bear to pass through the city was very early morning, at dinnertime when everyone was dining or attending the theatre, or on Sundays.

A smile lit Reed's face upon seeing her. His partner, John, had brought her upstairs to her brother's office and then left them alone. Reed rounded his polished mahogany desk and swept her into an encompassing hug. Rose relaxed within the safety of his arms, breathing in his sandalwood scent with a feeling of calm, and wondered why she hadn't simply told him three years ago.

"What trouble brings you to my office?" he asked, his chin resting against her head.

Oh, yes! That was why she hadn't told him. Her reputation for causing mischief, and especially for worrying her mother, seemed to hang around her like a well-worn cloak. Even if she'd been the epitome of resolute decorum and somber propriety since Finn's death.

She pushed against him until he released her.

Unfortunately, she really was in trouble this time, and not the small kind of sneaking out to see a bawdy show on the Common or go with Claire to a pub in a seedier section of the city. No, this was serious and sad, and it would hurt people she would give anything not to hurt.

Her face gave it all away, no doubt, for Reed furrowed his brow and lost his teasing manner.

"What is it, dear one?"

He pulled her toward one of the chairs and sat in the one next to it, not putting his desk between them, which she greatly appreciated.

Rose imagined he could hear the rising tattoo of her heartbeat as she tried to form the words to explain her awful deception.

"I have something I need to tell you that you must keep absolutely secret. For now. Also, something I need to ask." How she wished she was there as an excited bride, merely to request he walk her down the aisle in their father's stead.

"You have my full attention." His intelligent eyes were looking right into her own, their intense blue a mirror of hers. Sometimes, she wished she also had his brains.

"I fell in love," she began, not sure why it came out like that. She paused. Perhaps she should have begun with, "A few years back, I got married." Her union with Finn had been all about the fullness of her heart and her inability to fight her own heart's desire. So naturally, the first thing she confessed to her brother was her love.

"Yes," Reed prompted her, "with William."

She shook her head, and immediately, the tears sprang into her eyes and began streaming down her cheeks. Reed's shocked face caused her to bury her head in her hands.

"Don't you love William?" he asked, his voice tentative, even while he handed her his handkerchief.

Breathe deeply, she counseled herself. When she could speak, she said, "Yes, of course."

"Rose," Reed enjoined. "Explain, please."

She lifted her head and started again. "I fell in love with a man named Phineas Bennet. It was in the summer, nearly four years ago."

He reached out and touched her arm. "What happened to him?"

Of course Reed had immediately surmised something had happened. Elsewise, she would be with him still.

"He died, or I so I surmised. His ship went down, all hands lost."

"I'm sorry," Reed said and put his hand around her shoulders. "Are you worried something will happen to William?"

Oh dear! She had better figure out a way to explain this more clearly before she tried to tell her fiancé.

"No, well, yes," she said. "I do sometimes have that exact fear something will happen to him. However, that is not . . . ," she trailed off.

Say it, she ordered herself. *Simply speak the words.* "I married him."

She felt Reed's arm stiffen. "William?"

"No, Finn."

If Reed were the gasping type, she knew he would have done so, for she felt his intake of breath.

She rushed on. "I am Mrs. Phineas Bennet, and I have been for over three years."

"I see."

The disappointment was evident in his tone. She knew his quick mind was imagining their clandestine meetings, their secret marriage, the deception perpetrated upon her family and society at large, and her being a wife, not an innocent bride.

All of that was so like the Rose she used to be, she could barely countenance her younger self. Certainly, she was no longer that irresponsible, selfish girl.

Moreover, she hadn't even told Reed the worst part.

"Does William know?" he asked.

She swallowed. "No."

"Don't you think he should?"

"Yes."

He squeezed her shoulder with the arm still draped around her.

"I imagine that will be quite a difficult conversation. He is not expecting to marry an experienced widow."

Her brother had managed to put into words as delicately as possible his assumption she was not a virgin.

"As it turns out, I'm not," she said. Neither *experienced*, which she would rather not discuss with Reed, nor a *widow*, which he would learn momentarily. "Phineas Bennet has recently returned to Boston."

"He died 'or so you surmised,'" Reed recalled her words with the steel-trap brain for which he was famous.

In this instance, Rose knew the reality had momentarily escaped him because of the sheer inconceivability of the mess she'd got herself into. If not for the strange situation she was trying to explain, she knew her brother would have grasped onto those words immediately.

Dropping his arm from her, he stood up and began to pace. The energy radiating from her brother was palpable, and she waited for the barrage of questions or, worse, the angry scolding she soundly deserved.

Instead, Reed suddenly crouched down in front of her and took hold of her hands, looking with piercing intensity into her eyes.

"This scoundrel who wed you and abandoned you, where is he and what does he want by suddenly returning?"

Good God! Like a knight in battle-worn armor, Reed was going to take up her cause. How noble and not entirely inappropriate, given how Finn had cruelly left her in the dark for so long.

"I had never thought him a scoundrel, and it is hard to change my view of him, although it seems he has dealt with me badly. Finn's a shipbuilder and was on the *Garrard*. I'm not sure if you recall how it—"

"It went down south of Nova Scotia," Reed said.

Rose nodded.

"And you changed overnight into the unsmiling, quiet Rose whom no one recognized. Until William Woodsom came along."

"Until William," she murmured. Then, more urgently, she added, "I don't want to hurt him. Reed, I never meant to hurt him."

"Nonetheless, I fear William will be, and quite badly. You didn't answer me, however. What does Bennet want?"

"He said he will let me divorce him." She gave the only answer she could, for in truth, she had no idea what Finn wanted.

Her brother didn't seem convinced. "How much money does he want to keep quiet?"

She flinched at his tone. "He didn't say he wanted anything." *Including her.* Besides, asking for money wouldn't be like Finn at all. Or at least, she thought not.

"He was in England and heard of my engagement, so he returned."

"How kind of him?" Reed remarked, standing up once again. "Then you've met with him?"

She nodded.

"Alone?" he asked.

Rose swallowed. "Not really," she hedged. "Only in a public place." *Or two.*

"Is that why you were at The Parisien?"

Truly, nothing got past her brother. Moreover, Charlotte was an extra pair of eyes and ears for him.

She nodded again.

"My wife explained to me why you were there, but, frankly, it seemed odd you would want to engage the services of a French chef when I have one living in my own home."

Ah, yes. That did seem odd when her brother put it like that. She had no need of Chef Ober's skills at her wedding luncheon, not with Pierre at hand.

Reed crossed his arms. "I don't think you should speak to Bennet again. Tell me how to contact him, and I'll handle this."

That would be the prudent thing to do. Why did it make her feel like a coward and a failure? Moreover, prudence was such a difficult virtue to which she had never quite adhered.

When she said nothing, Reed added, "Rather than waste your time on this man who decided to come back from the dead when it suited him, I think you should focus your attentions on the man who wants to spend the rest of his life with you. You should go talk to William at once."

Rose felt the blood drain from her head. "Can you tell me what will happen next? How long does a divorce take? Can it be kept completely private?"

She took a deep breath and added, "Does Mama have to know?"

Reed grimaced.

"What happens next is I shall get Bennet's signature that he will not contest a divorce proceeding. The divorce itself takes only as long as the time for me to create the writ of the divorce agreement and get it before a judge. As for keeping it private, it will be on the court's docket but not necessarily in the newspapers."

"And Mama?" she persisted.

He closed his eyes for a long moment. When he opened them, his blue eyes appeared sadder.

"I think you should tell her, but I will leave that decision up to you. In any case, you should speak to William first. The man has a right to know everything about the woman he loves and intends to marry."

Again, the disappointment weighed heavily in her brother's tone, making Rose feel about seven inches high.

Considering her situation for the umpteenth time, Rose surmised, "Perhaps after William hears the truth, I will be merely the woman he *intended* to marry."

"Don't be melodramatic, Rose. William loves you, and I doubt something that happened in your life, no matter how terrible the fact of your hiding it from him, will cause him to change his mind about marrying you."

Chagrined, she lowered her head. Still, she would have sworn Finn loved her so thoroughly he could never have stayed away from her for years, letting her mourn as she had. *What did she know of a man's love?* Acrimony twisted inside her.

"I could divorce Finn and spare William the pain of ever knowing," she said, no longer caring if Reed thought her a coward. It was not about her, after all, but about keeping William from feeling the pain she was feeling.

"It could stay between you and me," she added, standing up.

He crossed his arms. "It could." Reed sounded weary.

"If it makes you think any better of me or of Finn Bennet," she said, lifting her chin, "we did *not* have a wedding night, nor did we do what would turn a woman into a wife."

Rose should be mortified at having this conversation with her very proper brother, except she'd heard from her sisters how even Reed had had his improper moments.

His eyes widened for a second. Then he nodded.

"Legally, that may make a great difference in your divorce," he said, his thoughtful tone showing he was treating this already as a case rather than as an emotional family situation. "Instead of a divorce, perhaps we shall pursue an annulment."

In another instant, his focus was back on her. "Even if physically you did not belong to another man, you gave your hand to him and took his name and signed a legal document. Personally, I think William should know that. It is up to you, of course."

Nodding, she sighed. "Finn lives above The Parisien. I suppose the only way for you to contact him is to go there. You can ask the staff, and they'll direct you to his room."

Reed gave her a sympathetic half-smile. "Don't worry, Rose. It may not seem like it at present, but everything will work out eventually. Will you trust me on that?"

Her brother had never lied to her. "I will. May I also trust you will tell no one until I speak with William? Not even Charlotte."

Instantly, he looked unhappy. "Yes, but in that case, do it soon."

After another evening of pondering her predicament, Rose concluded Reed was right. She could not leave William with a hood over his head when it came to her past. Especially not with Claire and now also Reed knowing, not to mention with Finn liable to pass them on the street at any moment and speak familiarly to her.

William being taken off guard was too awful to contemplate.

With her mind made up to confess, she couldn't stand to keep the secret from him a moment longer than necessary. When he agreed to a mid-day walk through the Common taking a break from the State House, Rose braced herself for the worst and hoped for the best.

"No, thank you," she said, declining his offer of strawberry-flavored shaved ice from a street vendor. Her stomach was already churning, and the idea of the overly sweet, syrupy cold ice hitting it only made it difficult to swallow. *How to begin?*

Glancing across the Common in the direction of Ober's restaurant, even though it was a couple streets away and not visible, she drew in a long breath.

"William."

"Yes, dearest."

"I need to tell you something that will come as a surprise, and an unpleasant one at that."

He faltered in his step, turning to look at her, and then he kept walking as did she.

"Go on," he said. "I'm sure I can handle whatever it is." He shot her an encouraging smile.

"Yes, I know," Rose said. "I certainly believe you can. A few years back, I met a—"

She was hit in the back of the head and spun around to see a child's ball made of rough canvas rolling away from her.

"What in God's name?" William began. "Are you all right?"

"Yes." She rubbed the spot where the ball had hit her, not only startling her but knocking askew her favorite straw boater and mussing her hair.

Glancing around, she expected to see a group of children playing, yet saw no one who might have thrown it. There was a couple on a picnic blanket. There were two girls playing with sticks and hoops nearby. There was an elderly couple strolling. There was Finn, darting out from behind a tree and gesturing at her.

Finn! She wrinkled up her nose. *What was he indicating?* Then, as he clapped his hand over his mouth and shook his head, she understood and turned quickly away. She couldn't let William know she knew Finn, not until she'd explained everything. Besides, he looked like a madman!

"Some mischievous boy, no doubt," William said, taking her arm and continuing the way they were going. "You were saying?"

Rose looked back over her shoulder. Finn was still shaking his head and putting a finger to his lips as if to shush her. Obviously, he didn't want her to tell William about him. *What should she do?*

CHAPTER ELEVEN

"You know, I think I would like that shaved ice after all," Rose said, turning to William. "Would you be a love and get me some? Lemon if they have it, please?"

He hesitated a moment at her capriciousness but almost instantly acquiesced.

"Certainly. Wait here." With that, William turned and walked back toward the edge of the park.

Rose took a step in Finn's direction, and sure enough, he hurried forward.

"Have you said anything to him yet?"

"No. I was about to. Why did you hit me with a ball?"

"Did I hurt you?"

"No but—"

"Then never mind that. Don't say anything more to Woodsom until I can speak with you again. Nothing. Tell him nothing. Do you promise?"

"What's this about?" she demanded.

"Can you come to my room later?"

Her head was spinning. William would be back any moment, and Finn was behaving so strangely.

"No, I don't promise anything. This makes no sense. Tell me at once why—"

"Come at six o'clock when the restaurant is busiest. No one will notice you arriving. Go again through the kitchen to the back stairs. In the passage to the second-floor dining room, there's an unmarked door. That's my room."

Finn looked her right in the eye, and she caught her breath at the earnestness shining back at her.

"Trust me, Rose."

Trust him. She did, or rather, she had.

"I will. I'll—" She saw William turn from the vendor. Quickly, she moved away from Finn, and he strolled in the opposite direction from her as if they'd passed each other without speaking. She waited for William to catch up.

"Thank you." She bit a huge mouthful of lemon ice from the small paper cone and promptly froze the roof of her mouth, causing her head to ache instantly.

"Ohh," she moaned while William watched her with a slight smile.

"Silly girl, put your tongue on the roof of your mouth."

Rose did as he instructed, and, in a few moments, the pain went away.

"Better?" he asked.

"Yes." She turned to look in the direction Finn had taken, and he was nowhere to be seen. Breathing a sigh of relief, she fell into step with William.

"Shall we walk up Commonwealth Avenue, and then I'll have to get home. My mother wants to discuss the wedding cake." She felt ridiculous telling such an obvious bald-faced lie. William stopped walking completely and frowned at her.

"You were going to tell me something. I think it was unpleasant, and also, if I'm not mistaken, important."

He was not a fool, and she was angry with Finn for putting her in this difficult situation. *Again.* She vowed to stop trying to distract William with falsities.

"Yes, you're correct, but do you mind if I put it off for another time?"

He touched her chin and held it, his lively eyes flashing with a shade of doubt.

"Sometime soon, Rose, yes? I have a feeling I need to hear whatever you were going to tell me. Is it regarding the *incident* you mentioned to me once, the one that left you saddened?"

William's words startled her. He'd remembered the conversation from their first date, despite her never having mentioned it again. If only she could tell him now as planned. Better yet, if only there was nothing to tell. She wanted her life back the way it was before the engagement party.

Right then, unseemly as it would be, Rose wished she could roll up onto the balls of her feet and kiss her dear beau. Her heart felt heavy with love for him.

"Yes, it is, and yes, soon. I promise. Please, though, don't worry about it." She offered him a small smile that she didn't feel. After all, there was plenty to worry about, but she would do that for both of them.

He was a good soul and didn't pester her or ask questions. Rose thought if she were in his shoes, she would have nagged at him until he told her.

"I won't worry, then, if you say not to. Whatever it is, it can't be too terrible. After all, everything has gone so smoothly, ever since I let you knock me over at the rink."

Rose laughed, recalling that day. She'd practically set her mind and heart against him, thanks to Maeve.

William threaded her arm through his.

"I love it when you laugh," he told her. "You become even lovelier if that were possible."

She felt the bloom in her cheeks, like a sweet heat, which he could put there with a certain look or a few words.

"Anyway," he added, "there's bound to be at least one fly in the ointment, after all."

Her happiness dimmed. This was an extraordinarily large fly.

"Am I invited home with you to discuss our wedding cake with Mrs. Malloy?" William asked.

She smiled as brightly as she could. "Do you truly want to go over the details of the wedding?"

He leaned over and took a bite of the shaved ice. Close to her, he licked his lips, and she wished they were alone so he could kiss her properly. She could tell by the look on his face he knew her inappropriate thoughts.

"Not really," William answered, then he tilted his head. "However, afterward, I'm counting on a moment alone with you in your back garden, right behind that lilac bush of which I'm so very fond. Or maybe before the cake discussion even begins." His handsome mouth rose on one side as he offered her his wickedest grin.

"A splendid idea," she agreed, grabbing hold of his hand and turning toward home.

Rose trod rapidly up the back stairs of The Restaurant Parisien, her heart beating time with her feet. The nervous excitement coursing through her reminded her of earlier days when she would have viewed this as a jolly adventure. However, the awful notion of betraying William soured any amusement she had in stealing through the restaurant's kitchen and up to Finn's room. This was beyond the pale now she was older and wiser, and an engaged woman at that!

Before she could change her mind, she knocked at the door, which was precisely where he'd described it to be. Finn opened it quickly and dragged her inside. Obviously he'd been waiting and listening.

For a moment, Finn held on, towering over her, solid, close, his fingers gripping her upper arms. Very easily, she could sink against him, and she knew he would wrap his arms around her.

"Release me," she nearly demanded. However, as the words sprang to her lips, he had already done so.

Securing the door behind them, he turned to her, and for a moment, she felt it, the old tingle low in her stomach, the frisson of warmth skating up and down her spine, the lightening and lifting of her spirit.

Her head spun. They were alone, in a small, plain room that smelled of food from the kitchen below. There was a small dresser with a coffee mug, a washstand, and ... a bed. Everything similar to his last room, as if it were nearly four years earlier. She swallowed.

Finn was staring at her, and she couldn't speak. If he did indeed take her in his arms, would she feel the same as when she'd been mindlessly in love with this man?

Her brain conjured William and his kisses in her garden the day before.

No, she decided, she would not feel the way she used to about Finn. Her heart belonged to another.

"Sit, please, Rose," Finn said into the silence.

There was no chair, so she lowered herself gingerly onto the edge of his bed.

He leaned against the dresser, crossing one ankle over the other.

"I'm sorry I had to stop you telling Woodsom, but the less people who know I'm here, the better."

A shiver ran through her. "Why?"

"I know this will sound crazy, and perhaps you will think me quite mad, but I believe I've stirred up a hornet's nest of trouble." He ran a hand through his sandy fair hair. "I went to see old Mr. Kelly yesterday morning. Naturally, he was astounded to see me alive."

No more than she had been!

"I thought it best to tell him to his face that the *Garrard* had been built incorrectly. At first, he listened to me, but then he seemed to think I was blaming him. I only wanted to make absolutely sure they hadn't used a similar design on another ship and wouldn't ever again. I told him I'd previously mentioned to the master shipwright about the design flaws, particularly the low freeboard, before we ever finished building her."

"What did he say?" she asked, while feeling this had nothing to do with her or William.

"He became red-faced, but with anger, not with shame."

"Naturally, he would be angry with the shipwright."

"That's just it, he was angry with me. Especially when I said I didn't think Master Builder Gilbert should be designing any more ships. Kelly asked me what I wanted. I told him I was looking for work, and he said I'd never work in a Boston shipyard again."

"What?" Rose jumped up. "That makes no sense. Why would he not want to know about the flaws and errors?"

"I don't think anyone at his yard lost their livelihood over the sinking, did they? No one was fined or punished."

Rose thought about the newspaper articles to which she'd devoted much time, reading and rereading to make sense of losing Finn.

"No one was held accountable. The disaster was blamed entirely on the weather. And everyone at the yard professed great surprise that a ship of her quality could go down."

"Her quality!" Finn spat out, thumping the dresser's faded wooden top with his fist. "I've been working with builders the past few years who would've laughed that ship's design right off the paper and would never, absolutely never, have put men on board her."

Then he shook his head. "Actually, there was almost nothing on paper! We worked from a wooden half hull model to build the *Garrard*. No written plans at all."

Jamming his hands into his pockets, he looked agitated. "They call it *practical* building here in the states. In England, it's all done by engineers and draftsmen who understand how ships float and why they sink."

She sat back down, trying to make sense of what he was saying. He looked so distraught, but the terrible tragedy was in the past, wasn't it?

"I understand you're bitter, Finn, and now you're being stopped from getting employment here, yet what has any of this to do with my telling Mr. Woodsom about you?"

"I think someone tried to silence me last night."

"*Silence* you?" Her words came out as a surprised croak. "What do you mean?"

He looked uncomfortable yet he stopped fidgeting, yanked his hands out of his pockets, and crossed his arms again. "I can't be entirely certain."

"What do you mean?" she asked again, her voice barely more than a whisper.

"I told you I still have strange dreams. Sometimes," he began, then stopped. Groaning, he added, "God, this is embarrassing."

"Tell me," she encouraged.

After a pause, he continued. "Sometimes, I think I'm still afloat on that damned piece of wood, especially when I'm dropping off to sleep or right before waking up. Other times, I imagine I'm being restrained on the fishing vessel sailing farther and farther from—" he broke off and glanced away from her to stare at the floor.

"Anyway, the dreams seem so real. And I've been known to drift off into one even during the daytime."

He lifted his head. His stormy blue-gray eyes stared into hers, waiting for her response.

She didn't have to consider for long. "That seems perfectly natural given what you went through."

He shrugged. "Some people would call me insane."

"Obviously, that's not the case," she said. "You're as sane as anyone."

"On my way back from the shipyard after meeting with Kelly, I thought I was being followed. I saw the same man on the trolley ride home, and I believe I saw him later in the restaurant dining room. Two nights ago, I thought I heard footsteps pacing outside my door. When I checked, there was no one there, only the empty hallway."

Rose considered a moment. "People do walk down hallways without meaning mischief, especially when the passage leads to a dining room."

He smiled. "I know. Even if I was followed from the shipyard, no one knows I live here. Except you. Still . . . ," he trailed off.

"Is there something more?"

Finn nodded. "Last night, I was heading home, just a block away on Temple when two men tried to grab me." He gestured toward the window which faced the street. "They were trying to pull me toward a carriage."

"To rob you?" Rose asked.

He locked his gaze upon hers. "No. I think to kill me. I can't explain why I think that."

Inexplicably, she wanted to wrap her arms around him and comfort him. Instead, she curled her fingers tightly in her lap to stop herself.

"You didn't want me to tell Mr. Woodsom in case that put him in danger. Is that right?"

"And you, too, of course. If you tell someone, then it will be apparent that you know about me. At this moment, no one knows we were ever married so I believe you're safe."

"Except for meeting you on the docks and here at the restaurant in broad daylight, with the entire restaurant staff watching. And having you throw a ball at my head." She tried to lighten her tone since he seemed so grim.

It worked. He smiled ruefully. "What else could I do? Shout out to you, 'Hey, Rose!'" Pausing, he sighed. "You haven't told anyone about my return, have you?"

She wrinkled her nose.

"Rose?" he prompted.

"I did tell Claire," she admitted. "I had to talk to someone."

He groaned again. "Will she tell anyone?"

Rose thought of Robert and Franklin. Most likely Claire wouldn't tell her twin brother, but what if she confided in her beau, too?

"I don't think so," she said. "I'll go see her later and tell her absolutely not to. She never told anyone about our marriage," she added to reassure him.

He nodded. "That's good."

She might as well let him know the worst. "I did speak to one other person."

Frowning, Finn waited for her to tell him.

"I have spoken with my brother."

Finn uncrossed his legs and stood straight, and the room instantly shrunk in size.

"You told your brother that I'm alive?"

"Yes," she said quietly, "and that we're married."

When his eyes widened, she reminded him quickly, "It had to be done for us to obtain a divorce." She shrugged. "Actually, I'm surprised he hasn't already paid you a visit, except he is most likely getting the paperwork in order first. Reed is very thorough."

"What did he say?"

That you're a scoundrel. The words floated through her mind, and she knew a petty wish to hurt Finn for how he'd hurt her.

"He was disappointed in both of us. Naturally."

"As any big brother would be. I'm sure he had choice words for your husband."

She flinched at the word, as now their marriage seemed nothing but sordid and duplicitous.

"What shall I do? Should I tell him about this threat to you?" Rose knew Reed would shout the alarm from every corner if he thought her to be in danger. She would lose all her hard-earned freedom to boot, and any restrictions or odd behavior would ensure that William would have to know immediately.

"You know his character. I don't."

"My brother is working to obtain a divorce for us as quickly as possible. I don't know if telling him about this possible danger will make any difference."

Suddenly, he reached his hand out to her, and unthinkingly, she took it, letting him draw her to her feet.

"I'd best get you safely home," he said, as the tiny space became too small for the two of them, both trapped between the dresser and the bed.

They locked gazes for a moment, blazing heat sparked without warning, making Rose nearly gasp aloud. She lowered her eyes, hoping he couldn't hear the way her heart was thumping.

"What will you do next?" she asked the threadbare carpet, noticing it for the first time.

"I need to speak with someone whom I can trust at the shipyard. I think I know who."

"What if you're wrong?" she asked, still avoiding his eyes.

"Then I'll be dead, and you won't have to worry about this any longer, nor whether you can legally marry Woodsom."

She raised her gaze, horrified. "Don't say that! You've already been dead to me once. I didn't like it the first time."

"I'm sorry," he said, his voice low. "That was a poor jape. I know I made mistakes. If I could go back and do it differently, I would."

"Would you?" Rose stared at him.

"Yes," Finn said adamantly, sounding sincere. "As soon as I began to work and put money aside, I meant to contact you, and then, like an ass, I got injured."

She glanced down at his leg. "How did it happen?"

"Because I was stupid and incredibly careless. I let my mind wander, thinking of . . ." He shook his head. "It doesn't matter, does it? The next thing I knew I was nearly crippled. It took months to heal and to walk again, and then only because of the strong shipbuilders' union in England. They made sure I was taken care of. As I convalesced and more time passed, I began to rethink my coming home."

"Why?" *How could a few months have changed his mind about returning to her?*

"As time stretched on and on, I assumed you thought me dead and were going forward with your life. Rightly so. I was still months away from getting enough money to book passage home, and on top of that, I was half lame. Quite frankly, given how we began, I thought you'd be better off without me."

Given how they began.

Rose frowned. They had begun their association with attraction and excitement that quickly became love, and then even more quickly to becoming husband and wife. Yet they'd always stayed insular, only the two of them. *Was that what Finn meant?*

"I see," she uttered. She didn't understand exactly, but she appreciated the fact Finn wasn't so cocksure of himself, no longer thinking his way had been the right way.

However, when he made a small movement toward her with that appealing look on his face, Rose didn't like the softening feeling inside her.

Trapped, she couldn't back up, with the mattress pressed into the backs of her legs.

"Truly, I am sorry," Finn repeated as he took both of her hands in his then gently tugged her the last few inches toward him. "Sorrier than I can ever express."

Unable to bear the painful memories that arose when staring into his familiar gaze, she looked down. He was so close, the tips of his leather shoes disappeared under the hem of her dress. *What was happening? Was she perhaps in one of the dreams she used to have almost nightly?*

The feel of his hands, slightly rough, of his thumbs stroking across her knuckles brought Rose back to the present. *This was real. He was real.*

When they were chest to chest, she was forced to look up at him or continue to stare mutely at the buttons of his shirt. Swallowing, she glanced up.

Finn released her then, but only so he could encircle her slim waist with his own large, capable hands.

She closed her eyes at his touch. How often had she thought of this moment and cried, sobbing into her pillow, knowing she would never be close to this man again? Yet here they were, his breath blending with her own, his lips only a hand's span from hers. Countless times she had dreamt of exactly this!

Whereas *his* dreams had been scary and violent, hers had been heartbreaking. Tantalizing fantasies that taunted her night after night, precisely as he was teasing her now. Sometimes in her dreams, they were picnicking in Arlington or sitting on a bench on the Common. Once, while looking at his handsome face, feeling so grateful he was finally with her again, she remembered clearly saying, "If this is only a dream, it will kill me."

At that precise moment, she had awakened, absolutely devastated, with tears streaming down her cheeks, and foolishly vowed never to close her eyes again.

So why was it she dared not look at him?

"Open your eyes," Finn commanded.

She shook her head.

"Rose," he implored.

She opened them as he asked and fell into his soft gray-blue gaze.

Inevitably, he bent low and tightened his hold on her at the same moment his lips claimed hers. She breathed in the scent of him, oak mingled with sea air, and was drawn further under his spell.

Finn slanted his mouth, and she tilted her head, allowing the heat of his lips upon hers to seep into her soul. His hand on the small of her back pressed her closer still. With his other hand, he cradled her head in his large palm and deepened the kiss, slipping his tongue between her lips.

So familiar, this heady sensation as his tongue swirled around hers. Unable to help herself, Rose sucked it deeper into her mouth. He moaned, or she did.

William!

"No," she managed in a necessarily muffled voice before Finn released her head. Pressing her hands on his chest, Rose shook her head.

"No, no, no," she said again, and he relaxed his hold upon her. "Let me go," she added, even while she made no move to step away.

He held up his hands as he let go of her entirely.

They stayed silent, breathing hard, staring into each other's eyes.

"I have to go," she whispered finally. In two steps, she was at the door, ready to flee.

"I'll see you home."

"No," she said, yanking open the door. "If there is someone watching, they may see us together. I'll be fine."

Or maybe she would never be fine again. *What had she done?* And worse, now she couldn't tell William about Finn at all, not while there was even a hint of danger. She prayed Claire had indeed held her tongue.

"Rose, I—"

"Goodbye," she barely uttered the word before she was fleeing down the back stairs and through the kitchen.

A minute later, she pushed her way through the crowded streets and headed home.

CHAPTER TWELVE

The next day, Rose practically ran into the Art Association Committee's headquarters at the Athenaeum. Claire was in her usual spot by the large window reading letters from would-be artists interested in exhibiting. Of all Claire's voluntary activities about the city, this was her favorite.

"I need to speak with you immediately," Rose said, scattering Claire's papers as she grabbed her friend's hand. Two other Athenaeum volunteers looked up.

"Not here. In the coat room," Rose urged.

They ran down the polished floor and sequestered themselves behind the rack of the other ladies' jackets and capes. Rose noticed Claire's cream-colored silk dolman with its fetching fringe and felt at once reassured by its familiar beauty. Everything in the world hadn't changed.

"Have you mentioned our last conversation to anyone?"

Claire's eyes grew wide. "You mean about Phineas Bennet's return?" she asked in too loud of a voice for Rose's liking.

Wincing, she shushed her. *Finn Bennet and his return and his kisses!* That was what she'd thought about all night long between fitful dreams.

Then Claire giggled. "Don't tell me he's dead again."

"Claire!" Rose protested. "This is not a manner to make a jest over."

"Sorry, I was simply so shocked the last time that I can't imagine what you could possibly say to astonish me further."

"Be serious, dear. You have said nothing to anyone, not even to Franklin?"

"Of course not," Claire said.

Rose breathed a sigh of relief. "I knew you wouldn't, but I had to be sure."

"Why? I thought you were going to tell William immediately."

"I can't now. Finn thinks someone isn't pleased that he's come back."

"I don't understand."

"He thought the ship should never have been launched. He told me so before he left." She paused, thinking of all the families who'd needlessly lost loved ones, the young men in their prime. "And he was right."

Claire absently straightened a coat hanging nearby before running the silky sleeve through her fingers. "How does that cause a problem at present?"

"He's not certain," Rose said, "yet after he went to his old shipyard to speak with the owner, someone may have followed him back to his room. What's more, he thinks some men tried to abduct him."

Claire frowned. "Abduct him?"

What did that tone in her friend's voice mean?

"Now he wants you to keep him a secret from everyone." Claire said.

Rose paused. "Well, yes, because it could be dangerous."

Claire's lovely eyes narrowed. "Are you certain he doesn't want you to remain silent because he wants you to stay married to him?"

Rose wrinkled her nose. "That's ridiculous. If he wants to stay married, he should give me an indication."

Claire tilted her head. "Or simply ruin your relationship with William."

"That may happen either way," Rose pointed out. "If I tell William of my marriage, he may walk away. If I don't, I'll have to hide it, and then tell him eventually anyway." She paused. "Oh, I see what you mean. You think it will be much worse if William learns Finn has been here for a while and I didn't tell him."

"Won't it?" Claire had moved on to smoothing the collar on a long-forgotten, out-of-fashion gentleman's frock coat.

Rose pondered her friend's words. Finn was not the devious type. He'd always been open and forthright. *Before he pretended to be dead for nearly four years!*

"In case Finn is correct, dearest Claire, and someone does wish him harm, please don't tell a soul. I would hate to have you in any danger because of me."

"It wouldn't be *because* of you," she remarked pointedly, "but I will not say a word. If there *is* a threat, then you mustn't go anywhere near Mr. Bennet. If someone is indeed watching him and sees you in close quarters," Claire trailed off with a shake of her head.

Rose nodded. "I know and I'll be—"

The door opened and Mrs. Taylor came in with her fur stole over her arm.

"Allow me," Rose said, taking it from the older dame and hanging it carefully.

"Thank you." Mrs. Taylor eyed her up and down. "I didn't realize you ladies had taken on the role of coat room attendants."

Claire and Rose laughed as if it was the funniest thing they'd ever heard, until Mrs. Taylor, assured of her own wit, left them.

"All right, then," Claire said, "back to work."

"You promise to—" Rose began.

"Yes, yes! To remain silent. However, you must promise to keep your distance from Mr. Bennet until we are sure there is no risk."

"That is prudent," Rose agreed, although she'd never been cautious before. She certainly could not give the requested promise. Nor could she have kept it.

As she hurried to India Wharf the following morning to Reed and Charlotte's home, Rose acknowledged she would throw herself in head first, to do whatever it took to help Finn, whether he wanted it or not. Anything except let her brother know what she was doing.

Most assuredly, she did not want to encounter him, for he would astutely get too many details out of her and then forbid her from doing anything that seemed even remotely threatening.

Luckily, Rose knew Reed would be at his office by that time of the morning.

Charlotte welcomed her in. "I'm so glad to see you," she said to Rose, and as always, Rose felt her gracious sister-in-law meant it wholeheartedly.

It had to have been difficult for Charlotte when her life changed from being a busy journalist to a full-time mother. From being out in the world, sniffing out stories to staying at home sniffing soiled diaper cloths.

Rose winced. It would be her turn next with William—to bear children and clean out the diaper pail. Yet in the space of a heartbeat, it was Finn's face she saw as the father of her children.

Shaking her head to clear her thoughts, she set down her satchel.

"Whatever is all this?" Charlotte asked, as Rose opened her leather bag, filled to overflowing with her collection of newspapers. She deposited them onto Charlotte's highly polished living room table, creating an unsightly heap in the clear gray light reflected from the ocean spreading out beyond the windows.

"This is the little matter I mentioned on the telephone," Rose said, wondering how she could really approach this subject without giving away her entire duplicitous story.

"It doesn't look like a 'little' anything. But first, the niceties. Would you care for some tea?" Charlotte asked, walking toward her kitchen door.

"Of course," Rose assured her. "I'm in no hurry." After all, she'd let years of lying build up. She could use a few more minutes to discern her best course of action. "However, I'd prefer coffee," she called after her, remembering Charlotte's French housekeeper's special way with the rich brew.

Charlotte must have asked Jeanine to bring in the refreshments, for she returned to the living room even before Rose had finished removing her gloves and short embroidered cape.

They took seats on the settee in front of the low table.

"May I?" Charlotte asked, indicating the worn leather satchel.

"Certainly," Rose said. "That was my father's, by the way."

"Mm," Charlotte said, clearly uninterested in anything but the contents. She fanned out the folded pile of newspapers that had managed to get tattered and creased at the edges while remaining in the bottom drawer of Rose's dresser.

Rose watched her sister-in-law. At one time, she'd read and reread each one of the articles about the *Garrard* until she thought she knew every image, every line of content.

Jeanine came in carrying a fully laden tray.

"Lovely to see you, Mademoiselle Rose," she said with her thick French accent. Then she placed the tray at the far edge of the table where she could find room, and the strong aroma of the coffee chased away even the pungent scent of the salt air.

How Finn would like this home, perched on the edge of the ocean, Rose thought. Then she reconsidered. Maybe after what he'd been through, that would be the last thing he'd enjoy, awakening to rolling waves just beyond his bedroom. There was so much she didn't know about him. How did he take his coffee, for instance? Did he eat green vegetables? How often did he bathe? Did he prefer fish or fowl? Spring or fall?

It mattered not. All these things she already knew about William.

Hiding her anxiety, she smiled at the pleasant-faced wife of Charlotte and Reed's chef.

"Thank you. It is always a pleasure to see you, too." She glanced at the tray. "Are those Pierre's fairy cakes, the same ones from my . . . ," she faltered momentarily, "from my engagement party?"

"*Oui*, he has been trying a variation. With almonds and vanilla instead of orange zest. What do you think?" Jeanine knew Rose was attending a cooking school as she'd had a long discussion on the best flour for roux with Pierre one afternoon while visiting her brother.

Picking up one of the small bite-size cakes, Rose was distracted by the rustling as Charlotte turned over one paper after the other. She took a hasty bite. Unfortunately, with the task ahead of her stealing away everything except anxiety, the sweet concoction tasted the way she imagined sawdust would.

Still, Rose beamed a false smile and proclaimed them, "Delicious!"

Satisfied, Jeanine poured them each a cup of dark-roasted coffee before heading upstairs to check on the youngest children.

"Do you want to tell me about the common theme I detect in your collection?"

Rose detected no duplicity in the question. Reed had kept his word and had said nothing to Charlotte. How to begin?

"I took an interest in the sinking of the *Garrard* a few years ago," she began, deciding not to reveal too much if possible.

"I remember it. A terrible accident," Charlotte said, glancing past Rose's head to the ocean outside their window as if some trace of the ship would be there even then.

"That's exactly it," Rose said quietly. "I can't help wondering whether it really was an accident."

Charlotte's astonished face made Rose try again. "I mean, obviously, it was not intentional. No one would want those men to die. However, I wonder whether the sinking could have been prevented. If it's possible the ship's design was not up to standards."

"You mean whether someone, such as a shipbuilder, was negligent," Charlotte asked, cutting right to the heart of the matter.

"Precisely."

Charlotte frowned, glancing down at the papers on her lap then looked at her sister-in-law with narrowed eyes.

"Why would you think that, Rose?"

Why, indeed! "When Mama told me the ship had gone down that day, I was so shocked. I couldn't believe it. In this modern age, for such a thing to happen."

Charlotte nodded. "Even in this age, terrible accidents happen that are no one's fault. That awful train crash in Revere, do you remember? I think thirty people died and scores more injured, and all they were doing was riding a train. Or what about the Pemberton Mill in Lawrence."

They both took a moment to consider the four hundred souls who'd perished when the behemoth of a building crashed down in an undulating crest of bricks and machinery. People said the destruction was accompanied by a noise like deafening thunder on an otherwise normal day on the banks of the Merrimack River.

"There are so many others unfortunately rattling around in my head, accidents I wish I could forget, but let's not become melancholy like the last pea at pea time," Charlotte instructed, picking up her cup. "Tell me why the sinking of the *Garrard* is of such interest to you."

Rose stared. Charlotte was pinning her with a particularly questioning gaze. She had to either lie now directly or lay it all out in the open.

She opened her mouth, then shut it. What if she endangered Charlotte in some way and her brother's beloved wife, mother of his children, came to harm? Rose would never—could never—forgive herself. Plus, her brother would murder her.

She cleared her throat, then sipped her coffee and cleared it again.

"I," she paused, "I cannot tell you."

Charlotte rolled her eyes. "How did I know you were going to say that? That's what every informant I've ever questioned has said right before he or she has spilled their innermost secrets."

Rose's own eyes widened. *Was that true?* Would Charlotte somehow get her to reveal everything? Then Charlotte laughed and reached out, touching Rose's hand to reassure her.

"I'm only fooling," she said. "If you cannot tell me why you care about the men on this particular ship, then tell me what you are hoping I can do for you."

Rose nodded. That was more than generous of Charlotte, offering to help without knowing why.

"Perhaps if I explain first what I think, then you can tell me if there is a way to go about proving or disproving my theory."

"Yes," Charlotte agreed. "Let's put one flat brick under another."

Rose stared at her.

"That is to say, that sounds like a good plan," her sister-in-law clarified.

Choosing her words carefully, Rose explained how she'd known one of the sailors, "Mr. . . . *um* . . . Mr. . . . Tim . . . Tim Bennet," before he left and how he had told her the ship was top heavy. She also relayed how no one at the yard would listen because the expense to change the vessel's construction once it had been started was too great.

"After the sinking, if you read the papers," Rose continued, "you'll see that not a man interviewed from the shipyard mentioned any fault with the ship's design. It's Kelly's yard, over in East Boston. However, ships have made it through far worse storms than that one. Why, as soon as the waves started to churn, the fore deck was swamped and under water."

Charlotte stared at her, and Rose realized her mistake.

"I mean, it surely would have been if what my friend Tom said was right. *Before* he left, I mean."

"Tim, you mean."

"I beg your pardon?" Rose asked mystified.

"You said his name was Tim."

"Did I? How silly of me!" She took a huge gulp of the brew and proceeded to choke and splutter.

"Don't have an apoplectic fit over a misremembered vowel." Rose smiled weakly.

"So, you would like me to discover whether anyone at the yard knew of the faulty design and kept mum about it. In essence, you think someone is to blame for the sailors losing their lives, including this man Tom. Or Tim."

"I do. But I don't know who. And it may be a conspiracy of more than one."

"It would have to be," Charlotte said. "No one man designs and builds a ship, nor an ill-conceived mill building."

"Oh dear," Rose exclaimed. "I almost wish I hadn't said anything to you. You have to be extremely careful. Reed would never forgive me if anything happened to you. Nor would I forgive myself."

"Why do you think anything could come of my digging around a little?" Charlotte asked, and Rose saw she already had a journalistic twinkle in her green eyes.

"Because men may have died needlessly."

"Yes, but people don't commit mass murder on a whim. Why would anyone knowingly send men to their deaths? Usually money is involved if something nefarious is afoot. Perhaps someone benefited from the sinking."

"How could anyone benefit from that?" Rose wondered aloud.

Charlotte looked thoughtful. "Believe it or not, people can make money over just about anything."

Rose shrugged.

"I suppose my not telling Reed what I'm investigating is imperative?" Charlotte asked.

Rose realized a sense of discomfort in asking a wife to withhold information from her husband, especially as, in this case, she'd already asked the husband the same thing. She couldn't bring herself to say the words asking Charlotte to do that. Rather, she could do nothing more than look down at her hands, noticing only then how she was crumbling the rest of the fairy cake on her plate. Dropping the pieces, she brushed off her fingers.

"Because you don't want to explain your prior friendship with the deceased Mr. Bennet?" Charlotte asked.

Rose flinched slightly. Hearing even Finn's last name on her sister-in-law's lips made Rose wish she'd had her wits about her to change it entirely. It was too late now.

"Honestly, Rose, I cannot imagine Reed having a burr under his saddle after . . . what?" Charlotte glanced at the newspaper on top of the pile. "After nearly four years. He's not such a stick that he'd begrudge you a little youthful flirtation."

No, Rose thought, *but what about a little youthful marriage?* Reed was not laughing that one off, she knew. And if he thought there was anything untoward to investigate, he would be beside himself.

All she could do was shrug slightly. "I would rather keep this between the two of us if at all possible. At least for the time being."

Charlotte nodded. "May I keep these so I can refresh my memory on the details and learn some names of the significant people at the shipyard."

"Of course," Rose said, noticing how Charlotte seemed to radiate with barely concealed excitement over having an assignment fall into her hands.

"Give me a week," Charlotte said, "and we'll see what I can find out. For now, no more talk of secrets and disasters. Tell me about the upcoming wedding. Any new developments?"

Rose took a deep breath. *Secrets and disasters. Hm,* that about summed up any thought of her engagement to William. What could she say? She launched into a discussion of her dress and of William's mother's idea for the celebration feast, all the while feeling as if she were acting a role—the part of the blushing bride, when in truth, she was already a beleaguered wife.

Charlotte didn't go to the shipyard to begin her investigation as one might expect. Rather, on instinct and from a keen sense of how the world worked, she drove her carriage from her home on India Wharf up Atlantic Avenue, straight to Commercial Street and to the offices of the Insurance Company of North America.

Despite its headquarters being located in Philadelphia, Charlotte was well aware of the prestigious and busy branch nestled in the heart of Boston's wharves and shipping industry. If anyone had information on the sinking and any subsequent financial settlement regarding the *Garrard*, it would be the ICNA.

She settled a dazzling smile upon the first clerk she encountered and a few minutes later, upon his superior. Within a short while, she was seated at a desk with records of all claims made after the *Garrard*'s sinking. It was a goldmine of information.

Naturally, Kelly's yard was represented and had been reimbursed by the underwriter, as well as the ship's owner, Mr. Dilbey. When she saw a private individual's name, she took note of it with a slight frown and a feeling that, unfortunately, her intuition would be correct. Someone had made money off those men's lives, someone who'd gambled that the ship would sink and had won. Even stranger, she was sure she'd read the name before in one of Rose's saved papers.

Adjusting the green shaded desk lamp, she compared the names to the ship's manifesto from the newspaper, and then the real mystery began.

CHAPTER THIRTEEN

Claire and Rose waited a tad impatiently, arm in arm on the sidewalk next to Thompson's Spa on Washington and Court streets. It was their favorite place for a doughnut and a drink although they weren't allowed to actually go inside the males-only cafe. They'd given Robert their orders instead.

"I'll have the egg phosphate," Rose had declared.

"You're joking," Claire had said, eyes wide. "That's a man's drink."

"How can a drink be a man's or a woman's?" Rose had shot back. "Especially if it's nonalcoholic." She'd gestured at the sign that stated "This is a temperance bar" in case there was any doubt. "Anyway, I was only teasing. I knew you'd raise an eyebrow. I'll have the egg lemon, please, Robert."

"I'll have an orangeade, dear brother. And don't forget the doughnuts."

They'd handed him two dimes each and waited.

"There," Claire said, pointing to a bench from which two men got up and walked away. "At last. Let's sit."

In another moment, Robert returned, followed by a soda clerk carrying a tray.

"You know," Rose said to the young man, "if your establishment would let us come inside, it would save you these extra steps."

"It's all right, miss. I don't mind. If you came inside, two lovely ladies such as yourselves in particular, it would be bedlam and mayhem and every other kind of trouble. If you know what I mean. You'd simply be a distraction to honest men trying to slake their thirsts."

Robert cleared his throat nervously. "Take your things, ladies, so this nice clerk can get back inside before we all get in trouble."

Rose shrugged before helping herself to her glass and her plate off the tray. Claire did the same. Halfway through her snacks, she saw Finn come out of a nearby alley that housed the Bell in Hand, which definitely was not a temperance bar.

Before she could process seeing him, he ducked into an office across the street. The unexpected sight of the man set her pulse to racing. It was still so very strange to know he was alive and breathing.

She tried to make out what type of business he'd gone into, fairly sure it was a newspaper publisher. After all, this was informally known as "Newspaper Row." Of course, she was nearly certain whatever he was doing, it had something to do with the *Garrard's* sinking. *Didn't everything in her life suddenly have to do with that cursed ship?*

She stuffed the doughnut into her mouth, chewing with her cheeks puffed out like one of the chipmunks that ran about the Common.

Should she investigate? What about Claire and Robert, who had taken a seat next to his sister with his own selection, a cup of Russian tea and a piece of pie?

She swallowed with difficulty and sipped her drink to wash it down, keeping an eye on the business's doorway and trying to listen to Claire's chatter about Franklin's superior intelligence.

"Superior to what?" she heard Robert ask, and it was the first time he seemed to show a spark of wit and not merely go along with his twin's opinion. Rose smiled.

At that moment, Maeve came walking along with her aunt, Franklin's mother. *How fortuitous!* Perhaps Maeve and Robert could be a match if only they took a slight interest in one another.

Robert stood at once, and Rose and Claire joined suit as soon as they'd wiped the crumbs from their mouths and brushed them from their laps.

"Good day to you all," Maeve said, glancing warily at Rose as she always did since their encounter at the Lowell's party.

Still feeling a tad ashamed of her behavior, Rose had tried to make amends already. And this was a good day to do more than that.

"Maeve, Mrs. Brewster. How lovely to see you? Can Robert get you both a refreshment from Thompson's?" Rose asked, smiling sweetly and being uncharacteristically chipper.

Four pairs of eyes stared at her, but she blinked at them all. *What?* she wondered. Truly, she was more known in the recent past for being somber and subdued, but she could be gracious and thoughtful, even in the middle of Washington Street.

Claire spoke next, directing her remark to Franklin's mother. "The doughnuts are most delicious. I do recommend them most wholeheartedly."

Mrs. Brewster glanced at the front of Thompson's, then back at Claire with a scowl, tugging at her short, fitted bustle coat. "They won't do for my waistline, I'm afraid. Rather thoughtless even to suggest."

Claire gasped, although Franklin's mother continued as if she hadn't heard. "I have an advertisement to place for a new housemaid," she said, speaking only to Maeve. "I can't seem to keep a girl these days. I'm stopping at both the *Daily Advertiser* and the *Courant* so I'll be a few minutes. You may stay here with your *friends*." And with that, Mrs. Brewster hurried off.

Rose noted with worry that Franklin's mother wasn't exactly warm toward Claire. In fact, she was downright rude and dismissive. She hoped the old biddy—who, truthfully speaking, wasn't that old yet acted like a biddy nonetheless—didn't stand in the way of Claire's fondest desire. *The idea of having her for a mother-in-law though, how awful!*

Maeve stood a tad awkwardly in their midst.

Rose opened her mouth to offer her a seat when Robert cleared his throat.

"Surely, I can get *you* something from the Spa," he offered.

Claire and Rose exchanged a glance. *How wonderful!* Perhaps Robert wouldn't need her matchmaking help after all.

"Why, you're only a little fatter than my sister," he finished.

Fatter! Dear God. Rose nearly groaned aloud. *What an imbecile!*

Maeve gasped, and Claire swatted her brother with her handbag. Rose knew her own eyes must be as wide as dinner plates because Maeve's were certainly bulging. The young woman looked positively apoplectic, and Rose couldn't blame her. For Robert to even comment on Maeve's body at all was utterly inexcusable.

Taking a deep breath, Rose tried to think of something to help the situation.

Claire simply took Maeve's hand and said, "If only I had your figure, I would be in heaven, so feminine and shapely."

Maeve seemed to take that well.

"Perhaps I will have a lemonade," she said, not offering Robert any money for her drink. She merely stared hard at him until he turned and went inside.

Rose breathed a sigh of relief. At that moment, she saw Finn emerge from the door across the street and head down Washington Street away from her.

"I've just caught sight of an old friend with whom I'd lost contact," she told Claire and Maeve, hoping her best friend understood her meaning. "I'm going to run and catch up. Excuse me, ladies."

Without waiting for a reply and admitting to herself she was behaving impulsively, Rose took off at an unseemly trot. She didn't want to lose sight of Finn on the busy street. After he turned right onto School Street, she feared she had, indeed, lost him. Scanning the crowd of pedestrians, she spotted him cutting through the old Granary Burying Ground and did the same.

Giving a nod to Paul Revere's statue as she had since she was a child, she increased her pace when Finn crossed the street and entered the Common proper. She could go no faster, not with her fashionable corset and heeled shoes, so when he began to outpace her, she gave up all sense of discretion and called out to him.

"Finn."

He stopped and turned at once. When he saw her, he rushed back in her direction.

"Is something wrong?" he asked.

Wrong, indeed! She realized, in a moment of impetuousness, she'd done precisely what he'd asked her not to. She'd demonstrated to anyone watching that she knew him.

"Oh," she murmured. "Nothing actually. I simply saw you and . . . ," she trailed off uncertainly when his face became a scowl of disapproval.

"Good God, woman. It's not safe," he muttered, already looking around them. "Haven't I told you that?"

Plainly, he didn't want to see her anyway, and now he was angry.

"Where can we go?" he asked suddenly.

So he *did* want to see her. That lifted her heart. She considered.

"I'll walk toward the Frog Pond, there's a thick clematis bower there. We can see if it's deserted."

He nodded. "You go first then, and I'll join you." Minutes later they stood in close confines, the leaf-covered trellis above them like a protective arch.

"I saw you on Washington Street," she told him.

"I went to the *Post*'s archives to read about the sinking. I wanted to see who said what."

She nodded. "I have every one of the local paper's coverage for weeks after the sinking. I saved them all."

His eyes widened momentarily as he realized what that meant. He now understood how she had scrutinized every line for information of him.

"I'm sorry," he said. "Truly, I am."

She lowered her gaze. She wanted to say it was all right, but the pain of his having let her think him dead bubbled to the surface anew. She tried to tamp it down, not wanting to shed another tear over Finn Bennet.

"If you would like to have the entire collection, I will bring them to you." Then she remembered they were no longer in her possession, and she was not about to tell him she'd spoken to Charlotte, even if she hadn't mentioned his name. Finn would not approve. She would simply wait for her sister-in-law to finish with them first.

"That would be most helpful." He offered her a gentle smile.

They stood in silence, and she wondered at her rapid pulse. Staring at his closed mouth, she couldn't deny she wanted him to kiss her again. Whenever she was in close proximity to this man, all she could think about was getting closer.

Rose felt her cheeks grow warm as he studied her.

"You didn't mention me to anyone else?" he asked.

"Of course not. And you don't have to ask. I'm not stupid. I used to be quite adept at all this secrecy," she finished bitterly.

It used to be *her* choice to hide Finn from everyone in her life. Now that she wanted to drag their relationship out into the light, she had to keep her mouth shut. It was intolerable, but she had no choice except to endure it.

"Stupid? No. Adept? I would have said you were, yes, until you called my name aloud a few minutes ago in the middle of the crowded street."

She rolled her eyes. *Maybe she was stupid.*

"After all, Rose, we simply don't know how any of this will turn out."

"What do you mean by that?" She heard the cantankerous tone to her own voice yet couldn't help herself. Not that long ago, her future had been perfectly set. Then Finn had arrived, tossing everything into uncertainty.

"Precisely what I said, I don't know. If I can't determine who is behind this whitewash, I may have to leave. I don't know how else to keep you safe."

She gasped. *Disappear again?* Only this time, she would know he was alive and would be unable to move on with her life. Neither free nor belonging to anyone.

"Without seeing me? Without a goodbye?"

"To protect you? Yes. Without a backward glance."

How could he be so cold?

"If you abandon me again with nothing resolved, Finn Bennet, I swear I will shout our marriage from the rooftops. You may have a life overseas that captured your interest and, for all I know, someone there has your heart, too." It wasn't the first time she'd wondered if he'd remained faithful or found himself some sweet British lass.

"However, if you choose that life over this one without giving me a proper divorce, then I warn you, I will ask my brother to use any legal means he can to prosecute you."

She felt tears welling up and added, "For abandonment."

Rose backed a step away from his shocked face. "And for cruelty." Then she continued, "You may not want me for yourself, but there is a decent and kind man who does."

She felt her emotions had got the better of her and turned heel, running out of the bower and along the wide path of the Holmes Walk.

Finn caught up to her in seconds.

"Rose," he said, not loudly yet with an insistent tone that halted her steps.

Taking a deep breath, she turned. *Gracious!* The sight of him might forever make her heart skip a beat. Or would she get used to his being among the living?

He took a step closer while still remaining a good three feet from her.

"To me, you are still mine," he said, his blue-gray eyes boring into hers. "Do you understand that? The moment I looked down from the rigging of the *Francis* and saw you, like a dark-haired witch, staring back at me, I knew you were meant for me."

"You left me," Rose protested, anger warring with sadness, making her absolutely wretched. "You left me. Left me! For so very long."

She watched him swallow, and his cheeks reddened.

"I can't believe we're having this conversation right in the middle of the damn Common, and you being an engaged woman." He looked heavenward, then back into her eyes. "I made a terrible mistake, and I'm asking your forgiveness for something unforgiveable, for making you suffer."

Finn ran a hand through his fair hair. "When we parted, you were still such a giddy young woman. After the ship went down and I lay on the deck of that damn fishing vessel with nothing to do but think, I realized you most likely regretted your hasty action in marrying me. You as much as showed me so. And I knew at that moment, if you didn't, then you should."

She opened her mouth to interrupt him. However, he didn't let her talk.

"Much as I wanted to be your equal, I was a laborer in comparison to your father and brother. You knew from the outset your family wouldn't accept me with open arms. Believe me, I understood you were trying to protect *my* feelings by keeping us a secret. I didn't think the situation would be any different when I came back. Still, I fully intended to do exactly that. Right up until this happened." He gestured to his leg.

Rose found herself taking a step toward him.

"If I had returned," Finn continued, "it would have been worse. You never would have let me actually claim you as my wife the way things stood, and honestly, Rose, I couldn't stomach the sneaking around, hiding how much I loved you."

She took another step in his direction, wondering if her own cowardice had caused their current situation.

"I'm sorry you felt you weren't good enough to be with me. I always thought you were. I was just afraid—"

"I know, love." He offered her a small smile. "It doesn't matter. When I was with you, I felt like a king."

Rose smiled, watching as he reached out a long arm toward her, nearly touching her cheek before letting his hand fall.

"After the accident, with nothing else to offer you, I decided I needed to be like McKay or Curtis, so I studied and worked as quickly and as hard as I could, I promise you that. Always with the idea that I would come back to you a better man. One with a promising future."

She shook her head at his reasoning. Even she had heard of Donald McKay and his record-setting clipper ships, although the other shipbuilder was unknown to her. In any case, she hadn't needed a *better* man. Only Finn, just as he was.

"I took too long, Rose. For that I will be eternally sorry. As soon as I earned a degree in naval architecture, I booked passage on the first liner home."

Home. "To Maine," she reminded him. "Not to me."

"To see my father, yes, and to get my thoughts in order. I knew what I faced here."

Rose sighed. "You came back with what purpose?"

"Don't you know?" This time, when Finn reached out his hand, he did touch her cheek. He stroked it lightly with the back of his fingers, sending tingling sensations coursing through her body. Then he started to pull her into an embrace.

"Take your hands off her," William's voice sounded harsh and very close.

CHAPTER FOURTEEN

Even though her fiancé's words were not directed at her, Rose jumped back as if touching fire, feeling all the color drain from her face. How could William possibly be there? Why *would* he be at that precise moment?

She looked at him. The expression he wore was nothing short of murderous. Her stomach sank like a stone in a pond.

William grabbed Finn by the arm, and Rose cried out, not knowing what would ensue yet terrified it would be violent.

Through it all, Finn remained silent. Equal in height to William, he simply stared at the man who currently held his upper arm in a tight grip.

Cocking his head, William asked, "Who *are* you?"

Finn's gaze flew to Rose's, then he looked back at William, his demeanor remaining calm.

"Release me. We don't want to embarrass the lady."

William glanced at her. "Rose, tell me now, who is this man?"

All the moisture left her mouth. The only thing she was certain of was this was not the time nor the place to confess to William.

"A friend, an old friend," she stammered.

At last, William dropped his hand from Finn's arm and focused only on Rose.

"Old friend, you say? How is it that I have never seen him before, not at any gathering or ball or party—" He broke off abruptly and looked at Finn again. "Wait. I have seen you before. At our engagement party, before the speeches. You were loitering by the doors, talking to no one."

To Rose, he said, "He was at the Tremont, yes?"

"I didn't know he would be there." This confrontation was exactly what she had wanted to avoid. Tears welled up in her eyes.

"I returned to Boston very recently," Finn spoke up. "I apologize. I should not have come uninvited to your party."

"Agreed," William said. "It was a private gathering. Your name, sir?"

Rose held her breath. She was desperate not to lie to William. He deserved only the truth. On the other hand, Finn might be pushed only so far and then blurt out that he was her husband.

"Phineas Bennet," Finn said, his tone uncharacteristically quiet.

"Today," William persisted, "why did I find you touching my fiancée?"

Rose started to speak, but Finn interrupted her. "We encountered each other by chance, and since I had not spoken to her at the Tremont, we were catching up. I'm afraid I got carried away. Again, entirely my fault. Please hold the lady blameless."

"I do," William said. "She has never given me cause to doubt her." He took hold of her arm, lacing it through his own.

To Rose at least, it was apparent that Finn bristled, a flash of hostility crossing his handsome face. For a moment, she thought he might drop his conciliatory demeanor and move to break her and William apart.

"It was good to see you again, Mr. Bennet," she said, the words sounding forced, crossing her tongue like sandpaper.

"I don't think you should meet again," William said, staring hard at Finn, "unless you are in the company of friends or family. Not if you can't keep your hands to yourself."

With uncharacteristic rudeness demonstrating how upset William really was, he turned on his heel, taking Rose with him locked to his side. With long strides that forced her practically to run to keep up, he swept them through the Common toward Beacon St, presumably with her mother's house as their destination.

She didn't dare even turn her head to glance back at her husband.

For a few minutes, they walked in silence until William began to slow his pace. Finally, when out of sight of those in the grassy park, he stopped and turned to her. She thought he would be accusing and quite rightly so.

"I apologize," he said against all expectations. "I acted badly back there," he continued. "In my defense, I was beyond surprised to witness him reach out and touch you as I approached."

Grateful William was not an angry, mistrustful man, Rose melted against his side.

"No, I am the one who is sorry. I should have stepped farther away from him. I was too familiar with Mr. Bennet, but he is, as I said, an old friend. From my late teen years."

William smiled weakly. "Ah, your wild years."

"My what?" Startled, she pulled back, then saw by his smile he was teasing her. If only he weren't so spot on.

"As a young lady, you were quite fizzy," he told her, "and then you calmed and then you became far too somber. Yet we solved all that, yes? You are precisely perfect, in my eyes, Rose Malloy."

"Thank you." She could barely say the words as sadness caused a lump to well in the back of her throat for the second time in a few minutes. Perhaps the Good Lord had sent him to stop something inappropriate from happening.

"How . . . timely"—she was going to say "odd" and changed her mind—"that you happened upon us like that?"

"Miss Norcross pointed out which way you'd gone," he said, not realizing how she flinched at the words.

Maeve! She had watched Rose leave Thompson's Spa, trailing behind Finn and apparently not too discreetly. When William happened along, Maeve must have sent him after her, perhaps with malicious intent.

"I know how much you like the pond, so I headed this way. I didn't see you at first. Then suddenly, you appeared on the walkway with that man behind you."

It was most likely Maeve still harbored resentment over William having broken up with her and wanted, in turn, to destroy his engagement. Stupidly, Rose had offered her the perfect invitation to meddle. She would be more careful with their relationship, and William's feelings, in the future.

Finn wanted to throw back his head and howl. Clenching his fists to keep from physically separating Rose and Woodsom, he turned away, unable to watch as they walked together, arm in arm. It had been one thing to know of the man and even to see him at the Tremont, but quite another to have her fiancé come between him and Rose to stake his claim.

This all-overish pain was exactly what he deserved. Still, it stung all the same. And despite knowing how this muddle had come to be, Finn felt real anger surge through him from his head down to his toes.

Dammit, what a mess! He hadn't lied to Rose when he'd said he couldn't blame this other fellow for loving her. She was everything a man could want. She was everything!

Like an idiot, he'd let go of the best woman who would ever cross his sorry path. All he could do now was try to bring justice to the families of the men who'd died. Despite what he'd said to Rose, he wasn't prepared to walk away, certainly not because of a threat.

As for his marriage, Finn shook his head. He didn't know if there was a way to save it. Wasn't even sure he was supposed to try. After all, Rose and blasted Woodsom were a perfect match. She'd looked so damned happy at her engagement party. Until she saw him!

Finn started back toward Park Street and the closest trolley, all the while cursing himself for the pleasure he'd felt at seeing her, even when he'd already vowed to stay away. His destination was the North End and Liam Berne's old bedsit. Although as Irish as potatoes and whiskey, Liam had refused to live with fellow immigrants in East Boston, preferring to nestle in with the Italians whose food and women he preferred.

If his friend no longer lived there, hopefully someone would know where he currently abided. For at that moment, feeling as alone in Boston as if he were still adrift on a hunk of wood in the Atlantic, Finn needed a friend.

While she dressed the next morning, Rose promised her own reflection she would stop obsessing over Finn. The disgust she'd felt toward herself at being caught by William overshadowed any pleasure she'd experienced in her husband's company. She must trust that Reed would handle the divorce with all due haste and that Finn would deal with the repercussions from the shipyard over his jarring return from the dead.

As for her, she had a wedding to plan, a fiancé to cherish, and a best friend who needed her aid in bringing about her own marital bliss. Rose decided to ask her mother what she knew of Mrs. Brewster and also her sister, Mrs. Norcross, Maeve's mother. Perhaps there was some reason that Franklin's mother was set against Claire.

Searching for her mother, she hastened into the parlor, expecting to find Evelyn perusing the morning papers with a cup of tea as was her custom. Rose stopped still as a Greek statue, even holding the breath she had gasped into her lungs at what she saw.

The tableau before her was unlike anything she could have imagined. Her respectable, widowed mother, dressed in a demure mauve morning gown, sat on the smaller of their two sofas. Beside her, seated much too close, was Ethan Nickerson. Evelyn was turned with her body toward him, and he toward her. And they were holding hands! What's more, there was no one else in the room. No friend or confidante, no chaperone of any kind.

How positively extraordinary! How unthinkable!

At her daughter's entrance, Evelyn glanced Rose's way.

"Dear one," her mother exclaimed, removing her hand from Nickerson's grasp but not swiftly, nor with guilt. Instead, she did it with slow and deliberate grace, and then the gentleman in question stood up to greet the youngest daughter of the household. He bowed slightly, a pleasant smile on his distinguished face.

Rose recovered from her surprise, releasing her breath and moving forward until she stood before the older gentleman. Offering a polite nod of her head and a friendly, "Good day, Mr. Nickerson," she took her mother's outstretched hand in both of hers.

"Mr. Nickerson and I are going to marry," Evelyn said without preamble as if it was the most natural and expected news in the world.

Rose felt her mouth drop open. When she recovered a second time, she nodded, glancing from the beaming man to her smiling mother. *How had this come about?*

At last, she found her voice. "That's wonderful, Mama. Congratulations. Also to you, Mr. Nickerson." She ignored the impertinent flurry of questions swirling in her brain. She also tamped down the image of her father's adored face. Oliver was long dead, and her mother was vibrantly alive. More than that, Evelyn had been alone for a long time.

"When will you marry?" Rose asked.

If her own wedding was to be postponed because of her divorce—or worse yet, cancelled—then perhaps her mother could make use of any of the arrangements she and Elise had already made.

"I'm not sure, dear. After all, I can't leave you alone in this house any more than you wanted to leave me."

In the span of a heartbeat, many things became clear: why her mother was not anxious about her youngest child finally flying from the nest and her recent preoccupied disposition. Perhaps Evelyn had been pondering her future, or even her past, and considering what it meant to become another man's wife. Of course, this explained her mother allowing herself to be monopolized by Mr. Nickerson at every gathering and each event they both attended. For years!

"We could sell this house," Evelyn continued, "and you could live with Mr. Nickerson and myself at his home until your wedding day."

Rose felt herself pale and had to sift through the myriad feelings her mother's words evoked, with the initial one being abject dismay. How awful, to move along with her mother like an unwelcome spinster! Fervently, she thanked God she was not one. Her second feeling was amazement—her mother would no longer reside on Beacon Hill as she had since the age of twenty-one, but rather in Cambridge. Mr. Nickerson's large home was across the river on Brattle Street, a Greek revival-style mansion that seemed massively oversized for two people.

Lastly, Rose felt sweet relief wash over her like cool rainwater. She would no longer have the overarching worry of leaving her mother alone. Moreover, the cream on top of her Bakewell pudding was knowing Mr. Nickerson was a retired merchant—and an impressively successful one—who had opened a string of emporiums around Boston and another two in Philadelphia. Surely, his being in trade would soften her family's reception of Finn as a shipbuilder, even if he were only to be known as her former husband and not her current one.

"Or you could live with Elise and Michael in the interim," her mother continued, oblivious to the thoughts swirling in her daughter's head. "It's obviously too crowded at Reed's."

Rose had to smile as her mother shuddered slightly. Evelyn had never approved of her son's home on the wharf. While Rose thought it quite a charming abode, she was glad she didn't have to be foisted onto any of her married siblings. She was perfectly capable and old enough to remain home, alone.

"We'll worry about that later," she assured her mother, noticing with amusement her mother's raised eyebrows, perhaps due to the uncharacteristic calm and levelheadedness of her youngest. Rose was no longer a child, and it was time her mother recognized that. "It will be a welcome relief to turn from planning my wedding to yours."

Mr. Nickerson coughed, and her mother blushed prettily.

"I wouldn't dream of treading on the spectacle of *your* wedding day," Evelyn said. "As for us," she glanced at her groom, "there won't be a wedding ceremony, per se. That would be unseemly. Some will frown on us marrying at all. In any case, I certainly won't be walking down the aisle in a new dress. Nor does Mr. Nickerson have any desire to stand at the altar in a morning suit. We have both had that experience before, and those days are far behind us."

"Exactly," said the reserved gentleman before expounding further, "We plan on having a small civil union, only the two of us and our immediate families, of course. It is not the type of ceremony young people ever consider."

Rose almost rolled her eyes. Little did he know she had already done precisely that type of wedding *sans* family. And she'd loved it. The day was etched in her brain, perhaps stronger than any other.

"I can't believe we're really doing this," Rose exclaimed, feeling giggly, lightheaded, and a little terrified all at once.

"You're making me the happiest man in the world," Finn said.

"It's the same for me," she assured him, knowing her mouth was wearing a generous smile she could not hide.

They'd entered the courthouse hand-in-hand.

"No regrets about not having your family around you, then?" Finn asked.

She remembered looking into his perfect blue-gray eyes and saying, "You are my family now."

He'd given her a lopsided grin, and she knew he was pleased.

"What about your *father and brothers?" she'd asked.*

"I doubt they would've come down from Portland anyway. I'll take you up to meet them someday soon."

Then they were ushered into the justice's office, where the process was over in minutes.

Mr. and Mrs. Phineas Bennet.

In the end, she'd never met her husband's family. If they'd gone to the memorial service for the *Garrard,* she did not know.

"Dearest, you look as if you're a hundred miles away," her mother said. "Did you need me? Do you want tea?"

Mr. Nickerson remained standing while Rose dithered. Now what? She had wanted to talk privately with her mother about delicate matters. She could do neither with her mother's *beau* standing by.

"I merely came in to tell you I was going to see Claire. I'll see you later, Mama. Good day, Mr. Nickerson." She hurried to the door, then turned back, "Again, congratulations to you both." She meant it with her whole heart.

Rose was still contemplating the unexpected turn of events when she strolled into Claire's foyer and was told by the housekeeper her friend was in a terrible state.

Red-eyed and retired to her room, Claire would see no one except Rose who was shown upstairs immediately.

"What's wrong? Why didn't you send for me?" Rose demanded, sitting on the bed beside Claire, who lay stretched out, her hand to her forehead, looking positively wretched.

"Are you ill? Feverish? A headache?"

Claire closed her teary eyes and moaned, "I will never be Mrs. Franklin Brewster."

With Franklin's dragging feet and fearsome mother, Rose feared as much but still asked, "Why do you say that? Franklin dotes on you."

Claire's free hand slammed upon the lace counterpane.

"He has *doted* long enough, and I am sick of it! It is humiliating," she fumed. "He should declare his intentions or release me to find someone who will. Don't you think?"

Yes, Rose did think exactly that, although this didn't seem the time to confirm it. Nor was it the time to tell Claire of her own mother's imminent marriage. It might be like rubbing salt in a wound to know even an aging widow could secure a proposal.

"Franklin may be slightly slower than another man would be," Rose began, "yet I still believe he intends to ask for your hand, and I think I am correct in believing you would like to be his wife."

Claire sighed mightily and lowered her hand from her forehead. She fixed Rose with her red-rimmed green eyes.

"I would like to be his wife, and, truly, it is not because of his unhurried courting that I say I will never be Mrs. Brewster." Claire grimaced. "No, it is because of the current Mrs. Brewster, his dragon of a mother."

Rose would have smiled if it weren't so serious.

"What has happened?"

"It is what hasn't happened. She has not taken to me. Not one whit."

Rose nodded, wishing more than ever she'd been able to get some insight from her own mother. "I don't think her reticence has anything to do with you, however. In case you haven't noticed, Franklin's mother is like buttermilk, sour beyond belief. Why, I doubt there is a female in all of these United States whom she would deem good enough for her son."

Claire remained silent a moment longer. At last she said, "Still, it is I whom she has snubbed."

"How so?"

Drawing herself up to sitting, Claire rested her back against her white-painted headboard.

"The dragon is holding a tea for young ladies at her home and did not invite me."

Rose felt her eyebrows rise involuntarily in surprise, and her cheeks grew warm in anger on her friend's behalf. Still, she hoped and prayed it was unintentional, despite doubting that could be the case.

"Maybe this is a special group? Individuals to do with a particular cause, perhaps?" she asked. "After all, I had not heard of this tea, nor was I invited." Rose didn't need to point out how, as a Malloy, there was not usually a gathering of young women to which she wasn't included.

"I think the only thing *special* about this tea is that you and I have not been invited. Maeve was, of course."

"She's Franklin's cousin, so she doesn't count," Rose offered. "Perhaps she is serving as hostess and these are friends of hers." Puzzled, she decided to delve further. "I'm sure if we put our minds to it, we can find out more. In any case, how did you learn of it?"

Claire's face clouded over. "That's the worst part," she confessed. "Franklin and I were out riding yesterday, with Robert chaperoning of course, and he mentioned he hoped to see me at his home next week and would do his best to find a reason to drop into the gathering."

"I see. And you had not the foggiest idea to what he was referring."

"Precisely," Claire said. "I felt like a fool when I explained I had no knowledge of 'the gathering'. Franklin's face became quite flushed. Naturally, it put a damper on the rest of the ride, and soon, we parted. If he has true feelings for me, he should make his mother aware of her utter insufferableness and demand she treat me better."

Rose was taken aback. This was the most heated she'd ever seen and heard Claire, who was normally so easygoing and, to her mind, a tad too passive, especially when it came to Franklin.

"Good for you," Rose said. "It's about time you took a stand."

"Whatever can you mean?" Claire asked. "I've done nothing except give up the idea of becoming the wife of the man I love."

"If he lets you give up, then he was certainly not the man for you. Besides, your strength will show when we attend this tea party."

"What do you mean?" Claire's cheeks colored. "We were not invited."

"I mean, dear friend, that you will take a stand against Mrs. Brewster treating you disrespectfully, and I will certainly stand with you. Then, whichever way it goes, you shall have your answer. If Franklin behaves badly, by which I mean does not stick up for you, then you will know it is best to break off any association with him. Because if that is the case, he will always be a mama's boy and too weak for you."

"Oh Lord," Claire said, perhaps not wanting to bring about such an ultimatum.

"Are we in agreement?" Rose plunged ahead, feeling quite happy she could focus on helping her dearest friend rather than dwelling on her own miserable problems. "Come, say you will step up as a true Appleton and stop this hand-wringing nonsense."

"Well . . . ," Claire hesitated.

"What do your parents say about this? Do they like Franklin?"

Claire shrugged. "I don't speak to them about such things. I don't have a close relationship to my mother as you do yours. You know that. And neither of my parents are overly concerned with when or if Robert or I ever marry anyone."

Unfortunately, Rose knew Claire was right. Certainly, Mr. Appleton was not about to step in and ask Franklin's intentions, and her mother had no reason to form an attachment to Mrs. Brewster nor see if she could pave the way clear for her only daughter. They were the type of people who should never have had children, Rose thought unkindly, or at least not sensitive ones such as Robert and Claire.

"As soon as we see which way the wind is blowing, if it is an ill-wind, then I shall find you a more suitable beau by next month. I promise you." Moreover, she meant it. Claire was lovely and smart, and Rose could think of at least three young men whom she'd seen watching her friend intently. More than one of them would be happy if Franklin stepped aside.

Claire issued another large sigh.

"I don't want another one. Even with his awful, scaly dragon of a mother, I love him."

Rose could see why Claire fancied him. Franklin was good-looking and tall and could carry on a conversation. What's more, he made a handsome living and would inherit a lovely home.

"Nevertheless, this is not to be borne," Rose insisted. "I believe he has had enough time to be a bachelor and I also think his mother has had quite enough say in the affairs of his heart. We do this and we take a stand, or I fear you will be a doormat to these people forever."

"A doormat! Gracious." Claire did not look pleased at the characterization.

Rose was glad to have her friend's full attention. "When is this gathering?"

"Next Wednesday, at eleven."

"Come hell or high water," Rose declared as Claire gasped at the wording, "we shall be there next Wednesday promptly at 10:50 to partake of Mrs. Brewster's tea. After all, your beau practically invited you."

However, it was neither hell nor high water that Rose encountered next, but rather the irate visage of her eldest sister.

"When were you going to tell me?"

CHAPTER FIFTEEN

The sharp tap on her bedroom door in the early evening had not given Rose any indication of who was on the other side. If she'd known Elise was going to march into the room as soon as she opened the door and demand an answer to such a vague question, Rose might have hidden under her four-poster bed or have feigned absence entirely.

"When were you going to tell me?"

Rose let the myriad of things she had not disclosed rattle around in her brain for a moment.

"Tell you what?"

"That Mama was getting married."

"Oh, that." Rose actually breathed a sigh of relief. That was something she could actually discuss.

"Yes, of course, *that!* What else could be so important? You must have had a clue, living under the same roof. Did Mr. Nickerson come here often?"

Rose shrugged. "I suppose he did. However, I didn't know about the intended marriage either until this morning.

"How romantic," Elise murmured and sat down unasked on her sister's bed. "And how fitting."

"What do you mean?"

Elise tilted her head, offering a wry smile. "With my slightly odd path to love and marriage, blackmail included, and Sophie falling for an engaged man and let's not forget Reed going all the way to Colorado to capture Charlotte's heart and then having to rescue her from that madman. Given all of our untraditional courtings and alliances, Mama finding love and hiding it from us for years . . . ," she trailed off. "Why are you looking like that?"

Rose swallowed and tried to relax her face.

"Like what?" Belatedly, she realized her eyes had widened and her mouth had grown slack. Was every Malloy destined to some dramatic romantic adventure? Moreover, was she following in her mother's footsteps, or rather was her mother following in hers?

"How did you find out?" Rose asked her.

"Mama used the *telephone*," Elise said and paused, giving Rose time to consider.

Their mother never used the "infernal device," as Evelyn referred to it after Reed had paid richly to install them in all their homes. His intent was to ensure his sisters and their mother could always reach him as well as each other.

"Yes!" Elise confirmed when Rose exclaimed in wonder. "Mama was quite concerned you would blab about her engagement before the rest of the family knew, and feared we would feel slighted or deceived somehow. She decided the telephone's expediency was suddenly a useful thing after all. When I picked up, I heard her saying, 'Clear the line, will you please clear the line?'" Elise chuckled. "She sounded quite imperial."

"How unlike her," Rose said, feeling rather miffed her mother thought she would gossip. In truth, though, she would have told Claire immediately if her friend hadn't been so upset.

"In any case," Elise continued, "Mama called me and Reed and sent a telegraph to Sophie."

Rose sat beside her sister. "So, what do you think about Mama and Mr. Nickerson?"

"I was a tad shocked at first, to tell you the truth. I suppose I'm simply used to Mama being alone. Still, I think it quite wonderful to have a colt's tooth and want to live a fuller life at her age."

"Yes, me, too. I'm very relieved she'll have a companion."

"And not some stuffy old matronly companion either but a man! A quite lively one at that, if their behavior at the last dance was any indication."

How had Rose missed that?

With Elise being so accepting of new attachments, was this the time to mention Finn?

She squashed the notion at once. If only she could. With the mysterious threats and with William still not knowing about Finn, Rose couldn't say anything. How convenient it would be if she could travel back to her younger self and tell her to open her heart to her family. If Rose had told her family about her love for Finn, they would have supported her when she thought him dead and rejoiced with her upon his incredible return.

No doubt, if her entire family had known of their marriage, if she had let that happen, then he would have hurried back immediately to Boston to claim her.

In that case, she would have missed out on meeting William, a notion that saddened her to even consider. She could not regret the love that had bloomed between them, nor all the special things they shared.

"Rose," Elise's voice called her back to the present. "Are you crying?"

Dear God, was she? Yes. She felt the moisture on her cheeks. How could she explain to Elise that thinking of her youthful love with Finn and her more mature love with William had evoked such intense sadness?

"Are you all right?" her sister asked, her tone soft and gentle.

"Mama's new start has made me nostalgic, I suppose," Rose hedged.

"Quite so," Elise agreed and patted her arm. "Anyway, I must be off home or Michael will think I've run away."

"As if," Rose said, knowing her sister was as besotted with the handsome banker as the day they'd married.

Elise sighed. "I could never leave him because I cannot imagine my life without his lovely smile." A warm reddish tinge crept across her cheeks. "Still, I am allowed to imagine a day without supervising our household and our children and the two cats and the parakeet. Can't I?"

Both sisters laughed.

Finn had never been the naïve or romantic sort, at least not until the day he'd met Rose Malloy. Yet going to Hull Street in the North End, within spitting distance of the Old North Church, and expecting to find Liam the same as he had been nearly four years before was most likely a naïve fool's errand.

Finn entered the same black door under the flat lintel that still looked out of place next to the graceful arches over the other front doors. Inside, he saw the same hallway with its scuffed wooden floor, and he knocked on the last door on the left.

A dark-haired woman with a child in her arms answered after a few moments. She didn't smile or even offer a greeting, merely stared at him challengingly while holding her young boy in her arms as a shield.

"I'm looking for Liam Berne," Finn said.

Her face relaxed instantly.

With a thick Italian accent, she answered him, "Sweet Mother Mary, I thought you were here for the rent."

"No, I—"

"Liam Berne," she spat the words. "I know him. Or used to." She glanced down at the child, and Finn realized the boy was not a wee toddler as he'd thought by his size. More likely a lad of about four or five, underfed and stunted.

Could he be Liam's?

The boys' dark eyes were those of his mother, not the pale brown he remembered from his friend. Still, Finn couldn't take his gaze off him. What if he'd given in to Rose on the last night they were together? He might have left with his child growing inside her. He wouldn't have known for months until he reached England and then not until he wrote to her and she to him. He would have come home immediately to a family of his own instead of years later to an estranged wife who was ready to begin a life with another man. She would have had to tell her mother and her siblings, and then . . .

"If you see him," the woman interrupted his thoughts, "tell him a little of his gullyfluff—you know, his pocket change— would go a long way to feeding his son."

Finn nodded. He definitely would tell him. "Do you know where I can find him?"

"Doesn't he still work at the shipyard?" she asked, then let the boy slide down her hip, until he stood beside her, keeping hold of her skirts with his small hands.

Finn smiled at the lad, then regarded his mother. "I think so, but I don't know for certain."

She tossed her head. "Is he too high and mighty for that now?"

Liam, high and mighty? "I don't understand what you mean?"

"With all his money and his fine house, does he still work at all?"

Finn tried to understand what she was saying. Had Liam changed professions or come into some money? "Can you tell me where he lives?"

"Not around here, that's for sure." She paused. "Are you his friend?"

"I used to be."

She nodded, then gave him a curious, interested look. "Do *you* have any money?"

He nearly laughed, but the idea she might beg a stranger kept him quite sober.

"Not much," he confessed. Yet she would probably consider the savings of a shipbuilder to be quite a significant sum. He'd spent as much time as he could spare away from his studies to earn a decent living, and had saved every farthing while away.

Since disembarking in the States, with the uncertainty of when he would begin to earn again, Finn was trying to spend as little as possible of those savings.

The woman shrugged, making a slight moue of dismissal.

"Liam lives in the Back Bay on Marlborough Street. Number 397." She stepped back, already turning away. Then she glanced at Finn once more.

"If you see him, tell him *grazie molto poco* from Tessa."

With that, she tugged the little boy inside and slammed the door.

Sweet Mary! Marlborough Street in the Back Bay. How could Liam get a house there? And if he was doing so bloody well, why wasn't he feeding his son? He'd hoped to find Liam at the yard when he had gone to see the owner, but then he'd been given the bum's rush and told to leave in no uncertain terms. He didn't even know if Liam worked there anymore.

Luckily, with nothing else to do, he could go find his old friend. For 5 cents a ride, it took only three electric trolley cars for him to get to the corner of Commonwealth and Hereford Streets. After a two-block walk, he found himself on the relatively quiet Marlborough Street, staring at what could not possibly be Liam's home.

Finn whistled sharply. *What in the hell?* There was nothing modest about this four-story brick dwelling with its lavish miniature front garden behind a wrought iron fence. The arched doorway with a brightly polished knocker awaited.

He took the five shallow steps and knocked, not sure what to expect. A young woman came to the door, dressed in the plain black gown and pinned white apron of a housemaid.

"Yes?" she asked, her tone neutral, although she did take a sweeping look at him from his dusty shoes up his worn pants to his shabby jacket. Recognition they were equals flashed in her eyes.

A lance of regret pierced him. Instead of worrying for the future, perhaps he should have spent a little of his hard-earned money to spruce himself up. No doubt Rose looked at him as a failure, too.

With shame clogging his throat, he asked, "Is this the residence of Liam Berne?"

"It is," she answered. "Who wants to know? The tradesman's entrance is around back, if you're here to do work."

Finn could not help frowning. *Liam with his own tradesman's entrance!*

"No, miss." He didn't want to embarrass the girl, but enough was enough. "I'm not actually here to do any work for Mr. Berne. We're old friends."

Her look was still doubtful, but she said, "I see, sir, my apologies. If you want to come in and wait a moment, I'll see if he is at liberty to visit with you."

She stepped back and held the door open wide. After he entered, she secured it behind him before leading the way down the hall to the first door on the right.

"You can wait in there," she offered.

Finn entered a room that was exactly as he expected it would be in this part of Back Bay. Polished wood floors barely visible around the edges of a thick, colorful Persian carpet. White trim, painted walls, velvet furniture with dark scrolled legs that looked freshly waxed, high ceilings, and a good-sized fireplace, which today was not lit since the weather was fine.

He definitely did not want to sit on the tufted sofa after having his bum on the trolley cars.

"Would you give me your name, sir?"

He turned, having forgotten for a moment why he was there. "Phineas Bennet."

She turned on her heel. He heard her leather soles trip quickly up the stairs and then, a short while later, what sounded like furniture crashing onto the floor. Heavier feet pounded across the landing upstairs and down the stairs. Liam burst into the room.

He stopped a foot inside his parlor and stared.

"Fuck," he said and slowly shook his head. "It *is* you, isn't it?"

Liam appeared the same as he ever was and also completely different, in fine clothing and boots that looked to be the best money could buy. He'd always complained about his feet hurting. They couldn't possibly hurt anymore.

"Aye," Finn answered, "but is that *you?*"

Liam narrowed his eyes. "How is this possible? How can Finn Bennet be standing in my home four years after he died?"

"How can you be a rich man on Marlborough Street only four years after I left you as a lowly whittler? Now that's a tale I'd like to hear."

Liam hesitated, then his face split into a grin and he stuck his hand out. Finn took it and they pumped their arms up and down vigorously. For the first time since leaving his father's home in Portland, Finn felt welcome.

"Will you sit?" Liam asked before pressing a button on the wall.

Finn gestured to his own clothing. "I would hate to ruin your sofa fabric."

"Nonsense," Liam said and sat, gesturing for to do the same.

Taking a seat on the opposite side of the fireplace, Finn shook his head.

"You really have landed in it, haven't you?"

Before Liam could answer, the same maid who'd shown him inside stepped quickly into the room.

"Madeira," was all Liam said to her, and once again, she vanished.

Finn smiled again. They'd never drank anything except ale.

"Are you going to tell me how this is possible?" He gestured at the lavish surroundings.

"I will, I will." Liam cocked his head. "If you tell me how you're not a ghost. I still can't believe I'm looking at you. After the sinking, I remembered thinking, *Damn, I told the unlucky blighter not to sail.* If you'd only listened to me."

Another servant, a slightly older woman, brought in a tray with a decanter full of luscious red wine and two crystal goblets. She set this on the table between the men.

"Shall I pour, sir?"

"No, I will," Liam said, not looking at her.

Still, she stood waiting.

"Thank you," Finn said.

Liam burst out laughing. "She's not waiting for you to thank her for doing her job. She's waiting for me to dismiss her."

Finn felt himself redden. He was perfectly happy to thank anyone who waited on him or showed him kindness, and he wasn't too keen on someone who didn't. He wondered how Rose treated her servants, as they'd never been together in such a situation. Just as quickly, he decided she must be as kind to them as she'd been to him.

"You may go," Liam told the woman.

She nodded and nearly made it to the door when Liam said, "Wait." Then he turned to Finn. "Will you stay for dinner?"

Finn thought about it. What else did he have to do? Even though he might wish to be sitting with his old friend in an Italian café in the North End—and even though something about this new wealthy Liam might rub him slightly the wrong way—a meal together would set things to right, he was sure. He nodded.

"Set another place," Liam told the woman, and she exited with the slightest nod of her head.

Liam leaned forward and poured a generous amount of the heady red wine into both glasses before holding one out to Finn.

"To being alive," he said.

Finn nodded and took a sip. It was sweet and nutty and fruity all at once. For some reason, it reminded him of Rose, and he had a feeling she would enjoy it.

"Tell me," Liam said, "and don't leave anything out."

Finn did as he was instructed and explained his entire adventure, leaving out only any mention of Rose, which seemed like omitting his reason for surviving. When he got to the part about thinking men were trying to kill him or at least shove him into a carriage, Liam exclaimed aloud.

Then he asked, "Did you report it to the police?"

"Not yet."

"Whyever not? The first thing I would do is talk to the local force."

Finn considered. *Why hadn't he?* Because he wasn't sure what was real or whom he could trust, or even that the police wouldn't somehow make it worse. And the more people who knew about him, the more endangered Rose might become.

He merely shrugged. "Your turn, old friend. How did this come about?" Finn gestured his wine glass toward the opulence of the room once again.

Liam offered a wry smile. "Investments."

"Really?"

Liam took another large draught of the madeira. "Yes."

"In what?" Finn asked.

Liam blinked and said, "Transportation. Railroads out West, electric trolleys on the East Coast."

"I take it you're not at the shipyard anymore."

Liam hesitated. "Strangely enough, I am."

Finn felt better about his friend. Many a man would give up honest work under such circumstances.

"I don't have the same position, though."

"Oh?" Finn wondered what else Liam could do. "No longer making models?"

Liam grinned. "That's old school, right?"

Finn was surprised. "Yes, you're right. Where I was in Britain, they thought our method was barbaric. Engineers, architects, draftsmen, that's the proper way. So, what do you do?"

"I'm the yard's master builder, directing those engineers, architects, and draftsmen."

Finn flinched. "How is that possible?" he blurted out before he realized how rude that sounded. Yet he knew Liam's training was basic compared to the university studies he'd undergone. Liam was more of a woodworker than anything.

However, his friend didn't look offended. "Yard seniority, partly. We lost some key people on the *Garrard*." He paused. "Like yourself. Then some left for other yards, Goat Island is big, and there's Brooklyn, of course, and even down to Norfolk. Gilbert left, too. He's a consultant at the Navy shipyard in Charlestown. But I'm still at Kelly's."

"So, you check the plans and mark them up?"

Liam chuckled and finished his glassful, then poured another.

"No, I basically shuffle papers from one fellow to another and sign when necessary. Pay is decent."

Finn was feeling a little sour, thinking of the choices he'd made that had caused him to lose Rose and his job and have no foreseeable future in Boston. He had nothing but a degree and a six-inch scar on his leg.

They were called in to dinner while Finn was thinking how different his life would have been if he'd let Liam remove him from the manifest as he'd offered to do. By the time he'd taken a seat at Liam's cloth-covered dining table, Finn realized how guilty he would have felt if he hadn't been on board to see for himself that no one could save the ship, nor those men and boys. He shook his head.

"What is it?" Liam asked, as a course of fish soup was set before them, steaming and fragrant.

"Choices," Finn said. "Paths we choose."

"I'm glad you came to see me," Liam said, tackling his soup with gusto.

"I went to the yard, too," Finn told him

Liam paused with his spoon midway between the bowl and his mouth, then he slurped his soup off the spoon and smiled broadly.

"I'm sorry I missed your visit. I bet they were surprised to see you."

Finn tasted a few spoonfuls, realizing he had quite a hunger.

"Surprised is not the word. I didn't see anyone I knew. Walsh was away from his desk, and there was a new secretary to old man Kelly, a bug-eyed fellow—"

"Marty," Liam said, grinning. "Good chap."

"I suppose," Finn shrugged. "He took me to see Kelly, who wasn't sure he knew me at first, then when I told him who I was and what I thought of the *Garrard*, he nearly took my head off with anger and said I'd never work at the yard again. Or at any local yard for that matter."

"What? That's outrageous," Liam said. "Why would he do that?"

A servant brought in the next course, roast duckling with fingerling potatoes and carrots.

Finn waited while she picked up the bowls and set down clean plates, looking idly at the dead duck with a measure of compassion. He, himself, had about as much prospects.

"Because I told Kelly the *Garrard* should never have sailed. The design was faulty and someone, probably Gilbert, should be held accountable."

Liam nodded thoughtfully. "Maybe someone already was."

"What do you mean?"

His host cut up a piece of duck breast and chewed it thoughtfully. "Well, we lost Bradley and Decker. Maybe divine retribution for building a crap ship."

A shiver of shock ran up Finn's spine. Those men had only followed orders and had died for it.

"I don't believe that." Finn sipped at the new glass of wine set before him. "I think that someone high up should be held accountable. Don't you? Remember how young some of the apprentices were? Just boys really." He rubbed a hand over his eyes, wishing he could erase the faces of those young ones, the fear he'd seen . . . "You lost friends, didn't you?"

Liam set his fork down. "Of course, but I'm awfully glad you're not one of them. You were my best friend at the yard."

Finn considered. "Maybe you can help me to get a job."

He watched an expression dance across Liam's face, a quick shadow of a thought or a mood.

"No," Liam said. "Best you should move on. If the higher-ups don't want you, you should go elsewhere. What about Portsmouth?"

So much for best friends. It would have been nice if Liam had offered to put in a word. However, he was probably right about higher-ups. If Finn's name was blackened by Kelly, no one would hire him in the area. However, he had no interest in Portsmouth. Not at the moment anyway. Not until everything was settled with Rose, one way or the other. Then, if he were going anywhere, it would be back up to Maine. They were still designing cargo vessels in the Downeaster style in Portland, ships a man could hold his head up high for building.

Finn drained the glass of wine as he realized he was still hoping there was a way he could hold onto Rose. But hope was a fool's emotion.

"What about you?" he asked.

"What about me?" Liam sounded slightly tense.

Feeling more relaxed by the wine and warm food, Finn nearly laughed. His friend had no way of knowing nearly every other thought in his head was of a certain lady, and thus, naturally, he wondered if Liam had a woman of his own.

"Have you found someone with whom to share your success?" As soon as Finn said it, he recalled the woman in the North End.

The edge left Liam's tone when he responded. "I see, you mean what about me and someone of the fairer sex? I've got my eye on one. Maybe two. And I've been known to escort a certain well-heeled lady to the opera. Her family isn't too keen on me, but I may change their minds yet. That is, if I feel like bothering. I'm not really ready to take a rib yet."

"What about Tessa?" Finn asked. He almost added, "and your son?" although that would be beyond offensive. He'd already crossed the line of propriety by bringing up the woman.

Liam recoiled at the name. "How in the hell—?"

"I apologize." Finn held up his hands in apology. "I went looking for you at your old digs and met her."

"I see." Liam nodded. "She's a bit rough, don't you think?"

Finn thought about it. "She had a pretty face. She sent you a message by the way."

"Oh?" Liam looked unconcerned as he sipped his wine. "What did she have to say?"

"Really? Do you want to know?"

"I do." Jokingly, Liam braced himself against the arms of his chair as if against a nor'easter.

"She said that she needs money for her boy."

Liam blanched, his face at once losing all traces of humor. "I don't even know if he's mine," he blurted out. "You saw him. He looks just like her and no one else."

"*Could* you be the father?"

"I suppose," Liam allowed, shoveling a candied carrot into his mouth.

"He looked hungry. They both did," Finn persisted.

"Well, damn," Liam said, dropping his fork. "How am I supposed to enjoy my meal now?"

Finn chuckled. "You're not. You're supposed to high-tail it over there tomorrow and give them some money, which you plainly have and they don't."

"Damn," Liam repeated.

"The boy could be yours. They could live here with you."

"Not a chance in hell, mate. She might've been with every bloke on Hull Street, and that guttersnipe could be any of theirs, too."

Finn tried again.

"Still, it wouldn't hurt you to give them some money, would it? If the father *is* a resident of the North End, it's doubtful the man will have a cent to spare. Not like you."

Liam sighed. "You're right." He started eating again. "It's no fat off my bacon if I give them a few dollars."

Suddenly, the rest of Finn's meal tasted like sawdust. He'd hoped Liam would be a little more magnanimous, but at least Tessa and her son would get something, if Liam was as good as his word.

In any case, Finn had his own problems to deal with. "I guess I'd best be going."

Liam shook his head. "No, no, hold on, none of that. Don't go getting all morose on me. You are alive, Finn Bennet, and that's the best thing in the world. Let's figure out what you're going to do next, right? Obviously, you can't stay here in Boston if you can't work at the yard."

Finn was taken aback. Was Liam still set on pushing him out of the city, and after only just discovering he was alive?

"If not Portsmouth, how about going into the transportation industry?" Liam continued. "I tell you, it's still a boom."

"I'm a shipbuilder," Finn said, unable to keep the firmness out of his voice as well as a strain of bitterness. "Besides, I want to see justice for those who died. Don't you?"

"Of course. If there are men left alive who didn't sink with the ship and who are to blame in any way, then yes, they should be held accountable."

Finn laid down his napkin and stood. "We won't be solving my work problems tonight, so I'll be going."

Liam stood up, too. "I insist you spend the night. Where are you staying anyway? At your old rooming house on Bowdoin Square?"

"No, it was full up." Besides, the memories of Rose in his arms there would have been torture. "I have a room above an old friend's business."

"Where?" Liam persisted. "In case I need to reach you before I hear from you again."

"I'm above The Restaurant Parisien."

Liam looked surprised. "Great food."

Finn nodded.

"Anyway," Liam continued. "Stay here tonight, and we can put our heads together in the morning on what to do next. I know a lawyer, if that helps."

Considering he'd never needed the services of one before, it seemed quite odd he might have two handling his business, one for a divorce and one to sue on behalf of the men and boys who died on the *Garrard*.

Finn declined. He wasn't sure why. Maybe because it stung too badly to think how Liam had stayed behind and made his fortune and even worked at the very yard at which Finn couldn't get employment.

If he'd avoided the test sailing, would he own a house such as Liam's in the Back Bay and have Rose in his bed?

He didn't know, but he didn't want to stay under Liam's roof. As he started the walk toward the trolley stop, he also didn't know why something about his friend had made him uneasy.

Returning to The Parisien, Finn considered his own constant anxiety. *Was it paranoia? Madness?*

Rose's sweet face materialized like a vision before his tired eyes. Even if he could win her back from the seemingly perfect Woodsom, he shouldn't try. Not if he loved her. Not if he wanted what was best for her—a luxurious life with an entirely sane and whole husband.

CHAPTER SIXTEEN

Rose looked up from perusing the late afternoon's newspapers with her mother to see Charlotte entering the parlor.

"Good day, Evelyn, Rose," Charlotte greeted them. "You're both looking well."

"There's my favorite daughter-in-law," Evelyn remarked mischievously, since she only had one son. Still, they all chuckled. "Come, have some tea with us." She glanced at the clock on the mantle. "Or maybe something stronger? A little sherry?"

Evelyn went toward the button that would ring the bell in the kitchen summoning their cook. Emily was no doubt reading the penny paper, as was her custom at that time of day, and drinking coffee.

"I don't want to intrude," Charlotte protested. "I had hoped to have a word with Rose though."

Evelyn paused, her finger hovering next to the call button mounted on the wall covered in a cheerful flower-embellished wallpaper.

"Is anything the matter?" She looked between Charlotte and Rose.

Charlotte smiled. "Your expression so resembles Reed's whenever Rose's name is mentioned. Do you both jump to the same conclusions that mischief is afoot?"

"I'm afraid they do," Rose said.

Evelyn smiled slightly. "You know our Rose."

Charlotte nodded. "I do indeed. However, there's nothing to be concerned about."

Rose hoped not. She fidgeted with the napkin in her lap, wondering how long her mother would linger before Charlotte could disclose any news.

Her sister-in-law took a seat. "I have a question about the wedding, a small detail."

How kind of Charlotte not to break her confidence, nor worry Evelyn Malloy with talk of nefarious dealings from the long-ago past.

Besides, maybe there were no nefarious dealings after all, and Charlotte would tell her such.

"We'll have tea anyway," Evelyn said, finally pressing the button, "and then I must get to my ladies' gardening meeting. I'm sure you and Rose can work out anything after that. If she lets you guide her, Charlotte."

Guide her, indeed! Would the family always think of her as the five-year-old who managed to climb onto the roof's eave and get stuck until her father rescued her? Or the twelve-year-old who remained on a train to Baltimore after the rest of her siblings had disembarked. When her mother found out about Finn, which eventually she would, Rose would most likely be marked as interminably and incorrigibly flighty.

After the maid arrived with the tea tray and they all had a cup and a biscuit in front of them, Charlotte eyed Rose, who felt as though her skin would burst if she didn't soon find out what her sister-in-law had discovered, if anything.

"I can't believe my last one will soon be married, but it is due time," Evelyn said.

Charlotte gave her a warm smile. "I for one greatly missed the lighthearted girl I met when I first moved to Boston. She seemed to disappear overnight to be replaced by a quite serious and solemn young woman. Lately, with Mr. Woodsom, however, it seems we have her back again."

"True," Evelyn agreed. "He has been good for our Rose."

"You are both speaking as if I am not in the room," Rose reminded them.

"That's because we speak only truths we don't mind you hearing," Charlotte assured her. She focused on her mother-in-law. "If I am not speaking out of turn, I am happy as a rattlesnake in a mouse hole at hearing *your* good news."

"A rattlesnake?" Evelyn repeated.

Charlotte cleared her throat. "That is to say, I'm very pleased you have found a companion once more."

"Oh, you are referring to Mr. Nickerson," Evelyn said, and Rose detected a soft blush upon her mother's cheeks. *How sweet.* "I have known him for a number of years," she explained, "and believe we still have a few good ones left to spend in each other's company. A little closer company than we have enjoyed as yet."

Rose choked on her tea. Had her mother just referred to the marital bed and sharing it with Ethan Nickerson? She was still coughing when Charlotte leaned over and thumped her twice on the back.

"Thank you," Rose managed. Then to change the topic, she drew their attention to something she'd just read in the paper. "Clara Barton is coming back to Boston. She'll give a talk at Harvard in two weeks."

Both the others perked up. "I would love to go," Charlotte said.

"As would I." Evelyn paused. "I'll purchase tickets for the three of us and invite Elise as well."

"And Claire too, please, Mama," Rose requested. Although her friend wasn't always so patient for lectures, Miss Barton's stories of the war purportedly brought even grown men to tears, and any distraction for Claire would be a welcome one.

At that moment, however, Rose wanted more than anything to hear Charlotte's disclosure.

"Mama, what time do you have to be at your gardening meeting?"

Evelyn brushed the crumbs from her fingers and stood up.

"Now, in fact. I shall see you both anon. I'm taking the carriage. Does that suit you, dear one?"

Rose stood and kissed her mother's cheek.

"Fine. I don't have any plans. If I do go out, it won't be far."

"I can always give her a ride," Charlotte offered.

As soon as they were alone, Rose nearly pounced upon her sister-in-law.

"Do you have anything to tell me?"

"Of course. Let's get right to it, shall we?" Charlotte pulled a notepad out of her satchel. "Naturally, large sums of money were paid out because the ship was fully insured. The underwriters paid the expected collectors—the yard that built her and the ship's owner, one Mr. Dilbey. However, there was one not so expected." Charlotte paused, then asked, "Do you know a Mr. Liam Berne?"

The beat of Rose's heart increased at the mention of his name.

"I don't," she said truthfully. "At least, not personally. However, I have heard his name mentioned."

"Oddly, the man should be dead," Charlotte said, scanning her notes.

"Why do you say that?"

"His name was on the ship's roster that was printed in the paper, along with your Mr. Bennet's."

Rose flinched at hearing "your" attached to Finn's name coming from Charlotte's lips.

"However, apparently you were wrong twice," Charlotte added.

"What do you mean?"

"Neither a Tim nor a Tom," her sister-in-law said, regarding her sharply. "A *Phineas* Bennet perished upon the *Garrard*. I suppose he is the one who mentioned Mr. Berne to you."

Rose looked down at her lap where she fiddled with her fingers. Of course, Charlotte would have looked at the list.

"It was a long time ago," she muttered.

"Indeed," Charlotte said. "In any case, Liam Berne received a hefty amount of money from the ship's underwriter. He signed the receiving document himself." She eyed the youngest Malloy sister. "Naturally, I am wondering how a dead man collected money. I shall take a trip to the yard that built the ship as soon as I have some free time."

"Kelly's yard," Rose intoned, thinking of how the yard's docks and moorings and even its sheds and cranes were etched in her memory? And now she had the new recollection of finding her dead husband sitting there, alive and well, on a bench.

She realized Charlotte was still staring at her. Rose hedged, "I suppose he didn't sail on the *Garrard* that day."

She couldn't possibly explain how she knew Liam Berne hadn't been on board when even the papers hadn't. She sighed.

Charlotte cocked her head. "Why do you think this Berne fellow bet against his own yard's creation?"

"I couldn't say." Indeed, it sounded like a nefarious thing for Finn's friend to have done.

"This might be a case of fraud or perhaps something even more reprehensible," Charlotte suggested.

"What do you mean?"

"Why would a shipbuilder take out insurance on the vessel he was to set sail on? How would he ever hope to collect since the policy was only payable for catastrophic destruction?" She tapped her pen's nib against the paper, unmindful of it leaking as she stared into the middle distance between them. "Yet Mr. Berne did precisely that."

"Very strange," Rose agreed. "So perhaps he never intended to go on it."

"Perhaps," Charlotte agreed. "Still, to take out that type of insurance could only mean a lack of faith in the vessel's seaworthiness."

That was true. Why else would Liam have insurance on the ship he was helping to build? Yet to make money off the deaths of the others, that was unthinkable. She recalled he offered to help Finn stay behind as well. He must have known he wasn't going to set sail long before he told Finn. Otherwise, why would he take out insurance? She shivered.

"Was it a lot of money?"

"Quite substantial," Charlotte confirmed. "Enough to set oneself up comfortably without needing to worry about an income."

Rose had no choice. She would have to meet with Finn again to tell him about this development. If Liam Berne had collected a large sum of money, perhaps he wouldn't want Finn telling others the ship had been designed poorly, particularly if it became known Liam might have stopped others from sailing that day and saved their lives.

A day later, from a vantage point across the street under the awning of a small green grocer's, Rose watched the doorway of Monsieur Ober's restaurant. After a relatively short and boring vigil, she was rewarded when Finn emerged and immediately spotted her. She watched him shake his head in disbelief and then gesture from the other side of the street for her to follow him.

He strode to the end of the block and then into the bookstore on the corner. She entered a few moments later. In the back, behind the stacks of classics, she found him waiting.

"What on earth are you doing?" he berated her.

"I wanted to speak with you."

"You were in broad daylight standing like a beacon on the sidewalk."

"Perhaps only a beacon to you," she retorted. "Most people assumed I was squeezing the peaches and checking for mealy apples."

He rolled his eyes. "Well? I hope putting your life in danger was worth it."

He was being melodramatic. Surely no one was spying on them at that moment. Idly, she pulled a book from the shelf beside her and opened it.

"I wanted you to know I spoke with Claire, and she's told no one of your return."

He eyed her steadily. "That's good. Thank you. And what about you?"

"Of course I haven't." She slammed the book closed and replaced it. "No one except Claire and Reed. However, I would like to tell William, as you know, and as soon as possible."

"Yes, I am aware," he said.

Was that a snippy tone she detected?

He crossed his arms and leaned against the brick wall between the stacks. "Is that all you wanted to tell me? Which hardly seemed worth the risk by the way."

"No, that's not all." She glanced around her. "My sister-in-law has uncovered something interesting."

"Your sister-in-law? Reed's wife?" Finn's eyes started to bulge.

Rose knew this wouldn't go smoothly until he understood. "I did *not* tell her about you. I merely asked her to look into the event of the *Garrard's* capsizing and see if there was anything untoward or nefarious. She's good at that sort of thing."

"I see." He rubbed his temple a moment. "What did she discover?"

"Charlotte found that your friend Mr. Berne was listed as one of the recipients of an insurance claim regarding the *Garrard.*"

Finn straightened slowly, cocking his head. "He received money."

She nodded. "A great deal of money, according to Charlotte, making him quite comfortable. It's public record. She gave me the name of the company that paid out."

He was silent.

"It's important, isn't it?" she asked.

"I think it proves someone besides me didn't think the ship was designed correctly. Liam lied to me, very recently, in fact, and most likely, he lied to me four years ago, too. Who else was on the policy?"

"The ship's owner and the yard owner."

His handsome brow furrowed, and she wished she could smooth it. Wished she could run her fingers over his face and then into his thick hair. It was not her place to do either anymore.

"If Master Builder Gilbert's name isn't on the policy, no one can know whether he profited from the sinking. Moreover, Liam told me he is over at the Navy yard in Charlestown, plying his craft," he added bitterly.

"Mr. Gilbert should have been held accountable four years ago," Rose said softly, imagining their lives if her husband hadn't disappeared. "What will you do next?"

"Talk to Liam, I suppose."

She found herself shaking her head. "Not alone, I hope."

He actually laughed, though it was a grim sound indeed.

"Liam is no giant, Rose. He's on the slender side and not particularly daunting. Besides, right now, even a giant would be no match for my ire."

"I only ask that you be careful. I'm certain you won't let me go with you, nor ask for help."

"Right on both counts." He reached out and touched her arm briefly, a quick stroke upon her wrist. "Truly, I'm grateful."

"Perhaps if you tell the police about Liam," she pointed out, looking at her skin where he'd touched it. It was tingling.

"If it comes down to my word against a shipyard owner's or a wealthy businessman's, I don't fancy my chances. No doubt the police will think me merely a disgruntled builder who came back hoping to cause trouble. And how are they going to protect me from an unknown threat? Or you, for that matter, if anyone found out we were married and someone tried to force my hand by threatening you."

When he put it that way, she supposed he was right.

Finn took a deep breath. "About the insurance claim, do you have proof, something in writing?" His question dragged her back to the present.

He looked more hopeful than she had seen any time they'd spoken. The painful feeling around her heart eased slightly.

"I don't, but as I said, it's public knowledge according to Charlotte. You can go to the office of North America Insurance if you like and see for yourself."

He nodded. "I'll do that."

They stared at each other a minute. Rose had nothing more to tell him, but she found herself reluctant to leave his company. Yet how would she feel if William were seeking out and keeping company with a former lady love? Utterly devastated and rightfully so.

"I must go," she said. "I'm sure Reed will contact you soon."

"He knows how to find me, I assume."

"Yes." She looked into his lovely eyes. "Finn, take care. Let me know how everything works out." The words sounded so distant, and she almost imagined this was their last meeting.

He smiled wryly, the corner of his mouth turning up slightly.

"How am I to contact you if I need to?" he asked.

"I guess you can go to Reed's offices at Scollay Square. And I, you?"

Finn thought a moment. "You can always send word via anyone at Ober's. A note telling me a place and time, and I'll be there."

She gave him another small smile and turned to leave. Suddenly, he grabbed hold of her upper arm.

Expectantly, Rose turned back. *Would she find him looking at her with love in his eyes? Was he going to sweep her into his arms and kiss her?*

However, upon his face was a look of consternation, not adoration.

"Speak of the devil," Finn said in a low voice, looking past her and out the small four-paned window in the brick wall.

"What's the matter?" she asked.

"Liam," he whispered.

"Here?" Rose turned around to peer out the same window into the side street. She saw only passers-by, moving quickly.

Finn shrugged, "I thought I saw him."

"That would be an incredible coincidence," she said.

"Unless he'd been watching the restaurant and saw me, and then saw you."

He frowned, staring out the window for another moment before focusing his attention on her once again.

"Never mind. I don't think this is a good idea, being trapped in this bookstore. On the other hand, I don't want you heading off down the street on your own in case he follows you. Where could we go where no one will see us?"

She hadn't expected that. Their "business" was concluded. She should ignore his dubious suspicions and leave. Instead, she found her mind casting about for a place they could go.

"The Natural History Museum?" she suggested.

"In the Back Bay? Why? What made you think of that?" he asked.

"I have no idea, but it would be quite deserted in the middle of a weekday."

"Too far," he said.

Rose puffed out her cheeks and blew the hair off of her forehead. *What was close by?*

"We're close to Faneuil Hall and Quincy Market."

Finn shook his head. "Only two of the busiest places in Boston."

"All the better not to be noticed," she pointed out.

"You're right about that, but we won't be able to hear each other above the din."

She narrowed her eyes. *Hear each other about what exactly?* Moreover, why didn't *he* think of somewhere? She tried again.

"The Old South Meeting House?" she suggested. "Not the most interesting museum in the world so perhaps not heavily attended."

"I wasn't asking to go sightseeing, so before you suggest the following, no to the Boston Museum, the Museum of Fine Arts, and the Music Hall, too."

"Well, then, Finn, why don't you—"

"Park Street Church," he interrupted. "It's quiet and directly around the corner."

"Fine, we'll—"

"You go first. I'll watch to see if anyone follows you. Choose a pew in the balcony on the far right under one of the arched windows, and I'll join you shortly."

Finn spun her around by the shoulders and gave her a little shove in the direction of the store's front door. She mumbled to herself about hard wooden pews and musty old churches, no matter how pretty. Still, she did as he asked and made her way to the church nearby, up the steep granite steps of the brick building, and past four towering columns.

Pausing at the tall double doors under the white marble lintel, Rose glanced behind her, flicking her gaze upon people walking by. No one seemed to be taking any notice of her, so she entered between the four shorter pristine columns into the cool interior.

As expected, the building was nearly empty at the odd hour, with no regular service scheduled. The church's interior was a tad boxy and plain for her liking, but she was not there to sightsee. Taking the stairs to her right, she walked along the length of the nave on the balcony level.

Rose sat next to the enclosed organist's box, resting her hands on smoothly polished railing in front of her. From up there, she could see anyone coming along the central aisle. However, as the minutes went by, no one came. At least, not the man for whom she waited.

As her anxiety grew, her pulse started to race and a lump formed low in her throat, nearly choking her. Wiping her moist gloved palms back and forth on the polished railing for the umpteenth time, she realized this unfortunate delay was all too reminiscent of waiting for Finn to return from the sea and then his never coming.

Heart pounding, Rose jumped to her feet, unable to bear the agony of waiting a moment longer, certain now Finn wouldn't come. She could feel it down deep in her bones. However, she refused to do anything rash, such as return to his room to find him.

Instead, she hurried home, casting worried glances over her shoulder the entire way. *Blast Finn and his ridiculous theories!* No one was following her, and there was no threat.

CHAPTER SEVENTEEN

Rose held firmly to Claire's hand when it seemed her friend might turn tail and run as they approached the Brewster's front steps on Brimmer Street. The evidence of the mysterious tea party was made clear by the garlands of flowers draped along the wrought iron fence, as well as hanging jauntily over the front doorway.

"Come, dear, let's stick to the plan," she admonished and yanked Claire to her side before ringing Mrs. Brewster's front doorbell. They were fifteen minutes early. On purpose.

Indeed, Rose had been ready to go for the past few hours, welcoming any distraction that took her from pacing across her bedroom, back and forth. She'd practically worn a path in the rug since Finn's disappearance the day before. Helping out Claire was a far better use of her time than worrying over her husband. The man could take care of himself.

Lucy, the Brewster's regular housekeeper, opened the door.

"Miss Appleton," she said with a slight curtsey and a welcoming smile, "and Miss Malloy. Please come in. You're the first to arrive."

So, the staff at least didn't know of Claire being snubbed. That was a blessing in any case.

"Everything is ready in the front room," Lucy continued. "May I take your capes?"

"No, thank you," Claire spoke for them both. They were wearing lightweight mantelets, Claire's in deep green and Rose's in dove gray, and were perfectly comfortable indoors.

"Please go on in, then. You both know the way," Lucy added with a friendly nod. "Miss Norcross is in there, and I'm to wait here to welcome guests."

"Thank you," Rose said, and they headed into the first room on the left.

Tastefully decorated with vases full of fresh flowers, there was a sideboard laden with refreshments, and no one in the room except Maeve, who turned at the sound of footsteps. Her face blanched of all its color when she saw who'd walked in, giving Rose a small measure of satisfaction.

Without hesitation, Rose gave Franklin's cousin her grandest smile, hoping Claire was doing similarly.

"So glad we are right on time, by which I mean a little early. It wouldn't do to have Mr. Brewster's special friend, Miss Appleton, not be here to greet the guests when they arrive, would it?"

Maeve still said nothing, although her mouth opened as she looked from Claire to Rose and back again.

"Are there any last-minute things with which you might need our help?" Rose continued, dropping Claire's hand when she was sure her friend was quite steady and not about to flee.

Wordlessly, Maeve shook her head.

Rose looked from Claire to Maeve hoping one of them would pick up the conversation and ease the tension. Alas, no.

Taking a few steps closer to the buffet table, Rose surveyed the offerings of tiny finger sandwiches and baked cheese biscuits, a pitcher of champagne-and-rum-spiked Roman punch, a covered teapot for the temperance gals, and, sadly, blancmange. She rolled her eyes.

Was there anyone who actually enjoyed that bland concoction?

Thankfully, next to it was a three-tiered plate of chocolates with the distinctive blue and silver ribbon laid around the pedestal proclaiming them to be Randall Chocolates from Newbury Street. Her favorites!

Come what may, Rose would have a few of those before the day was through.

"It looks as if you have it all quite under control," she said. "As expected. We were so pleased when we heard you were going to host. It certainly wouldn't have been seemly for Claire to do so, of course, being a little premature in some people's eyes. Obviously, it's quite a task these days for Mrs. Brewster, given her age, don't you agree?"

"I . . . I . . . ," Maeve began.

"If only she'd had a daughter," Rose finished, turning to beam at Claire as if that would be rectified soon.

At last Claire found her voice. "Franklin said he would try to stop by while I was here. Do you know if he is at home?"

Rose was proud of how Claire had worked in how her beau expected her to be at the party. She gave her friend an encouraging smile.

"I don't know for sure," Maeve said. "Would you both like some punch? I think I'm going to have some." With that, she turned away and helped herself to a generous glassful of the intoxicating lemony champagne beverage, spooning a dollop of meringue on top from the porcelain bowl sitting at the ready.

She took a large gulp and then another before downing the potation entirely. When she faced them, she had meringue clinging to the space between her thin upper lip and her pointy nose. Rose would be damned if she'd tell Maeve.

Claire, however, was more generous. *"Um, "* she began. "You have—" and she started to gesture to her own lip.

"Are you saying Franklin invited you?" Maeve asked.

How rude, Rose thought, as if there was any question Claire should be invited.

"What a strange question," Rose answered before Claire could speak. "Naturally, Mr. Brewster knew Miss Appleton would have been invited to any gathering of ladies at his home. Why do you ask?"

"I think I hear my aunt calling me," Maeve said in a faint tone and disappeared from the room still clutching her empty glass.

"Yes, you go tell the ol' biddy," Rose murmured as soon as Franklin's cousin had disappeared.

However, Claire looked shaken. "You don't think Mrs. Brewster will throw us out when she hears we've come, do you?"

"She wouldn't dare," Rose said. "Franklin would be furious. Besides, you were recently at a Wetmore ball. At Chateau-sur-Mer, for goodness sake!"

Claire brightened. "True."

The sound of footsteps caused them both to face the door and in came Lucy with two sisters of their acquaintance, followed by another young lady of good reputation. In fact, as more came in, Rose noticed they all had a few things in common: their age, their family status, which was not surprising, and their brown locks. All brunettes, not a one as dark as the Irish Malloys, nor flaxen as the Appletons. Every single one, a chestnut brown.

While young ladies were still arriving, Franklin suddenly entered. The girls all parted like hens before a rooster. Except for Claire. She stood her ground and waited for him to come up to her.

Good girl, Rose thought.

Franklin's genuine smile of admiration warmed Rose's heart. This would work out. It had to. Obviously, he cared deeply for Claire, and she, him.

"I'm so glad you came," he said to Claire, then glanced over her shoulder. "It looks like a fine spread, and I'm sure you'll enjoy yourself. Moreover, it is nice simply to have you in my home. That doesn't happen often enough."

Whose fault was that? Rose wondered. If only the man were more assertive.

Claire smiled up at him. "I'm glad to be here and ever so happy you stopped in."

He grinned at her, and for a long, awkward moment, they seemed to forget anyone else was there, as they stood staring into each other's eyes.

Rose observed the other guests. The ladies were murmuring, frowns upon their unblemished faces, talking behind gloved hands. It became painfully clear what they were saying. They'd been led to believe Claire and Franklin had broken off their association, and that he was freely searching for a wife.

The tea was a gathering of eligible daughters from good homes, but was Franklin supposed to attend the tea and choose one, or was someone else going to do the choosing? Maeve perhaps or—?

Mrs. Brewster, with Maeve trailing behind, glided into the room, her face a thunderous scowl when she took in the sight of her son and Claire. Her appearance instantly brought to a halt both the happy couple's long dance of gazes and smiles as well as all the disgruntled whispering.

Recalling herself, Mrs. Brewster took in the ladies with an encompassing smile.

"So glad you all could come. Please, let Annie serve you whatever tempts your appetite from the buffet."

Sure enough, a slender girl had appeared beside the sideboard as if by magic, apron starched, kerchief in place, and ready to serve the upper echelon of Boston's society. The ladies surged forward like hungry hogs at a trough.

However, Rose kept her eyes on the drama unfolding in front of her. Mrs. Brewster's smile died and, grim-faced, she ordered Franklin to accompany her out of the room. Moreover, with extreme discourtesy, she did not greet either interloper, and Rose couldn't help making a sour face at the woman's broad back as she exited.

Maeve, for her part, almost looked contrite. Perhaps she was only doing what her aunt had requested by hosting the party. Or perhaps her expression was due to the Roman punch she'd imbibed unsettling her stomach.

After sidling up to the end of the sideboard, Rose offered the beleaguered and strangely familiar Annie a commiserating smile.

Then, she darted her hand in and snatched up a chocolate, which she quickly popped into her mouth. Thus fortified, she waylaid Maeve, steering her toward the corner of the room and away from Claire, who had struck up a conversation with one of the guests.

"These ladies," she said to Franklin's cousin, "they are all of a type, I noticed."

Maeve let her gaze drift over the roomful of women happily munching on tiny sandwiches.

"Yes, I suppose so," she said vaguely.

"They are all here at Mrs. Brewster's special invitation, correct?"

"Yes, they were invited by my aunt," Maeve allowed.

"I would ask you the purpose of this tea, except I have surmised it is so Franklin's mother can choose him a bride. Is that also correct?"

Rose ignored Maeve's astonished expression at how plainly and boldly she was speaking, yet she could see no virtue in tiptoeing around this unpleasant business.

"I will take that as another yes," Rose added when Maeve said nothing. "Moreover, from Franklin's behavior, he was unaware his mother was bride-shopping. What I can't understand is why Mrs. Brewster is set against Miss Appleton. Surely, Claire is above reproach."

A shadow flickered across Maeve's face.

Ah-ha, thought Rose. *There* is *something*. At the very least, there was some matter Maeve and Mrs. Brewster had discussed. Whatever it was, if it was about Claire's reputation being sullied or her nature being less than good, it could not be true.

Maeve tried to move past her, but Rose stepped quickly sideways.

"I don't know anything," Maeve insisted.

"In the same way you didn't know anything about William Woodsom's kissing habits? Or how about meddling in my association with him by sending him chasing after me the other day? What did you hope to gain by that? I am starting to wonder if you are carrying a torch for my fiancé."

Maeve pursed her lips. "I never would have thought this before, but I am not sure you're good enough for Mr. Woodsom."

Momentarily, Rose had no words. *How dare Maeve Norcross say such a thing!* However, she quickly regained her wits.

"Fortunately, it is not your place to judge my merit, nor to judge Miss Appleton's, for that matter."

Maeve gave a toss of her head.

Rose had had enough of this game. "Unless you want me to tell this entire gathering how you once threw yourself at Mr. Woodsom and then lied to me about who kissed whom, I suggest you tell me what Mrs. Brewster has against Miss Appleton."

"You wouldn't!"

"I would," Rose insisted.

"It would cause a terrible stir. A vulgar thing to do, right here in my aunt's parlor."

"I don't mind stirring things up at all. I care only about my friend. There is no better girl in the world than Miss Appleton, and any man would be lucky to have her."

"Fine," Maeve spat out. "I'll tell you."

However, she had raised her voice, and whatever Franklin's cousin was about to say, false innuendo or not, Rose was certain she didn't want the rest of the guests to hear.

"Let us take a stroll in the Brewsters' gardens, shall we?" She leaned very close to Maeve and added, "I suggest we take our little *tête-a-tête* outside."

Maeve pursed her lips then stalked out of the room, leaving Rose to follow. She glanced back at Claire and gave her a reassuring smile. Better to get to the bottom of this than let it continue.

Five minutes later, Rose was ready to weep. It was all her fault Claire might lose her heart's desire. *Her* fault! Someone had seen Claire sneak out repeatedly about four years ago, both early and late, over a period of a few months, taking her carriage, which would be gone for hours. No doubt that someone was a servant, one who lacked loyalty to the Appletons and had moved on, taking her gossip with her.

Unfortunately, that servant had ended up at the Brewster home in time to "save" Franklin from a terribly bad match with an immoral, disreputable female. For, of course, there was only one credible explanation for Claire's comings and goings—she had been secretly meeting a man.

Except she hadn't! Rose had.

Maeve finished speaking, and still Rose remained silent. Claire had lent her the carriage to go and see Finn on more than one occasion. Whereas Rose knew own her mother would be watching her like a hawk, Claire, with her rather indifferent parents had assumed no one would notice or care if she borrowed their town carriage at odd hours.

Now Rose could only wonder with dread who else was privy to this terrible blight upon Claire's reputation.

"Does Mr. Brewster think ill of Miss Appleton?"

"Not that I know of. In truth," Maeve said, "I don't approve of taking the word of a servant. I never have. Most are too flighty and stupid to give their words such credence. However, my aunt says they have no reason to lie, either."

Rose could barely focus on Maeve's words. *How could she fix this for Claire?* What's more, how could she do so without bringing down the condemnation of Boston's elite upon her own head and, worse, besmirching the Malloy name?

Her mother would be heartbroken. Elise would be beyond disappointed. Reed would kill her.

Perhaps she could speak with Mrs. Brewster and convince her of Claire's purity without offering up her own misguided actions as proof of her friend's innocence.

"Personally," Maeve continued, seeming unable to stop being the center of this drama once she'd been thrust onto the stage, "I don't care a fig if my cousin has fallen in love with Miss Appleton and vice versa. Whatever happened four years ago is ancient history."

If only that were true.

Regardless, Rose looked at Maeve in a kinder light.

"What does Mrs. Brewster plan to do with the information?"

Maeve shrugged. "She cares only about saving Franklin. She has vowed to tell him of Miss Appleton's 'sordid past' if he indicates he will offer for her."

Rose felt the blood drain from her head. The only thing saving Claire so far was that Franklin was a most unhurried man, dragging his feet for so long. However, today, with their showing up uninvited and with Franklin standing in the middle of the room, looking only at Claire . . .

Good God! Franklin was speaking with his mother at that very moment.

Rose picked up her skirts and hurried back into the house, hearing loud voices as soon as she entered. In the hallway, right outside the closed doors to the party, Claire stood, a stricken look upon her lovely face. Franklin appeared no better.

Rose was too late. They had exchanged words.

"There is nothing more to say," Franklin said, his tone uncharacteristically severe.

"In that, sir, you are correct." In turn, Claire's voice was loud, which it never was. She barely glanced at Rose as she turned away.

"Come along," her friend said firmly, "we are leaving."

Rose stayed rooted to the spot. This could not be happening.

At that moment, Annie appeared from the kitchens, eyes averted as she moved past the unpleasant scene, carrying a pitcher of lemonade and returning quickly to the party, closing the door behind her. Rose immediately knew she was the one who'd gossiped. She had looked familiar because four years earlier, she'd worked for the Appletons.

Claire stalked toward the front door and yanked it open. When framed by the light from outside, she turned, looking back at Rose and then at Franklin.

She was magnificent, Rose thought, standing tall, head up, eyes flashing.

"I hope never to set foot in this house again," Claire said, her voice sounding like ice and steel. "Nor speak to *any* of its inhabitants. Come along, Rose."

Rose opened her mouth to protest, but this Valkyrie was not to be disobeyed. Still, she gave Franklin one last beseeching glance. Surely, he wasn't going to let Claire simply walk out of his life.

However, the usually affable man looked anything but. His mouth was set in anger, his chin thrust forward, and his face clouded in a myriad of emotions—no doubt shock and sadness among them.

This was all Rose's fault, yet there was nothing she could do at that moment in the hallway of the Brewster mansion. It was too awful. She followed Claire onto the front step, hearing someone close the door behind them. Every young lady at the gathering must have overheard the terrible altercation in the front hall. The civilized tea had become scandal-water of the worst kind and would be all over Boston by nightfall.

Claire Appleton had been set aside by Franklin Brewster on the grounds of impropriety.

Tomorrow would be even worse.

No family in Boston would welcome her and, certainly, no young gentleman would take her for a wife. Claire would have to leave the city.

It should be Rose who was driven out like the indecent woman she was.

As soon as they got a few yards away from the Brewsters' front door, Claire began to cry in earnest. Silent tears streamed down her face. She didn't try to stop them or wipe them or hide her face behind her gloved hands. She simply cried and walked, and kept on crying and walking, right past Rose's carriage, right on toward her home.

Rose hurried along beside her, feeling at an utter loss, not knowing what to do. How she despised this unfamiliar and decidedly wretched sensation of helplessness!

After one agonizing sob rent the silence, Claire stopped. She stopped walking and she stopped her tears. Then she turned to Rose.

"I have wasted my time on that man."

Rose had not expected that statement. She'd expected her dear friend to lash out at her for ruining her life.

"What did he say?" Rose's own voice sounded choked.

Claire squeezed her eyes shut for a moment before opening them again.

"When Franklin returned to the parlor, he beckoned me to follow him. I saw at once something was wrong. As soon as we got into the hall, he closed the doors behind us and turned on me like a jackal. He said he had been fooled by my genteel demeanor and lovely face."

Rose swallowed. Franklin must have said a lot more than that, but Claire merely slipped her arm through Rose's and continued walking in silence for a little while. Giving her friend time to gather her thoughts, Rose waited for her to continue, offering her the inadequate comfort of squeezing her gloved hand.

At last, Claire said in a much softer tone, "Naturally, I was stunned and I told him so. He asked whom I was meeting secretly four years ago." She paused. "Can you believe the gall? I said, 'Four years ago? Why, no one.' 'That's not what I've heard,' he said, and he sneered at me."

She shook her head in wonderment. "Franklin actually sneered and said his mother told him about my illicit undertakings. I asked him quite seriously, 'Are you mad? Have you lost your senses?' Then he said, and I promise you, these were his exact words, 'I thought you might do me the courtesy of disclosing who it was who beat me to your virtue.'"

She was breathing heavily and gripping Rose's arm more tightly than she probably intended.

Rose wanted to cry, too. Franklin must have been incredibly hurt and shocked to say such a thing, as would any man have been at hearing such a shocking thing about his beloved. And from his heartless mother, no less.

"It sounds like a misunderstanding. A terrible one," Rose added, "but not an irreparable rent in the fabric of your relationship. Surely, after all this time—"

Claire snorted. "Exactly. *All this time.* My virtue, indeed! My biggest virtue was patience, waiting for Franklin Brewster to declare himself."

"How did you leave it with him?" Rose asked. "I mean *before* saying you were never setting foot in his house again?"

"Franklin said whoever my lover was, I had better hope that man still wanted me for . . . ," her voice faltered, "for he no longer does."

Oh dear!

"You know he doesn't mean that," Rose said. "He was angry and hurt."

"Franklin should have trusted me." Claire's tone was now one of utter disappointment. "I told him I would not dignify his filthy, mistrustful question with an answer. Let him stew in his doubts. Let him imagine me . . . lying with every . . . every man . . . in . . ."

Claire broke off and was crying again. Fat, hot tears were splashing onto Rose's sleeve. They were no longer strolling but striding quickly at Claire's pace, and in another few minutes, they were at the Appletons' front door. Many people had passed them and not once had her friend looked away or tried to disguise her tears.

Worse and worse. Truly, all of Boston would learn how Claire had been cut by the Brewsters. Even if Rose shouted all her own wickedness from the pinnacle of the State House dome, right above William's own small office, the damage to Claire was irrevocable.

And added to it was their stroll across Beacon Hill presenting an unstable female, a public breakdown, and hysterics.

The only one who could truly fix this was Franklin Brewster, himself, if Claire was to have any future, and it would have to be done in an extremely public way.

CHAPTER EIGHTEEN

"Rose. Rose."

"Sorry," she turned to William. "What did you say?"

She realized he must have repeated himself, as he'd had to do all evening. She was beyond distracted and unable to concentrate on anything except Claire's dilemma. Moreover, she couldn't even discuss it with William, as she couldn't possibly tell him how she knew Claire was not the one who'd been sneaking out to see a man.

He gave her his most patient smile. "I asked if you needed a coat, yours or mine?"

They were outside enjoying an early evening concert. Unfortunately, she'd heard the same music with Finn. At present, Rose was seated on a chair on the lawn of Leverett Park, with Elise and Michael, Reed and Charlotte, and William. Four years earlier, she'd been leaning against a railing on a balcony on Hanover Street.

Instead of quietly enjoying Tchaikovsky surrounded by friends and family, as was currently the case, she and Finn had been alone, their thoughts solely on each other. The beautiful music floating up from the park below had been merely the musical accompaniment to their holding one another, their impassioned kissing, and, yes, even a little exploratory touching.

Tchaikovsky was the only common thread, but the notes were tying her younger self to her newly engaged self quite tightly.

It was beyond disturbing. When she recalled her husband kissing her during the second movement of "Francesca da Rimini," and, at the same moment in the score, William happened to turn to her, Rose tilted her face to receive his kiss—in public—the division of time blurring between the past and the present.

Naturally, her fiancé had looked shocked, until she'd feigned a yawn as if he'd misread her intent all along.

When he took her hand in his at precisely the same point when Finn had stroked his fingers down her spine, she'd shivered.

"No, I'm not cold. Thank you," she told her fiancé when he offered her a coat.

How oddly Rose was behaving. And not for the first time. It was disconcerting. However, it was not something he couldn't tolerate. William had admired her when she was slightly wild. When he'd first come from England to live in America, he'd seen her at events when she was the tender side of eighteen. He'd watched her dance too closely in some cases, laugh too loudly always, and speak her mind to a group of adoring males.

What's more, he'd adored her bubbling spirit.

Then he'd left the area for a time, gone to school on the Continent, and come back only to find a very different Rose Malloy, somber, subdued, and absolutely never laughing. Even though she'd lacked the old spark of gaiety, he'd still admired her, still found she dominated his thoughts until he'd finally decided to make her his.

William had worked damn hard to make sure she smiled and danced and enjoyed life. He loved the more mature Rose. Yet lately, she'd become subdued again, even a little distant. When he asked her about any troubling thoughts, she professed her complete happiness in their relationship.

Yes, it was disconcerting.

Tonight, they were at a favorite pastime, listening to music, this time at one of Mr. Frederick Olmsted's masterfully designed parks. Seated with her family, eating syllabub from tall chilled glasses, William could swear Rose was somewhere else in her thoughts. She'd shivered yet declined his offer of a coat. Now, so keenly aware of her strange moodiness beside him, he might as well be listening to some tune the old cow died of as Tchaikovsky.

More than anything, he wanted to be alone with Rose, stare into her incredible sapphire-blue eyes, and find out if there was anything at all wrong, anything he could do. After all, they had become friends. The best of friends, something he hadn't expected and, thus, cherished all the more.

If Rose had a problem, he had a problem. If he could solve it, he would do so.

Unfortunately, like *the incident* she'd mentioned once when he'd first started courting her and the secret she had started to tell him more recently only to change her mind, there were barriers between them. William didn't like secrets or barriers, especially between him and the woman who would be his wife.

He leaned down and murmured so only she could hear, "Can we take a stroll?"

He felt Rose stiffen, sensed her pulling away.

"Aren't you enjoying the concert?" she asked him.

"As much as you are," he said wryly, wondering how bad things were if she didn't want to steal a moment alone with him.

"It's grand," she whispered over enthusiastically, and William felt a little sick inside at her obvious pretense. "Let's stay here and finish our dessert," she added.

Damn. Well, perhaps this was not the time to open an old wound or to create a new one. Whatever it was that was bothering her, she would disclose to him when she felt ready.

Rose was no coward, he knew that, so he had no doubt she would broach the issue eventually.

Rose wanted to cry. Desperately, she wished she could take a walk with her beloved, holding his hand as they traversed the many paths, and kiss him on one of the quaint bridges or under the maple trees. She fervently wanted to simply enjoy their love for one another.

Instead, there was an ugly scar on her heart, and if she didn't handle things correctly, it would ruin William as it had already destroyed Claire's happiness.

If they walked alone, he would question her. He was a smart man, and she was being far too careless in her behavior for him not to have noticed something was definitely wrong. And preoccupied by what to do about Franklin and Claire, she knew she was even quieter than usual.

Why, Rose had realized everyone was clapping at the end of a piece only when the loud sound finally penetrated her brain, and belatedly, she'd joined in.

She'd already sent a note to Franklin that morning, asking him to meet her somewhere discreet. She could risk no speculative gossip, yet she also didn't want to return to his home where the dragon resided and ruled and where prying servants might be eavesdropping.

Of course, in her note, she hadn't used the term *dragon*, but only with great restraint.

By the time her little party of concert-goers had departed Rose's home on Mount Vernon Street and set out in multiple carriages for the park, Claire's beloved had not yet agreed to speak with her.

It seemed an interminable evening, except for the pleasure of William's sweet attentiveness, if only he didn't look so concerned. If only she deserved him.

As she'd hoped, upon returning home, there was a briefly penned reply from Franklin.

Yes, the Bijou Theatre, mid-morning.
F. B.

At 10 a.m., Rose climbed the stairs to the second-floor lobby of the theatre on Washington Street. While a bit plain on the outside and housing an ordinary row of shops below, the building sported no less than twenty-one arched windows in the three upper floors. In fact, the Bijou's interior was so luxurious as to be a little gaudy, with its mixture of masonry and wallpaper, its innumerable carvings, and an ornate central chandelier that looked as if it were descending from a fool's cap.

Rose eyed it all fondly. She'd watched more than one hilarious Gilbert and Sullivan comic opera there, as well as many a play. What's more, she thought the acoustics to be quite good.

Franklin was already present, speaking with a gentleman in a top hat, who moved away as she approached.

"Miss Malloy," Franklin said and bowed slightly. "That was Mr. Keith. Do you know him? The owner? I'm helping with a few minor improvements. Or rather, my late father's company is, of which I am its head."

He looked nervous, and the jittery path of his conversation proved him so.

"Mr. Brewster," Rose began, swallowing her own nerves, "may I call you Franklin? I believe we have been close enough acquaintances for such familiarity."

"Yes, we have," he said, his voice sounding strangled. "Please do so."

By God, he was choked with emotion. *That was a good sign!*

Rose was determined to make this right for Claire. Her friend had proven herself to be a saint yet again. When Rose had tried to apologize to Claire for the stain on her friend's otherwise unsullied reputation, for having ever let her get mixed up in Rose's own sordid indiscretions, Claire had held up her hand and silenced her.

"We are closer than sisters, are we not?" Claire had asked. "I did nothing wrong, and even you, although rather unorthodox, I know you did nothing immoral either. Yes, you were impetuous, but you were following your heart. Honestly, how many girls our age could have married such a virile, handsome man as Phineas Bennet and yet not given him their innocence?"

When Claire had put it that way, Rose had felt almost virtuous.

"We did nothing wrong. What's more, I can lend my carriage to whomever I please," Claire had insisted. "Whenever I please. And the dragon and her son can go to devil!"

Rose had never heard Claire speak thusly. If she had even a little of her friend's courage and righteousness, she would find the wherewithal to mend this rupture.

"I must tell you a grave misunderstanding has occurred, and an egregious injustice has been perpetrated upon our common friend, Miss Appleton."

Franklin's eyes widened at her customary way of getting right to the point, which was not admired by everyone. In this instance, however, he seemed to appreciate they would not be wasting time circling the matter at hand.

"I think there has been no misunderstanding," he challenged. "For I have it on good authority, with an eye-witness no less, that the information I have been told is absolutely true."

How deeply would she have to elaborate to clear this up?

"The eye-witness may have reported truthfully what he or *she* saw," Rose allowed. "However, the perception, or rather, the *interpretation* of what was seen is positively false. This, I know, because I was involved."

Fully prepared to confess her part in the mischief, still, Rose hoped she did not have to.

Franklin walked in a circle, no doubt his version of pacing, and then he stood before her once more.

"I love Claire," he confessed, surprising Rose that he would say the words to her. "However, even if she would have me after the other day's disastrous encounter, I cannot enter into this marriage." He paused to cross his arms and thump his own shoulders.

"No" he stated again, "I cannot enter a marriage with this dreadful hint of impropriety in her past."

Rose felt as if this same drama were playing out in her own life. With real curiosity, like a cat pawing at a particularly sticky cupboard door, she asked, "So if Claire has had a prior relationship, which I can assure you she has not, does that make her an unsuitable choice to be your bride?"

"No," Franklin said with an emphatic shake of his head. "It's not that. If she had a prior relationship, I would only want her to be truthful and tell me. If she'd lived in Africa or spoke Chinese or had been in love with another man, I would want to know."

He frowned at the floor, and Rose could see his struggle. He loved Claire and wanted her, but he was a rational man and a cautious one.

Franklin took another circular stroll before he stopped again.

"I thought we had been honest with each other in all things, more so than other couples," he continued. "Some chaps I know simply marry a girl for her pretty face, and that's that. They don't tell and they don't ask, and I think they have poorer lives for living as strangers. Naturally, Claire has asked me about my, *uh*, my history with the fairer sex."

A profound blush appeared on Franklin's cheeks. "And I told her honestly. Similarly, I asked her and thought I knew everything about the woman I love. Until my mother suddenly told me Claire had been sneaking out at all hours. I know it was years ago . . . ," he trailed off, then seemed to come to a decision as he adjusted his vest and tugged at his coat.

"If she could keep a secret like that, then how can we have a true marriage of the minds and hearts?" he asked Rose.

The man was perfectly correct, of course. Rose *should* have told William about Finn, dead or alive, when she first let him become serious about her, when she started to open her heart to him, and certainly before they became engaged. It would have always been between them, even if Finn had really been dead. Her eyes teared up at what a mess she'd made.

"Miss Malloy, I'm so sorry," Franklin said, pulling a handkerchief from his pocket and handing it to her. "I did not mean to cause you distress."

"Oh, no, you haven't. At least not as you think. My emotions are not for you and Claire, for you will hear in a minute that, luckily, your situation is easily rectified. I'm crying rather self-centered tears, and I apologize for doing so." She dabbed at them.

She was a Malloy, and like her brother, she fixed things for those she loved.

"I will be forthright with you, as you have been with me," Rose began. "Claire did indeed keep a secret from you because it was not hers to tell. She *did* sneak out in her carriage on numerous occasions, but only in order to lend it to me. Honor bright, it was I who had a secret association with a young man four years ago."

Franklin had the grace to keep his face impassive so as not to embarrass her.

Rose was almost through the worst, so she plunged ahead.

"I didn't want to tell my mother about my attachment, and so, unthinkingly, I relied on Claire to help me. It was a terribly selfish thing to do in retrospect. However, four years ago, it seemed merely like an exciting adventure. I never meant for Claire to suffer any consequences. I hope you will believe me."

Franklin stared at her, his intelligent eyes scanning her face, seeing her pain and her regret. After a few moments, he nodded.

"Of course I believe you," he said at last, and a weight dropped from Rose's shoulders.

"I am so grateful you contacted me," Franklin continued. "I have been half mad with doubt and disbelief. Claire is the best kind of person anyone could wish for in a friend and in a wife, and she speaks often of her love for you. I can certainly picture her selflessly and without regard to her own reputation doing as you have described to me."

Rose nodded. *What an understanding man.*

"I am extremely glad I eschewed etiquette and came over to secure a dance between you and Claire at that party so long ago," she told him. "For you are indeed worthy of our Claire."

Instead of seeming pleased, however, Franklin's expression looked tortured.

"I said terrible things to her. I have wronged her, and I didn't have faith in her in the face of my mother's condemning words and blasted witness."

He looked as if he might start to tear his own hair out. Rose considered what Claire had said in anger and weighed that against all the months and months of her friend loving Franklin Brewster.

"I am certain Claire will forgive you. She loves you, and that love cannot simply stop in one day. However, you must soften your mother toward her, too. It cannot be easy for either of you when your own parent disapproves."

Merely the fear of such disapproval had caused Rose to behave badly toward Finn and hide her love for him.

Franklin nodded. "I will tell my mother the truth and demand she apologize to my future wife, and that will be that. I mean to marry Claire, and my mother had better get used to the idea, or she'll find herself minus one son, a daughter-in-law, and any future grandchildren."

Rose smiled genuinely for the first time in days at the idea of Claire's dream of marrying and having children finally coming true. Then she recalled the greater problem.

"All the young ladies at that absurd tea party overheard your conversation with Claire. If you mean to win her back *and* remove the blemish on her reputation, you had best do something public and large. Otherwise, you know what will happen? People will think you merely a besotted fool who accepts Claire *despite* her soiled past. And if that is the case, even after marriage, she will not be welcomed in society's parlors. She will be a pariah, and you will both have to leave Boston."

Franklin looked slightly shocked, his face paling from its early rosy blush. However, he clearly understood the gravity of the situation.

"I will make it clear it was not her but—" he broke off and stared at her as Rose took a stricken step back.

Her heart started to pound and the blood left her head. *Good God!* Franklin would tell everyone it was she who had the secret assignations. He would do that to save his love, as he should, and then the Malloys would be the pariahs.

Yet he started again. "I will make it clear she was only lending her carriage to help a less fortunate. I promise, your name will be left out of it. You brought us together to begin with, and now, you've done it again. Or at least I hope so. Claire and I will owe you a debt of gratitude."

Rose felt the tears well again. How kind of him to say so, when it was her thoughtless actions that had nearly driven them irrevocably apart.

"Don't worry. I know exactly how to repair this," Franklin said, the twinkle back in his brown eyes.

With all her heart, Rose hoped so.

She also fervently hoped her next conversation with William would go as smoothly.

Most of all, she wished she could stop wondering why Finn had left her waiting at the church and whether anything had happened to him. However, she had to remind herself he was not her responsibility or her concern anymore.

The knock at his door caused Finn to jump up from his bed where he had spread out his reading material. Boat-building books on one side, newspaper accounts on the other.

"Who is it?" he called out, wondering if he should have obtained a firearm.

"Reed Malloy."

Finn's face twisted into a grimace of regret. He'd been expecting Rose's brother, but still, the man was an unwelcome visitor. Like a downpour on a July fourth celebration.

Yet Finn had no one to blame except himself. He had done everything wrong from the moment he'd been rescued, and it had led to this moment. The moment when he would lose Rose.

Pulling open the door, he looked at a tall man with Rose's dark hair and intense blue eyes. He didn't know whether to hold out his hand, but Reed didn't, so Finn kept his own by his side.

Rose's brother gave Finn a cursory glance up and down, sighed, and then asked, "Shall we meet here or do you want to come to my office?"

Finn moved sideways and gestured for him to enter.

"You were expecting me, I take it?" Reed quipped, stepping into the center of the room and setting down his portfolio on the bed cover.

"Yes. Rose mentioned she'd spoken to you."

Her brother's glance was sharp. "She was supposed to stay away from you."

"Except for one or two brief encounters, she has done so," Finn said, feeling all at once irritated at having to apologize for seeing his own wife.

A flash of his feeling must have shown on his face. Rose said her brother was perceptive and sure enough, he pushed his coat back, hands going onto his pockets, and an expression of utter displeasure set firmly on his face.

"The only reason I didn't greet you with a blow to your face is that you left my sister with her innocence intact."

Finn's mouth opened briefly and then he snapped it shut. Reed Malloy certainly laid it all out.

"I'm surprised she talked about that with you," Finn said tightly.

Her brother shrugged. "We are a close family, and I believe she told me in order to stick up for you, to convince me you aren't as terrible a scoundrel as I think you are."

"I'm not," Finn said, then felt annoyed at himself for being defensive. He didn't really owe this man an explanation. Or maybe he did.

"I love your sister. I always have. If I hadn't thought we could make a good life together and that I could provide for her,

I wouldn't have married her. That's the truth. However, over the past few years, I've realized she can certainly do better than me."

"Agreed," Reed snapped. "Is that why you played dead and broke her heart? Do you have any idea what a sad state she was in? You put her through hell." His eyes sparkled with pure anger. "I may just thump you anyway."

Finn took in the words. "I wouldn't stop you." In fact, he would let Reed pummel him. It might make them both feel better.

"What sort of man marries a woman like our Rose and then doesn't keep his word to her? That doesn't sound like a man my sister would love?"

Her brother wasn't going to make this easy.

"It's a long story, one I won't bother you with. Yet I will ease your mind, Mr. Malloy, by saying I believe your sister has made a decent choice in husbands. In *both* instances."

The words came out bitterly, but there was nothing Finn could do about that. Thinking of his Rose going off with the perfect William Woodsom was a continuous ache.

"I have time to hear your story," Reed insisted, "or at least the part about how you decided to abandon my sister."

Finn sighed. "Very well. When I finally reached England, it was already months since the sinking of the *Garrard*. I was desperate to get back to Rose. At the same time that I figured out how to earn passage home, I also discovered I could make something more of myself. I intended to return home first, of course, and was going to ask Rose if she would go with me to the university in Scotland. I was working to earn passage back." He remembered the flash of pain, the disbelief. "Then I got severely injured."

He paused. *Did Reed really want to hear anymore?* The man looked to be absorbing every word.

"The longer I was gone and the longer she believed me dead, the harder it was to disrupt her life. In truth, I began to think she would be better off without me. And seeing her current choice for her next husband, I would say I was right. The man is a descendent of English nobility, for Christ's sake."

Reed Malloy just stared, saying nothing at first. Then he spat out, "What a load of bullshit!"

Finn backed up a step at the man's vehemence.

Rose's brother continued, barely taking a breath. "If my sister loved you, then why did you need to better yourself? Not for her sake, I guess, but for your own. You were a selfish bastard to do what you did. Can you convince me otherwise?"

Finn felt his blood start to boil, and the back of his neck prickled. *Convince the man?* He thought about it. Was that what he wanted to do? Did it matter now if he made Reed believe he wasn't an utter cad?

No, it didn't. Not a whit. The words spilled from him anyway.

"After my convalescence, I found a place to study to become a master builder. I seized the opportunity to be more than I was, and it *was* because of Rose, if not directly for her. When we were together, she was ashamed of me and couldn't bring herself to introduce me to you and the rest of the world as her husband."

Reed nodded slightly, which was enough encouragement for Finn to finish.

"Since I've lost her, none of what I did makes sense anymore. I am a trained naval architect, and a good one, but I could have come back and kept my Rose and been quite happy as a shipbuilder at the yard. I find that without your sister," he trailed off and sat heavily upon the narrow bed, feeling all the wind go out of his sails. There was no need to finish his sentence and lay his heart bare.

Finn stared at the wide pine floor and saw nothing. "I suppose I will go up to Maine where my father lives. There's plenty of shipbuilding there. I know one thing, I can't stay here."

"Because it would be too painful to see her," Reed surmised.

"Worse," Finn said, lifting his head and looking his brother-in-law square in the eye. "Because my being here would cause her pain."

Reed's eyebrows lifted nearly into his hairline.

"I have seen it every time she looks at me. My coming back has caused her nothing but distress."

Finn realized the ache he was feeling was not truly physical. Centered in his chest, a dull throbbing made it difficult to breathe—it was the keen loss of Rose.

Reed said nothing. Then he also sat on the edge of the bed next to his leather portfolio, glancing at the scattered books and papers with cursory interest.

"I've spent some time reading the accounts of the sinking," Finn explained, "and learning precisely who said what. I appreciate what your wife found out."

Reed jumped up again as if he'd been scalded. Wearing an expression like a thundercloud, he demanded, "What does Charlotte have to do with this?"

Finn thought the man's eyes would pop out of his head.

"I'm sorry if I've spoken out of turn. I assumed you knew Rose asked your wife to determine if there was anything shady. And Mrs. Malloy did exactly that."

Reed ran a hand over his eyes and then through his hair before he spoke again.

"What did my wife find?" His tone was clipped.

"Insurance fraud," Finn explained, thinking of Liam's elegant house and how slippery the man had become, never at home when Finn went looking for him. "It has nothing to do with my divorce from your sister. Shall we get on with it? I assume you have something for me to sign."

For a moment, Reed looked as if he wasn't done with the prior subject, but then he leaned over and started to undo his satchel.

"Yes, I have brought an agreement for an uncontested divorce. If you sign it, then I can file in the court and—"

One of the six lower panes in the room's only window shattered inward with such sudden force that both men ducked. The brick that caused the damage skidded to a stop in front of their feet. A piece of paper was tied to it with twine.

Reed bent down first and picked it up as Finn crunched over the glass, raised the sash, and looked out, craning his neck one way and then the other to see if anyone was running away. No one looked the least bit suspicious.

When he turned, Reed had untied the note from the brick, which he placed by the door. Then he handed Finn the paper.

"Message for you, I take it."

Finn shrugged, only wishing Rose's brother hadn't been there when this unsavory event had occurred. He scanned the writing, a mere two lines:

If you want to stay alive, leave Boston.
Don't tell a soul or your delicate flower perishes.

Finn didn't have to read it twice to understand what the threat implied. Someone had seen them together at the bookstore and knew who she was.

"What is it?" Reed asked.

Finn looked up from the note and directly into a blue gaze that so resembled Rose's eyes he couldn't speak. Yet he couldn't possibly hide this from her brother, her protector. Wordlessly, he handed over the paper.

It took only a second.

"What in blue blazes!" Reed exclaimed. "Who the hell sent this?"

"I wish I knew," Finn said. "I told Rose we must not be seen together and not to tell Woodsom or anyone about my return because it might put people in danger. I was too late."

"Why does someone want you to leave?"

Finn frowned. "Because the *Garrard* never should have sailed. Somebody besides me knew it and let us go to our deaths anyway. Except I'm not dead, and that's a problem."

Reed considered. "Even if you divorce my sister, she won't be safe."

Finn agreed. "Until I leave or die."

Reed shook his head, folded the paper, and tucked it into his coat pocket. "Even then, I doubt it. It seems merely her *knowing* you is the issue, not being married to you. The absence of your person will not erase the fact she knows you survived. I imagine whoever is responsible for threatening you, and her, will have no compunction about getting rid of Rose even after you leave. She is the proverbial loose end."

Finn's pulse seemed to race as he took in Reed's conclusion.

"What do I do? Stay and she is in danger. Leave and she is in danger."

Reed crossed his arms over his chest. "You could leave and save yourself, and let me worry about my sister."

"No." Finn would not explain why or try to make this man understand that despite past appearances, he was not the kind to abandon a woman. "She is *my* wife."

"For now," Reed muttered. "I admire you for not running from this mess. However, your question remains valid: What are we to do?"

Snatching up his satchel, the divorce papers still inside, Reed headed for the door, only glancing back when his hand was on the doorknob and still Finn hadn't moved.

"Well, man, don't just stand there. Are you coming?"

Finn felt adrift, clinging to the wooden board from his own doomed ship, helpless and with no control over his destiny. The nausea that had plagued him returned with a vengeance, and all he could do was breathe deeply and try to ignore the black seed of despair the note had planted inside him.

Was this really happening?

"Where?" His voice sounded like a jack plane running over thick timber—rough and raw.

"First thing's first," Reed said. "I have friends in the city's police force. We'll take your troubles there. I want to hear everything about this from the beginning, but you might as well say your peace to the constabulary at the same time. Agreed?"

Finn thought about the ramifications. Going it alone had been futile, and he didn't think Rose's position could get any more precarious than it already was. He grabbed for his coat.

"Agreed."

CHAPTER NINETEEN

"What were you thinking?" her brother demanded the minute Rose walked into her own front hall from an exciting cooking class on slow-simmered soups.

Considering all the things swirling in her life at that moment, she kept her mouth closed. Any one of a number of her thoughts could prove damning.

"Into Father's study. Now," Reed said and turned on his heel.

She nearly stuck her tongue out at the back of his head, but she was too old for such behavior, no matter how satisfying.

"Close the door, please," he said as soon as she entered a step behind him.

Such dramatics, she thought, while shutting it firmly.

"Yes, dear brother. To what do I owe the pleasure?"

"Don't you 'dear brother' me. Are you trying to get yourself killed? And what about my wife? How dare you bring Charlotte into this!"

Stuff and bother! He knew.

"You've spoken to Finn," she surmised.

"Indeed I have," Reed intoned. "This is not the simple matter of my taking some papers over for the man to sign, is it?"

Rose looked at her shoes. Such a lovely shade of turquoise, peeking out from under her hem.

"Well?" he asked.

"You seem to know everything. What do you want me to say?" Then she looked up at him as it dawned on her he'd actually met her husband. *At last.*

Despite her brother's expression of abject displeasure, Rose couldn't help asking him the question she'd longed to four years ago.

"What did you think of him? Did you like him?"

Reed stared at her as if she'd truly lost her mind. What's more, he stayed mulishly silent.

Stepping forward, she took her brother's hand.

"Doesn't he speak well with a lovely cadence? And he's clever, didn't you think so? Were you taller than him, or he, you? I can't tell. Did you walk together? Did you notice his limp? He didn't have that before he went away, and I still haven't asked him—"

"Silence," Reed ordered.

She pressed her lips together to stop herself speaking, chewing her lower lip while she waited.

With an expression of exasperation, her brother wrenched his hand free.

"Stop being a gadfly. We are not here to discuss the merits of Mr. Bennet."

"Oh, but we could be," she persisted. "After all, I married him. Can I not be a little curious as to your opinion of him?"

He rested his backside against the desk, his long legs stretched out in front of him, and crossed his arms.

"Well?" she persisted, suddenly dying to know something of Reed's opinion.

"All right!" he snapped. After a few moments, he said, "Bennet seems to be a forthright individual. Quite surprising, considering his treatment of you."

Rose waited. And waited. Reed stared her down.

"Is that all? I asked you—"

Her brother raised his hand to halt her. "I neither liked him nor disliked him. I was, however, angry he has put you in danger. He speaks as any normal human does, I suppose, except with a slight accent, mid-Maine, I'd warrant. I believe we were of a similar height although we did not stand back-to-back and examine our reflections and postures in the mirror."

Rose giggled at the notion.

"I noticed his limp, yes, when we walked to the police station."

"Oh," she sobered immediately.

"I asked him to relay his entire tale to a detective, which he did." Reed rolled his eyes. "In answer to the question I previously skipped, yes, I do believe he is clever. Yet I cannot say I admire him. He has compounded one error with another."

Rose wrinkled up her nose in dismay, the pit of her stomach feeling knotted.

"I am sorry you do not admire him. What errors do you mean?"

"The ones you already know. Marrying you secretly, pretending to be dead for years, and then coming back bringing danger with him, and, of course, meeting you privately."

Feeling her cheeks grow warm, she was about to say they were never truly alone when she realized that was not the case. However, he *was* her husband so it wasn't a terrible offense.

"The potential danger is not Finn's fault," she protested. "You know the whole story now. What will the police do next?"

"That is not your concern. Moreover, no one knows the whole story yet. Do they? This is an ongoing matter, and more than ever, you need to stay clear of Bennet."

"But—" she started.

"You have to," Reed insisted. "I was with him when a threat was made both to him and to you."

She surged forward and grabbed Reed's hand again.

"What threat? What was it?"

"He has been told to leave the area and talk to no one or *your* life will be imperiled."

Her thoughts were whirling. *Would Finn disappear again in order to protect her?*

"With the police on hand, there is less danger, don't you think?" she asked.

Reed sighed. "Perhaps whoever is threatening him will act even more quickly."

How cavalier of her brother!

"How was this threat made? Did you see the person?"

Reed shook his head. "A brick through Bennet's window with a note attached. Crude but effective."

"I see." She would have been terribly frightened by such an occurrence if she'd been there when it happened. "No one was hurt though?"

"No," he said, his voice calmly quiet. "Not yet."

She couldn't suppress a shudder.

Reed felt it through their joined hands and pulled her to him, resting his chin on the top of her head.

"I am trying to help fix this mess." He patted her back.

"I know." Rose pressed her check against him. Reed could mend any issue. She'd come to believe that, ever since their father had passed.

"You know Mama intends to marry Mr. Nickerson."

She felt her brother relax and knew he was smiling.

"I know."

Not for the first time, Rose pictured her mother living elsewhere.

"It's an interesting development."

"A welcome one, I think," Reed said. "Do you agree?"

She pulled away from him. "I am extremely relieved she has found someone to keep her company. Yet how unexpected. I thought at one time someone mentioned him being interested in Elise."

"What? That's absurd." Reed shook his head. "Nickerson could be her father. He was around the house because of his interest in Mother, not Elise."

"That does make more sense. It also means Mama and Mr. Nickerson have been hiding this for quite a long time." *Longer than her own hidden marriage to Finn, in fact.*

She blinked up at her brother, wondering if that helped in her defense.

"That doesn't excuse *your* behavior, not one whit." Reed knew exactly what she was thinking. "The circumstances are very different. Our mother will be wed with the full knowledge and blessing of those who love her. In any case, you want out of your marriage so why try to justify what happened in the past? How could it matter what I think of Bennet?"

Out of her marriage. Yes, of course, because she loved William. Then again, could she honestly say she loved *only* William? Certainly, some ghost of a feeling existed for Finn, some connection between them that wouldn't let her stop thinking of him, some spark that sizzled when he was close.

It was wrong! She belonged to William now.

Reed groaned. "If I had a penny for each of your wayward thoughts! Why, I can practically see them in your eyes." He sighed. "Luckily, I don't know what's really going on in that adorable head of yours, or I would be the one who needed to be locked up. Simply stay put, stay safe, and I'll let you know when you are divorced and Bennet has departed our fair city."

With a pat on her shoulder, he left.

It might as well have been a pat on her head as if she were a child.

Or a pet.

Rose fumed. Then a dreadful thought entered her brain. Since even the Boston constabulary also knew about Finn Bennet, she had no choice but to tell William.

"I've caught you at last," Finn said to Liam as his friend alighted from a carriage and started up his own front walk.

Liam froze, then came forward with a smile. "What do you mean?"

"I've dropped by a couple times only to be told you're out."

"I do still work at the shipyard. You know that. Moreover, I have social engagements as well."

Finn couldn't shake the feeling Liam had been dodging him. The only reason he was seeing him now was because Liam had been dropped off in front by someone else rather than driving around back in his own carriage and disappearing inside through the back entrance. "I have left a message or two."

"Really?" Liam's brows drew together. "I didn't see them. I'll have to ask my servants. Someone will be fired."

"That's not necessary," Finn said. "I'm talking to you now."

"Shall we go in? I could use a drink."

Finn considered. "No. I can be brief."

"Is something wrong?" Liam faced him squarely.

"You lied to me. About your fortune."

Liam continued to look him in the eyes, his nostrils flared, and then he blinked.

"Yes, I did."

"Why?" Finn shot back.

"Because if you knew how I got the money, you would think poorly of me."

"Why would that matter?" Finn watched Liam carefully.

He shrugged. "I don't want you to blame me for the *Garrard*. We both had friends on board who died. I didn't want that to happen. I hope you believe me."

"You stayed behind. Why?"

Liam looked at the paving stones under their feet. "You know as well as I do that ship wasn't built right."

"It was built *exactly* as designed," Finn shot back. "The men built it right. It wasn't their fault. It was designed wrong."

"Agreed. I knew it, maybe more than most. The wooden version I made—*Christ!* It wouldn't stay afloat in a barrel of water if you dropped in a pebble beside it."

"So you stayed behind," Finn spat out the words with disdain.

"I didn't want to die," Liam stated plainly. "I'm a coward. Is that what you want to hear?"

"Maybe you're a murderer," Finn said softly.

"No!"

Finn took a step closer. "You did know better than most, didn't you? Enough to take out an insurance policy on the *Garrard*."

Liam looked around. "Shall we go inside?" he asked again.

"I'm done here. You go into your comfortable home bought and paid for with blood money."

Liam paled, and Finn added, "As for me, I wouldn't be able to spend another moment under your roof."

Finn started to turn away, then he asked, "With all that money, why do you still work at the yard?"

The color leached from Liam's face. "It's my job."

"Strange answer for a wealthy man. Here's another question, are you behind the threats telling me to keep my mouth closed?"

"No," he said, but Finn could tell by his demeanor Liam was hiding something.

Whoever threw the brick knew about Rose. Liam hadn't known about her before Finn's last visit, although he could have found out somehow. After all, Finn himself had told Liam where he was staying, then all he had to do was watch the restaurant.

"Just so you know, I've been to the police department."

Impossibly, Liam seemed to go a shade whiter. Finn hoped his statement would cause Liam, or someone else involved, to leave Rose alone at the very least.

"That makes no difference to me," Liam said. Turning on his heel, he rushed up his own front steps and disappeared quickly inside.

Franklin had set things up perfectly. Or so it seemed. Unfortunately, Claire was not cooperating, and Rose was beside herself with frustration. All her friend had to do was show up at the Boston Theatre, not far from the Bijou where Rose had met with him. Franklin had chosen the right venue. It would hold three thousand of Boston's finest patrons, and the theatre itself was rather magical, declared more than once to be "the finest theatre in the world" by journalists and theatre enthusiasts.

Rose was certain she could fit her entire home into half the lobby, which was all graceful arches and colonnades. However, the interior mattered not a whit, nor the people inside the theatre, not if Claire wasn't one of them.

Franklin's grandfather had helped with the building of this second Boston Theatre and thus, the owner had seen his way clear to grant Franklin a favor of epic proportion—front row seats for a sold-out show of Edward Bulwer-Lytton's *The Lady of Lyons*. More importantly, an advert in the evening's playbill would be the crowning glory of his plan.

If only Claire was not sitting in her room moping.

If only she would put on the gorgeous dress Rose had helped her choose for the splendid night.

If only time was not trickling away at an alarming rate.

"I simply do not feel like going out tonight," Claire stated. "Particularly to such a public place, and more importantly, as a horse's third leg. Unnecessary and awkward for you and William."

Rose thought she had already overcome all these objections.

"This is a special occasion. These tickets were procured as a gift, and it would be an insult to the giver if we were not to go. You and I are the ones going, and William has kindly agreed to escort us. If anyone is the third leg, it is him."

Claire merely flounced across the room, doing it better than anyone had every flounced before, and Rose was ready to throttle her.

"Please, dear friend, let me help you into the gown. We don't want to miss the opening. I believe it's a ventriloquist. Also, besides the play, there will be lovely music."

"And everyone who was at the dragon's party will no doubt be there as well."

Rose ignored the remark and began to undress Claire and then dress her.

"If one of those wretched creatures so much as looks sideways at me," Claire continued, "I will bop them on the top of the head with my reticule. My most heavily beaded one, at that."

"Yes, of course," Rose murmured, making Claire stand still as she eased the gown up over her undergarments, turned her friend, and proceeded to button her up the back.

"You look gorgeous."

Thank God Claire had her hair done earlier, or they would have been late for sure. It was set in a most becoming style, up at the front, with glorious golden follow-me-boys curling down her back.

"What matter if I look gorgeous?" Claire protested.

Rose thought a moment. "Because if any of those twits from the party are there, they must see you are the most divinely perfect young lady in Boston and know that soon, you will be snagged by the best young man."

She was careful not to mention Franklin's name as that resulted in tears despite Claire's attempt to keep up a state of indifference only mitigated by an occasional outburst of fury. Both conditions were preferable to despair and tears. Moreover, Rose definitely did not want Claire to have red eyes on this momentous evening.

A tap at the door drew their attention.

"Come," Claire said.

"Mr. Woodsom is here," Claire's maid informed them and disappeared.

"How kind of him to pick us up at my house." Claire seemed to rally. She checked herself in the mirror, added sparkling diamond ear bobs, and grabbed her beaded evening satin cape with fur trim. And the aforementioned beaded reticule.

Rose watched her. "William is, indeed, very kind," she agreed, trying to ignore the sinking feeling in the pit of her stomach. *How kind would he be when he learned of Finn?*

"Well," Claire said, "you're the one who wanted to get moving. Don't stand there like a stone statue."

CHAPTER TWENTY

Twenty minutes later, William helped them down from his carriage and escorted the two friends inside the large theatre. They barely had to wait to check their capes and coat, and then they made their way to the bar. People were still drinking rum snowballs and champagne as the house lights started to flicker, calling everyone to take their seats.

As expected, the usher led the three of them down the left aisle to the front row where four seats were empty.

"I actually prefer the first row of the balcony," Claire said, turning briefly to look at the mass of humanity at their backs. "You can watch everyone and still have a good view of the stage, although this is rather exciting, too. I do hope none of the actors sneeze or are particularly slobbery speakers."

She giggled, and Rose knew the frothy snowball they'd shared had gone straight to Claire's head.

Her best friend always was a light imbiber. Luckily, the alcohol-induced contentment meant Claire had missed the loud whispers that had occurred, as well as the sudden silences when they'd walked down the aisle. Boston's finest were talking and, no doubt, passing judgment on Miss Appleton.

However, Claire didn't miss the fact there was an empty seat on the other side of her. In fact, she moaned a little loudly.

"It's terrible. It looks as if I had an arranged date who has changed his mind. No one will look at that seat and not think of Franklin Brewster. Please," she beseeched, grabbing Rose's hand, "let's all move over one, and let the empty seat be on the other side of William."

"As you wish," Rose said, glancing back at William. Soon, it wouldn't matter and they could rearrange themselves again if all went according to plan and Franklin joined them in the front row. She had one last thing to do.

"Quick, your playbill." She opened hers and nudged Claire with her elbow to do the same. "Let's take a look. I always like to see what we're in for."

"Go ahead," Claire said, "tell me if there's anything interesting," and she tucked hers away under her right leg, rearranging her gown on top of it.

Rose rolled her eyes. Claire was supposed to see the "ad" from Franklin nestled amongst those for soft hats and stiff corsets, bottled beer, blanket wraps, and chewing gum, as well as the ever-present treatment for sore feet and corns!

Rose found it almost immediately. In boldfaced type, with a sketch of a church steeple and two hands clasped, was the message:

Claire Lilith Appleton, loveliest, sweetest, and purest woman in all of New England if not the world, I ask the honor of your hand in marriage so everyone will know the high esteem in which I hold you. That you could help a friend in need at risk to your own reputation, that you could love a man such as me, who does not deserve you, that you could entertain my proposal of marriage, it is all that I can ask.
Franklin M. Brewster

Rose's mouth opened. The fake advertisement was a tad long and must have cost a pretty penny. Did Franklin really have to mention a "friend in need"? Everyone knew she and Claire were the best of friends! It was almost as if he had put "Rose Malloy" in large type.

On the other hand, it would go a long way to softening Claire's resentment and pain.

"Take a look at this page," Rose began, and the house lights went down. "Sweet mother," she muttered.

"What *was* it?" Claire whispered.

Rose wasn't sure what was going to happen next. Franklin hadn't told her. Suddenly, a bright light shone directly in her face, blinding her.

She couldn't see what was going on, yet everyone started to clap.

They should never have switched seats. Obviously, a stagehand was supposed to turn the light onto Claire.

What was everyone clapping for?

Then she heard Claire exclaim in surprise.

"What is going on?" Rose asked. If only the stupid light wasn't in her eyes.

Claire said nothing, sitting still and silent.

"It's Franklin," William said, his tone full of mirth. "He's come out on stage with a bloody armload of roses. It looks like a hundred."

"This woman you see bathed in heavenly light," Franklin started and then paused. "*Um*, actually, the woman beside her," he added, and blissfully, the spotlight moved off of Rose's face and onto Claire's.

Still, Rose blinked and tried to make out anything besides the ghostly white spots before her eyes.

Claire must have looked equally uncomfortable for in a loud voice, Franklin suggested, "Perhaps you could simply turn the house lights back up."

In a moment, they flickered and then came up full strength. Everyone clapped again.

"This woman seated before you is my own true love." Standing at the edge of the stage, he spoke directly to Claire. "You have read the playbill, my dearest?"

Staying silent, no doubt in a state of shock, Claire shook her head, and Rose could make out a panicked expression on her friend's face. Panicked and bewildered!

Oh dear!

Rose thrust the program into Claire's hands, and she started to page through it.

"Never mind, I'll read it," Franklin announced, and he did so.

Rose thought the words sounded far better coming from Franklin than they had in print.

When he finished speaking, the orchestra in the pit began to play softly, and the pure strains of Paines' "A Romance of Springtime" floated through the theatre.

Franklin, quite dashingly, jumped off the stage to land at Claire's feet. He took her hand and pulled her to stand in front of him.

Then, still in his loud stage voice so all could hear, he said, "Miss Appleton, will you marry me?"

Rose had a moment's fear Claire was going to deny him, but her expression was neither one of discontentment nor rejection. Rather, it was merely discomfort at the closeness and loudness of her beloved's voice, blaring at her. Nevertheless, her face broke out into a beaming smile, so becoming Rose was once more overtaken by her friend's beauty.

Then quite softly so only Rose, Franklin, and maybe William could hear, Claire said, "Yes."

Nothing happened. Rose started to clap, but the rest of the audience remained silent and absolutely still because no one had heard Claire's reply.

"She said yes," Franklin announced to the audience. "By God, she said yes!"

The theatre erupted in thunderous applause at last, whereupon he thrust the massive bouquet into Claire's arms and then seemed at a loss. His public performance was over, and apparently, he hadn't thought what to do next.

Rose and William quickly moved over so the two newly engaged could take their seats, and the house lights went down again.

"Well done," William muttered to Rose, who suddenly wanted to laugh as her spirit felt lighter than it had in weeks. Franklin's proposal had not been without its issues, but it had worked. The evening was a resounding success.

Claire set the flowers and the playbill at her feet, keeping one gorgeous red rose on her lap, and let Franklin hold her hand as the orchestra stopped playing and the first act began.

Well done, indeed!

At the intermission, William and Rose left Claire and Franklin alone to digest that they were now quite publicly a couple.

"Do you want some refreshment?" William asked.

So happy for her friend, Rose felt as if she'd drunk twelve glasses of champagne already. However, there was always room for one more.

"Burnt champagne, please," she asked him, "and if they have one—"

"I know," he interrupted. "A strawberry in the glass. Where will I find you?"

"I'll go to the powder room, and most likely be back here before you." She glanced around her. "Second arch on the right."

"Second arch," William repeated, offering her a smile before he wandered off.

Rose watched him, unable to keep from smiling, too. *Sweet man!*

No doubt there would be a line in the ladies' room, but probably not as long as the one in which William would be waiting for beverages. In a few minutes, she had checked her hair in a massive gilded mirror, adjusted her corset, smoothed her stockings, and pinched her cheeks. As she exited the powder room, three things happened in quick succession.

A man she'd never seen before appeared at her elbow.

"Mrs. Bennet?"

His words were enough to stop her feet while her heart instantly began to race. Then the second thing happened: another man took her arm from the other side and started to steer her toward the theatre's exit.

"Scream and I'll shoot you," the first man said, and he seemed to be pressing a pointed object into her side. Even through her gown, corset, and shift, she could feel the hard metal.

A pistol? How utterly absurd! In the middle of a crowded lobby! Absurd or not, Rose could barely breathe for fear at what was happening.

In a moment, they were on the staircase above the main entrance when the third astonishing thing happened: Finn appeared before them.

"Gentleman, make a scene here in front of all of Boston and you'll hang for sure." He looked them up and down. "I wouldn't worry too much. A standard drop won't break your neck, that's true, but hopefully it will knock you out before you start the unpleasant business of suffocating at the end of a rope."

Immediately, Rose felt the man on her right release her arm, and in another instant, they disappeared into the crowd.

"Are you hurt?" Finn asked.

"Dear Lord. Dear Lord." It was all she could say, over and over. She couldn't even breathe properly, only able to take shallow quick breaths. Terror mixed with relief, and the next moment, she was in Finn's arms, leaning her face on his chest, feeling his strength envelop her.

"I'm so sorry," he murmured against her hair, and she nodded. It wasn't his fault.

"They know who I am," Rose told him.

"What?"

She lifted her head and stopped speaking into his jacket, which she noted was a well-made evening suit. "I said that they know who I am. They called me *Mrs. Bennet.*"

His jaw clenched, and she rested her head against him once again because it felt right and the familiar scent of him calmed her galloping heartbeat. She finally took as deep a breath as her clothing would allow, and some of the terror dissipated.

"What are you doing here?" she asked, looking up at him.

"Believe it or not, I like the theatre. Did you think I was merely an uncultured barrelman?"

She knew Finn was jesting in order to distract her from reliving her fright.

"I never thought you were uncultured," she returned, "but perhaps a tad salty."

He offered her a wry grin. "Of course, my seat in the balcony isn't quite as good as yours, in the front row for all to see, but I had a good view."

Rose felt her face grow warm. "That blasted light."

His eyes crinkled. "You looked like a Greek goddess. Your hair shone like polished onyx, and the light turned your gown into fiery copper. In a word, gorgeous."

She sighed. "It was supposed to be about Claire." If he was so interested in how she looked, then why . . . ? "Why didn't you show up at the church?"

Again, his jaw tightened, then he spoke, "I decided it was best not to go after you."

"Whyever not?"

"I don't want to frighten you anymore than has already happened this evening," he said. "When I came out of the bookstore, I did see a man trailing after you. One of these goons, I think. He watched you enter the church. I decided not to follow you inside. Instead, I waited to see what he would do. When he took off at a run to the nearest streetcar, I did, too."

"Then he wasn't following me?" Rose pointed out.

"I'm certain he was going to tell someone he'd seen us together. I did the only thing I could think of, I jumped on the back of the same car as him, and it took us right to the shipyard."

"Kelly's?"

"No, the Navy yard at Charlestown. I lost him in the mass of workers."

Rose couldn't suppress the shiver that trickled down her spine causing her to shudder.

In response, Finn stroked her back, leaving a trail of warmth from her shoulders nearly to her derrière.

"Truthfully," he added, "I didn't just happen to the theatre tonight. I've been keeping my eye on you since we last met at the bookstore."

The sound of glass shattering interrupted Finn, and then William's furious voice spilled over them both.

"Step away from my fiancée."

CHAPTER TWENTY-ONE

William had waited and grown concerned. After procuring their drinks, he'd returned to their meeting point by the second arch. Five minutes later, and with his glass half empty, he'd headed toward the ladies' room and lingered uncomfortably a minute outside the entry. Still, no Rose, although plenty of other females gave him curious or disapproving looks.

Finally, he'd started to wander around the lobby. Then, at last, he'd spied her glorious copper-colored silk gown. However, as he closed in on her, his eyes seemed to be lying, for *his* Rose was in the arms of another man, being held extremely close.

Rage, white hot and blinding, rushed through him. As he reached the pair, who didn't apparently notice his approach, William dashed the glasses down onto the floor behind his betrothed. It was the most civilized thing he could do in light of the explosive anger boiling in his heart and threatening to result in a brawl, right there in the lobby of The Boston Theatre.

"Step away from my fiancée."

As the pair broke apart, William directed his focus on the only person who mattered.

"This is the second time I've found you with this man."

Rose had appeared quite contented resting against the chest of Phineas Bennet. Moreover, her old "friend" seemed quite content holding her.

As she moved toward William, her lovely face pale with guilt, her dark eyes huge, his heart sank to his shoes. There was something terrible and destructive happening, and his world was about to change, unless . . .

"Rose, say something." He heard the pleading tone in his own voice.

Yet it was Bennet who spoke. "She was threatened and nearly abducted. I helped her. She's a bit unsettled."

William spared the man barely a glance as he watched Rose's face for some small indication everything was going to be fine.

"Who threatened you?" His perfectly normal question felt anything but. "*Why* would someone threaten you?"

Finally, Rose found her voice only to lose it a moment later. "Because I—" She stopped abruptly and looked to the man behind her for answers.

That alone cut William like a blade.

"This has something to do with you," he said to Bennet. "She has been put in some danger because she knows you. Have I surmised correctly?"

Bennet looked at Rose and then back at him before nodding.

The electric house lights went up and down. The audience, both those who were and those who weren't fascinated by the tableau being played out in the lobby, returned to their seats to watch the second half of *The Lady of Lyons*.

The three of them remained where they stood.

"Who is this man?" William demanded.

Rose's cobalt eyes filled with tears, which terrified him further.

"Not here," she whispered at last. "Please. Just take me home."

For a moment, William felt a surge of surprise. He could almost believe it was Bennet she was talking to. And that he, her fiancé, was merely the interloper.

Without another word, she walked stiffly toward the coat-check counter and waited for him to catch up with the ticket stubs. William tipped the young lady and eased Rose into her velvet evening cape, barely touching her because suddenly, she seemed like the most fragile, brittle creature in the world. Worse, she stared at the floor while he did so.

"May I take your arm?" he asked.

She glanced at him, tears glistening on her cheeks, and nodded. In silence, they left the theatre.

It was the longest ride of his life, with Rose's occasional sniffling being the only sound other than the horse's hooves and his own heartbeat, which seemed to be pulsing loudly in his ears. His misery was made worse when they reached her street without having spoken.

Then, she broke her silence. "No," she said almost angrily. "We should go to your house."

Without a second thought, William drove them to his home on Phillips Street where, for the most part, he lived alone with two servants and occasionally hosted his parents when they were in the States. Neither of them mentioned the utter impropriety. It simply wasn't done, and yet, they did it.

Finn watched them leave and then strolled out into the nighttime air, not sure what to do about the rush of anger that left his heart pounding. Anger at himself mostly. Frustration at how powerless he felt, a feeling that was foreign and entirely distasteful.

Catching sight of himself in a store display window, he suddenly realized the foolishness of having spent hard-earned money on an evening suit he would doubtless never use again. He could have hung about the lobby and saved Rose from those idiots while dressed in his usual clothes. Yet he'd felt the need to live up to her expectations of what a man at the theatre looked like, on the mere chance they might meet.

He certainly hadn't planned on holding her in his arms.

It hadn't mattered one bit. She had left with Woodsom.

Rose waited silently while William turned on the lamps in the dark parlor. The most modern of incandescent lighting suddenly allowed them to see each other clearly. They stood staring at one another.

"A drink?" he offered, then frowned, perhaps recalling what had recently happened to their last drinks and why.

"No." Her voice was so faint, she tried clearing her throat. Still, she could only look at him. Whatever she said next, nothing would be the same between them.

"Are you ready to talk to me?" William seemed a little hesitant, as if he dreaded her answer.

Rose had spent so much time thinking about this moment, so why on earth didn't she have the right words to tell him? Gentle words. Apologetic words.

She continued to gaze at him for another long moment. His face was pale, the dark smudges a sharp contrast. If only she could ease his pain.

"I am truly sorry," she began, for she truly was. Beyond anything, she wanted William to be the laughing, jovial man he'd been when she'd met him.

"Is this the important thing you nearly told me the day we had Italian ice?"

Rose bowed her head, amazed he remembered. After their walk, they'd kissed in her back garden and discussed wedding plans with her mother. If only she'd told him then.

Finally, she nodded.

"And what stopped you?" he asked.

"The ball to my head."

William frowned.

"Finn—Mr. Bennet—threw it. He wanted to stop me from telling you he'd returned."

"Why?" His voice was raspy, with a hint of anger in his tone.

"I'm sorry," she repeated. "He is in some trouble, and he thought that I—or even you—could be in danger if anyone found out we knew he was in Boston."

"Why isn't this making sense to me?" William asked. "This has something to do with the incident that made you very sad in the past. We almost talked about it once."

Rose took a breath, nodded, and still she could barely get anything past her suddenly numb lips. But she did.

"Phineas Bennet. He is my husband."

William took a step backward as though he'd been struck. He shook his head as if trying to ward off the pain, and a dark lock of hair fell over his forehead, making him look boyish, making her wish she could take back her words.

"Rose?" He stared at her, the hurt that was etched on his face cut straight through her. It resembled precisely the anguish she'd felt when she lost Finn to the cold ocean. Except William had not lost her. She was still his, if he wanted her.

For long moments, William searched her face before dropping his gaze to the thick rug under his feet. Yet not before she saw how his eyes were glistening. His pain, and knowing she'd caused it, struck her with wrenching agony.

"No," he whispered. Then again louder, "No!" He raised his chin, looking right at her again, a mask of anger in place of his confusion and sadness. "What is the meaning of this?"

"I'm sorry. I was going to tell you—"

"That you were *married*? When? *After* our wedding? On our honeymoon, perhaps?"

She'd never heard such a tone from William. At least, not directed at her.

Rose crossed her arms over her chest, suddenly chilled.

"I thought him dead, long dead. Even my family didn't know about him. No one did. So, in the beginning, there seemed no point in saying anything."

"In the beginning, perhaps, but after I asked you to become my wife. Surely then!" William paced the length of the room. "No *before* that. How about when you let me fall in love with you?"

"I . . . I cannot defend myself. I didn't want people to know what I had done."

"People?" he repeated, his voice raised. "I am not 'people'!"

"I know." Rose didn't know what else to say. She had used him terribly.

William paced away from her, seemingly trapped by the four walls. At the far corner, he turned.

"I wanted to give you everything," he said loudly, nearly shouting. "Experience everything with you."

"As did I. As I still do." It was true. She loved William Woodsom, and right then, in his anger, he was magnificent. His passion for life was something that had helped her to come back from the frozen world she'd slipped into after Finn.

"Is that so?" He stalked closer again.

She nodded, fascinated by this uncivilized creature who had materialized before her.

He practically roared as he swept a porcelain vase off the nearest table. She jumped as shards scattered across the floor.

"And yet you have already experienced some things, and let me believe otherwise."

Ah! His pride was rearing its head at thinking he had been duped out of being her first lover if not her first love. She understood enough to know that was important to a man, especially one of William's standing.

"No," Rose said, glad she could at least give him this. "I agreed to marry you with my virtue entirely intact. A virgin wife the first time, a virgin bride for you."

This made him pause, stare hard at her, but then he practically spat out his next words.

"Then Bennet is an idiot."

She started to shake her head when he closed the gap between them, pulling her into his arms with none of his usual playfulness. Within seconds, while he gripped her upper arms, he crushed her mouth beneath his.

Rose knew he meant to punish her, and she allowed him to be hard and fierce, and then, she wound her arms around his neck and held him close. Her body melted against his as it always did, and he deepened the kiss, slanting his mouth, teasing hers open.

His tongue swept hers, tasting her, and she relished him. His hands released their tight hold on her arms and circled behind her, languidly drifting up and down the silken bodice of her gown.

At last, she felt the tension in him draining away.

When long moments had passed, William gently nipped her lower lip, sucking it briefly into his mouth before he rested his forehead on hers. Together, they breathed in unison.

"Thank you," he said.

Flinching at his gratitude, Rose leaned back to look at him. "What could you possibly be thanking me for?"

"Thinking you'd had marital relations with Finn made it worse. Your telling me you are still an innocent makes me feel less of a fool."

She reached up and stroked his handsome face. "You are no fool, Mr. Woodsom. If I could go back and do things differently with you, I would. I would tell you I was a widow, and then, after fainting with shock at our engagement party, I would tell you I thought I'd seen my dead husband's ghost."

"That would have been prudent." Against all odds, William smiled down at her, albeit a sardonic and sad one. "You have never been prudent, and I knew that." He captured her hand on his cheek. "I've never before kissed a married woman."

Rose tried to smile back and failed. "Yes, you have. Quite a few times actually."

His mouth twisted in a wry grimace. "I suppose you are right."

He released her, and as he did so, the chill and the fear and the sorrow returned. How much she depended upon him to shelter her. He had healed her heartache, and she'd grown accustomed to feeling whole within the circle of their love.

"Would you care for that drink now? I know you don't want whiskey, but perhaps brandy. It seems you have much to tell me, and I, for one, could use a drink."

Normally, Rose would say no to such a hard drink, preferring fruity wine or champagne or even absinthe. At that moment, however, a mature person's brandy sounded perfect, and she told him so.

"While I'm sure I've awakened the servants, I think I can trust them to leave us alone. Shall we venture into the kitchen for a snack?"

He asked her this as he dispensed them each a generous pour of amber liquid from his sideboard and handed her a crystal glass.

They tapped glasses, and Rose took a sip, letting the brandy trail warmth down her throat. She coughed.

"If you like," she agreed. "I would like to see what kind of 'snack' you know how to make."

He smiled, genuinely this time, and she wanted to cry again. How lovely was William's smile. How many more times would she see it?

They wandered down the hallway to the kitchen, where he set down his glass upon the center chopping block. Rose watched him rummage through the cupboards, go in and out of the large pantry, and open each of the compartments of his newfangled refrigerator as if he'd never looked inside before.

Eventually, he had an assortment of pickled foods, cheeses, bread, and even jam and cookies, all on a large plate. They sat there at the kitchen worktable and ate while sipping their drinks.

It was a strange and enchanting meal, and Rose savored every moment of it. This was how it would be with her and William, relaxed, a little whimsical, easy. If they were still to marry.

She could not let this, nor him, go. William was all she would ever need.

"How long were you together?" he asked suddenly.

"Five months," Rose said quietly. "But married for barely a month."

"We've been together longer than that," he pointed out.

She nodded.

"An yet you didn't engage in the act of man and wife?"

She felt her cheeks grow hot. "I couldn't be a real wife to him," she admitted, squeezing her hands together in front of her. "My family knew nothing of him, and I feared the very thing that happened. That he would disappear, except I would be left . . ."

Rose couldn't say it, even to William.

"You'd be left *enceinte*?"

"Precisely. I would have broken my mother's heart and shamed my siblings."

He sliced some cheese, offered her a piece, then popped a slice into his mouth, following it with a cookie.

"Amazing no one ever heard of this marriage," he remarked.

"Because we kept it secret. Actually, *I* did. I didn't want my family to know I'd married in haste in case they disapproved."

William pondered that a moment yet seemed to understand.

"You are right. They most likely would have." He paused. "And still will."

"No." She shook her head. With so much time to ponder Finn and how she'd treated him, she could not agree. "I was wrong to do what I did. I should have gone to them first, *before* I married." She twisted her fingers together. "I made Finn feel—"

"Dammit!" William swore softly. "Honestly, Rose, I don't care what Bennet feels. Then or now. He was a blackguard to marry you without your family's permission, especially as young as you were."

She pressed her lips tightly together. He had a right to be angry, and she would not waste her breath defending Finn. Instead, she spread butter and some thick strawberry jam on a slice of bread and munched on the sweet treat. It was exactly what she needed to steady her nerves.

They continued to eat in strained silence that eventually, almost miraculously became comfortable again. Hours later, they'd ended up back in the parlor. Having swept up the vase into a pile by the fireplace, the sat side by side on the sofa, nearly emptying the decanter of brandy.

"I'd best be getting you home," he said.

"I wonder what time it is." Rose considered whether her mother or her brother might have called the police already.

"We left the theatre early," William reminded her. "It's only," he glanced at the clock on the mantle. "*The devil!* It's nearly 2 a.m."

Still, neither of them jumped up. He took her right hand in his and ran a thumb over the ring that had sealed their engagement.

"What happens next?" he asked.

She sighed, having dreaded that question.

"Reed is seeing to my divorce."

"You said your family didn't know."

"I needed my brother's help after Finn returned."

"Finn," William repeated the name softly, as if learning a new word.

Rose wish she could stop herself from saying it. It was like a curse word between her and William. She'd already told him about the ship's sinking and where Finn had been and how he'd returned to save her from bigamy.

Or that was the reason she gave, not knowing for sure why her husband had, at last, come home.

She'd also told William about the oddity of Liam staying behind and making a fortune.

"Perhaps this man is behind the threats," he'd surmised, "and sent those thugs to the theatre."

As they got into William's carriage, both a little tipsy and exhausted, Rose couldn't believe how the evening had turned out. She felt closer than ever to this wonderful man.

Resting her head on his shoulder, she closed her eyes for the short drive. In a few minutes, they arrived at Mount Vernon Street, dark and quiet. She loved the sight of her house as it came into view, with a single lamp left on at the front.

"I love this house," she said, recoiling slightly at the loudness of her voice in the darkness.

William chuckled. "You, Miss Rose, are a little inebriated."

"Then we had best get you home," she declared.

"That makes no sense, but I agree. We both need some sleep. Tomorrow, or rather, later today for it's already tomorrow, things will look different."

Rose noted with dismay he hadn't said things would look better. *What was he thinking?*

He walked with her up the front steps and stood with her while she opened the door.

His hand on her chin, he lifted her face and looked into her eyes.

Her breath caught. *Was William going to tell her they were finished?*

CHAPTER TWENTY-TWO

William's next words calmed her. "I love you."

"I love you, too," Rose told him without hesitation.

"Then we'll leave it at that for now." He kissed the end of her nose and then seemed to reconsider, capturing her lips with his own for a tender assault.

As she tried to wind her hands around his neck, however, he stopped her and gently sent her inside before closing the door behind her.

Finn slammed the door as he left his room early the next morning, unable to shake the anger that had dogged him since watching Rose leave the theatre with Woodsom. Somehow, he had thought after he had rescued her—*after he had held her in public!*—she would go home with him. It was an irrational, foolish thought.

From the moment they'd spotted each other four years ago, he'd been the unexpected object of Rose's devotion, despite her hiding their association from her family. More than flattering, her attention and affection had been astonishing, incredible.

Finn had basked in the love she'd shone upon him and had returned it a hundred-fold. Even after the years apart, it twisted his gut every time he witnessed her spending her precious attention on Woodsom.

Yes, he could plainly see she loved the man, but could she truly feel for Woodsom as deeply as she had felt for him? Worse, did her new love supplant her old love for him?

It's your own damn fault, he reminded himself. *Your own insecurity cost you everything.*

The thought flitted through his brain as it did every day since returning to Boston. However, it was still sorely difficult, nearly impossible, to believe it was too late.

Reed Malloy had kept the divorce agreement secure in his portfolio that day at the police station, and Finn hadn't brought it up. He had told the detective what he knew and then he'd left.

Apparently, what with two thugs going after Rose, nothing had changed. After all, what could the police do? There were no suspects except for Liam, and he was as dodgy as an eel. They would question him, maybe they had already, but to what aim?

Today, Finn intended to track down Master Builder Gilbert, if the man worked, as Liam had said, at the Navy shipyard in Charlestown. Easy enough to reach by trolley although he wasn't sure if they would let him onto the yard or exactly what he hoped to discover. A full confession of incompetence from Gilbert was highly doubtful, but perhaps the man would at least demonstrate some humility and remorse for the lives lost to a terrible design.

"State your business," a sentry said to Finn when he reached Gate 1 on Water Street.

"I'm here to see Master Builder Gilbert," he'd offered, peering past the man so he could see all the way down First Avenue, which spanned the yard's entire length.

"Is he expecting you?"

Absolutely not. That was one thing Finn was certain of. No one expected a dead man.

"No, and I'm not sure he'll know my name. I used to work for him at a yard in Eastie. May I meet with him?"

The guard sighed. "You a civilian?"

"Yes," Finn told him.

"That's ok. There are plenty working here nowadays, but you'll have to be escorted. Wait here." He disappeared inside the guard hut. When he came out, he had an official-looking ledger. "Can you write?"

Finn bristled. "Of course."

"Don't get hot," the sentry said. "As many as can, can't. Anyway, write your name here," and he handed him a stubby pencil.

After Finn scrawled his name on the line and wrote the date, the first sentry gestured to another guard.

"Take him to the Muster House."

"Muster House?" Finn questioned him.

"Gilbert's clerk said he should be on one of the upper floors with the civil engineers. Mind your step. We've got a lot of work going on around here."

"None too soon," Finn muttered and fell into step beside his escort.

The place was outdated compared to where he'd worked in the United Kingdom. The Charlestown yard had nearly been closed in the last decade, which would have been a shame, he thought. At present, the yard did mainly rigging work for the Navy, producing tons of rope. Yet no naval ships were built there anymore, not from scratch, for the dry dock was too small.

"There's more activity going on than I thought there would be," he said to the silent man beside him, gesturing to the docks on their right.

"Got about sixteen commercial vessels right now, and doing repairs on four for the Navy."

That explained the question from the first sentry. Civilian builders were employed there to keep the place open, working on merchant vessels. They continued down First Avenue until they turned left onto Fifth Street. Up ahead, on the right was a small, three-story circular building with a turret on top.

"The Muster House," said the guard, who left him at the door and promptly turned around and went back the way he had come.

Finn entered and nodded to two men who seemed to be doing something official for the Navy, perusing ocean charts as well as land maps.

"I'm looking for Master Builder Gilbert," he told them.

"All the way up, third floor," said the one closest to him, attaching a piece of string to a map with a pushpin.

Finn climbed the circular stairs in the middle. As he breached the third floor, he saw men at desks positioned by the many windows. He recognized Gilbert at once, sitting at a table with two others, drinking coffee and laughing. It was the laughter that twisted Finn's stomach.

"Mr. Gilbert," he said as he approached his old superior, a man in his late forties with a thick moustache and spectacles.

Gilbert looked up and blanched a sickly pale. Instantly, Finn knew the builder had been warned of his return for he had neither a hint of puzzlement as to who Finn was, nor did the man's eyes bulge in wonder at the resurrection of a dead man.

Either Mr. Kelly or perhaps Liam had spoken to him already.

Finn decided to take a different tack, as if pulling on the sheet ropes in hope of catching a fairer wind.

"I don't know if you remember me, my name is Phineas Bennet. I worked at Kelly's yard years ago. I always paid careful attention to your work," he said, hopefully with pointed meaning, "and I would very much like to work here under your tutelage."

Gilbert wrinkled his brow. No doubt he had been expecting heated accusations of incompetency.

Finn held his breath. Perhaps the man would employ him, thinking by doing so, he could keep Finn quiet. If Gilbert sanctioned him, even letting him work at the yard, maybe the threats would stop and he could breathe more easily over Rose's safety. Finn could continue to seek justice in the meanwhile.

"Yes, I remember you," Gilbert said with a measured tone. "You were a good builder."

Around them, the other men paused in their work, watching silently.

"I'm better now," Finn said. "I have an advanced degree from Glasgow University."

Gilbert's eyebrows rose. "Really? That is impressive."

Finn nodded, hating to deal with this man who'd caused the death of boys as young as 14. Still, he couldn't survive if he couldn't work. If Gilbert went against what Kelly had said and hired Finn, then he'd have a chance at a new beginning.

"We might have some work for you here, but we're not building ships." Gilbert crossed his arms over his narrow chest. "We don't need even a loftsman at the moment. For old time' sake, though, I can put you to work. Do you want sails or rigging?"

Finn swallowed. All that study to make rope or sew canvas!

While he hesitated, Gilbert explained, "Won't be improving this yard until the appropriations act comes through, and then it'll be for tools and water pipes and such. Maybe dock repairs. What we need is a new dry dock and electric lighting. All these damn gas lamps are a hazard!"

Finn nodded. "I'll take whatever work I can get." He had a bit of money saved anyway, and working near Gilbert meant he could continue to pursue some measure of justice for those who'd perished aboard the *Garrard*.

With that, he began his first day in the immense concrete building known as the Ropewalk.

Rose didn't remember going upstairs nor undressing, which apparently she hadn't. When she awoke, it was late the next morning, nearly lunchtime, and she was sprawled across the top of her bed, still in her scrumptious copper gown. Now, a wrinkled mess.

It took her a moment to remember what had happened. When Rose did, she groaned. Then she recalled even more and groaned again before burying her head in her pillow.

William now knew she was married. Two men had tried to abduct her, most probably to kill her. Finn had saved her life.

Rose was supposed to be at her cooking class, but that thought didn't cause her even to lift her head. There was no point in trying to get to school. She would never make it before the end of the lesson.

Then she remembered the only good thing: Claire and Franklin were well and truly engaged. Claire's reputation was salvaged, too, and there would be a wedding to plan.

Perhaps a wedding to cancel as well. Her own.

Why so much bitter with the sweet?

A knock on her door caused her usual response. "Yes?"

"It is I."

At the sound of her mother's voice, Rose sat up. Should she stop and strip off her gown and get under the covers? That would take too long. Besides, at her age, she would not earn too much disapproval for her late night.

"Come in."

Her mother sailed in carrying a cup of tea on a saucer. She paused at the sight of Rose in her evening dress, however she did no more than raise a delicate eyebrow.

"For you," Evelyn said, approaching her daughter and holding out the teacup.

"Thank you." Rose would have preferred coffee, and her dear mother knew that, but Evelyn would never be disabused of the belief that tea was the best remedy for anything. And if not that, then a glass of sherry.

Taking the cup, Rose sipped. The milky sweet brew actually did immediately make everything seem better. Perhaps her mother was correct after all.

"You were out quite late, I take it," Evelyn said without rebuke.

"William and I went to see *The Lady of Lyons.*"

"Mm," her mother murmured. "Which ended at half past eleven, I believe."

"Did it?" Rose asked vaguely. Then to distract, she added, "Franklin Brewster proposed to our Claire, directly before the performance."

"Mm," her mother said again, still looking at her bemusedly. "I read about it in the morning papers. While you were still soundly asleep."

"Of course." Rose drank more tea. "Did they reprint Franklin's pretend advert from the playbill?"

"They did," Evelyn confirmed. She cocked her head and observed her squirming daughter. "There was also talk of a certain other theatergoer being accosted in the lobby and of broken glassware."

"Oh?" *What could Rose say?*

Evelyn narrowed her eyes. "You weren't hurt, I can see that. Do you want to tell me what happened?"

"Nothing to tell, really," Rose began. Merely her fiancé finding out she had a husband after her husband saved her life by rescuing her from armed men. "Are the police looking for those men?"

By the expression on her dear mother's face, Rose had put her foot in it.

"Men?" Evelyn repeated.

Damnation. Rose should have read the story in the paper before she said anything.

"The ones who accosted me," she offered, her voice trailing off as her mother leaned forward and put her hand on Rose's arm.

"The paper said you were being restrained by one man when William approached and dropped or threw down champagne glasses behind you. He then quickly removed you from the theatre."

No one had noticed the two men with the gun. That was just as well. Moreover, the interpretation of Finn restraining her rather than comforting her was excellent for her reputation and for William's pride. Rose certainly wouldn't argue the finer points of what had occurred. She was only thankful she hadn't mentioned the gun to her mother.

"Yes, of course." *Should she tell her mother about Finn now that William knew?* "I meant, are the police looking for the man, the one man, the one who restrained me?"

"I don't believe so. It was simply a small side note, perhaps two lines. The paper indicated William handled it, and that was that."

"Correct." Rose finished her tea and set the cup and saucer down beside her bed. "I believe it's time I got up."

She swung her legs over the side of the bed and hoped her mother would take the hint and leave her to her morning's toilette, even if it was nearly noon.

However, Evelyn was not letting her get away too easily.

"I know you are nearly a married woman, but you must still take care, Rose. You cannot be alone with William until all hours, at least, not unless you are out in public."

Rose opened her mouth to protest, yet she could think of nothing to say. She knew she had no moral ground to stand on.

"Yes, Mama, I know. I'm sorry. It won't happen again."

"Furthermore, you can't have unseemly people accosting you at the theatre," Evelyn added.

"Where *should* they accost me, Mama?"

Her mother's eyebrows drew together, exactly like Reed's. Then in the next instant, they relaxed as the words sunk in.

"That is not even the least bit amusing," Evelyn said, despite the small smile playing about her lips.

"No, Mama. Honestly though, I was on my best behavior. Beside it wasn't my fault," Rose finished.

"No, dear, it never is. Only remember this, your reputation is your most valuable commodity, even though you have secured a marriage proposal from a most wonderful gentleman."

"I will do better," Rose promised.

"Thank you. We wouldn't want anything to jeopardize your future."

It was definitely not the time to tell her about Finn.

"Yes, Mama."

An hour later, Claire came bounding into the dining room where Rose, feeling incredibly hungry after everything that had occurred, was having poached eggs on toast and sausages.

Her friend squealed with delight as soon as she saw her. Jumping up, Rose had her arms around Claire and was hugging her in mere seconds.

"You're getting married!" she exclaimed.

"I'm getting married!" Claire returned.

"Let's sing it this time," Rose suggested, and did, "You're getting married!"

"I'm getting married!" Claire echoed.

"Perfect, shall we add more lines and make a real song of it?"

Claire laughed with sheer delight, and Rose had never seen her happier. Was that how she'd looked when she'd been Finn's newly wedded wife? Was that how she'd acted after William had proposed?

Upon consideration, Rose thought it would be splendid if she and Claire could feel that same glowing happiness *without* the benefit of a man. However, she wouldn't spoil her friend's happiness by philosophizing about that particular point. After all, Claire had waited a long time for this day.

"What happened during the intermission?" Rose asked.

The instantaneous blush on Claire's face told the story.

"So you kissed?" Rose surmised. "What else?"

Claire giggled. "We kissed some more, and then this!" She thrust out her hand so Rose could see her engagement ring, a large glowing opal with diamonds encircling it, all set in a thick gold band.

"It's gorgeous."

"I know." Claire beamed. "Then we talked about a date. Next May."

Claire would make a lovely spring bride. Rose would pray for a mild winter and early thaw. "We'll start planning immediately, if not sooner."

"Moreover, we are most decidedly *not* going to live with his mother. I think we'll take a place in the Back Bay because the cost is so dear here on the Hill. Perhaps you and William can reside there as well, and we can be neighbors again."

Claire twirled in a circle for no reason at all, looking like a child on Christmas morning. While she spun, she talked.

"Tell me, why didn't you return for the play's conclusion?"

Rose sighed. She didn't want to relive it.

"Are you hungry? Come, sit down and eat something."

"I'll sit," Claire said, and she did. "I'm not hungry, however, and don't change the topic. Where did you and William go? Was there kissing involved?"

It was Rose's turn to blush.

"Ah-ha."

"Well, not at first. Didn't you read the papers?" Rose had read over the papers her mother had mentioned earlier, and she and William were mentioned by name. Finn was called the "mystery man."

"Of course I did. I clipped out any news of my engagement and put copies in my trunk. Why?"

Rose pushed a sausage around with the tip of her knife. "I'm afraid I was part of a 'scene' in the lobby last night."

Claire sobered at once. "Tell me."

"I'm sorry to say Finn was correct about men wishing him harm. They found me and tried to abduct me."

"Dear God!" Claire reached out a hand and touched Rose's arm. "Were you hurt?"

"As it turned out, Finn was at the show last night, as well. He scared them off."

"Thank goodness!"

Rose nodded. "Then William found us. Together. Hugging."

"Dear God!" Claire said again.

"Indeed! The remainder of my evening was spent with William, explaining everything I've kept hidden from him for so long."

Claire nodded. "So he knows everything?"

"He does, and he was unbelievably kind and understanding. We ate alone in his kitchen, and he forgave me. I didn't get home until very late—or rather, very early this morning. Mama has already had words with me about that."

"I'm so sorry." Then Claire lowered her voice. "Because of the newspapers, does your mother know about . . . you know?"

"No. Still only you, Reed, and now William. I can't see any reason to tell Mama until the situation is resolved. She'll only worry."

"You should go to the police." Claire sounded emphatic.

"Most likely, I should." Rose considered going to the station and giving the police a description of the villains. "Yes, I will. Today, I suppose. I expect my brother will be demanding some answers from me and from Finn, too, for that matter. That is, if Reed read the society pages."

Could she not escape the mess in her life for one day?

"Never mind all that," Rose said, ready to put it behind her. "When are you going to meet again with the dragon? I believe she owes you an apology."

"Soon. I will be gracious and not make her grovel. Too much."

"That is kind of you." Rose grabbed Claire's hand and admired the ring again. "We must go show Mama. She is thrilled for you."

Before they could do so, Reed's solid frame filled the doorway.

"Hello, you two. Congratulations are in order, and I read how your engagement was accomplished with such style," Reed said to Claire, whose cheeks reddened again.

"Thank you." Automatically, she held out her hand to show Reed her ring, causing an amused grin to brighten his expression.

Dutifully, he took Claire's hand and pretended to examine the ring with great interest.

"A fine-looking one," he declared. "Has our mother seen it yet?" he asked, turning to Rose.

She shook her head, her heart sinking. If he knew of the engagement, then he, no doubt, knew everything.

"We were just going to—"

Reed interrupted her. "I need to speak to my little sister," he said to Claire. "Why don't you go find Mrs. Malloy and show her your ring."

Claire looked from Reed to Rose, who nodded before watching her best friend head for the door.

"Please tell Mr. Brewster I said he is a lucky man," Reed added.

Claire gave a smug smile over her shoulder before disappearing down the hallway.

Turning back to Rose, Reed appeared nearly as angry as concerned.

"What happened last night?"

Rose sighed. "Not you, too."

"Yes, me, too. I suppose Mother was worried, seeing your name in the newspapers, and I also suppose the mysterious unnamed man was Bennet."

"Correct on both counts, Attorney Malloy."

Reed grimaced. "Not a time for witticism."

"It's not what you think. Finn didn't harm me. He saved me from a couple of men who tried to kidnap me from the theatre."

"Kidnap you? Dammit all!" he fumed. "I was actually planning on seeing him today to have him sign the papers, then Charlotte pointed out the incident in the morning's *Post*. We can only hope anyone threatening you will understand you care nothing for him once your marriage ends. And as quickly as possible."

He ran a hand through his hair. "Nearly kidnapped?" Then he swore again. "Bennet has brought nothing but trouble."

"That's not fair," Rose protested. "If not for Finn last night, I don't know if I would be speaking to you now."

"If not for him," her brother said, his teeth practically grinding together, "you'd be a happily engaged lady with no worries of being kidnapped."

True yet beside the point.

"If I hadn't married him—" she began, breaking off when she heard a gasp.

Too late, Rose realized her mother had entered the room.

CHAPTER TWENTY-THREE

Rose and Reed turned as one at the sound of their mother storming across the floor with Claire trailing behind her.

"Married! Married?" Evelyn said repeatedly, getting louder. "Married!" The tenor of her voice betrayed her shock. "That's why you were out until the wee hours. You eloped with William!" She sounded thoroughly peeved.

Intent on disavowing her mother's assumptions, Rose opened her mouth, but Evelyn stood before her, nose to nose.

"That was very wrong of you, Rose Olivia Malloy, after all the time Elise has put into planning your wedding. I am most disappointed in your behavior."

Rose felt all the blood drain from her head. If her mother was upset at her secretly marrying William, how much worse would she take the news about Finn?

"And think of how let down people will be," Evelyn continued beginning to pace. "All those who were coming to the ceremony and to the luncheon."

Claire stepped forward, her eyebrows knitted in confusion, and Rose's heart began to pound. She could practically see the gears turning—and sticking—knowing what her friend was going to say before she said it, yet utterly helpless to stop her.

"I don't understand," Claire began, and Rose lifted up her hands to ward off the words. "How could you marry Mr. Woodsom when you are already married to Mr. Bennet?"

Rose smacked her own forehead with her palm and held her hand there, head bowed, shaking it back and forth, knowing the consequences that would follow. Everything had changed in that instant.

"Married to *whom?*" her mother practically shrieked this time. She looked at Claire. "Mr. *Bennet?* Who in God's name is this Mr. Bennet?"

Turning back to Rose, Evelyn demanded, "What is the meaning of this?"

Dear God! Those were precisely William's words. Before Rose could speak, Evelyn rounded on her only son.

"Did you know about this? Of course you did! Nothing gets by you. Obviously Claire knew," she said, gesturing at the diminutive blonde, who looked a little sick at having spilled her friend's secret.

Evelyn threw her hands up in the air. "Have you all gone mad?" she raged. "We have planned a wedding, a large one. How can Rose be *already* married? To a man whom I've never heard of? Does the whole household have to crumble when I relax for five minutes?"

Reed and Rose exchanged a look as Evelyn finally paused to take a breath.

"Nothing's crumbling, Mother," Reed said.

Evelyn headed for the closest chair, tossing herself down and closing her eyes.

"So close to getting four of them respectably married. So close." She continued to murmur this to herself.

Rose lifted her head and glared at Claire, who seemed to have shrunk into an extremely small version of herself.

"I'd best be going," she whispered to no one in particular and darted from the room.

Too right! And it was the only time in Rose's long relationship with Claire that she'd had unkind thoughts about her best friend. Particularly thoughts about strangling her.

Rose shared a very different look with her brother, glad for the first time that he'd already been apprised of the situation. This moment would have been infinitely worse, like a deluge instead of a thunderstorm, if she'd had to deal with both Reed's interrogations and censure as well as her mother having a conniption fit.

The siblings approached Evelyn on either side. Reed took one of her hands in his, and Rose crouched down and held her mother's other hand.

"Mama, I was going to tell you *after* the situation was resolved in some manner, one way or the other."

"Dear God," her mother said, not opening her eyes. "A situation."

Rose looked to Reed for assistance. His expression proclaimed, "I told you so," yet he proceeded to pat their mother's shoulder.

"It's not as bad as it sounds," he said. "Actually, it *is* rather bad. However, not without remedy. What's more, I'm handling it."

"Our Rose is married," Evelyn whispered, and a little moan escaped her. "Since when?"

"Is that detail really important?" Rose asked.

"Four years," Reed responded, and their mother flinched as if she'd been struck.

"Not exactly four," Rose corrected, glaring at Reed. "Almost. Yet I thought I was widowed for nearly all of them."

At that, Evelyn's eyelids snapped open. "Sherry," she ordered.

"But, Mama, it's not yet two o'clock," Rose pointed out, recalling her mother's usual rule about drinking spirits early in the day.

"Sherry," Evelyn repeated. "Immediately."

Reed nodded, so Rose jumped up and ran to the sideboard where they kept the sherry service. She quickly poured a generous amount of the sweet liquid into one of her mother's delicate short-stemmed green glasses.

Not another word was spoken until Evelyn had taken her first sip and then another.

"I will not pry into the whats and wherefores," she said at last. "Only tell me, are you still marrying William?"

"Yes, Mama," Rose didn't hesitate. "If he will still have me."

"He knows about your . . . about this other man?"

"Yes, Mama. He found out last night. I stayed late with him to tell him everything."

Evelyn sipped again. "I see. And he still wants to marry you?"

Rose sighed. "It would seem so."

Their mother turned to Reed. "You are procuring your sister's freedom?"

Reed nodded. "I have the papers ready for Mr. Bennet to sign."

Rose started slightly, wishing for some reason Reed hadn't said Finn's name again.

Evelyn took another sip and then abandoned the pretense and drained her glass entirely.

"Then we will put all this behind us. As soon as you are div . . . free, we will proceed as planned, and no one outside our immediate circle need be the wiser regarding your youthful indiscretion."

Her mother got up and left, still clutching her sherry glass. She must have been quite upset for she didn't offer Rose a smile of encouragement or even spare her a backward glance.

"She is very disappointed in me," Rose said. A bubble of sadness expanded in her chest.

Reed wrapped his arm around her shoulders.

"I'm sorry she found out that way. Mama was shocked, obviously, but only because she wants you to be happy with William."

"I know." Rose considered the current state of affairs. "I'm sure you want to get on with serving Finn the papers. Should I go to the police station and tell them about last night?"

"Yes, absolutely. In fact, I'll go there with you first. You never know what nefarious types might be hanging around. I always hated it when Charlotte went to the station on investigative business."

I should tell him Charlotte hasn't finished investigating. I should tell him right now.

"I'll be ready in a minute," she told her brother. "Let me get a hat."

Coward, she berated herself as she left the room.

"This is larger than we imagined," Reed said to Rose when they finally left the police station. "Do you understand that?"

"Of course, I'm not dim witted." She hurried to keep up with her brother's long stride.

Men had died last night.

That had been a shock to learn from the police. Although finding out it was *not* Finn had been such a relief, she felt lightheaded.

Reed took her directly to his office nearby with strict instructions to wait for his return. Then, he headed for The Parisien, divorce papers in hand and determination in his expression.

Rose did exactly as she'd been told and waited. When her brother returned, she would be almost a divorcée, needing merely the judge's gavel. However, when Reed came storming back, he declared himself unsuccessful.

"The slippery scoundrel wasn't there. Promise me you'll stay far away from him until this is over."

Luckily, he hadn't expected her to disobey and so hadn't waited for her verbal promise, which she pointedly did not give. Instead, she waited precisely an hour, browsing aimlessly in the shops close to The Restaurant Parisien, and then entered the dimly lit dining room. Rushing up the back stairs to Finn's room, Rose heard voices before she even crested the top step. When she did, she saw . . .

Finn and William!

As she came into view, William's gaze swung toward her. He stood in the hall, facing Finn, who was looming in his own open doorway, arms crossed. Both men looked heated, angry.

"What are *you* doing here?" William asked her, irritation lacing his voice.

She stopped in her tracks. Before she could answer, Finn spoke up.

"Don't speak to her that way."

William's full attention returned to Finn. "You shut your mouth," he ordered in clipped tones, sending him a baleful glare. "Rose is *my* fiancée, and I will speak to her however I see fit when I find her sneaking up to another man's room."

"To her *husband's* room," Finn pointed out unnecessarily.

William offered a hollow-sounding laugh. "In name only, or so she tells me."

Fin's jaw clenched, and both men looked to Rose again, each one wearing an expression of betrayal.

She ignored the insult to Finn's manhood. It was not her concern at that moment.

"I came because I have more information. One of the men who tried to abduct me the other night has turned up dead. He was shot and his body dumped in the harbor."

"Christ!" Finn said.

William stared at her as if he didn't know her.

"Do you hear yourself? Is this the life you want to lead, talking of men being murdered and bodies in the harbor?" He shook his head in wonder. "And then you came directly here, to the center of all the danger in your life. For God's sake, Rose, why?"

She swallowed. But William was wrong. She wanted the peaceful life she'd had before Finn's return, filled with nothing more than cooking and music, and being with William and her family. It was all she wanted. However, she couldn't have any of that until the threat had passed.

"Reed thinks some important person was worried his identity would be traced through one of those—what did you call them?" she turned to Finn, "Those *goons*. I thought it important to tell you. The other one was most likely killed as well and perhaps his body went out to sea."

Rose glanced nervously at William since she'd started talking about dead men again.

"You should have sent someone in your place," he said, his tone still sharp. "I'm sure your brother doesn't know you're here."

True on both counts. Reed would be livid, and she shouldn't have come. However, Rose had yet to be able to refrain from seizing on each opportunity to see Finn in the flesh. It was still a miracle every time she saw him, as if he had truly arisen from his grave, hale and hearty.

"Reed did come here first," she looked at Finn, "but you weren't here."

"I was at work," Finn said, surprising Rose. Immediately, though, he directed his attention back to William.

"Rose can come see me whenever she likes," Finn stated, obviously trying to get under her fiancé's skin.

"You say that because you're a selfish bastard," William practically growled. "What about her safety?"

Finn tilted his head. "When she's with me, I keep her safe."

William made a sound of disgust. "She'd have been better off if you'd stayed dead."

Rose gasped. "You're both speaking as if I'm not even here."

"Better for you, maybe," Finn retorted, ignoring her words and still addressing William. "It's harder to take someone's wife when that someone is still alive."

"No," Rose protested, wanting to correct him.

William said nothing. He simply cocked his arm and punched Finn squarely in the mouth. It happened so fast that Finn neither ducked nor swerved. In the blink of an eye, blood was flowing where his own teeth had cut into his lip. At the same time, William shook out his hand as if in pain.

Rose ran forward, putting herself between them as Finn started to roll up his sleeves.

"No," she said again, this time to both men. "Stop it. Please."

"You are worth fighting for," Finn said.

William still said nothing, but he held her gaze as she turned her back on her husband and looked at her fiancé squarely.

"Please," she beseeched him, putting up her hands, touching his solid chest. "This will solve nothing."

William's eyes darkened. "It will make me feel better."

Was that a flash of humor?

However, Finn was close against her back, and she could feel the tension coming off him in waves. Any moment, he would put her aside and lay into William. They were evenly matched, and it would be awful.

"It won't make *me* feel better," she assured William. "Please, go with me now."

William's eyes narrowed. At the same time, she felt Finn take a step backward.

"Please," she said again. "I don't want either of you hurt."

William's mouth hardened into a straight line.

What had she said wrong?

"That's fine," he told her. "You stay and conclude your business with your *husband*."

With that, William left, not sparing a backward glance for either of them.

Silence enveloped her and Finn for a few seconds. Then he muttered, "Touchy fellow, isn't he?"

Rose turned and slapped his cheek hard, smearing the blood across his face and leaving a wet trail on her palm. Finn grabbed her wrist when she held up her hand, not to strike him again but to look at the evidence of what she'd done.

Her arm was shaking. All of her was shaking, Rose realized. She wanted to cry but not in front of Finn, who had caused so much misery.

"I'm sorry," he whispered, still gripping her arm. "I deserved that. But not from him."

She looked up at his face. It was a sight to see, with his upper lip cut and a bruise forming at the edge of his mouth. His thick dark blond hair was standing up on his head and mussed everywhere else.

She wrenched herself free and ran after William, hearing Finn's footsteps behind her.

Catching up to her fiancé on the busy sidewalk, Rose called out to his quickly departing back.

"William, please wait," she beseeched. They couldn't leave it like this, not with him furious at her.

He halted and turned, but there was no inviting expression on his face.

"I will not stand here in public and discuss this," he said calmly but firmly. "I'll talk to you later, Rose. In private."

Then he stalked off stiffly without his usual self-assured gait, which always bespoke of a confident William Woodsom, son of English nobility.

Rose stared after him until he disappeared into the horde of other Bostonians. She didn't call him back to her—or even try to. *What could she say after all?* She let her tears fall, her insides aching for how she'd hurt him.

Realizing Finn was at her elbow, standing in broad daylight with his battered face for all to see, she wiped her cheeks with her handkerchief.

"Should I go after him?" she asked, not caring she was asking her own husband for advice on matters of the heart.

"No," Finn said. "The man loves you and he has his pride, which has just been sorely wounded at seeing you come to my room. Give him overnight to think on it."

Then Rose felt his hand touch her arm, and she whirled around to face him, feeling all her sadness transform in a flash to anger.

"*You* did this to him! *You* stayed away until he'd asked for my hand, and then you wouldn't let me tell him. I will never forgive you for this." Rose cared not at all for the people who paused or looked at her during her tirade. Let them stare.

Finn ran a hand through his hair and then said quietly, "You should not have come to my room."

"Oh," She stomped her foot. "Are you blaming me for this mess? I thought it best you knew the extent of the danger you're in and that you've put me in, as well. I certainly wasn't inviting a repeat of the manhandling from the last time I visited you."

"Manhandling?" he asked, his expression hardening. "Is that what you call our kiss? I suppose next you'll say I forced you to marry me and had my way with you. Except, wait, you're still a dried up, prudish virgin."

"How dare you!" she roared causing an entire family to shy away to the far edge of the sidewalk. He was being entirely unfair since she'd never been a prude. As for dried up—

"Perhaps you're no longer an innocent!" Finn was now in high dudgeon, his voice as loud as her own. "Did you give your precious virtue away to Woodsom, knowing your family would accept him as your deflowerer far better than they ever would me?"

Without waiting for her next comment, he turned heel and went back inside The Parisien, barely limping, his back ramrod straight.

Rose stared after him, taking gulps of air and waiting for her emotions to settle, along with her racing heart.

In the span of minutes, she'd had both the men in her life walk away from her in anger. *Was she to blame for all of this chaos? Or was Finn?*

One thing was certain, William didn't deserve the pain he was in. *Would he ever forgive her?*

CHAPTER TWENTY-FOUR

Charlotte took the North Ferry from Battery Wharf. Upon disembarking on Eastie's Border Street, she easily found Kelly's shipyard after a short walk.

Entering through the main gate, she asked a young man walking hurriedly with a planer in his hand for directions to the owner's office.

"What's this about, miss?"

"It's missus, to be precise, and I would like to speak either to Mr. Kelly or to the yard's overseer about the *Garrard*."

The young builder nodded solemnly. "I wasn't around when it went down, but the pall of it still hangs over the yard at the mention of her name. Sad business."

"Agreed, sir. And all hands lost?"

"Yes, ma'am. Mr. Kelly isn't here, hardly ever is anymore. You might have luck speaking with Mr. Walsh, our overseer. If you come this way, I'll find out if he's in his office. A busy man, as you might expect."

"Naturally. I won't take up much of his time. Was he the overseer when the *Garrard* went down?"

"Yes, ma'am. The very same."

Ten minutes later, Charlotte found herself seated before a weathered desk, having to peer past a large decorative glass bottle with a three-master inside of it in order to see the overseer. Mr. Walsh was seated on the other side, his black eyes taking her measure. He seemed none too pleased, either. His tone, however, was polite when he spoke.

"What can I do for you, ma'am? Something about the *Garrard*?"

"Yes, precisely," she turned slightly to find the young man still standing by the door clutching his metal planer with both hands.

At her inspection, Walsh said, "Back to work, Murphy."

When he left, the overseer muttered, "These apprentices. They don't know what hard work is!" Then he focused on Charlotte once again. "Now then, ma'am, what is this about?"

She scooted her chair a few inches to the left to better see him. "How do you choose who goes out upon a test sail?" Charlotte asked.

The man's eyebrows rose high. "That depends."

"Upon?" she prompted.

"Upon the vessel's size, the newness of design, how far out the test will take her. For the most part, the master builder doesn't go unless requested by the owner. That is, the one who commissioned the ship, not the yard owner. A few riggers and carpenters go, and a skeleton crew mans every position. Sometimes we provide 'em, sometimes the ship's owner does. Sometimes the owner himself goes."

"I see." Charlotte glanced at her notes. "Did the vessel's owner go out on the *Garrard* on her fateful maiden voyage? There was none such listed in the paper."

The overseer wrinkled up his forehead. "No," he said with surety.

"Nor the master builder, Mr. Gilbert?"

"Why, no," Walsh said.

"Also, none of the crew were from the owner's company? They all came from the yard. Why was that?"

Walsh's face reddened. "I can't say for certain. Maybe they had none available for this particular ship until it would go into service."

"I see. So only men from the yard died. Mostly young ones, it seems." She scanned her notes. "A large number of apprentices, too. Is that normal?"

"No," he started. "I mean, I don't know why that would be the case."

"That's ridiculous," Charlotte interjected. "You are the overseer. You were here at the time. Don't the manifests go through you."

"Sometimes," he said, "and some go through our master builder. As it happens, this was Mr. Gilbert's project. He could put on board whomever he liked."

"Or take off, as well, I suppose."

"What do you mean?" he asked, pulling at his collar and fanning himself with the first piece of paper he grabbed.

"If someone's name was on the ship's manifest, is it possible they were not on the ship?"

"Unusual but not impossible, especially with this type of voyage that didn't have the actual crew. Look, wouldn't you rather speak with Mr. Kelly about all this when he returns?"

Charlotte narrowed her eyes. "Yes, I would like to speak with him. However, I saw your name mentioned in more than one paper as the representative for this yard, and I felt you had an outstanding command of all the circumstances."

After all, to her way of thinking, the owner of the shipyard would be interested only in protecting its reputation and glossing over anything out of the ordinary, and Mr. Gilbert would have his own reputation to defend, especially if he had any fault in the matter of the ship's design. Neither would offer up any nuggets of information that hadn't already been in the paper.

"By the way, sometimes an overseer goes on a voyage, as I understand it," Charlotte pointed out, fixing him with a questioning look. "Why didn't you go on the test sail?"

After a pause, Mr. Walsh hung his head. "I should have. Always felt badly that I hadn't. Not that I think I could have done something those on board couldn't. You say there were many apprentices. That may be true, but there were experienced men as well." He sighed.

"By the time the ship was ready, I was to be married the following Wednesday, which cleared me from having to go since the ship was supposed to be out nearly four weeks."

Charlotte pursed her lips. He seemed genuinely remorseful.

"You shouldn't feel guilty, sir. I'm sure your wife was relieved at your being spared."

"Aye."

"You are familiar with the manifest."

"Yes, went over every name after the sinking. Needed to say a goodbye."

"To your knowledge, then, were all the men who were named actually on the ship?"

Walsh wrinkled his forehead again. "I have tried not to think overmuch about who was on or not since then. But there were two on the manifest who weren't on the ship. Their families were notified immediately or even knew ahead of time they weren't on board."

"Can you tell me why they didn't set sail?"

"Not for any nefarious reason, ma'am, I'm sure. One, a rigger, came down with a fever that morning, and, well, I guess he was young as you say, fifteen years old, perhaps. His mum was the one who came to the yard and said he couldn't go. The other man, a ship designer, was removed on the order of Mr. Kelly, I believe."

"That would be Mr. Berne," Charlotte said.

"Aye, how did you know?" His eyebrows rose once again.

She smiled and shrugged as if it were inconsequential. "So that change must have happened at the last minute. Otherwise Mr. Berne's name would have been removed from the manifest, correct?"

"Yes, probably the decision was made the night before, after the yard secretary had retired. He would have been too busy in the morning to redo the manifest."

"Do you know why Mr. Berne was removed?" Charlotte paused with her fountain pen over her paper.

"Not a clue, ma'am. Could have been due to a bender the night before. Could have been a hundred reasons. Lucky man, though."

"Yes, I suppose he is." She decided to press her own luck. "Mr. Berne still works here, doesn't he? I would like to have a quick word with him if I may, and with Mr. Gilbert."

"As to Master Builder Gilbert, he has moved on, and I couldn't say where he is. However, I can get Mr. Berne to speak with you."

The overseer lifted his telephone, speaking to someone in another building on the yard. He asked succinctly if Mr. Berne were available, mentioning how there was a journalist there to see him about the *Garrard*. He waited a few moments. "I see."

His expression tightened before he gave her what she could only think of as a blank stare.

"Oddly, he left early today, not long ago, in fact."

"How peculiar, and precisely when I wish to speak with him, too." She stood up. "I appreciate your time." She nearly left a message for Berne along with her calling card. However, the idea of this stranger, who had escaped death to collect a large sum on an insurance claim and who had gone missing from his job, showing up at the home she shared with her husband and children stopped her cold. A little caution concerning Mr. Berne was in order.

"I will come another time to speak with Mr. Berne," Charlotte promised. "And Mr. Kelly as well."

Rose had thought she would have to seek William out at his home or worse, appear at his office under the scrutiny of the State House secretaries. Instead, as she finished drinking her coffee the next morning and poking at a dish of sliced fruit, the housekeeper announced Mr. Woodsom was in the front hall.

Rose glanced at her mother, whose face was a picture of concern, before pushing her chair back and scrambling for the door.

"Invite him to have some tea and porridge, of course, if he's hungry, dear," her mother called after her.

Rose doubted he would want either. She'd spent the night wondering how to make amends for her inexcusable actions, half dreading seeing him again, yet now he was there, she couldn't wait to lay eyes on him. He was her beloved, after all.

She stopped short in the foyer. William looked terrible. Clearly, he hadn't slept or taken the time with his grooming that morning. His hair was charmingly in disarray, his clothing unkempt, and dark circles under his eyes. And it was all her fault.

"Where can we speak privately?" he asked, his tone flat.

"In my father's study," she answered at once. She knew Evelyn would expect him to pop in to greet her first. William clearly looked in no condition to do so.

"Jillian," she addressed the maid, "please show Mr. Woodsom to the study and get him some tea or whatever he'd like. I'll be along directly."

She watched him trail along behind the young woman, looking defeated even from behind, and not the man with boundless energy and a zest for life she'd come to know and love.

With guilt weighing heavily like a wet wool cape, Rose poked her head around the dining room door.

"Mama, I'm going to have a private chat with William for a few minutes. He's not feeling quite himself today, a touch of indigestion perhaps, so he's not going to stop for breakfast with us."

"Tell him to have some ginger tea," Evelyn said, "or chamomile. Emily can brew him some directly."

"Yes, Mama." She turned to leave.

"Rose," her mother added, narrowing her eyes, "there is no tea that cures a broken heart. I know that from experience."

Indeed. Both she and her mother shared the experience of widowhood and the long pangs of heartache it caused.

"I know, Mama. Unfortunately, I know." She paused, about to confess to her mother that things were not going smoothly when she thought better of it. Before turning away, Rose forced a smile. "Nothing for you to worry about."

As she walked along the hallway to the back of the house, she realized those were the precise words she'd said to William that day on the Common when she should have told him the truth about Finn's return. The words were a lie then as they were now. There was plenty of reason to worry.

Upon entering the stud, Rose closed the door behind her. William was slumped in the comfy tufted seat that faced her father's desk. She had sat in it many times to converse with her father when she was a child—exciting, lengthy discussions that had fueled her spirit.

With his back to the door, despite his height, the top of William's head was barely visible above the high overstuffed back of the seat. Rose decided not to take her father's leather chair and put the barrier of the desk between them. Instead, she rested her behind on the edge of the desk on the same side as William and gave him her full attention. She had made this mess, and she would deal with the dire consequences.

And they *were* extremely dire. She understood that all too well.

William's fingers were steepled together, and he was staring at them intently.

Rose looked at them, too, seeing a little bruising on the knuckles of his right hand. She knew better than to mention it, despite dearly wishing she could take hold of those bruised fingers, kiss the marks, and tell him how sorry she was.

At last, William looked up at her.

"I've been thinking of the irony that I found out about Bennet during *The Lady of Lyons.*"

Rose hadn't thought about it, but he was right of course. The play was about betrayal and a woman caught between two men.

"Am I the jilted marquis?" William asked softly. "And is Bennet the one returning as the hero who wins your love?"

"This is not a play," she reminded him, although the similarities struck her as eerie.

"You married this man you barely knew," William said, his tone even and precise, "and he deserted you for over three years. He returns bringing nothing but heartache and potential danger. Now what? What are his intentions toward you?"

"I don't know."

Silence hung between them like a thick curtain for a long moment.

Then William said, "I guess that's not as important as this question: Do you still love him?"

Rose hesitated, and that seemed to be all it took to push William over the edge into despair. He stood up abruptly and paced the room.

"Perhaps I always sensed there was something you were holding back from me. Not this, of course! This was beyond imagining."

"I am sorry," she repeated, thinking she would be apologizing to him for the rest of her life.

William nodded, still walking around the room. "You thought him long dead?"

"Yes," she said, nodding for emphasis.

"Now that you know he's alive, what are your thoughts?" He stopped pacing to stand before her and gaze into her eyes.

She took a deep breath. She owed William the absolute truth.

"If he hadn't vanished into the sea, I believe I would be with him still."

"Yet he did vanish," William reminded her and then fell into silence. After another moment, he took her hands in his.

"Do you love me?"

"Yes," she answered without any hesitation. "I love you. You must believe me. I never would have become engaged to you if I didn't."

"I believe you love me," he said. He pulled her close, his gaze locked on hers until the last moment when his lips found her mouth.

Familiarity and warmth, Rose felt safe and relieved, reveling in the sweet pressure of his mouth against hers. He was still *her William*.

The kiss went on until he raised his head, and she saw tears glistening in his eyes. Her stomach clenched.

Good God! Was that a kiss goodbye?

"Do you love Bennet?" he asked again, more directly this time.

Did she? "I loved him tremendously when I was eighteen."

"That's not what I asked," William pointed out.

"I don't know. It has been years since I had to examine my feelings for him."

"You must have felt something since he returned. What are your feelings now, Rose?"

Turmoil swirled through her. What William wanted her to do was beyond difficult. It would tear her apart if she truly delved into her emotions. She had avoided scrutinizing her own heart and her depth of feeling for one man over the other, just as she'd avoided comparing the men themselves.

Finn was Finn—the man who had captured her every sense with her first glance of him, their first words, first touch, first kiss. Everything had been intense, charged, all encompassing, so different from her idle flirtations before him, and she'd had quite a few of those. She'd pledged herself to him forever and thought her life over when his ended. Rose had cared for both their hearts better than he himself had done.

Love Finn? Why, he was sewn so deeply into the soul of her being that as soon as she'd discovered he was alive, she had ached with wanting to see him, to touch him, to breathe alongside him. She'd felt driven to be near him despite herself.

But William! Standing before her, he was sweet love and laughter, as well as sensual desire. He gave her everything she wanted, and she had given him all that was left of her heart in return, trusting this time she would have a chance to experience the full joy of living with a man.

With William, everything seemed possible in their future, and she'd eagerly looked forward to their wedding day so they could begin their life together.

"I am torn," she whispered, then cleared her throat. "I wasn't sure what I felt when I first saw him again. Mostly disbelief and then anger. Honestly, though, and you deserve my honesty more than anyone alive, a part of me still has feelings for him."

She realized she was wringing her hands and tried to stop by fisting them at her sides.

"How can my heart belong to both of you? It's not possible, is it? It's certainly not moral. How can I love you so much and yet still feel a deep attachment to him? It is bewildering, yet you want and need the entire truth, so yes, I do feel love for him, too."

There, she'd said it. It was a terrible thing to say to her fiancé, but she couldn't pretend she loved William solely or that Finn had no place in her heart and mind.

He closed his eyes a moment. When he reopened them, she saw in their depths that he'd made a decision, and a shiver of despair ran through her.

"As an only child, I never learned to share," he began, and she found herself shaking her head, knowing where this was leading. "I never had to be second in my parents' love. I can't be second for you. Moreover, I won't share even a tiny bit of your heart with Bennet."

"William, please—"

"I can't," he said, his tone desperate yet definite. "You were mine, but not wholly. I suppose I could have lived with that if he were dead. If you carried a small torch for a lost husband, I could bear it."

Again, Rose tried to speak and William stopped her.

"I am not making this decision willy-nilly, I swear to you. I have spent every moment considering. I thought to speak to Bennet and come to terms with the man. Then, seeing you there, realizing you were comfortable enough with another man to show up at his dwelling, to watch you place yourself between him and me." He shook his head. "Even to lump me in with the bastard, hoping *neither* of us got hurt."

His voice broke slightly, along with her heart.

"Please," she said, "I didn't mean—"

William touched her lips with one finger.

"Circumstances being what they are, sweet Rose, I won't settle for less than the whole of you. I'm sorry, but I simply can't. I am releasing you from our engagement."

She didn't want to be released from their engagement. Rose closed her eyes, feeling one tear and then another escape to roll down her cheeks. She felt William wipe them away, and they stood together in silence for a long moment.

At last, she garnered her courage and opened her eyes once more to look into his dear brown ones.

"I wish I could tell you my heart was entirely yours," she said. "You deserve that."

William said nothing at first. Then he murmured, "Love and pride," which she instantly recognized as the secondary title to Edward Bulwer-Lytton's play.

"I wish you could accept what I can offer you," she added, still clinging to a shred of hope.

He shook his head.

Rose swallowed back more tears.

"I can tell you, William Woodsom, you will always, always have a place in here." She touched her breastbone. "And if I am ever to love again, whomever I'm with, he will have to share me with you."

The anguish on his face was no doubt mirrored on her own.

"I am so sorry," she whispered. *How could she ease him, soothe him?* "I got engaged to you in good faith and would happily have lived my life loving you and you alone."

He took hold of her hand and raised her fingers to his lips for a gentle kiss.

"You are an incredible woman, Miss Malloy. Know that I wish you only the very best. I wish you joy and love and peace. I will never forget you."

God, he was really going to end this. He was giving her up, and there was nothing she could do, for she could no longer lie to him and, clearly, only absolute dominion over her heart would keep him by her side.

"And I, you," she told him, gazing into his eyes to memorize them, seeing the warm flecks of gold in the tawny depths.

Without another word, William turned from her and departed the study. Rose sunk to the ground and wept openly.

CHAPTER TWENTY-FIVE

"She is as she was four years ago," Evelyn said into the telephone in her front hall. "I can't console her. I can't bring her out of it. She is going through terrible pain. Please come at once."

Those were the words that had summoned Claire to Rose's bedside. Rose knew this for Claire quoted them to her, as they sat on her bed, holding hands, both crying, with Rose feeling so sick and nauseated she couldn't imagine ever getting out of bed again.

Her mother's statement to Claire had been quite correct. She was in terrible pain, both mental and physical. All of her body ached with the loss of William.

She couldn't fathom whether it was worse than the first time her heart had been broken.

"Forget Mr. Graham and his ridiculous 'health crackers,' forget tea and even sherry," Claire stated, dabbing at the corners of her own eyes after crying silently along with Rose. "It's something stronger you need to bring you back to life. I shall go procure for us some brandy."

This caused Rose to erupt in torrential sobbing again until she managed to convey that she and William had last drunk brandy together.

"Fine, whiskey it will be." With her face streaked from drying tears, Claire left the room only to return a short time later with a decanter from Oliver Malloy's study and a tray of biscuits from the kitchen.

"I've sent your housekeeper out for a surprise that will delight you, I know. Meanwhile, drink this." Claire poured a very large amount of the clear liquid into the empty water glass that Rose kept by her bedside.

"Where's yours?" Rose asked, eyeing the glass and sniffing it. "This has been sitting around since my father died."

"That's called *aged*," her friend declared. "It makes wine and liquor better. Go on. Drink up."

Wrinkling her nose, Rose took a sip and coughed, nearly spilling some on her counterpane.

"Try again," Claire said. "After a few sips, everything tastes good or at least drinkable."

Rose took another swallow and let it burn its way down her throat and into her chest. And then, for good measure, another. She knew it couldn't thaw the ice that had encased her, making her feel chilled, despite a warm bath and a warming pan to heat her sheets. Nor should it. She'd lost William, and it was all her own fault.

For a few more minutes, they sat together, with Rose sipping and pondering her lonely future and sipping some more.

"Your turn," she said, at last handing the nearly empty glass to Claire. "Go on, try it," Rose added, then burped and unexpectedly laughed out loud. "It's de-pisc-able."

Claire laughed. "What did you say?"

"I said that the whiskey is deth-pixable. Oh, you know what I mean."

Claire took a small sip. "God, it's awful! Like I imagine poison would taste." She sipped it again. *"Hm!"*

"It hasn't helped anyway," Rose said, wanting to lie down. She did exactly that.

"I'm sorry," Claire said, gazing down at her. "I wanted us to be happy brides together."

Rose let the tears trickle down the sides of her face and into her ears.

"I shall never be one. I am entirely done with men."

Claire made a *tut-tut* sound. "Please don't say that. You are still young and—"

"No," Rose stated. "Don't say it." She paused, feeling as if her bedroom were spinning. "I need water. There," she said, sitting up and gesturing across the room, "in the pitcher."

Claire jumped up and brought it over. However, since her glass still held whiskey, Rose could think of nothing to do except drink from the pitcher, which she did, slurping from its sloped side.

She handed it back before wiping her mouth and chin on the back of her hand.

"Better?" Claire asked.

"Maybe," Rose said. "I feel strange though. Not good strange, either. Whiskey is denifitly not for me."

"*Denifitly*," Claire repeated and giggled.

"Stop." Rose lay back down. "Secondly—"

"Wait," her friend interrupted her, "what was the first point?"

Rose considered a moment but couldn't recall.

"Never mind that, secondly, both of these men knew how much I loved them, and each . . ." Her words caught in her throat. "And each was able to leave me. What does that tell you?"

Rose began to cry again, hiccupping while she did so.

A knock at her door made no difference to her emotional state, and she didn't care when Claire answered for her.

"Come in."

Evelyn entered holding a tin container that could only be one thing.

"Ice cream," Rose's mother announced. "Strawberry, as requested."

Behind her, the housekeeper carried a tray with bowls, spoons, and napkins.

"Set it on the bed, thank you," Evelyn said. "We have everything we need."

Rose sat up again, plumping her pillows behind her and resting against her headboard.

"I don't feel well at all." She used the edge of her bed cover to dry her face.

Her mother, wielding a large silver spoon, started to scoop the frozen concoction into the three bowls. She divvied up the entire quart and then placed the spoon in the empty container, and the container, on the floor.

"I can understand why you don't feel well," she gestured toward the whiskey decanter on the bedside table before handing Claire and Rose each a bowl and spoon. She picked up the last one for herself. "While ice cream cannot solve problems, it can certainly make them easier to bear. Good thinking, Claire."

Rose didn't think she could eat anything. However, she touched the tip of her tongue to the first spoonful, and before she knew it, she'd polished off half her portion. It settled her stomach, although her head still seemed stuffed with wool.

"I have something else for you," Evelyn said. She reached into the watch pocket in the seam of her bodice and withdrew tickets that had been carefully folded in a piece of cream-colored paper. "You may have forgotten, but Miss Barton's lecture is tonight."

Rose groaned.

"Dearest, this will take your mind off of everything. I promise. She is an excellent speaker, despite the topic being grim, to say the least." Her mother shook her head. "I'm sure she'll discuss the war for a little while, but I believe she will speak mostly of her work at Johnstown after the flood. It will be fascinating."

Evelyn held her spoon as if she were about to conduct an orchestra and read from the printed sheet: "Clara Barton was the first of the relief workers to arrive, a mere three days after the catastrophic failure of the South Fork Dam in Pennsylvania.

As it turned out, over two thousand people had perished, and many more were still in peril, causing Clara and her Red Cross to remain for five months."

Rose suppressed a second groan. Her own troubles were slight in comparison to a wall of water and debris 60 feet high bearing down on an entire town at the speed of a fast-moving locomotive. Would hearing about death and destruction change her perception of how hopeless her own life seemed at present? She doubted it.

Finishing her ice cream, she let Claire take her bowl from her.

"Do you want to go?" Rose asked her friend.

Claire looked torn between enjoying the lecture with its no doubt gruesome details, supporting sketches, and mesmerizing photographs and supporting Rose's desire to stay home and wallow in her misery.

"Yes," the petite blond said, "I rather do."

Thus, Rose found herself out in the world when she believed she should be at home in mourning. The decent thing to do was put a black shroud over her head, cover the mirrors, and stay indoors for the next decade. Instead, wearing a plum-colored dress with a small lightweight cape, she entered the main lecture hall of Harvard University, fighting past the throng of those still hoping to secure a ticket.

They had picked up Elise on the way over, and the four of them located seats halfway back in the center section.

"Perfect," Evelyn said. "I'm so pleased you came, Rose, aren't you?"

"Yes, Mama," she said to humor her mother. Yet in truth, nothing could banish the heaviness she felt, the near-crushing knowledge she and William would not marry. The ever-present feeling of loss was a familiar one, a terrible overarching sensation she had hoped never to experience again.

Still, her brain could entertain other thoughts while her body remained listless and her heart torn and battered.

"I'm sure it will be enlightening to listen to Miss Barton."

It occurred to her that, as with the cooking school's Miss Farmer, Miss Barton was another spinster who enjoyed a full life without the benefit of a husband. Rose nodded quietly to herself. She could do the same.

As soon as the seats were filled, Clara Barton entered the room and stood before them. At age 69, the "Angel of the Battlefield" still looked capable and vigorous. Her voice was strong and her presentation lively. It seemed only a few minutes had passed when, in fact, she'd been speaking for nearly an hour and a half. She allowed questions and gave answers. Then, to everyone's chagrin, it was over.

"I don't know about you," Elise said, to the three of them, "but I am exhausted merely listening to her. I don't know how she does it. I feel I am quite a lazy good-for-nothing."

They all chuckled, except Rose. She, too, felt positively drained.

"I only hope to be so spry at her age," Claire pointed out. Miss Barton had paced the stage for most of the lecture, and regaled them with anecdotes she'd endured the year before in Pennsylvania with as much gusto as thirty years earlier during the War Between the States.

"I wish it wasn't so crowded," Evelyn mused. "I would like to have spoken to her personally a moment, and even have heard her thoughts on women gaining the vote."

"You are right, Mama," Rose spoke up. "See, she has already been beset by well-wishers. We had best leave before we're crushed."

The four of them exited the building and began a brief walk across Harvard Yard to where their carriage was parked.

Evelyn took Rose's hand. "I'm proud of you coming out like this."

Elise's ears perked up. "Why? Are you ill?" she asked her youngest sister.

Rose reddened, having momentarily forgotten Elise didn't yet know about any of her misfortune—Elise, who had planned the now non-existent wedding down to the smallest detail.

"Oh my mouth," Evelyn muttered, having realized her faux pas.

Before Rose could begin to explain, Maeve appeared in front of her. She greeted everyone, paying particular attention to Claire who would soon be related by marriage.

"Wasn't that a stupendous lecture?" she commented. Not waiting for an answer, she added, "I admire Miss Barton tremendously, although I know I could never venture into such territory as she did." Then her gaze focused on Rose, who could read at once in Maeve's expression that she knew.

"My condolences on your association with Mr. Woodsom coming to an unfortunate end. Such a shame."

All four ladies, especially Elise, gasped at her ill-mannered words.

"Still wearing his ring, I see," Maeve continued. "I would have thought it in bad taste."

Rose stared down at her hand and her treasured engagement ring. She hadn't yet thought to remove it.

"I will tell you what is in bad taste, Miss Norcross," Evelyn Malloy said, "bringing up my daughter's private business out in the open for anyone to hear. Like a common fishwife. I would have expected your mother to teach you better than that. Good evening."

Leaving Maeve rightfully red-faced and chastised, Rose's mother took her daughter's arm and hurried their little group past Franklin's cousin without another glance.

Their somber party remained silent until they reached their carriage, and then Elise began firing questions as quick and targeted as a soldier's bullet.

Too soon, Rose had to relive it all, watching her sister's face turn from incredulity to sorrow as she heard what had occurred.

"How could Maeve know so quickly?" Rose wondered aloud.

Claire, who had remained silent through everything, cleared her throat.

"I believe I can explain that. It's my fault. Maeve lingers at Franklin's house like a fly on manure. I think she has more freedom around my future mother-in-law than in her own home," she conjectured. "Anyway, I told him a very short version of what had happened only because Franklin asked if the four of us could go out tomorrow night," she explained, barely glancing up from her lap.

"When we had finished speaking in the parlor, we found Maeve in the hallway as we made our way out to his carriage. I suppose she had been listening in on our conversation. I promise, if I'd known she was anywhere around . . . ," Claire trailed off looking quite forlorn.

Rose touched her friend's hand. "It is fine. You kept my confidences quite securely for years, and I know you are not a gossip. The news of my broken engagement was bound to make the rounds sooner or later. I am not worried about Maeve or her opinion. She is all sour grapes anyway."

Privately, the notion of Maeve still hankering after William gave Rose pause. If William did take up with Maeve, Rose wondered how she would bear it. She couldn't! She would have to poison Franklin's cousin with arsenic in her tea or catch her off guard and push her into the harbor.

She couldn't even take cheer at the outrageousness of her own thoughts. Instead, Rose sat with her fists clenched in her lap. At any given moment, she felt so close to crying, she could do nothing but breathe deeply while longing for the sanctuary of her bedroom.

Rose decided to give William his ring back by way of a go-between, for going to his home and seeing him would be too painful, and if he wouldn't see her, that would be even worse.

The next day, Rose caught one of their two maids going out to the shops on the cook's errands and diverted her to William's house in the Back Bay. However, Bridget returned still with the blue box and the exquisite ring inside.

"He's gone," Bridget told Rose.

"Gone?" she repeated stupidly, as if the word was beyond her comprehension.

"Yes, miss. His housekeeper said he's left for an extended trip to the Continent."

"I see. Thank you."

Rose took the box the maid held out to her and walked slowly back to her room, aware though unconcerned by the numb feeling that seemed to have stolen over her, leaving her lethargic and disinterested.

Wondering how she would ever look at her engagement ring again, she put the lovely little box in the back of a drawer of her wardrobe along with all her hopes and dreams for her life together with William.

He had truly left her.

CHAPTER TWENTY-SIX

Rose knew Reed had tried and failed the next day and the next after that to catch Finn at his room. Frustrated by the man's inaccessibility, her brother reported he'd slid the envelope containing the divorce papers under Finn's door with a stern warning note to sign and return them immediately to Reed's offices off of Scollay Square.

Rose tried to care whether she was a married woman or a divorced one, but with her engagement broken along with her heart, she found she could not raise much concern over her marital status.

What did it matter? Without William, who had been the sunshine in her life, what did anything matter?

She wondered how she could survive not having him in her life anymore.

That last thought came and went with a stark realization—if she could learn to live without Finn, she could live without anyone. Even her dear William.

In the days that followed, Rose did not return to the Boston Cooking School, causing Miss Farmer to send one of the teachers to check on her health. Suddenly, Miss Spencer was admitted into the foyer.

Trying not to be rude, Rose asked the instructor to kindly thank Miss Farmer for her concern and said she would be back at the school the following day. She did not mean it.

Two afternoons later, Miss Farmer, herself, showed up on the Malloy doorstep, and Rose was mortified when Jillian announced her.

"May I intrude a moment?" the assistant principal asked after she was shown into the sitting room.

"You are not intruding," Rose said, jumping up to meet her. She did a mental check on what she could offer her to eat and drink. "Would you like some tea or coffee, or perhaps a cup of cocoa?" she added, as Rose remembered the woman's love of chocolate.

"We also have delicious lavender biscuits. I didn't make them. Our cook, Emily, did. She has Mrs. Lincoln's cookbook. Such a fine one. The book, I mean, although, of course, Emily is a fine cook, too. I've been reading it ever since I started at the school. I *am* coming back. I know I told Miss Spencer I would return yesterday, but I . . . that is, I . . . oh dear."

Miss Farmer's face was placid as she allowed Rose to ramble on before finally stopping for a breath.

"You are a superb cook," the assistant principal said unexpectedly.

Rose took a small step backward. She was diligent, persistent, and dedicated when at the school. That was certain. However, Rose hadn't believed her skills were in any way out of the ordinary.

"I don't like to think of you giving up," Miss Farmer said. "Yes, I will have cocoa, please, if you'll join me, and I hope you'll tell me what's bothering you."

"Yes," Rose said at once, for she greatly admired this woman and had found her to be wise and comforting and unflappable from the start, even when another student set her own hair on fire trying to caramelize sugar.

Thus, without too much awkwardness, Rose found herself seated with Miss Farmer on the sofa, drinking cocoa and discussing her sad situation.

After Rose came to the part in which she discovered William had left the country, Miss Farmer *tsk-tsked.*

"That is an unhappy story indeed. However, it is not the whole of *your* story, is it?" She set down her cup. "You are a good cook, and that has not changed whether you are engaged or not. I understand about heartbreak and disappointment, but you must not let either define your person. Many young people let that happen. I did not."

Rose most certainly had let her widowhood define her for years, and as Fannie said, she could see herself letting it happen again with her newly broken heart. Rose wanted to stay tucked in bed in her room and go over in her mind in detail every minute she'd spent with William.

Should she ask Miss Farmer about her own heartbreak? Of course, there was the stroke at a young age that had caused Fannie to stay in bed for a long time and to live with a limp. Rose knew little else except the woman had never married.

"Why did *you* start to cook?" Rose ventured a safe topic.

Miss Farmer smiled. "Necessity, my dear. I needed to do something."

That struck a chord with Rose.

"What's more, as with you, it turned out I had an aptitude for it. However, I had to blunder along for years without tutelage. You do not. In the few months I've known you, I have seen greatness. Your meringues are light yet firm, and your *vol-au-vents* with seasoned fish are, in a word, divine. Not to mention, perfectly puffed, and I would give up an entire meal for a slice of your strawberry sponge."

Rose felt her cheeks grow warm with the effect of Miss Farmer's compliments.

"Thank you."

"You won't give all that up, will you, not because of something entirely unrelated happening in your life? I understand about staying in one's room, although it was forced upon me due to my health. I hated it. *You* have a choice. Use your talent to pull yourself out of any melancholy that has gripped you. That's my suggestion. These lavender biscuits are every bit as good as you said, by the way." She popped another into her mouth and stood up.

"I must be off. Thank you for your hospitality and letting me offer unsolicited advice."

Rose stood as well. "No, Miss Farmer, it is definitely I who am thankful. Your words and your kindness have indeed made an impression on me."

They walked toward the foyer.

"Then I will see you tomorrow in class?"

"Yes, you will." And this time, Rose meant it.

"That infernal bastard is dodging me," Reed said, storming into his bedroom where he knew Charlotte was reading by the window, her favorite place for quiet time when their children were in bed.

"What kind of talk is that with children in the house?" Charlotte admonished him. "You sound like a sore sheriff hunting down a slippery thief."

Reed shrugged. "A hotheaded attorney, perhaps."

"Yes precisely, or an exasperated farmer at reaping time with not a field hand in sight."

He blinked at her. *Exasperated farmer?*

"I can't stand it," he told her. "Rose is slipping back into that morose state that makes me fear for her future and her sanity, and my mother is considering not marrying Mr. Nickerson so she can stay home and tend to Rose as if she is an invalid. What my sister needs is a swift kick."

"Gracious. You *are* in a state. First of all, your sister is perfectly within reason to mourn her engagement and the life she had planned with Mr. Woodsom. He was ideal for her, and it is doubtful his like will come along again."

Reed felt a twinge of compassion for Rose. His wife was correct. One could not simply replace the ideal person. He could not imagine life without Charlotte, and at that moment, no doubt, his sister was unable to imagine her life going forward without William. Yet go forward she must. Except Bennet was the blockage.

"I have no doubt you will get the signature from Phineas Bennet eventually, even if you have to wait him out on his doorstep. After all, you showed great determination in coming out to Colorado and making sure I took in Lily and Thomas when I was too dense to see the right path."

He sat down beside her, a small smile already on his face.

"How do you do it, Mrs. Malloy?"

"Do what?" Charlotte asked, putting a marker in her copy of *The Scarlet Letter.*

"Disarm me, distract me, make me realize I overstate my problems?"

"Did I do all that?" She blinked and gave him her sweetest smile.

"Indeed," he said, eyeing her book. "I'm sorry I interrupted your reading."

Grimacing slightly, Charlotte lay it down on the table. "It is all heavy-handed sin and guilt. *Bah!* I'm not sure I can finish it anyway. Honestly, I much prefer Mr. Twain's *Huckleberry Finn,* no matter how the critics tout Mr. Hawthorne."

"Finn!" Reed repeated. "You've brought me right back to where I started."

"Shoot," Charlotte said. "Then I'd better try some more distracting." She stood up and embraced her husband, placing a searing kiss on his lips.

Putting his arms around her, he pulled her closer. *Mm.* He felt like purring when he held Charlotte. Slanting his head, he deepened the kiss and finished by nibbling on her lower lip.

"I love your lips," he told her when they broke apart. "That was some quite good distracting," Reed added. "However, I still feel as though I need a bit more disarming."

She grinned.

"Of course, Mr. Malloy." Charlotte wrapped her arms around his neck and drew his head down for another kiss.

"I need your help," Reed said, a long time later when they were lying wrapped in each other's arms, Charlotte's back resting against his front.

"What? More disarming?" she asked, stifling a yawn. "Aren't you tired?"

He chuckled and stroked his fingers across her bare shoulder.

"No, I meant I need your help with Rose and Bennet, and the dead men and Berne, and the yard overseer whatever his name is."

"Walsh," she supplied.

"Yes, him, too. Wait, how do you know his name?"

"Shoot," she said again.

Reed swept his hand down to rest on her pert bottom. He circled it with his warm palm.

"Nice," she murmured.

"I'd hate to have to spank you," he said into her ear. "For withholding the truth."

He felt her freeze in his arms.

"Spank me?" she repeated, and the breathy tone of her voice demonstrated her interest. In another moment, she pressed against him more firmly.

He groaned, then grumbled, "You're not supposed to sound so pleased about it."

"Well, if done correctly with a strong but kind man and a willing woman, I've read—"

"Charlotte," Reed interrupted. "Please tell me what you know about Walsh and why you know it."

She sighed. "Does this mean you're not going to spank me?"

He rolled her onto her stomach, pulled his hand back, and swatted her lightly on her rear.

"*Hm,*" she said, thoughtfully into the pillow.

"What do you think?" he asked, although he felt himself grow hard again and wondered at the unfamiliar source of his arousal.

"It *is* an interesting sensation," she admitted. "It caused a general warming and tingling that seemed to travel from my posterior forward to my—"

"I meant, tell me about the yard overseer."

"Oh," she said, and then giggled uncharacteristically. After a second, she regained her composure.

"Now that the cat is out of the bag, I can tell you when Rose came to me to investigate the sinking of the *Garrard*, I not only went to the insurance office, as you heard from Mr. Bennet, I also took a trip to East Boston."

"Dammit all! That was dangerous and rash and dangerous," he added again for emphasis. "Yes, I know I said dangerous twice. You should have come to me. She's *my* sister, and this is *my* problem."

Charlotte stiffened. "She is *like* a sister to me. I consider her to be *my* family, too. What's more, I didn't know there would be any danger in looking into the circumstances of a ship that capsized four years past. How could I know?"

"True," he conceded. "And you discovered how Berne received insurance money and then went to Kelly's yard?"

"Yes," Charlotte agreed.

"And you met with the overseer, Mr. Walsh?"

"He was quite forthcoming. Although when I tried to speak to Liam Berne, he had left early. Quite inconvenient."

"Good, I say." He didn't want his wife getting mixed up in this any further, not with bodies floating in the harbor.

"Not good," she said. "I left everything at loose ends, and I feel badly about it. Why don't we go together to Mr. Berne's house and—"

"No, I forbid it." He knew it was the wrong thing to say as soon as he said it.

"You what?" she sputtered.

"Two men are already dead as well as an entire boatload drowned. I don't want you within a mile of Berne. Nor do I want you going back to Kelly's. Do you understand me, Charlotte?"

He could see the mutiny in her eyes and changed tactics. "You have our children to consider," he reasoned, drawing her body close to him again, "and I would hate to have to find a new wife to be a mother to them, not to mention tend to my needs."

"Tend to your needs indeed! Mr. Malloy, you are beyond the pale!"

Reed grinned against her hair and lowered his hand to her bottom once more.

"I thought *this* was beyond the pale," he said, gently smacking her delightful rear again. "I don't think wanting to keep you out of harm's way is unreasonable to any degree. It is simply my loving you with all my heart."

He felt Charlotte soften against him and then press against his shaft expectantly. No more talk of his sister's incredibly complicated life. Tonight, Reed would succumb to the charms of his incredibly wonderful wife.

Finn watched The Parisien from his vantage point across the street. If he thought laying low, being respectful to Gilbert, and working a lowly job in the Ropewalk would cool things off, it hadn't. Precisely the opposite.

The day before, someone had placed a dead fish in the pocket of his jacket, which he'd hung in the Ropewalk's utility room. Tonight, he'd been followed home. Of that, he was certain.

After another few minutes, he watched a heavy-set man enter the restaurant. Only a few minutes later, he came out, looked up and down the street, and left. He certainly didn't seem to be a man who wanted fine French cuisine.

Pulling his collar up and his hat down, Finn dashed across the street, down the alley, and into the back entrance. As he charged into the kitchen, Louis looked up. He scowled.

"You are very popular, my young friend, but I cannot have people coming and going looking for you every day and night."

"The man who was just here, he asked for me?"

"He did." The chef turned back to his worktable, chopping something Finn couldn't see.

"Sorry." He started up the back stairs.

"Your lady friend's brother was here again, too," Louis called after him, "earlier today."

Finn sighed. He couldn't dodge the divorce much longer. Yet ending his marriage to Rose felt wrong on every level. He loved her, and somewhere deep down, she must still love him, even though he had bungled terribly and mucked up their lives.

Unlocking his door, it caught on something as he pushed it open. As soon as he saw the official-looking envelope, he didn't have to look inside to know what it contained.

"Damn," he muttered and tossed it onto his washstand. Reed Malloy was a persistent man, but at that moment, Finn was too exhausted to care. There'd been no joy in his life recently, except Chef Louis' cooking, and far too little rest.

At that moment, he decided to skip the former and opt for the latter. Removing his boots, Finn sprawled across the bed, then rolled onto his back. A sigh escaped him, and he let his eyes drift closed, intending to relax merely a few minutes before getting some dinner.

In his dream, Rose stole into his room, unable to stay away, and he held her and told her how much he loved her. Finn was not surprised to feel a hand shake him into wakefulness. Plainly, the eyes peering out of a face masked by a kerchief and staring down at him were definitely not his lovely wife's.

What's more, he didn't feel Rose's perfect lips pressed against his temple but rather the cold, blunt steel end of a gun. *Was this the end?*

"I could blow out your brains before you even wake up," grated the intruder's voice.

CHAPTER TWENTY-SEVEN

Not the honeyed words Finn was hoping for.

"You could. Rather loud though," he pointed out. "There are probably a lot of people in the dining room, not to mention the staff."

"I'm not afraid of a few cooks," the man muttered, holding up his free hand, large and calloused, and demonstrating how well he could make a fist. Clearly, he worked a tough job for a living. Judging by the size of him, maybe he was a stevedore.

"Besides you're talking fimble-famble. The restaurant's empty," the brute told him. "It's the middle of the bloody night."

He'd slept longer than he'd imagined. And now, Finn had best get himself out of this mess.

"Who sent you?"

The man might have smiled. Finn couldn't tell in the darkened room.

"Not important" he said. "Here's the message—too many people know you're alive. You've done a lousy job of hiding."

"If you kill me, each and every one of those people will know I've been murdered, and some of them may even give a fig. You can't kill everyone who knows about me."

"True, and the boss knows that. You've taken a job instead of leaving. Boss knows that, too."

So clearly, this man's boss wasn't Gilbert, who had given Finn the job.

"You can't kill me, and you can't starve me out since I've found work. And I have no family here for you to threaten."

This time Finn was certain the man smiled, and the brute's next words gave him chills.

"No family, mate, but there is your pretty Rose."

Finn kept his tone placid. "Not mine anymore. That's old news."

He started to sit up, and the man put his beefy paw onto Finn's chest.

"Here now, what are you up to?"

"Let me prove that Rose is nothing to me anymore. I've got divorce papers."

Finn shoved the man's hand aside and sat up. Reaching for the envelope, he tore it open and found Reed's note about taking the signed documents straight to his office. He put that aside and showed the intruder the first page.

"Right there, 'Rose Malloy versus Phineas Bennet in a suit for divorce.'"

Over his handkerchief mask, the man's eyes scanned the document while his bushy eyebrows drew together. So long did he peruse the page, Finn began to believe the goon couldn't read and was only looking for some word he knew.

Helping him out, Finn pointed to the word *Rose* and said, "That's all legal, do you see?"

After another moment, the man agreed. "Looks to be, yes. So?"

"So your boss can stop threatening her because she's nothing to me, nor I to her. At the risk of getting my brains blown, as you say, I'm telling you I won't investigate anything more about the *Garrard* or anything to do with her sinking. I'm simply working at the shipyard, and that's it."

"Boss don't want me to kill you tonight or give you a bash on the smeller. Looks like you've already had that done to you anyway." The intruder gestured with the end of the pistol to Finn's cut and bruised face.

"Nah, he wants me to fix it so you can't work," he finished.

Finn's heartbeat, already racing from being awakened by a thug, sped up further, and sweat broke out on his back. He wasn't about to let some faceless coward who sent goons out to do his dirty work take anything more from him.

As the gunman shifted his weapon toward Finn's knee, he erupted into movement.

Shoving the larger man with all his strength, Finn had the benefit of surprise even as they both hit the floor in a tangle. Straddling the intruder's expansive chest, Finn thrashed out at his head with his fists, over and over, until the man's arms went slack and his head lolled to the side.

Grabbing for the gun as he arose, Finn stepped away from the prone figure, his bum leg aching from the tussle on the floor.

Christ Almighty! He just wanted to get back the girl he loved and then design a few goddamn ships. *Was that too much to ask?*

Dressing quickly, he slipped the gun into his coat pocket. He wasn't about to try anything stupidly heroic. Heading straight for the police department, he showed them the gun and convinced a detective and a sergeant to return with him to his room.

Gingerly, the detective pushed the door open while Finn peered past him.

"Fuck!" he swore. The man was gone.

"Mama, you are not going to change your plans to marry Mr. Nickerson. Do you hear me? You are not!"

Rose had returned from class to find Evelyn wringing her hands.

"I have decided I can't leave you. Not alone in this enormous house."

"The house is quite reasonably sized, and I assume I will still have an allowance from Father's will and can keep Emily and Jillian, although I may let Bridget go, as two maids seems an excessive number."

"Maids and cooks are not family," her mother reminded her. "Besides Emily and Jillian go home at the end of the day. If you terminate Bridget, you will be all alone at night."

"Then I won't. Or I'll think about it. I don't have to decide at this moment. Why are you suddenly in such a state, Mama?"

Her mother sighed. "It was one thing to know you were moving out to live with your husband, and I with mine. It is another for me to be the one to move out and leave you here, a single girl."

A widow, Rose nearly said, as that was how she had become used to thinking of herself for so very long. *Before* William. And ever since he'd left the States, and her, she almost felt like one again.

"Not simply a single girl," Rose pointed out. "A divorced woman." *Or nearly so, if Reed would get on with it.* "As such, it is perfectly appropriate for me to stay here alone. What's more, I love this house and can think of nothing better than remaining in it and caring for it. I want to continue to dine where we have had so many lovely meals together and to sit in Father's study, where I still sometimes think I can smell his aftershave."

Her mother stared at her. Then she smiled. "Maybe it is I who is afraid to move on. I have lived here a very long time."

Setting down her shopping bag, Rose considered her mother a moment. "Do you love Mr. Nickerson?"

Her mother blushed prettily. "I do."

"Then you must marry him and enjoy many years with him. His house is lovely. All it lacks is your warmth." She clapped her hands with enthusiasm. "Once you are there, it will feel like your home because you will make it so."

Her mother looked unconvinced.

"Think of the gardens," Rose added. "All yours to putter in."

"I do *not* putter," her mother admonished, though a flash of keenness crossed her face. "Mr. Nickerson does have some fine planting beds, not to mention an Italian-crafted fountain."

"Knowing how everything has turned out for me," Rose confessed, "if I had the opportunity to start a new life with the man I love, I wouldn't hesitate. And neither should you."

Her mother crossed her arms and stared. "How did you become so grown up and wise, my little flower?"

Rose simply smiled. She wished she hadn't learned all her lessons the hard way. However, since she was staying put on Beacon Hill, she thought about her new plans for her old home.

"Mama, if I do wish to redecorate or change anything around, you won't mind, will you?"

"No, of course not. You will be mistress of No. 7 Mount Vernon Street, and you can do as you please."

Rose nodded. It was actually more than a little thrilling, the notion she was to become an entirely independent woman with no one to whom she would answer. *Good grief, she could barely conceive of such freedom.* She might redecorate the sitting room in a fashionably medieval style. Or with some Empire pieces that had recently come back into style. Or perhaps an exotic oriental décor.

Squinting, Rose let her gaze wander around the room and imagine it.

Hm, maybe she would just get a cat.

"I'm going to put on an apron and try out a recipe I learned today," Rose told her mother, who had long since stopped appearing shocked that her well-bred daughter liked to work in the kitchen alongside their cook.

"I may have to send someone out if Emily doesn't have everything I need, such as coriander."

"Will we be having your creation for dinner?" Evelyn asked.

"I do hope so, if it comes out well." Rose picked up her bag with its fresh fore-quarter of mutton, kissed her mother's cheek, and hurried down the hallway to the kitchen.

It did turn out well, and when Reed and Charlotte arrived unexpectedly later in the evening, they enjoyed a taste of Rose's mutton curry.

Speaking freely since everyone in the room was well-aware of Rose's marital status, Reed explained how he had been unable to contact Finn in days.

"Do you think he has found employment?" her brother asked her.

Rose shrugged. "I couldn't possibly know. I doubt he's at Kelly's yard where he used to work, as he told me he was tossed out."

"Strange," Charlotte said. "Even though I was questioning the overseer about the *Garrard*, he didn't mention being visited by one of her ghosts, back from the dead."

Rose considered. "Finn said he only spoke with the owner."

However, now her curiosity was piqued. *What was Finn doing with his days?* Reed was certain he was still in Boston, as confirmed by Chef Louis. Moreover, Finn had mentioned he was at work on that terrible day she'd encountered William outside her husband's room.

Her previous compulsion to be near Finn had vanished. Not surprisingly, her anger with him over hurting William had extinguished any feelings of excitement and wonder at seeing her dead husband among the living. Regardless, she supposed she could move things forward and become a free woman more quickly if she spoke with him herself. She could certainly stomach her indifference and insist he march himself over to her brother's offices with the signed papers.

First, Rose had to find him.

Charlotte pointed out Walsh's office as she walked onto the East Boston shipyard, this time in the reassuring company of her husband. After coming to an understanding that they would work together to help Rose, they decided to revisit Kelly's. However, the office was locked.

Reed asked one of the yard's only visible workers, hurrying past with a bucket of tar, where they might find the overseer.

"Mr. Walsh went on an unscheduled holiday," the man said. "That's all I know," he added as if expecting a follow-up question. "Grabbed his stuff and took off for parts unknown."

"Then you don't know when he'll be back?"

"No, sir." The man set his bucket down. "With old man Kelly never here no more, and now Walsh gone, I don't know as how this place'll continue."

"I suppose we could go find Mr. Kelly at home," Charlotte wondered.

"I hear he's taken to his bed after some bad news. Took his health right from him."

"Maybe Mr. Walsh has not left the area yet for his holiday," Reed suggested. "Where does he reside?"

The man stared hard at Reed, and it occurred to Charlotte he was not meaning to look aggressive, but, rather, he was wearing his thoughtful expression.

"I can tell you that," the man said, wiping a grimy hand under his nose, leaving a streak like a tar moustache. "Moved out of his walkup on Everett Street a few years back and bought hisself a fine house, on Bunker Hill. Quite the place, I hear Not sure I'd want to go away if I lived there."

The back of Charlotte's neck prickled. A few years back, perhaps four? Maybe Walsh came into quite a bit of money? Even though his name wasn't officially on the ship's insurance policy.

"That must have made Mrs. Walsh quite happy," she said. What's more, if Walsh went away without his wife, perhaps she would receive them in her home and be forthcoming on their good fortune.

The man let loose a short laugh. "I doubt that, as our overseer's never been married. There ain't no Mrs. Walsh."

With that, and a quick tug on the front of his cap, he picked up the bucket and strode away.

Charlotte felt her stomach drop, an unpleasant sensation that often assailed her when she at last understood something. Particularly if that something was abject evil.

Obviously, Walsh was a consummate liar. Moreover, he'd known how unstable the ship was and had let young men go to their deaths needlessly. She would bet her last laying chicken he'd been paid handsomely from the insurance money, a generous cut paid either by Dilbey, the ship's owner, or by Liam Berne.

"I know that look. What are you thinking?" Reed asked her.

She told him about Walsh's wedding excuse for not going on the *Garrard*.

Reed took her arm in his, and they turned toward their carriage.

"I suppose Berne was put on that policy and yanked off the boat not so much because he's a ruthless blackmailer or even smart enough to cook up insurance fraud, but because he was duped into being the patsy should anyone ever start asking questions."

"Most likely," Charlotte agreed.

"And when do you think the overseer will return from his time away, dear wife?"

"Never," she surmised.

"Most likely," Reed echoed her words. "I think we should send the police over to Dilbey's place before he disappears, too, if it's not already too late."

"What of Mr. Kelly?" she asked.

"I don't think he had anything to do with it. He was making good money every year until the disaster, and he wouldn't have risked his yard's reputation on a one-time payoff."

"You're probably correct," she said. "What of Mr. Gilbert?"

Reed shook his head. "I'm not sure. What do you think?"

"He, too, must have known the boat was poorly designed unless he was utterly incompetent. What's more, a yard overseer couldn't order the likes of Finn Bennet to build a ship incorrectly. Gilbert had to be party to this terrible scheme to give the orders. Tantamount to murder, isn't it?"

"I believe a judge and jury will see it that way, yes."

"For all three of them?" she asked.

Reed nodded. "Maybe four. Perhaps we can get Berne to tell us more if he understands it will save him from being held accountable."

"Good idea." Charlotte climbed into their carriage. "Should we try speaking to Mr. Gilbert at the Navy yard?"

"Yes. With a goodly sized police presence," Reed suggested.

Waving slightly at Chef Louis in his white uniform, busy at his stove, Rose went up to Finn's room.

The door was ajar. Inside, the chamber looked nothing as it had when she'd been there last. Instead of tidy and shipshape, as Finn called it, his things were strewn about as if someone had been looking for something. The chair she'd sat upon had been tipped over, and even his mattress was askew.

Not knowing what else to do and hoping Finn would return while she was there, she set to righting the place. She began by putting his clothing back in his chest of drawers and that was when she found the locket.

With a gasp, she retrieved it from the back of the top drawer, pulling the familiar chain out with a trembling hand. She didn't have to open it. She knew what was inside, a lock of her own hair, which she'd given him along with the locket and gold chain on their wedding day, a memento and hopefully a talisman to keep her husband safe. She recalled years earlier how bitterly she had cursed the abysmal job it had done of bringing Finn back to her after the ship went down. Then she'd thought of it no more.

Apparently, he'd kept it around his neck, and it had survived the shipwreck and his rescue and his years in the British Isles. Then apparently, when back in Boston, he'd removed it.

The fact that the gold locket, shining in her palm, was still in his ransacked room meant this had not been a robbery, or at least not a very thorough one. Someone had been looking for something specific or perhaps merely intended to scare him.

When she'd thoroughly straightened up the room to her satisfaction and still Finn had not appeared, she adjusted her hat, put on her gloves and went downstairs.

"Chef Ober," she said, wishing she didn't have to disturb him while he was working.

"Oui, mademoiselle?" He didn't turn.

"I apologize for interrupting you, but can you tell me where I might find Mr. Bennet?"

She saw the man pause in stirring his sauce before resuming a gentle motion with the spoon.

"Your brother asked me the same thing the other day. As did another man. Everyone wants Phineas. All for different reasons, I suspect." He looked up from the pan. "Why do you want to find him?"

Rose felt her cheeks grow warm. *Why did she want to find him?* She certainly didn't owe this man an explanation. Walking closer, she glanced at the sunny yellow sauce with flashes of rich orangey-red.

"Saffron," she surmised. "How unusual. And expensive," she added.

Chef Louis beamed at her. "You cook?" he asked.

She nodded. "What are you making to go with this sauce?"

"Crispy chicken," he said. "I'll add a little roasted garlic."

"Some cardamom," she offered.

He raised his eyebrows. "Really?"

"Gives it a magical taste that no one can figure out."

"Yes," he nodded, smacking his lips once as if tasting it in his mind. "I can imagine that perfectly. Thank you," he added.

Rose smiled.

"Your man is at the Navy yard now. He works there."

Her man? Not anymore.

"Thank you, Chef."

As she exited, she considered her plan. At that hour, the streets were jammed with traffic, and her horse and carriage would go nowhere fast. However, with nearly two hundred streetcars threading their way throughout the city every hour, one was certain to be going her way.

Yet which way was the quickest? She could go left along Winter Street and back toward the Park Street Station. At the last moment, she turned right and headed toward Washington Street. Within minutes, she saw a streetcar marked No. 296 with "Roxbury and Charlestown" emblazoned on the dasher. *Thank goodness!*

Rose clambered aboard and paid her fare, nodding to the conductor before taking a vacant seat. The car wound its way through the financial district along Milk Street, through Post Office Square, and along Congress to Adams Square, before rejoining Washington Street. She sighed in frustration at the traffic and the number of vehicles of every type. What's more, every few seconds, it seemed, a pedestrian ran in front of the trolley.

Soon, they crossed Haymarket Square and passed the Northern Depots, turning right onto Causeway Street and left onto Beverly Street, all the while picking up people and dropping others off. Rose watched the conductor record each and every passenger's fare that he collected on the mounted register.

At last, they crossed the Warren Avenue drawbridge and passed through City Square onto Chelsea Street. Rose stood up impatiently as they traveled along the road bordering the shipyard. She disembarked at the corner of Bunker Hill Street and found herself trotting in haste the short distance to the Charlestown shipyard's main gate, feeling anxious as the late-day sun sank lower. Soon the yard would close, and she might miss him again.

The yard spread out before her, to the right and left, was enormous, like a small town. *How would she ever locate Finn?*

At the gate, a young man in a naval uniform came up to her.

"May I help you, miss?"

Rose didn't want to mention Finn's name. She hesitated.

"Yes, I'm trying to find," she hesitated, racking her brain for the name of the master builder Finn had mentioned, "Mr. Gilbert." He would know where Finn was.

"Yes, miss. Is he expecting you?"

"No," Rose said. "Yet it is important I speak with him."

After a moment's hesitation while he seemed to consider, the guard nodded.

"Master Builder Gilbert is normally in the Muster House." With that the young, straight-backed man marched off, and she had no choice except to follow him. The place was bustling with workers, and a few times, someone strode between them carrying a long skein of rope or a 2-by-6, and she nearly lost sight of her guide.

At last, he slowed his step in front of a round building that reminded her of a squat turret. Taking her inside, the guard led her up the stairs to the third floor.

"He's there, miss." He gestured to the oldest man in the room. "Master Builder Gilbert. This lady is here to see you, sir."

Rose faltered, as a mustachioed man with graying hair looked up from his desk, surveying her. As he slowly got to his feet, her head felt light.

What on earth was she to say to him now? That she knew Finn Bennet was alive? That she thought this man's incompetence had helped send men to their deaths? Perhaps she should counterfeit that she needed a ship built.

"I was sent by The Boston Cooking School," were the words that finally came out of her mouth. She nearly rolled her own eyes when she heard herself.

A couple of the other men in the room snickered.

Gilbert's eyebrows shot up. "On what business?" he asked, without any invitation for her to sit down.

In for a penny, in for a pound, Rose thought. "As you may or may not know, we have a nutrition program at the school. We are studying how sailors fare on . . . well, on sailors' fare. If you get my meaning."

The men laughed again. One said, "Gilbert, she wants to know if our boys stay healthy on Navy chow."

"Why would you want to talk to me?" he asked.

Quite right. Think, think, think. "We believe men need more vegetables in their diets. To stay healthy. Naturally, we would pickle them for long journeys. The vegetables, not the men." Rose laughed nervously.

To a man, they looked at her as if she had three heads.

She continued, "We are wondering if you can design space in your vessels for more . . . *um*, pickle jars."

"Are you serious?" Gilbert spluttered. "Look, Miss—"

"Malloy," she provided unthinkingly and then cringed. *How stupid of her.* However, if he recognized her name, he gave no outward sign.

"While we are very busy here, Miss Malloy, we aren't designing new ships for the Navy at this juncture. No galleys, no storage, no shelves for your pickled vegetables."

Rose was about to turn away, when he added, "However, I'll get my assistant to take you to the Stores Sergeant. I'm sure he'll be most interested in discussing the sailors' nutritional needs with you."

She nearly protested, but then, decided to play along. At least she would still be able to search for Finn.

"Wait here a moment," Gilbert instructed her before vanishing down the flight of stairs with more haste than she thought someone of his age could muster.

Rose merely smiled at the other men, who went back to their work, and then she waited in silence. In a few minutes, another man arrived, not dressed in a uniform as her first guide had been. Instead, he wore civilian clothing as did so many of the workers at the yard.

"Right this way, miss," he said kindly. "I've been told to take you to Sergeant Morrison to talk about supplies."

"Yes, thank you." Rose accompanied him down the two flights of stairs and out of the building. They crossed from one side of the yard to the other, traversing the main thoroughfare, and eventually, they ended up in front of a brick building without signage.

"The Stores Sergeant is in here, miss. You'll have to meet with him by yourself. I have to get back to work." He opened the door for her and stood back.

So, she wasn't going to be left alone to wander the yard in search of her husband. Rose sighed. Perhaps she could leave the Stores Sergeant quickly and head out on a hunt by herself.

"Thank you," she offered and looked inside. It was a dimly lit antechamber, from what she could see, and quite empty. Perhaps someone had been there recently, for bits of sawdust circled in the air, caught in the late-afternoon sunlight.

"Right in there, miss," her guide urged.

Rose took a step inside. "Sergeant?" she called out but was met by silence.

"I don't think he's here." She started to turn exactly as the door closed behind her.

"How rude!" Putting her hand on the knob, Rose found it to be locked. *Oh dear!*

"Sergeant?" she called out again hopefully.

Nothing and no one responded to her. She took a few hesitant steps forward until she was in the doorway of the next room, peering into the absolute darkness beyond. Considering the rest of the yard was bustling, it was unsettling to be in a confined space of stillness. *What was going on?*

Rose cleared her throat glancing again at the door behind her. However, before she could say another word, something that felt like a sack came down over her head. She shrieked but a hand clamped over her mouth, pressing the cloth that smelled like grain against her face, and a strong arm snaked over her chest, pinning her arms to her sides.

She was silenced and subdued, mad as a wet cat, and quite terrified.

She half-expected to have her throat slit or to be knocked unconscious. Instead, her silent captor pushed her forward at a slow shuffle. When they reached the other side of the room, she heard another door being opened, and then she was shoved by a strong hand placed in the middle of her back.

Rose fell unceremoniously to her knees at the same time as she heard the heavy door behind her grate closed.

CHAPTER TWENTY-EIGHT

Immediately, Rose yanked the sack from her head and gasped at the impermeable darkness surrounding her. There was not a ray of light anywhere. She didn't feel brave enough to stand up, so she crawled in the direction from which she thought she'd entered—hopefully, toward the door. Perhaps her abductor had gone to get a rope to secure her hands and feet and would return momentarily.

Suddenly, all of Finn's warnings became very real. She'd been foolish to come to the shipyard.

Crawling forward slowly, hampered by her skirt which kept getting caught under her knees, Rose eventually reached out and touched a wall, cool and firm. *Unfortunately, not a door.* Working her way up the wall, using her hands to inch higher and higher, eventually she stood upright.

Her pulse slowed a little from gaining her new vantage point. Whatever it was, it was preferable to being in the middle of the enclosure and not knowing what was beside her.

All at once, she heard a sound, a scraping of heels on the floor, down to her left and not too far away.

She wasn't alone!

Perhaps that should have calmed her. Instead, it terrified her. *Friend or foe? Man or beast?*

Of course not a beast, she scolded her wildly running thoughts, *and if not a friend, at least a fellow prisoner, so certainly not a foe.*

"Hello," she said into the pitch black, her voice coming out in a raspy whisper. She cleared her throat and tried again. "Is someone here?"

"Mmph," she heard. Someone was trying to speak but couldn't. Then more scraping sounds and frantic movements came out of the darkness.

"I know you're close and restrained," she said as calmly as she could. "I shall come to you."

With her heart pounding again, she shuffled slowly in the direction of the noise, keeping one hand on the brick wall beside her. Then something touched her head, and she shrieked, ducking and waving her hands above her head. Immediately, she thought of bats and other creepy creatures, yet her hands touched only ropes hanging.

Still, it unnerved her that something might sweep across her face, so she got down on her hands and knees once more and crawled toward the noises.

"It was nothing," she said, speaking to whomever she was approaching, the sound of her own voice keeping her calm. "Only a rope touched me, and I panicked."

"Mmph," came again, closer this time.

Reaching out a hand, Rose touched a booted foot, then another. She ran her hands up the legs, man's legs, realizing they were bound with rope, tied together securely. She didn't hesitate in moving closer, feeling her way up to someone sitting, leaning back against the wall, her fingers on his stomach and chest before finally brushing across a mouth bound by a rag. This, she untied, already knowing who it was.

Rose tugged off the gag and ran her fingers over Finn's cheeks.

"Are you hurt?" she asked, nearly kissing him, so glad not to be alone in the darkness.

"Just my pride," he said, his face inches from hers and utterly invisible. "Are you?"

She shook her head then realized he couldn't see her response.

"No, only frightened half to death. Who did this?"

"I don't know. Gilbert, most likely. Quickly, please. My hands are tied behind my back. See if you can work the knots loose. And hurry. I have no idea how long we have, but we don't want to be here when whoever locked us in returns."

"What is happening?" Rose asked, working as quickly as she could in the dark to free his hands.

"I'll explain when we're somewhere safe. Tell me how you came to be here."

"I came looking for you," she said, hearing him swear softly at her admission.

"God, I wish you hadn't."

She started to bristle at his words, pausing in her actions, and he urged her to concentrate.

"Come on, love, keep at it. I only meant I thought you were safe and far from here."

Rose continued to struggle with the knots at his wrists. They were expertly tied as only a seaman could do. Eventually, however, she worked them loose, although it seemed like hours had passed when she finally managed to free his hands.

Even in the dark, Finn made quick work of the rest of his bindings around his legs, while she pressed her hands against the firm brick and slowly stood up once again. Tentatively, she made her way along the wall at his back, seeking a door.

Having lost all sense of direction, she didn't know if she was going back the way she'd first entered or farther into the building. She came to some crates, which impeded her progress until she felt her way around them, and continued until she reached a corner.

"Rose," Finn's voice came out of the blackness, comforting her.

"Yes?"

"I'm nearly free," he said.

"I haven't found a door nor window yet," she told him.

After another few minutes of silence, she felt the wall change from brick to plaster and surmised she was touching an interior wall. In another moment, she felt a doorframe and then a handle.

"A door! I think it goes farther into the building though, not outside."

"Keep talking or humming or something," Finn ordered

Rose began to hum. In the darkness, with her senses heightened, she heard him approaching. Yet when his hand suddenly brushed her shoulder, she cried out before she could stop herself. When he took firm hold of her upper arm, she wanted to sag against his warm and comforting form.

Instead, she gritted her teeth. She would be strong, courageous even, and help get them out of the mess they were in.

Rose heard Finn rattle the door handle. Then all was silent, except for a brushing sound above her head.

"What are you doing?" she asked, keeping her voice low.

He seemed to pause in his endeavors. "Why are you whispering?"

"I don't know," she admitted, her voice still soft. "Maybe because I'm barely breathing."

Against all reason, he chuckled softly. "Well, keep breathing. I don't want to have to carry you out of here."

She couldn't help smiling into the darkness.

"*Aha,*" he exclaimed.

"What?" she asked.

"There's a key above the frame." Finn paused, scrabbling at the handle. "In case anyone gets locked in, I expect. Or maybe the key's been here since the place was built, and no one remembered it. First place I always look," he added. "Maybe it's a Maine notion."

There were more noises as he fumbled to get the key into the lock. Then, lovely as her sister Sophie's music to her ears, Rose heard the click of the tumblers as they turned.

Finn eased the door open, and what seemed to be blinding light shone through the opening.

Blinking, she looked past him, realizing the brightness was merely the last rays of the sun disappearing over the western part of the city and coming in through the side of ill-fitting window shades in the next room.

"I'd rather go back than farther inside," Rose said, still keeping her voice quiet.

Finn didn't speak at first, then he looked behind him, with the sunlight illuminating the confines of their makeshift prison.

Rose turned back, too. Another door was in the opposite wall, obviously the way she'd come in. Finn's ropes lay discarded in the middle of the small chamber. More ropes hung from beams and a few storage crates lined one wall.

"Which way?" she asked.

At that precise moment, they heard footsteps and the unmistakable sound of a key in the outer door.

Without a word, Finn grabbed her hand and hauled her into the next chamber. As he closed the door swiftly behind them and locked it, she heard the other door into their prison slam open.

"Finn!" she exclaimed as a bolt of fear slashed through her.

Again, he took her hand securely in his, and in the next instant, they were running across the floor of a small storeroom and out the other side into a narrow alley between two buildings. Those in pursuit would have to go back the way they came and around the structure, buying their prey a little time.

Finn clearly had a destination in mind. Without hesitation, he dragged her hell-bent across the gray granite of the yard, now deserted of any workers. She surmised it had taken her at least an hour to untie him! They continued across some short-cropped grass, across mud, too, until Rose thought she would rather drop and give herself up than take another step.

When they reached a massive wrought iron door, she looked up and realized where they were. The Ropewalk, the longest granite building in the entire United States!

Finn heaved open the door and dragged her inside before closing it quietly behind them. For a second, he paused, giving her a chance to catch her breath. The pungent smell of the tarred yarns, the oiled machinery, and the hemp was all encompassing and momentarily made Rose's eyes water.

Between heaving great breaths of air into her lungs, she asked, "How on earth did you know about—?"

"This is where I've been working," he told her. "It seemed safer to hide out here than to risk running across the yard and getting shot."

"But surely there are people out there who can help us."

"If someone wants to, they can shoot from the cover of any number of buildings while we try to make it from here to the gate. Whoever nabbed you could say you were a trespasser and they thought I was, too. The fact I'm employed here wouldn't be discovered until after we were both quite dead." Finn shook his head. "No, we can't trust anyone out there."

She supposed he was right.

As they started to wander through the cool stone building, Rose couldn't help gawking at the massive yet narrow structure, that was over thirteen hundred feet long, as Finn informed her. She'd never seen a masonry building so large.

Stretching before her were massive skeins of rope that ran the length of the building, disappearing farther than her eye could see. Under them were steel tracks upon which sat complicated carriages with rope wound in their interiors.

Moreover, all around her, there was still dust motes floating in the air, and Rose had the distinct impression the workers had only recently vacated the building.

Obviously, there were dozens of places they could hide.

"I've seen this place from a distance all my life," she said, "yet it's the first time I've been inside."

"Why would you?" he asked. "It's not exactly a sightseeing attraction."

He didn't hesitate in drawing her toward the building's center, filled with every kind of modern machine for drawing out the hemp and turning single yarn into multiple strands and for twisting those strands, eventually braiding them into strong rope.

She was still breathing hard from the run and glanced at him to see if he was doing the same. It had obviously been difficult for Finn, whose limp was more pronounced than ever, although she hadn't even noticed it when they were fleeing for their lives across the shipyard.

"Let's go in farther," he urged, and they went half the length of the first floor before he settled them down between two huge coils of strong, hemp rope.

Safely ensconced, Rose hunkered down beside him, sure no one could find them. And even if they did, she felt safe with Finn by her side.

He rubbed his shin a moment. Then he scooted forward, straddling his legs on either side of her, while she curled her own underneath her skirts, which she arranged around herself for warmth.

"We need to stay put for a while. When it's dark, we'll slip out," Finn said, bringing back the clamp of fear that had only just released its hold upon her. "Hopefully, whoever is behind this will assume we headed straight for the front gate."

"Stay put," she repeated, considering the very real yet unknown danger.

Her brother would be livid. *And William?* She couldn't even imagine what he would have thought, except this was precisely the type of situation into which he'd feared she would become entangled because of Finn. He would have been wrong in that case, for she'd walked into it herself, open-eyed, like a ninny.

"Yes," Finn added, "until the rest of the yard closes and empties out. I think the only way we can get out of here is under the cover of darkness."

She swallowed. *Good God!* Her mother would be frantic when she hadn't returned at teatime and missed supper as well. She could simply tell Finn she was leaving. After all, the true threat was to him, wasn't it? She'd been inadvertently caught in the same snare but by mistake. It had to have been a mistake!

If she walked out the door and found any workers still making their way to the gate, she would be safe to walk with them. She could probably stroll beside the first kind-looking man . . .

"I know what you're thinking, as you sit there fidgeting, but I can't let you go out there," Finn said, his tone brooking no debate. "It's too easy for you to be nabbed."

"I could simply—"

"With a man on either side of you, like at the theater, you'd be silenced and abducted without anyone noticing, even if there was a crush of workers. More easily so, in fact." After a pause, he added, "Please, don't be difficult."

Difficult? Any residual fear was quickly channeled into anger.

"*Me?* Difficult?" Rose snapped. "Whatever can you mean? I've been most accommodating ever since you reappeared at my engagement party."

"You were always willful, going out after dark when we both knew it wasn't safe. Not to mention headstrong, which I admit I admired about you. Even respected. It meant I could see you. I apologize for implying you've been anything but helpful in this situation."

Finn took her hands and held them both. "I can't let anything happen to you, not on my account." Then he glanced around at where they'd ended up. "Not more than what has already happened, at any rate. You've been safe and you fell in love, and you were happy until my return. I did not mean to wreck all that."

Rose stared into his familiar eyes, gazing so intently back at her.

"It wasn't all trifle and cream while you were gone," she said quietly. "I did not simply bounce back to living the way I had before we met."

Finn offered her a half-smile. "You *were* quite the social miss, as I recall."

She felt her cheeks warm. "I suppose I was." William had said something similar to indicate she'd been considered a bit flighty. "I was young."

"I'm not condemning you. You were doing exactly what a beautiful young lady without a care in the world should have been doing."

Rose sighed. "I feel as though I've aged a hundred years in the past month," she said.

"Oddly, you don't look a day over eighty-five."

She slapped his arm.

"In truth," Finn added, "I know exactly what you mean. I considered myself an adult before. Looking back four years, I think I acted like a child. I built ships. I saw you, fancied you, and fell in love in two shakes. And I married you without a nod to propriety."

At his mention of their marriage, Rose remembered the treasure she'd found earlier.

"I found the locket in your room. I can't believe it survived."

"My room?" He cocked his head.

"Yes, I went there first before I came here."

He sighed. "That was dangerous."

"As it turned out, the danger had come and gone." She explained about the state of his living quarters. "Was someone looking for something?"

"Not that I can think of. Most likely another attempt to scare me the hell out of Boston. Excuse my language." Then he shrugged. "I have nothing from my life before, except the locket."

"It's amazing you have it still."

"No," Finn contradicted her, staring into her eyes. "If I survived, it would, too. Not surprising at all. I never took it off, not until I came back and . . .," he trailed off.

"And what? Saw your wife at her engagement party?" Rose supplied, tamping down any guilt over William. She had no reason to feel badly in that regard.

"Something like that."

Still holding her hands, Finn now slipped his fingers between hers, so they were firmly intertwined. Pleasurable sensations feathered through her. They had both grown up and grown apart, but her body's reaction to him felt exactly the same. She knew what pleasant sensations would occur if he simply stroked the back of her hand with his thumb.

Then, as if reading her thoughts, he did so.

Even through her favorite gray gloves, he traced a heated path on her hand and then up her wrist. She clamped her lips around any sound that threatened to escape at his touch.

"I know I have no right to be jealous," Finn said, his voice low. "But seeing you with another man, it was . . . it made me . . . I couldn't stand it. I thought I would go mad or do *someone* bodily harm."

She nodded. Merely imagining him chatting up some young miss while in England or Scotland pained her.

Again, as if knowing what she was thinking, he said, "I want you to know I was faithful to you the entire time I was away."

His words were a gift that went a long way to assuaging her lingering resentment over the hurt he'd caused her.

"From the first time we kissed, I could never imagine being with any other woman," he confessed.

Finn dropped her hands and briefly closed his eyes, running his fingers through his short hair until it stood on end.

"Despite what you think, I know the worst thing I have done to you was not staying away. The worst thing I did was coming back and ruining your perfect new life."

"Then why did you?" Rose couldn't help asking, as any previous answer he'd give her had not been satisfactory.

"God help me, I knew my returning would destroy everything you had gained since I'd left, whether I reached Boston before your marriage or after. Yet I couldn't help myself. I couldn't let you slip away without seeing you again. Letting you know how much I loved you. How much I've always loved you."

Rose flinched as if he'd struck her. His announcement of loving her—at long last—felt pointless, almost an insult, and certainly too wretchedly late. The wheels were in motion for their divorce, and like those of a fully stoked steam engine, she didn't see how they could be stopped or even veer from the track.

Nor did she even want to stop the proceedings.

Anger at his timing bubbled to the surface once again.

"You are a callous bastard to say that to me now. Yet I was a selfish child, who thought I was a woman. I should never have married you in the first place. No matter what you say, Finn, I won't believe you ever loved me as I loved you. If you had, you could not have stayed away."

He grabbed her by the shoulders and looked her in the eye.

"You're wrong. My love for you and knowing you loved me, too, was what saved me from dying after the sinking. It was the only difference between me and the other men on that ship. When I got to Plymouth, I wrote a dozen letters while recuperating." He glanced away, then back into her blue gaze.

"I destroyed them all. Each time I finished pouring out my love and explaining about the ship's sinking and how I'd finally reached England, each time I realized how ridiculous it would be for you to receive a declaration from a half-crazed, delusional dead man. I was still having vivid nightmares and didn't know if they would ever stop."

"I would have—" she began, but he cut her off.

"Then I got injured, I was barely able to stand upright. A penniless invalid, prone to wild imaginings. That was the man I'd become. I was, in short, a disaster." His voice broke on the last word.

"It wasn't fair to you," Finn finished in little more than a whisper.

In the silence that followed, his grip relaxed, and he held her more gently. Rose stared into his stormy eyes, wishing impossible wishes while she did.

"I kept thinking of your joyful spirit," he added, "and your family, so precious to you, and your life here. I didn't fit in with any of it. Yes, I knew you would grieve, although frankly, I didn't comprehend the enormity of it because I couldn't conceive of you loving me that much."

She gasped. *How could he not have known what he'd meant to her?*

"I was sorry to cause you pain, Rose, and I still am, but I knew you would recover and live the life you were meant to have. With someone like Woodsom, not with me, a gentleman of the four oats, as they say."

Without wit, money, credit, or manners. A ridiculous saying, and one that certainly didn't sum up Finn Bennet.

Before she could speak, he placed one of his strong hands behind her head to cradle it and drew her forward.

"Through every minute of being away from you, I always loved you beyond anything."

Then he kissed her, and the years fell away. They were simply Rose and Finn in a stolen moment, expressing their ardor as they'd always done.

With her eyes closed, and the familiar sensation of his mouth upon hers, in that instant, everything was perfect. She breathed him in and pretended.

When at last Finn drew back and she opened her eyes, the memories rushed back of all that had passed. She recoiled, feeling as though she would burst into tears.

He frowned, most likely at seeing her devastated expression. Before she had time to do more than take in a deep breath, Finn kissed her again, this time teasing her mouth open with his tongue and, with her small acquiescence, sliding it between her lips to taste her more fully.

Rose sucked gently on the invader, as a spark ignited low in her body. Instinctively, she lifted her arms and laced her hands at the back of his neck. The bodice of her gown restrained her breasts, grown suddenly sensitive, and the fabric rasped unbearably against her stiffening nipples. A vivid image of Finn's mouth kissing her sensitive peaks four years earlier shot through her.

When his teeth grazed her lower lip, biting it gently, the spark deep within her erupted into flames. Feeling as if she would incinerate, wriggling against the heated torture that burned at the apex of her thighs, Rose sucked harder on his tongue and moaned aloud.

His hands finally, blissfully, touched her breasts, cupping them before stroking their plumpness through the fabric. It was not enough, only making her desire more frantic for release. She moaned again and whispered his name.

If only he could touch her skin.

She opened her eyes as he pushed her gently back to lean on the coiled ropes behind her. Then slowly, he raised her skirts, his fingers trailing along her stocking-clad thighs.

Was he trembling? Rose wasn't sure. I might be her own shuddering she could feel.

His shimmering gaze reflected the desire she felt, as well as the unspoken question.

In the middle of this danger, with threat lurking literally on the other side of the wall, Rose wanted Finn Bennet more than she ever had before. More than she'd ever wanted anybody. She nodded.

A small yet serious smile played about his mouth.

As if they had all the time in the world—or perhaps because it seemed time had suddenly stopped to give them a few minutes of paradise—Finn eased her skirts up the rest of the way, letting the cool air fan her briefly. She felt the chill for mere moments, only long enough to watch him undo his trousers and draw out his hardened sex.

Rose swallowed, her heart pounding while the rest of her throbbed with anticipation, and knowing exactly what she wanted. If Finn hesitated or asked permission, she might scream.

CHAPTER TWENTY-NINE

Finn separated Rose's drawers where they met at the apex of her thighs, feeling the dampness of her dark curls. His brain was awash in disbelief at what was about to occur. Sheer gratification, as well as gratitude, flowed through him when she arched and moaned as his knuckles brushed her cleft. Clearly, she was as ready as he was.

Positioning the head of his shaft between her legs, Finn wished he had time to prolong their lovemaking, to touch every inch of her skin, to taste her, to suck her soft breasts. But he couldn't. That they were doing this at all, at this time, was madness. Unexpected, miraculous, precisely like Rose, and he knew he mustn't dally.

Instead, he pressed into her, slowly and steadily. He couldn't help groaning with delight.

Her body tightened around him, and he had to grind his teeth to keep from climaxing immediately.

"Finn?" she said uncertainly.

Was he hurting her?

"Should I stop?" he whispered against her neck.

"God, no," she said. "Just . . . I don't know. It's strange, but wonderfully so."

She relaxed under him as he began to move, deep into her warmth and wetness, then drawing out again. He couldn't last long, that was painfully obvious. Yet more than anything, he wanted her to experience the joy of coupling.

He kissed the white column of her neck, and she arched it, exposing the vulnerability of her throat.

"Please," Rose said.

"Tell me," he murmured, barely able to think and unsure what she was asking.

"Can you touch me? Down there? At the same time as you . . . ?"

Frantically, he slipped his hand between their bodies, seeking her nubbin. He stroked his finger across its firmness, and she cried out. Loudly. Too loudly. Covering her mouth with his own to silence her, he continued his sensual ministrations.

"*Mmmm,*" she said.

"*Mm?*" he asked.

"*Mmm, mmm, mmm.*"

She was close, which was good because he feared he was closer.

Finn stroked her faster, while continuing to thrust deep into her slick, tight passage. All at once, she stiffened. He felt her body quivering under his as she cried out into his mouth. Then she twisted her head to break the contact and take in great gasps of air as she neared utter repletion.

When he knew her to be sated, when the pressure at the base of his spine could not be held back a second longer, he pulled out of his wife and spent himself against the coiled rope beside her.

As soon as Rose opened her eyes and focused on him once more, she smiled, a satisfied look upon her lovely face.

Quickly, he helped her rearrange her clothing and then attended to his own.

"That was quite unexpected," she said at last, glancing away and blushing as if he'd merely stolen a kiss.

Finn nearly laughed at her understatement. "That was extraordinary."

Rose did laugh then, a throaty, delightful sound that wound its way around his heart. When she spoke again, it was to give him an order.

"Tell me what happened to you today."

He hated to break the cocoon of placidity they'd created, but she was waiting for a response.

"A man held a gun to my head the other night in my room, so it's no surprise you found it ransacked. I had no doubt he was quite real and not a figment of my imagination when he threatened to shoot my kneecaps."

She gasped as if such viciousness had never occurred to her. And why should it have?

"Despite enlisting the help of the police, the intruder slipped away. Today, I thought I saw Liam here at the yard, precisely where he should not be, walking near the Commandant's house."

Rose nodded. "I know the one you mean, with the four chimneys. It has lovely gardens. I went to a party there once." She frowned. "Did he go inside?"

"No. If he had, I might as well have tossed myself into the ocean right then and there. If this corruption went up as far as the base commander, as high as admiralty, my goose was cooked for sure. But he went right past, directly to Gilbert's office. I asked myself why he was here instead of doing his job at Kelly's."

"I spoke with him today," she offered. "Mr. Gilbert, I mean, not Mr. Berne."

Finn grimaced involuntarily, imagining Rose at the Musket House, like a lamb to slaughter.

"No doubt why you ended up here." He couldn't help the hard edge to his own voice. "Did you ask for me by name?"

She shook her head. "I made up a story so I could look around the base, hoping to find you because —" she broke off, a strange expression on her face.

"Why?"

She hesitated.

"Why, Rose? Why did you come to the base and put yourself in such danger?"

"To ask you to sign the divorce papers," she said quietly.

Her words cut like a knife gutting a helpless fish. Even with Woodsom out of the way, she wanted to be free of him.

He couldn't blame her. Look where knowing him had brought her. Still, it stung.

"Anyway," she said, "go on, what happened next?"

"I waited for Liam to come out. Before he did, I was grabbed from behind, a sack crammed over my head. I was punched hard in the stomach so I couldn't breathe and dumped where you found me."

"I was, too," she said, "except I wasn't punched or trussed up as you were."

"Dammit!" The idea of her being manhandled by some goon made his heart pound and his blood boil.

Perhaps it was the look of shock on his face that caused Rose to add, "Sorry for interrupting again. Please continue."

He took a steadying breath. She was here with him. She was safe, except for his being unable to keep his hands off of her. With that thought, he grabbed hold of both her hands, realizing they'd made love with her gloves on. How strange!

"When I could breathe again," Finn continued, "I was already bound and gagged and in the storage room in the pitch black. Then you arrived and, honestly, at first, I was unsure . . ."

He didn't finish his sentence. In a flash, however, he saw she understood.

"You were unsure if I was real, weren't you?"

"Yes," he confessed. "Right up until you untied me." Her arrival had been too similar to so many of his disappointing dreams.

Rose offered him a smile in the waning light.

"I suppose real peril is better than believing it's a trick of your mind, yes?"

She did understand, and it felt like a massive weight lifted off his chest.

"Rose, you have no idea."

"What do we do now?" she asked.

"As I said before, we wait. I know the yard fairly well, but whoever did this knows it better. We need darkness to get out of here."

Into the silence that followed came Rose's next question. "Will you tell me about your injury?" She pulled one hand free of his and placed it upon the knee of his good leg.

He rested his hand over hers, imprisoning it. "It's not a very interesting tale."

"It wasn't caused during the ship's sinking," she pressed.

"No, it was my own stupidity. I let my mind wander while working." Looking up into her dark blue eyes, his breath caught in his chest. *How could he ever be worthy of this woman?*

She frowned at him, clearly not understanding his intense expression.

"Tell me," Rose persisted.

"I was wielding an adz."

"I don't know what that is." She gave a rueful smile.

"Why should you? It's a wicked tool, used by brutish men." He caressed the side of her face. "It's like a large axe, only heavier, made out of forged steel. It has a curved chisel head," he added, demonstrating the shape with his hands. "I was hewing timbers with it, *dubbing*, we say. That is, carving out the wood."

"Why am I already feeling a little queasy?" she asked, then added, "Go on."

"Unfortunately, I was not attending to the work at hand. My thoughts were like driftwood on the tide. I should have been concentrating. Instead, I was thinking of—" he broke off sharply.

Finn considered telling her how her face and the memories of them together used to fill his waking moments. That might be manipulative. He didn't want to make her feel guilty, nor become an object of her pity. Yet he wanted her to know he hadn't callously put her aside.

"I was always thinking good thoughts of being with you," he continued, and watched her nod solemnly, her large eyes never leaving his. "A moment's carelessness was all it took. Splintered my shin bone. Damn painful, too."

He lifted his trouser leg and rolled down his stocking. Rose gasped and put a hand on her own stomach. He had no doubt it was churning for the scar was ugly and deep, a white line, running crookedly across his shin about four inches below his knee.

"I was damn lucky it didn't chop my leg in half, but it wasn't a full blow. A knot on the timber deflected the blade. Unfortunately, right into my shin bone. As I said, though, it was a glancing strike."

Rose reached her hand slowly out to touch the scar, but Finn released his pant leg, covering the old injury. Grabbing for her other hand, he held them both in his again.

"I'm all right," he said. "There's no pain anymore except on the dampest of evenings when it throbs a bit."

"Yet you limp," she began.

He shrugged. "I lost a wedge of bone, but I had a fine physician. I was in Newcastle at the time and was treated at the Infirmary. Couldn't have asked for better."

He offered her a small smile. "As I said, I'm lucky not to have lost my leg, either to the adz or to amputation."

He could feel her tremble while she continued to stare at him in silence for a long time. Then he realized her eyes were glistening. Reaching up, he stroked her sweet cheek with his knuckles.

"Really, love, it's all right."

His words of comfort seemed to be her undoing. He watched tears fall from her eyes and course down her cheeks.

In an instant, Finn pulled her to him, taking her into his arms and settling her on his lap.

"Please, Rose. Don't cry for something that's over and done with."

Rose knew Finn was right, but couldn't seem to stop herself.

"I can't help it," she told him between sniffles.

She was crying for him and his pain, as well as for their lost years together, every lost minute, every lost hour, taken from them by the ship's sinking.

"Hush," he soothed. "It hurts me when you cry."

She sniffed and wiped her face on his shoulder. She couldn't tell him her tears were for more reasons than she could list, including how he'd let her believe him dead.

Regardless of his many reasons for staying away, a part of her hung onto the belief if he had truly had loved her, he would have come back sooner. Despite the intimacy they'd just shared, it was hard not to toss aside his excuses about being injured and then wanting to better himself.

If he'd loved her the way she loved him. *Had* loved him.

She pulled away until he released her, and she scrambled back to her own space.

"Forgive me," Rose said stiffly. "I'm behaving like a child. Of course, you've long since healed, and it's all in the past." The confusion clamoring in her brain, however, was nothing compared to the topsy-turvy feelings of her heart.

Or maybe it was simply the peculiarity of how intensely her body had reacted to Finn, despite how her heart no longer yearned for him as it once had.

"Nothing to forgive," he muttered.

"No," she agreed, keeping her own counsel. Perhaps not. Not anymore. Holding onto her pain over his betrayal was pointless, and she would make an effort to root it out.

"Do you know William and I . . . ? What I mean to say is that William has gone abroad, and we are no longer engaged."

Finn nodded, and she appreciated the fact he didn't gloat, nor did he offer condolences that they both knew would have been quite false.

They sat in silence again for a few minutes. Rose wondered what he was thinking. For her part, she was still amazed she was part of this dangerous adventure. What would Charlotte, who'd had her own share of intrigue, say about her abduction? She almost smiled at the idea of telling her how she'd untied Finn and, hopefully, how they escaped.

"You're practically grinning," he accused. "Are you enjoying this?"

"No," she shook her head. "Certainly not, although it is rather exciting and will make a good story. It's precisely something my sister-in-law would get up to."

Finn shook his head, and she could barely see his face in the dusky light.

"I don't think we got 'up to it' so much as got dragged into it, but I think it's time to get ourselves out of it."

She glanced around. "Shall we venture out? It sounds very quiet now."

He looked at her askance. "The walls supporting this building are three feet thick. We can't hear footsteps outside."

However, at that instant, they both clearly heard a door slam back against its framing in the direction from which they had entered. Someone had pushed open the iron door with great force.

Rose's heart started pounding double time, precisely when she'd been lulled into nearly forgetting why they were sitting on the floor in the middle of the shipyard's Ropewalk having a chat, as well as engaging in other marvelous activities.

"Now what?" she whispered into his ear.

"We wait," he said tersely.

In about a minute, the footsteps echoing through the building sounded nearly abreast of their hiding place, and Rose held her breath.

"We'll find them," they heard a voice close by. "They haven't left the yard. I'm sure of that."

Gilbert, she mouthed to Finn, who nodded in agreement.

"And when we do?" came another voice, unfamiliar to her.

"Accidents happen every day at the Ropewalk. Dangerous place to be," the master builder concluded.

Whoever was with him laughed.

Gilbert didn't. He sounded deadly serious. "As the authorities will see it, if that little miss wasn't here illicitly meeting her beau, she wouldn't have suffered the same fate as him."

"Which is?" asked the other man.

"The slicer will swing down and take off both their cursed heads."

Rose nearly gasped aloud, managing to stifle it with her own trembling hand. She stared silently into Finn's eyes.

"Perhaps they were locked in an embrace," Gilbert added, warming to his invented tale, "and didn't notice the rope slicer had broken free of its mooring. They died painlessly."

"Will they?" the other man asked.

"I quite doubt it," the master builder said, and his accomplice laughed again. "No bullets though," Gilbert warned. "This can't have the look of anything but an accident. Understand?"

"Yes, sir."

The two men were still directly next to the rope coil behind which she and Finn hid, and Rose wished herself anywhere except there.

In another moment, their footsteps had moved on. Unnecessarily, Finn put his finger to his lips to keep her from speaking, which she knew better than to do. Then he raised his head until he could see beyond the thick rope.

When he lowered himself again, he put his lips to her ear. "They are heading to the north entrance, about two hundred yards away. Not far enough yet."

She closed her eyes. She most certainly didn't want her head taken off.

"In another minute," he continued, his breath hot against the shell of her ear, "we're going to go quietly back the way we came."

Rose opened her eyes and looked at him, shaking her head. She made a gun out of her right hand and pointed at it with her left.

He leaned into her again. "You heard what they said. No guns." Then he paused and rested his forehead against hers for a second. "On the other hand, if it seems we're escaping, I suppose they'd have to shoot us and try weighting our bodies down in the harbor."

Rose shivered. Decapitation or death by drowning. She wanted to live. And to cook.

Finn eyed her thoughtfully.

"There are only two doors to the Ropewalk," he said, "and a quarter mile between them. We're already halfway there." He stood up and offered her his hand. "Come on, love. Let's get out of here."

They took off at a quick pace, despite his limp, moving as quietly as they could, though it was impossible to avoid the reverberation of their footsteps through the vast, silent building.

In fact, she was certain she heard the men chasing after them.

In a minute, they'd reached the south door and slipped outside. Finn took the time to close it and to lodge a piece of timber across the handle and through the latch, hopefully providing them enough time.

With luck on their side and Finn's knowledge of the yard, they made their way quickly toward the main gate. They passed the timber shed and were running across an open stretch of grass toward Second Avenue when Rose thought she heard the Ropewalk door forced open.

Distracted, she stumbled momentarily but had righted herself with Finn's hand on her arm when to her amazement, her brother appeared seemingly out of nowhere. He was flanked by policemen with their guns drawn.

CHAPTER THIRTY

Later that evening, on the sofa in her family's sitting room, sherry in hand and her mother at her side, Rose could scarcely believe the afternoon she'd had. It had been hard to let Finn go, even after the police had apprehended Gilbert and his accomplice, who'd run up behind them in the darkness, unaware of the police force waiting to meet them.

Even after Rose had been embraced by Charlotte, who was waiting in the guard's hut.

Even after they'd gone to the station and told the police everything.

Even after Reed had accompanied her into her home and bellowed so all the neighbors could hear, "What happened to you at the shipyard makes me so furious I want to thrash Bennet and lock you in your room for the rest of your life. You should not have been anywhere near the Ropewalk."

Even then, she felt as if things were dreadfully unfinished between her and Finn.

It hadn't been easy to watch him walk off into the night. They hadn't even had a chance to touch hands or speak privately.

She'd had no option but to let him disappear into the darkness. If she hadn't gone to the shipyard, Finn might be dead already.

That thought haunted her as she'd excused herself after dinner and readied for bed. Thankfully, she had gone and stuck her nose where some might say it didn't belong. Now, Master Builder Gilbert was in jail, along with some ogre of a man Finn said used to work at Kelly's yard.

According to Reed, the *Garrard*'s owner would be taken into custody, as well as Kelly's overseer, Walsh, if they ever found him. They had all shared in the hefty insurance claim. They had all committed manslaughter, and more recently, the ogre had apparently committed outright murder of at least two people of whom they were aware, dumping the thugs' bodies into the harbor.

In the quiet of her firelit room, Rose admitted to herself she hadn't thought of William when she had made love with Finn in the Ropewalk. Although she keenly felt the disappearance of William from her life, she realized she wasn't experiencing the same type of utter despair as she had after the supposed death of her husband.

No, this time, she was not entirely destroyed. Not because she had loved William less than she had loved Finn, but because she was more of a complete person apart from her heart's desire. As Fannie had said, she was still Rose Malloy, heartbroken or disappointed, engaged or not.

Moreover, Rose had the knowledge of having survived such anguish before, and she knew she would survive it again. It had taken a few dark days of worrying her mother and the rest of her family and, of course, Claire. Then Rose had decided she would not fall into the deep despondency that had taken over her four years earlier.

No, this time, she would rescue herself.

"I'm none the worse for wear," Rose told her mother for the umpteenth time the following morning. "It was truly not so terrible an experience."

Because she still had her head attached and her life intact. *What more could she ask for?*

There was also the not-so-small matter she had let her husband make love to her. She could speak to no one about this, not even Claire. She could only replay the momentous event and let a myriad of emotions roll over her like waves.

All that day, in fact, Rose couldn't shake the feeling Finn was near. She expected to see him at every turn, just as had happened at the start of their relationship four years earlier. Yet he was nowhere to be seen.

The rest of the week, she went to cooking class and helped ready her mother for her upcoming marriage to Mr. Nickerson and subsequent move across the river. Lastly, Rose went about the unpleasant task of composing notes to those who had sent her and William early wedding presents.

Still, no Finn.

A few days later, Rose deposited Claire on her doorstep after they'd supped on broiled lobsters at Crawford House's ladies' lunch. They'd also spent a futile few hours hunting at Parker Brothers and at R. Hollings for a present to mark her mother's special day.

"We should go to Amano on Hamilton Place," Claire suggested as they hugged goodbye. "Tomorrow, we'll find some perfectly exotic gift there from Bombay or Hong Kong."

After Rose agreed to another shopping expedition, she climbed back into her carriage. The sudden realization there was a note on the seat cushion barely surprised her. At least it wasn't attached to a brick. She glanced around but saw no one.

Meet me at The Quincy, Rm 504, five o'clock tonight. Tell no one.

Well, that was rather presumptuous of Finn, she thought, although she knew she would go, if only to remind him he owed her brother a visit and a signature.

Rose entered the magnificent seven-story hotel on Brattle Street, passing under its massive clock tower at 4:50 pm. It had been about five years since The Quincy House's last renovation, and she still thought it very *au courant*.

Making a mental note to suggest to Claire they lunch there the following week, Rose crossed the lobby, hoping she looked like a lady who was merely going to her room and then perhaps for a meal at the hotel's so-called New Café. Not like a woman about to meet her estranged husband . . . and lover.

Certainly, the only reason he could have called her to the hotel was to repeat what they'd done at the Ropewalk under more comfortable circumstances. Even knowing that—especially knowing that—she had gone willingly.

After telling the elevator operator—a woman about her own age in a smart uniform and cap—her desired floor number, Rose eschewed the small seat in favor of standing and waited. Inwardly, she felt about four years old, letting the "magic box," as she thought of it, lift her through the hotel.

Rose realized she was holding her breath only when she released it, as the elevator came to halt. The young lady lifted the bar, pushed aside the accordion grating, and then opened the wooden door.

Wandering along the carpeted hallway, Rose found the room easily enough but hesitated at the door. Her pulse raced at seeing Finn for the first time since their incredible escapade. She touched her jaunty hat, pinned slightly sideways on her head, and then knocked.

Once. Twice. Rose didn't make it to thrice before the door swung inward. Stepping swiftly across the threshold, she turned to see an absolute stranger, who immediately closed the door behind her and locked it.

Terror clutched at Rose's throat like an itchy scarf tied too tightly, and her fear was heightened by the extreme calmness of her captor.

The man had both hands in his pockets and leaned against the door as if this were the most casual and normal of circumstances.

"So *you* are Rose Malloy?" he said, looking her up and down almost insolently.

She swallowed and tried to hear properly past the loud pounding of her heart that resounded in her ears.

"You have me at a disadvantage, for I know not who you are."

"I'm not sure I shall tell you" he said. "I'm not sure it will matter."

Her blood seemed to freeze in her veins. Rose couldn't imagine what his intent was, but then, she also couldn't believe how utterly stupid she'd been to ensnare herself in this dreadful situation.

Yet another dreadful situation!

Reed would become a grey-haired man by next week.

She glanced around, thinking of escape and of what she could use as a weapon. There was little to see except highly polished hotel furnishings, a couple well-tufted chairs, and a bed. It had no separate sitting room, although a door undoubtedly led to an *en suite* bathing room, as the hotel was known for its luxury and comforts. She saw nothing that could help her unless she could barricade herself behind that door.

Women had few defenses, and Rose knew them all. First, bluffing.

"Apparently, you have no manners, and as such, I am leaving." She took a step toward the door and the stranger. Unfortunately, he didn't move. Instead, he smiled a scary little grin and crossed his arms.

She halted and backed up, walking toward the two spacious windows. She looked down, so very far down, to the busy street below. Scollay Square and her brother's offices were a mere few blocks away. So close, but Reed might as well have been in France for all the good it did her.

Escape was her next option although . . .

"I don't believe you'd survive the fall," the man said. "Maybe we'll find out shortly."

She shuddered. *Bastard.* Toying with her.

Breathing deeply, she considered what to do. Nothing had happened yet. Keeping her wits about her was her next defense, and hopefully, she wouldn't have to resort to violence.

"You know who I am," Rose said, stalling for time, "and you've been following me obviously. You put an unsigned note in my carriage. Why did you think I would come?"

"You tell me."

"Because you knew I would think the note was from someone else. Moreover, there's really only one person who might send me such a note and to whom I might go without question. And that person has very few friends or acquaintances."

The high cheekbones of her captors' face flushed a ruddy color. She was on the right path. After all, this had to be about Finn. William had been right on that count. All the danger in her life seemed to lead back to her husband. This man was too young to be Walsh, the missing overseer of Kelly's yard. So that left—

Rose bit her tongue. Should she let on she knew who he was, or would that put her in more danger? Liam Berne wouldn't need to kill her if he thought she couldn't identify him, would he?

"Why did you want to meet with me?" she asked, letting him believe her still in the dark as to his identity.

At last, he pushed away from the door.

"I want to know why Master Builder Gilbert is being detained in the city jail. I want to know if Mr. Dilbey is also being held. I want to know what has happened to Mr. Walsh."

She only knew the first and last names for certain. She knew Gilbert had been arrested at the yard. As for the missing overseer, he might have fled. And Dilbey, she knew not at all. Still, Rose said nothing.

"Well?" Liam Berne prompted.

She blinked. "I think you should be asking the city police. How would I know anything about any of those people?"

Liam's tone grew harsher. "Because Finn has come back to even the score, and you are Finn's wife."

"We are divorcing," Rose said bluntly, despite how odious it was to speak to a stranger about such a private matter. "In any case, I don't understand why bringing me here will help you get your answers. Why do you care what befalls these men?"

His face transformed into a sneer. "It's no matter to you, is it, why I care? But I'll tell you. Because I don't want whatever's happening to everyone else to happen to me. I did nothing wrong."

She nearly gave away her game of ignorance by telling him it was wrong to get rich off of dead men, but on that account, she held her tongue.

"I cannot help you, sir. I know nothing you don't already know, and I haven't seen Phineas Bennet recently."

"Is that so?" He ran a hand around the back of his neck and shrugged as if in discomfort. "I hope to hell you're lying because I want him to know I'm not going to disappear, nor am I going to prison. Not for doing as I was told. Not for staying alive."

Rose pursed her lips. Liam Berne was starting to sound deranged in his tenor if not his words, and his agitation was clear on his face.

"Again, I must ask why you wanted to meet with me. I cannot help you."

"You must," he said, taking a step toward her. "Finn will listen to you, won't he? It's as if all those lost souls have come back embodied by his person. I can imagine them all crying out for justice, urging him to it, but I have done nothing wrong, I tell you."

"If that is so, then why don't you simply go to the police and tell them what you know. Tell them who it was who took you off the ship's manifest. Tell them who put your name on the insurance policy."

Even as Rose finished speaking, she realized her mistake.

Liam's eyes seemed to catch fire, and he came even closer, causing her to back against the windows.

"You do know who I am, don't you?" His soft tone terrified her.

She shook her head.

"Yes, you do. I'm Finn's old friend, not that he believes me. You're going to help me make him understand. I didn't want to die then, and I don't want to go to prison now. Do you understand?"

"Yes, of course," Rose told him. The man must have gone insane with guilt—or with fear, perhaps—yet as far as she knew, he hadn't directly hurt anyone. "What do you want me to do?"

There was a rap at the door. When Liam showed no indication of hearing anything, she wondered if she'd imagined it.

"You'll help me then?" he asked, looking almost relieved.

Rose strained to hear another knock. Could the person on the other side of the door hear them? Perhaps it was a hotel maid.

"Help," she called out, her focus entirely on gaining someone's attention.

Another rap at the door, then the handle rattled.

"Rose!" Against all odds, incredibly, Finn was in the hallway.

At the same time, Liam took hold of her by her upper arms.

"If he won't listen to me, then we'll make a fair swap. My life for yours."

She gasped. "What do you mean?"

"I'll let you live, if he lets me live. Do you see?"

She nodded. *Yes, she saw clearly Liam Berne was mad as a March hare,* as her mother would say. In other words, he was becoming quite unhinged.

"Help!" she cried out again.

"It's too late," Liam said. "Too late for both of us, I suppose."

While keeping her pressed against the sill and imprisoned by his body, Liam leaned around her to slide the window sash up.

Rose felt the breeze off the harbor as it whistled past the hotel. It lifted the hair at her neck and tugging at her pinned hat.

Plunge backward to her death? No, thank you.

As terrified desperation seeped over her bringing the prickle of perspiration to her skin, she resorted to a female's final defense. She brought her knee up as hard as she could into Liam's private manly parts.

Instantly, he crumpled upon her, and she did it again with even more force. He nearly unbalanced her off the sill and out the window when he dropped to his knees, groaning in pain. At the same time, the door splintered open, and Finn hurled into the room, nearly falling over from the force of his entry.

His face, as he took in the scene, was one of confusion at seeing Liam already taken down.

Rose battled with the still existing urge to run screaming from the room or to lash out physically at whatever was in her path. Instead, she took a deep, calming breath and tried to clear the spots from her vision. Then she stepped over Liam where he lay sprawled and still groaning, and she moved directly into Finn's arms.

He hugged her tightly, and she reveled in the moments of relief, which were almost as exhilarating as the moments of terror. Then Rose pulled away.

No need to fall to pieces now. She was fine and, after all, she had dispensed with this threat quite capably by herself.

"Are you unharmed?" Finn asked.

"Quite. I believe this man is nearly a lunatic," she said calmly, as Finn looked from her to Liam. "He is clearly a danger to himself as well as to others."

Looking down, she straightened her jacket and adjusted her hat. "I'll ask the concierge to call the police while you guard him." She started for the door.

"Rose," Finn said, halting her steps.

Turning, she locked her gaze upon his. Everything around them was forgotten, as the moment seemed suspended in the *what-if* and *if-only* notions that had made up their entire relationship.

Then one of them yielded. She thought it was Finn, for he nodded as if in understanding.

With that, Rose walked out of the room, taking the stairs instead of the elevator. After speaking with a shocked concierge, she decided not to wait for the police. Instead, she left the hotel and the last vestiges of the dangerous mess behind her. Thinking it too late to catch Reed at his desk, Rose took herself home.

As usual, Reed had seen to the loose ends. She'd called him minutes after stepping in her own front door, and her brother told her he would not let her spend another evening answering questions at Boston District 3 headquarters. He would go in her place and help Finn if he needed it.

When Reed stopped by after breakfast the next day to escort Rose to give a deposition, he looked hesitant.

"What aren't you telling me?" she asked him on the way to the station in his carriage.

"I'm not sure how you'll take this, given all you've been through."

It was not like Reed to hedge rather than speak his mind.

"Please tell me," Rose asked.

"Bennet was waiting outside my office when I got there this morning. He signed the divorce papers."

Her brother's soft-spoken tone belied the life-changing event.

Rose stared straight ahead, far too many thoughts and emotions whirling inside of her to give voice to any one of them.

All that remained was a judge's decree. It came swiftly a week later, thanks to Reed's urging. At last, she was entirely free.

CHAPTER THIRTY-ONE

"I cannot believe you haven't spoken to him yet," Claire stated. "It's been weeks. Aren't you beyond curious to know how he ended up bursting down that door?"

Frankly, Rose *was* curious, but she was also sick of focusing on Finn. Not to mention tired of the black cloud that hung over everything to do with the two of them.

"I would far rather talk about how things are going with you and Franklin," she declared.

Claire immediately took on the wondrous glow that overcame her visage whenever she discussed her fiancé. However, as Rose's mind wandered to the proper length of time for letting custard set, she caught only the tail end of her friend's words.

". . . and that's why I always thought he was right for you. You can't fight the pull of first love, especially not one of that magnitude."

Rose had to shake the thoughts of cooking out of her brain. "What are we talking about?"

"About Finn and you, of course, and how he shaped your entire idea of what love is."

"Claire, dear heart, I want to stop talking about Finn and me. There is no 'Finn and me' in any case."

"Balderdash!"

Rose rolled her eyes. After signing the agreement in Reed's office, Finn had disappeared and made no attempt to contact her. Nor she, him. What's more, she had felt no compunction to do so. The long obsession with the man, as if he were in her blood and somehow coursing through her veins, was over.

William was still on the Continent. Finn was God knew where. And Rose was living quite happily alone after her mother had married and moved out the week before.

"I am utterly content," she assured her friend.

"Poppycock," Claire tried again. "You are the same woman with needs and wants and a heart, aren't you? You have been kissed, and you want to be kissed again, don't you?"

Rose smiled. She'd done a good deal *more* than kissing. And yes, she would very much like to experience more of that again. Presently, however, she simply didn't feel compelled to be with a man. She enjoyed dining with her friends and family. Moreover, she enjoyed her own company. Most of all, she liked doing whatever pleased her and answering to no one for the first time in her life.

Maybe when the newness of that freedom wore off, she'd start thinking of making an association with a man once again. Meanwhile, she'd acquired an adorable cat and named her Cocoa, for the puss had rich sable fur, which reminded Rose of the delicious hot beverage.

She tapped her chin. "You know something, I really don't think Maeve will ever suit Robert."

The two girls laughed uproariously.

"I agree. What were we thinking?"

"While Franklin is perfect for you, I believe Robert needs—"

"You," Claire suggested. "If you won't let me speak of you and Finn, how about you and Robert?"

That wiped the smile off Rose's face. *Could her friend be serious?*

After everything, would Claire still wish Rose upon her brother? How generous! How absurd! Moreover, would her friend be insulted by Rose's complete adversity to such an idea?

"Dearest," she began, "you know I love you dearly and have a fondness for Robert, since we practically grew up together, but I see him as a brother."

"A dull stick of a brother," Claire added, mirth shining in her eyes.

"Thank goodness," Rose said, sighing. "Truly, I thought you were serious."

"No, I cannot imagine the right woman for my brother," Claire said, "if one exists. You on the other hand—"

Rose held up her hand. "Here we go again."

"Well, I do think you have made two wonderful matches," Claire pointed out. "I am only sorry neither of them brought you the lifelong happiness I wish for you."

William would have, Rose was certain, if only he hadn't fled from the mess she had created, needing the soothing balm of thousands of miles of distance between them. He hadn't accepted the return of his ring, nor could she wear it, so it remained in its navy box in the back of her handkerchief drawer.

Finn *could* have brought her lifelong happiness, too. His very presence had made her happy. If only he hadn't let her grieve for him so long the grief itself overshadowed everything else when she thought of him. Admittedly, that had eased significantly with all they'd experienced since his return.

"I think it is up to me to bring my *own* happiness to my life."

Claire took her hand. "You are correct, of course."

Still, her friend sounded unconvinced.

Rose smiled. "Did I tell you about Miss Farmer's new idea?"

"A new way to cook beef?" Claire asked, pretending to yawn. "Are we braising, roasting, or wrapping it in pastry? Perhaps we're running it up a flagpole and letting the sun cook it."

Rose laughed. "I know, I know. I've bored you with every recipe I've tried, every nuance of spice, and each chopping and slicing technique I've learned. This is different."

Claire cocked her pretty head. "I'm joking, you know that. Do tell."

"I'm going to help her open her own school. I will be the assistant principal. We're going to do all sorts of new things, like show women how to put on a luncheon or a wedding reception. There will be lectures, too, morning and evening."

Her friend clapped her hands. "How exciting! I can perfectly imagine you showing people how to do the things you've learned. Miss Farmer is lucky to have you."

"Previously, I would have worried what Mama thought. Yet times are changing, and since she knows I've already been married, nearly widowed, and now divorced, I find she treats me more as a grown up. And adult women can be anything they want to be in this day and age."

"True," Claire agreed. Then she frowned. "I hope it's all right that I don't really want to do more than I am already doing. I simply want to be Franklin's wife and have his children, and keep a good home for all of us."

Rose hugged her. "I think that's perfectly acceptable. But I hope you will come into my new school and listen to a lecture on nutritious meals."

Claire reached over to lift the lid of a Randall's chocolate box and popped one in her mouth. "Of course!"

Rose's solitude and being left to her own devices could not last, not with a mother, a brother, and a sister all within a few miles of her. They stopped in to make sure she was fine, safe, well fed, even warm enough on the first chilly evening of autumn. Any excuse was good enough for them to interrupt her new routine of cooking school, lectures, testing recipes, reading, and futile cat grooming.

It was a Sunday afternoon, so she had her house entirely to herself, with no staff due back until six o'clock the next morning. Rose had only just closed the door on Charlotte and Elise, who'd dropped by together to entice her to go to the park with them and all their brood. To which Rose had replied with an emphatic *no*! She had two kinds of bread rising, nearly ready to bake, and a soufflé in the oven that needed tender love and care.

She had made it as far as her beloved kitchen doorway when her doorbell rang.

Rolling her eyes, she willed herself to have the patience of Job, and turned to answer the summons. She yanked open the door, ready to tell Elise absolutely—

Finn.

Utterly unexpected, the sight of him took her breath away. That in itself shocked her, the intense visceral reaction of her body to this man. Still. Again. *Oh bother!*

She forgot her manners and said nothing.

"Do you always open the door without first finding out who is on your step?" he asked, his gray-blue eyes dancing in the afternoon light.

"I thought you were someone else," she said, then wished she hadn't been so quick to explain herself. She owed him no explanation. However, it disturbed her for him to think she meant another man, as if she would jump from William to Finn to the mysterious "someone else."

"My sister and sister-in-law were here only a moment ago," she added, wishing she could simply stop talking.

In truth, Rose answered the door as often as her maid did, without any preamble, because she was not afraid. Not anymore. Not now Finn was out of her life.

So why was he there on her doorstep?

"Why are you here?" she asked, realizing belatedly how ungracious she sounded. Then she sniffed the delicious aroma of baked cheese, drawn through the house by the open door, and remembered her soufflé.

"Drats!" she exclaimed, before turning heel and dashing down the hallway to the kitchen.

To her delight the last grains of sand were only then dropping through her kitchen timer. Gingerly, she opened the oven door and sighed in delight at the perfectly pouffed cheese and herb soufflé. *Magnificent!*

With hands encased in thick oven mitts, she extracted the white porcelain dish and set it down gently on the cooling trivet on her counter before turning to quietly close the oven behind her. Then something happened she had never thought would happen—Finn Bennet was standing in the middle of the Malloy family kitchen, now *her* kitchen, having followed her inside.

"I hope it's all right," he began.

"*Shh,*" she said.

"Excuse me?"

"Speak more softly, please. The soufflé," Rose said, indicating the dish.

Finn shrugged, although he stared hesitantly at her creation.

"I have heard that a loud noise can make it fall," she whispered.

"That sounds unlikely," he muttered, then he cocked his head. "Let's try it."

"What if it sinks?" she protested.

"There are far worse things that can sink."

They eyed each other, letting a hundred thoughts pass between them. Then he smiled.

"Anyway, it will still taste as good, don't you think? Shall we?"

Rose shrugged, belatedly recalling how unfeminine her mother thought the action. Anyway, the idea of testing the soufflé appealed to her, and doing so with Finn appealed even more.

"Fine," she said in a normal tone. "First, try shouting."

Finn grinned, kept his gaze locked on hers, and then bellowed, "Rose Malloy is the most beautiful woman in the world."

Her eyes widened, and she grinned at him, then glanced at the soufflé. It looked precisely the same, a burnished brown on top and raised about three inches over the rim of the dish. Still perfect.

"My turn," she said. Looking around, she spied her smallest cast iron sauté pan. Snatching it up with both hands, she slammed it down on the counter with a bang.

They both leaned in to examine the eggy creation.

"No change," Finn said, "but if it had sunk into a flat mess, it might've been due to the vibration of the counter. That wouldn't have been a good test."

Even in this bit of fun, the precise brain of a builder was working.

"You're right," she acquiesced. "Anyway, that was more of a thump."

He surveyed the room. Hanging neatly from a cast iron rack were her steel pans and lids. He took down two lids, and with his hands directly over the soufflé, he clanged them together like concert band cymbals.

Nothing happened.

"*Hm,* I guess it was a myth." Rose would mention that to Fannie in the morning.

"Glad to be of service," he said, as he hung the lids back in their places. Moreover, he did appear quite cheerful.

Just like that, Rose saw him anew, through older eyes. Perhaps not a great deal wiser but, she hoped, less capricious. She still appreciated the man but for different reasons. What's more, in her mind, they were now at a new beginning.

She didn't even mind when Finn picked up a serving fork and used it to stab the soufflé. As the air escaped and it sank to the rim of the cooking dish, he stared at her with shocked eyes.

"Ballocks! I am sorry. I thought it was solid cake."

She laughed until she nearly cried. Then she grabbed two plates and served them both a generous piece. They ate in companionable silence for a few minutes, seated on stools in her kitchen.

"You were right," Rose told him. "It did taste just as good. Let's go into the parlor. You can tell me to what I owe this unexpected visit."

There, that was far more gracious, she congratulated herself, quite befitting the lady of the house. And she led him down the hall to her front room.

"It's a lovely house," Finn said, trailing behind her. "Well crafted."

"Thank you. I have lived here all my life."

As they entered the parlor, she spied her cat, curled up in the sunlight on the sofa. It lifted its head at the disturbance.

"Cocoa, this is Finn. Finn, Cocoa."

"A pleasure," he said to the cat, who put its head back down and closed its eyes. "Handsome-looking animal."

Why did it please her that he liked her cat?

"Yes, I think so, too. Will you sit?"

He did, which was how Rose came to be in her parlor on a Sunday afternoon with her former husband seated opposite.

"Truthfully," Finn started, "I have tried very hard to leave you alone, but you are in my thoughts daily."

She nodded. She would not confess to the same, albeit it was true.

"I hoped you wouldn't mind if I told you what I've been doing and find out how you are."

"All right," Rose said, feeling a little tentative at becoming drawn in by his magnetism too quickly.

"I have taken over Kelly's yard. The old man was quite devastated by all that occurred and by having a hand, however unwittingly, in such a great loss of life."

"Then he wasn't a part of the scheme?" she surmised. "Yet he seemed so unhappy at your return."

Finn leaned back in the chair, and Rose marveled again to have him in her sitting room, right there, on a chair where each of her family members had sat.

"When I appeared at his yard the first time, Mr. Kelly was shocked, plain and simple, and wanted to deny the truth by calling me a liar. Now, I'm his master builder. I foresee owning the yard within three years, if not sooner, as he is nearly ready to retire."

"That's good. You deserve it. I know you'll be successful." Her heart was entirely full of gladness for him.

All at once, she recalled how Claire started nearly every conversation of late with a question.

"I have to ask you something despite it having no import any longer."

Finn smiled slightly, leaning forward. "Of course, love, ask me anything."

How easily he still used that term of endearment? *With every member of the female sex or only her?* An emotion bubbled up in her, bittersweet and familiar.

"How did you come to find me at The Quincy? The floor I was on, the very room, in fact?"

"Oh, that," he said, appearing to have expected, or hoped for, some different question.

"It is quite a mystery to Claire and to me," she confessed.

Finn smiled slightly. "Tell Claire that after the incident at the Ropewalk, I spent every waking hour keeping my eye on you."

"You did?" It was news to Rose, although she remembered expecting to see him at every turn, and yet he was never there. Apparently, he *had* been, but had kept himself well out of sight.

"I knew the trouble wasn't over, I felt it in my bones. Liam had seemed scared when I'd last spoken to him, so I asked myself, what will he do now? And then there was Walsh, gone missing, according to your brother."

"He's been apprehended, did you hear?"

"Yes. I think he and Gilbert will hang for cooking up such wickedness."

She nodded, wondering if Finn had heard about the ship's owner. "I heard from my brother that Dilbey had gone along with the scheme and is expected to spend his life in jail for doing so."

"Yes, I know." He leaned forward in his chair and absently stroked the cat's head. "With Liam and Walsh still on the loose, I decided to spend my time keeping you safe. Or trying to. *Christ Almighty!* I'm only fit to lead blind monkeys. I'm sorry, Rose, I did a terrible job of it, and it nearly went very badly for you."

She eschewed his statement with a wave of her hand.

"That's not true. Honestly, your knock at the door reminded me I wasn't so far from help. Knowing someone was so close, it roused me from my panic into action."

"Rather good action, too, as I recall."

They grinned at one another.

"To your question," he continued, "I followed you to the hotel and then lost you only while you were in the lift. The operator didn't mind telling me what floor she'd delivered you to, after a minute or two of conversation."

Rose imagined him chatting up the young uniformed woman.

"You charmed the lady with your devilish good looks, didn't you?"

Finn laughed aloud. "Is that what did it? I thought it was my pleading for her to help me find my wife, whom I told her might at that moment be in the arms of another man. I didn't bother trying to explain about the danger I feared you were in. Adultery seemed to be enough impetus for her to help me."

Rose sobered at the mention of being his wife. Yet she would not ruin this easy repartee they had by dredging up the past.

"No doubt the lovely elevator operator helped you in hopes you would find me *in flagrante delicto*, and thus perhaps turn your attention on her."

He frowned. "I saw no lovely elevator operator. I see no loveliness anywhere except when I look at you."

Her heart seemed to skip a beat, and she swallowed nervously. Finn had a way of saying the most flowery sentiments as if they were simple fact. The trait was most appealing.

"How did you find which room?" Rose persisted, her words putting them back on safer ground.

His mouth lifted wryly. "Pure luck and persistence. I literally ran from door to door, knocking, listening, tossing some open if unlocked. Then I heard you, thank God."

Knowing he'd had her under his watchful eye, standing guard in the shadows, certainly endeared him to her. Luckily, she had saved herself, but the situation had nearly got out of hand. His timely assistance could as easily have been the difference between her remaining alive and not.

"As I said, after I heard your knock, I began to fight."

Finn nodded. "Liam never suspected you for a bully-trap, but you certainly handled him."

Warmed by his praise, she merely tilted her head and smiled.

"I was prepared to do whatever it took."

They stared at each another for a long moment. Abruptly, Finn stood up and crossed the space between them to crouch down before her. He took her hand, looking at it as if it were new to him, then he raised his gaze to hers.

"Now what, Rose?"

Indeed.

Her bruised heart was not ready. Too much had happened. Years. William. Pain.

Yet she looked at him, at his familiar handsome face, his earnest eyes, letting her gaze linger on the scar on his right temple and on his wonderfully skilled lips. Then she saw the hint of gold where his shirt collar gaped slightly away from the column of his neck. Instantly, she knew it was the chain that held her locket.

Something shifted inside of her, softening toward him.

Finn Bennet. Rose Malloy. Now what?

"We get on with living," she said. "No hiding, no sneaking, and no heartache, I hope, for either of us. We both deserve normal, ordinary lives, don't you think?"

For her part, between the Ropewalk and The Quincy House hotel, she'd had enough adventure to last a lifetime.

Finn frowned. "Ordinary? Rose Malloy, living an ordinary life?" He chuckled slightly. "That's inconceivable," he told her and brought her palm to his lips for a searing kiss.

EPILOGUE

Rose and Fannie were everywhere at once, or so it seemed, as they welcomed in the public for the open house of Miss Farmer's School of Cookery. Housed a stone's throw from the old school full of staff who wished them well, their new school had three new teachers, shining stainless-steel counters, and was perfectly prepared for their new mission stressing practical cooking over theoretical.

Bursting with excitement, tugging at her newly starched apron, Rose greeted newcomers, gladly talking about the cookbooks for sale with precise measurements. She had spent many hours transcribing recipes herself. No more *dash* of this and *pinch* of that. Teaspoons and tablespoons and measuring cups were the order of the day.

As regular middle-class women mulled about tasting the free samples, picking up schedules, and speaking with the teachers, Rose knew Fannie's dream of teaching housewives instead of would-be teachers was going to be a roaring success.

Incredibly, she had helped. More than helped. Rose was doing something authentic and useful with her life.

When she turned and saw Finn, the single male amongst the ladies milling about, she didn't even startle. Seeing him there in the middle of her happiness was almost expected, and she wanted to run up to him, hug him, and share her delight.

Oh, the scandal that would cause!

Instantly, his face lit up with a grin that must have matched her own. He strolled over to her.

"Isn't it wonderful? I won't even ask how you knew to come today. I am so happy to see you. The shipyard is going well? I knew it would with you at the helm. *At the helm*, ha. That's funny, is it not? Anyway, this school is going to be a shining example of practicality, usefulness, and, of course, deliciousness."

He laughed. "Take a breath, love. *You* are deliciousness, do you know that?"

She laughed along with him, her pleasure at their mutual success lifting her to giddiness.

"Come taste this." And she grabbed his hand and brought him to one of the sample tables. "Try this. It's known as Turkish Delight."

When he pulled back slightly, she added, "It's candy."

He opened his mouth, perhaps to decline the offer, and she popped a piece into his mouth, watching while he chewed the sticky treat.

"Isn't it scrumptious? Now taste this," she implored him before picking up a little doily with a sliver of frangipani cream pie on it.

"See its flaky crust. Taste the creamy goodness." She shoved it into his hands. "And this gingerbread, it's heavenly."

She crammed a piece in her own mouth and then tried to put some into his.

"Rose, stop. It's all delicious, but I didn't come here to stuff my face like a glutton, or to have you do it for me."

"Oh my goodness!" she practically shrieked. "Are you here to sign up for classes? You'll be our first male pupil. Miss Farmer," she began to call out looking around for her beloved mentor.

"No, Rose, please." He tugged at her hands and came away with more gingerbread, which he dutifully ate. "Good Lord. That is delicious!"

She knew he would love it. *Who could resist the surprise of lemon peel?*

Yet he continued tugging at her, until he had succeeded in spiriting her away from the hullabaloo into the next room where a few students were examining the clean and airy new classroom.

"I'm sorry, Finn, I'm just so excited."

"I know, love, and you have no idea how happy I am for you. But I didn't come to sign up. I came to ask you to go out with me. Tonight. I mean, after this event, whenever it ends. Out in the open, in public, where we might run into anyone and everyone. I'm inviting you to dinner," he paused, then added, "At wherever you choose, of course. Will you?"

Her heart was thudding loudly in her chest, and she was sure he could hear it. It had been difficult at first to pull her thoughts from the cooking school to Finn. Currently, however, he had her full and undivided attention.

As she looked at him and considered what he was asking, Rose felt a lightness shower over her.

Before she could say anything, Finn continued. "Since we first met, I've improved myself in some ways, yet become less than I was in others. I worried for two years whether my injury would be the deciding factor, the nail in the coffin, as they say. Then, there were other impediments to our future." He grimaced at stating the obvious.

"I've tried to hold back and to give you time, but more than anything, I want to start over with you, Miss Malloy."

He took her hand and cleared his throat.

"My name is Phineas Bennet. I have a university degree and solid, respectable employment. I can hold my head up with any of Boston's finest."

"My dear Finn, you always could." Rose took a step closer, not caring about any perceived impropriety. "You are *not* less than you were. You were perfect for me before," she paused.

It was true. He had always been perfect—this smart, hard-working, decent man. *How could she ever have been ashamed to go to her family and tell them she'd fallen in love with him?*

As for Finn's limp, while it might be a nuisance to him, it meant nothing at all to her, except that it caused him discomfort.

"You still are," Rose confessed. "Perfect, I mean, for me."

Finn's quick intake of breath proved he'd still had his doubts.

At her words, he pulled her into an embrace, there in middle of one of Fannie Farmer's brand-new cookery classrooms.

Without thinking, she melted against him, letting his arms encircle her.

Inclining his head, Finn claimed her lips, and she helped by tilting slightly so their mouths fit even more closely. They both ignored the gasps of onlookers.

A familiar tingle sizzled through Rose's body and down her limbs to her toes, a sensation of which she would never tire. And upon her tongue was the delectable taste of gingerbread. Warm, spicy, with a little biting edge and a perfect amount of sweetness—exactly like their love.

Finis

AN IMPASSIONED REDEMPTION
NOVELLA

and the rest of the Defiant Hearts series
including

AN INTRIGUING PROPOSITION
PREQUEL

AN IMPROPER SITUATION
BOOK 1

AN IRRESISTIBLE TEMPTATION
BOOK 2

AN INESCAPABLE ATTRACTION
BOOK 3

AN INCONCEIVABLE DECEPTION
BOOK 4

are available in print and ebook.

ABOUT THE AUTHOR

USA Today bestselling author Sydney Jane Baily writes historical romance set in Victorian England, late 19th-century America, the Middle Ages, the Georgian era, and the Regency period. She believes in happily-ever-after stories with engaging characters and attention to period detail.

Born and raised in California, she has traveled the world, spending a lot of exceedingly happy time in the U.K. where her extended family resides, eating fish and chips, drinking shandies, and snacking on Maltesers and Cadbury bars. Sydney currently lives in New England with her family—human, canine, and feline.

You can learn more about her books, read her blog, sign up for her newsletter (and get a free book), and contact her via her website at SydneyJaneBaily.com. She loves to hear from her readers.